ENCHANTMENT'S EDGE 2:
ORBUS'S WORLD

ENCHANTMENT'S EDGE

Volume 2: Orbus's World

Philip G. Williamson

Hodder & Stoughton

First published in 1997 by Hodder and Stoughton
A division of Hodder Headline PLC

British Library Cataloguing in Publication Data

A CIP catalogue record for this title is available
from the British Library

ISBN 0 340 68225 6

Typeset by Palimpsest Book Production Limited,
Polmont, Stirlingshire

Printed and bound in Great Britain by
Mackays of Chatham PLC, Chatham, Kent

Hodder and Stoughton
A division of Hodder Headline PLC
338 Euston Road
London NW1 3BH

PRELUDE

'Orbus!'

Though he yelled at the top of his voice, King Leth's words seemed not to carry far. They were absorbed into the all-surrounding bluish mist, deadened within the vast, silent emptiness of the place.

'Orbus!'

He was becoming hoarse from shouting. His fear constricted his throat and his cries were growing desperate, though he strove to conceal his anxiety from the two bewildered children who gripped his hands. The silence of this place chilled him to the core. Such was its nature that it seemed to amplify to shocking intensity the pounding of his own heart against his ribcage, the roar of the blood raging through his veins, and the almost deafening uneven rhythm of his breathing and that of his young daughter and son.

How long had they been here? At least an hour now, probably longer. It had been late afternoon when they had been cast from Leth's study into the eerie blue silence of the Orb. But this place defied any attempt to gauge time accurately, for there was nothing here. Neither sun nor stars, not even a sky. No trees, no breaks upon the perfectly level landscape, no sign of creatures living or dead. No shadows at their feet. Nothing save the veil of blue-toned mist and the blue wall, towering high, higher than Leth could comprehend, encircling them, forming ceiling and floor also and seeming, paradoxically, to be both close and far away.

The paradox did not end here. As he and the children approached the wall, no matter the ground they covered or the direction in which they walked, they came no closer. The boundary of the blue world-chamber remained eternally at the same distance from them, never nearer nor, when Leth turned to look back the way they had come, further away.

Leth walked on, keeping uppermost in his mind the hope of finding Orbus, the Orb's mysterious tenant. Without him Leth knew of no way of leaving the Orb. He was beset by a feeling of dread at the prospect of remaining here. As time passed the unrelenting uniformity of the place began to oppress him. He strained his eyes and ears, seeking something, *anything*, that would relieve the disorientating monotony of his surroundings and reassure him that he and his children had not been cast into a void.

But nothing changed, and Orbus did not appear. Leth was drained. The loss of Issul, the Krai invasion, Grey Venger and, finally, the coup against him, had left him at his lowest ebb even before he had inadvertently entered the Orb. He struggled to keep a grip on his sanity, and thought of the children at his side. More than ever at this time they needed him. Their understanding of what had happened was even less than his. For them he had to show fortitude, be the resourceful, protecting, loving father they knew and trusted utterly.

Orbus, why have you forsaken me?

Was he truly facing betrayal here, as he had in Enchantment's Edge? Had Orbus been building up to this all along? Was Orbus in league with Leth's enemies: with Fectur, the Krai, the demonic creature from Enchantment who led and drove them? Was he with one or more of the factions? Aligned with Grey Venger and the True Sept? Could it be possible? Had Orbus planned this from the beginning?

No, no!

Leth forced down his fear, reminding himself that it had been an accident that had cast them into the Orb. Orbus had not known. Even if he had planned to betray Leth, he could not possibly have contrived the random circumstances that had brought them here in such a manner. It was he, Leth, who had by chance permitted his children to enter his study. Jace, his daughter, had been attracted by the precious blue casket that lay upon his desk: the magical casket that was the gateway to this mysterious blue domain – Orbus's world. In his distraction Leth had neglected to return it to its secret compartment in the wall. And Jace had picked up the casket and, before Leth could stop her, had raised the lid, performing the fateful action that opened the way into the Orb, casting them here, all three. No. No one, not even Orbus, could have engineered that.

In the past Orbus had repeatedly cautioned Leth against allowing anyone near the casket. No one but he should know of it. Orbus had been passionate and unmovable on that score, for to know of the casket was to covet it and its secret at any price. And Leth had kept the secret almost until the last, telling not a soul, not even Issul. Jace had come upon it by chance, nothing more, and simple, childlike curiosity had been her only motivation in opening it. Besides, Leth reminded himself, if it had been Orbus's intention to trap him here he could have done it at any time.

Or had Orbus been watching and waiting all this time? Were his powers greater than Leth knew? *Had he sought to trap the children, Leth's heirs, too?*

The thought shook him, but again Leth fought it back. He would not believe it. He believed in Orbus, had come to trust him, had accepted Orbus's account of his genesis, his history and the history of Enchantment. He gave total credence to Orbus's story of his defeat by his adversaries, the other so-called gods of Enchantment, and his eons-long imprisonment in the empty blue of the Orb. Leth cast it over in his mind again and again, and could not permit that it had all been fabrication designed to lure him and the children here.

But he had only Orbus's word to go on, even so. And Orbus remained a mystery. He informed Leth purely to the degree that he chose, and was often less than candid when faced with penetrating enquiries. There were many questions that Leth had either been discouraged from pursuing or had failed to gain wholly satisfactory answers to.

Notably, on all past occasions Orbus had been here when Leth had entered the Orb. It was solely by Orbus's command that Leth had been able to leave and return to his study in Orbia palace. Why had he chosen not to appear now?

Orbus, where are you?

He cupped his hands to his mouth, drawing a deep breath, and called once more.

'Father, we want to go back now.'

It was Prince Galry, King Leth's young son, who spoke. He used the formal mode of address and his face was solemn and pale – indications of his struggle to combat the fear he felt. Galry was aged six, a robust, energetic, proud and handsome boy. But his eyes were red with the tears he fought to withhold, his lips tightly compressed, the lower one jutting forward and trembling slightly, despite his efforts. Galry had burst into tears of terror when they had first been transported here; he had been dazzled by the flash of blue light caused by Jace opening the casket lid, and had thought himself blinded. Jace, less affected, had simply gazed in silent awe. A year younger than her brother, Jace, who was so like her mother, Queen Issul, in both looks and temperament, had first asked to return home, and then had been keen to explore. Her tears had come a short span later, when she learned that there was nothing to be found, grew bored and discovered that her father was either unwilling or unable to return them to their home.

By that time Galry had overcome the worst of his fear. Sensing something of his father's anguish he had put an arm protectively around his little sister's slim shoulders, gently bidding her to calm and striving to distract her with nursery rhymes and word games.

Leth had been proud of them both. For some time as they walked the children had amused themselves, and provided Leth with much-needed distraction. They had sung songs together, played guessing games, chased one another. But the unrelenting tedium and strangeness of the place, combined with their father's continual calling and thinly veiled unease, had eventually begun to play upon their nerves. They had been silent for some time. Now Galry felt it incumbent upon himself to express what they both felt.

King Leth knelt and took them in his arms. 'We will go home soon,' he promised.

'But *when?*' protested Galry. 'I'm bored, Father. And I don't like it here.'

'And I'm hungry,' added Jace.

Leth gazed about him. This was something he had begun to consider early on. It was one of the reasons he had decided to walk rather than remain where they had first found themselves. But the further they went the more his spirits fell as nothing changed. Nothing at all.

Were they to starve here?

Leth strained his eyes, desperate to descry a break, a new feature in the boundless blue mist or encircling wall. Something, no matter how small, which might indicate a way out or a change or a suggestion that the queer bundled denizen of this domain had not wholly abandoned them.

Leth considered his last meeting with Orbus. It had taken place only moments before he and the children had been transported here. He had gone to Orbus in desperation, to reveal to him how he, Leth, King of Enchantment's Edge, had been gulled and overthrown by Fectur, the scheming Lord High Invigilate and Master of Security of the little kingdom. In an audacious coup Fectur had successfully appropriated power from the King and installed himself as Regent in Leth's place. He had declared Leth to be of unsound mind, had produced 'evidence' to substantiate his claim that Leth was no longer fit to rule, and had ingeniously manipulated circumstances to provide himself with the support of a majority of the most powerful members of government and faction leaders.

Fectur's next move, quite obviously, would be to remove Leth terminally, his heirs too. As long as the King lived he would be a threat to Fectur, but with Leth gone and Queen Issul lost and believed dead Fectur would have established an autarchy and secured permanent rule for himself.

Could this be his means of disposing of Leth? Had Fectur and Orbus worked together to trap the King and his children here, where no one could possibly find them?

It was a terrible thought. Leth recoiled from it. How would Fectur and Orbus now confront the advancing Krai and the unidentified god-creature from Enchantment which commanded them? With Orbus at his side could Fectur somehow halt their advance? After successfully executing his coup against the Crown, Fectur had spoken gloatingly to Leth of a possible change of policy in regard to the Krai. He had not enlarged upon the topic, preferring to allow Leth the torment of not knowing. Had he conceived some further devilment with Orbus?

Leth shook his head wildly to rid himself of these thoughts. Releasing the children he thrust himself to standing and glared at the encircling wall. Betrayal of such scope . . . he could not dwell on it.

'*Orbus!*'

His voice was absorbed into the hanging mist, as so many times before.

No, no, he would *not* believe it! Orbus had been dismayed by the news of Fectur's deceit. Orbus was himself endangered by the Krai advance, for the creature that led them was one of his ancient enemies and Orbus had yet to regain anything like his former powers. Many other enemies dwelt within Enchantment, and they would all have moved instantly to destroy Orbus had they known of his regenesis.

If Orbus was to be believed.

Leth told himself again that Orbus had no need of such a ploy. At any time he could have made Leth his prisoner, with the children as well had he simply commanded that they be brought.

But could it be that the god who aided the Krai was not unidentified after all, was not even Orbus's enemy?

Leth raged mutely, momentarily paralyzed by the notion, then again rid himself of it forcibly. He was surely now probing too deeply into the tunnels of madness.

Another thought came as he took his children's hands once more, this one more welcome: could it be that Orbus had actually brought the three of them here for their protection? He was fully informed about events at Enchantment's Edge, knew that Fectur would have to kill Leth and the children. But why no explanation? Why no sign of him?

Leth gave thought to Orbus's words at their earlier meeting: *'Ah, Leth, a few moments later and you would not have found me.'*

There had been an uncustomary delay between Leth's arrival and Orbus's appearance, and though Orbus had given no real explanation of where he had been going he had spoken evasively of his work upon an experiment of some sort. Now his words seemed laden with an import Leth had not perceived at the time.

Orbus had reaffirmed his own status as a prisoner here in this world, yet his manner had implied something more. In the past he had made no secret of his yearning to be free of the Orb. It was to this end that he directed the major part of his efforts. Could he have found a way of leaving it? Leth recalled an experience just a few nights ago – was it a week? Two? He was in his bedchamber, unable to sleep, and had stood at the window and gazed with troubled thoughts over the storm-ridden blackness of the city-castle and the low forest beyond, towards the distant, misted weird lights of Enchantment. And he had thrust himself impatiently back from the window and had seen – or believed he had seen – standing in the shadowed corner of the chamber the figure of Orbus, vague and indistinct. He had thought it was a vision. Even now he was not sure. But the figure had moved, had spoken briefly, and then had faded.

Had Orbus discovered a way to liberate himself from his prison world?

Leth's mind flew back further, to the time of his first encounter with the ragged-garbed tenant of the Orb. It was more than three years past, just prior to Leth's accession to the throne. His mother, Queen Fallorn, elderly and with her health beginning to fail, had summoned Leth to her chambers within hours of abdicating the throne in his favour. It proved to be almost their last conversation, for shortly afterwards Fallorn had succumbed to illness and within days had died.

In this meeting Queen Fallorn had revealed a great and profound secret to her only son, one of which she was the sole living custodian. It was something she bound him never to reveal to any other, save when and if the time came to pass the throne into the hands of his heir. It was a secret revealed solely to the ascending monarchs of Enchantment's Edge: the existence of the blue casket. Solemnly placing the casket in his hands, she had bidden him withdraw with it to his private study. There, when he was alone and assured of no interruptions, but under no circumstances before, he was to open it.

Intrigued, Leth had followed her instructions and, bewildered and amazed, found himself for the first time in the unearthly blue domain of the Orb, confronting the extraordinary creature who dwelt there. At that time, in a conversation both mesmerizing and bizarre, Orbus had seemed to mock Leth. He had made it plain that Leth was helpless there, wholly in his power. King and potentate though he might be in his own domain of Enchantment's Edge, within the world of the Orb he was as feckless as an ape in a cage.

Orbus then led Leth to infer that his world, the Orb, might be a prison of sorts, though he also enigmatically described it as an existence and a 'nowhere'. To Leth's enquiry as to whether he, Leth, was now a prisoner Orbus had given a cryptic reply, leaving Leth hardly the wiser. Subsequent discussions over the ensuing months had proved both enlightening and mystifying in equal measure. But always Orbus had made it plain that he was absolute master here, and that without him Leth was unable to leave.

And now the master had departed his house.

Leth bowed his head in despair, and slowly knelt and held his children again.

Orbus, Orbus, are we to die here?

PART ONE

ONE

I

Queen Issul strode from her office, through the reception chamber where her private secretary, Hullie, sat at her desk, and into the corridor beyond, where she turned and almost collided with the still figure of the Lord High Invigilate, Fectur.

'Oh!' The young queen took two steps back, quickly regaining her composure. 'Fectur!'

Fectur slightly bowed his head. 'My Queen.'

'What are you doing here?' She felt her anger rise. Anger that she should have let him catch her off-guard like this, anger at his presence, lurking like a felon at her door, and anger most of all at Fectur himself, for his schemings and manipulations, his deceits and duplicities that had brought so much suffering upon Enchantment's Edge and which, she had little doubt, had contributed immeasurably to the disappearance of her husband, King Leth and their two children.

And she felt fear, too. Fear of Fectur's power, the labyrinthine workings of his formidable mind, his unstated designs, the influence he exerted so insidiously in all areas of life, both within the great city-castle of Enchantment's Edge and beyond. A brilliant, ruthless man, Fectur, without conscience or scruples. She had learned in the most painful way that he was capable of anything. Absolutely anything. It was pure chance that had brought her back to Enchantment's Edge within hours of his coup against Leth. Leth and the children were gone, but she was not too late to force Fectur to relinquish the throne into her hands. A day more . . . would he still have done so, or would his power and confidence have been such that he would have openly defied her? Most probably, she reasoned, his men would have manned the city gate – she would have been led discreetly away somewhere; news of her return would never have passed beyond Fectur's ears.

She took some small solace in the knowledge that he was not infallible. Not quite. She had wrong-footed him with her return. Lord Fectur had taken a gamble, making his move against Leth in the belief that Issul would not be coming home, at least not yet. She had embarrassed and humiliated him. He had not risked standing against her, for to do so was to threaten the integrity of the Crown, and plainly he had lacked the support for that. He had achieved Leth's overthrow through guile, deceit and the ruthless manipulation of circumstances. Leth's state of mind had been the pretext, and Fectur had persuaded government, army and factions that he was acting in the best interests of the Crown. With Issul's return that argument could only be sustained by his stepping down voluntarily. But he would not be beaten. He would be taking careful stock, awaiting and creating his next opportunity. His instinct was that of the spider that sits concealed beneath its trapdoor, allowing its prey to step too close. His jaws had closed once upon the flesh he sought, but, impossibly, it had struggled free. Now he had withdrawn again into the dark, where he waited, patient, still, and ready.

Issul suppressed a shudder. She needed him. It was an unpalatable fact, but Fectur was invaluable, and therein lay his strength. Many of Enchantment's Edge's most skilled troops were under his direct command; his intelligence network extended everywhere, holding stores of knowledge and information that the Crown needed to function effectively; and his police and security system held sway over far too much of the little kingdom.

And now Orbus was proposing that, to have any chance of rescuing Leth and their children – and indeed, of saving Enchantment's Edge from the advancing Krai and their god – Issul must leave the city-castle again, this time to journey into unknown Enchantment. In effect Orbus was asking her to hand power and virtually complete freedom of choice back to Fectur.

The Lord High Invigilate stood motionless, his short stubby fingers linked before him, observing her with a smile of cordial hatred. 'You have heard the sad news?'

'Of Duke Hugo?' She gave a curt nod. 'Word arrived a short time ago.'

'Such a tragedy. A great loss, for Enchantment's Edge as much as for you and your family. My heart goes out to you all.' He tutted, but his eyes were blank, the pupils pinpoints. 'The poor Duchess. How will she take the news?'

'She will not be told yet, Fectur. Do you understand?' Mawnie – Demawndella – Issul's sister and the wife of Duke Hugo of Giswel, was confined in a state of delirium in her apartment within Orbia palace.

'The Duke was unwise,' said Fectur. 'The King's orders were explicit: to remain within the castle. For some reason Duke Hugo saw fit to disobey and launch a sally against the Krai. No doubt he believed he had good cause, but . . . he has paid the most terrible price. Many good men lost their lives, and Giswel Holt is weakened.'

'How many were lost, Fectur? Do you have more details than I?'

Issul had only recently received the news, brought by pigeon. Pigeon flights had ceased for some days, she had learned, for fear of interception by the Krai. Now the defenders of Giswel Holt reasoned correctly that the Krai would be unlikely to want to prevent this news reaching the capital.

'Some dozens, it would appear,' Fectur replied. 'Foot soldiers, horse troops and several knights. Prince Anzejarl has now divided his army into two. A considerable force remains outside Giswel Holt's walls, while the bulk of the army is thought now to be marching north, towards us.'

Issul took sober heed of this. The Krai could be here within days. The city-castle itself was a difficult prospect to lay seige to, situated as it was upon the vast, soaring scarp from which it and the kingdom drew its name. The season was late-harvest, so store-rooms were well-stocked. But the city-castle had become severely overcrowded with refugees who had fled from the towns and villages of the region which lay in the enemy's path. More still poured towards the city gate. And the Krai had access to much of the harvest, too, plus good supply lines leading back into the Mondane Kingdoms they had conquered before turning upon Enchantment's Edge, and to the Krai lands themselves. They had formidable allies in their ranks. Creatures of Enchantment, somehow under the command of Prince Anzejarl: slooths – monstrous winged beasts for which cliffs and walls were no obstacle. The slooths were fearless, fleet in the air, and deadly. Issul had already witnessed their effects in battle, and had received accounts of the panic and destruction that they had caused when Prince Anzejarl had unleashed them upon Enchantment's Edge and other, less well-defended towns. And there had been additional reports of huge, brutish troll-things moving with the Krai army.

What else? It had been established beyond all reasonable doubt that the Krai were led by one of the mighty god-beings who ruled Enchantment. The precise identity of this 'god' was undetermined, and the fact of its existence had not been made public for fear of inciting the populace and, worse, one or more of the factions. The factions had worshipped such beings before the practice was banned by Leth's forebear, King Haruman. Worship still continued clandestinely, and if it were officially acknowledged now that one of the so-called gods gave patronage to the Krai, and indeed led them to war against Enchantment's Edge, the consequences within the kingdom would have been catastrophic.

Rumour was rife, of course. Most of the factions were vociferous in their claims that the current strife was due to the gods being angered at the Deist Edict which prohibited worship. They had become even more vocal with the appearance of the slooths, and it served no one's interests, not even Fectur's, to have such knowledge broadcast. As it was, as far as she knew, even Fectur, though he might strongly suspect and even believe in the intervention of a god, had no actual evidence. It was Leth who, in discussion with Orbus, had confirmed the existence of the Krai 'god', and apart from these two, only Issul and Pader Luminis of the Arcane College were aware.

Orbus had told Issul that there were as many twenty-three of these beings dwelling in Enchantment. One was Triune, whom she had already encountered. They were Orbus's enemies, and he had himself been one of them before his defeat, banishment and separation from his soul. He confirmed that they were not truly gods, although their power, compared with ordinary folk beyond Enchantment's borders, was immense, and in that sense put them on the level of deities. He described them as nodes of consciousness formed out of the chaotic energies that created Enchantment, and declared that they were doomed, only half-knowingly, to forever wage war upon each other and the world in order to continue to exist.

Orbus did not know which of these beings aided the Krai. He informed Issul that outside of Enchantment's borders his ancient enemies were deprived of much of their power. Hence the creature which led the Krai, and which reportedly took the form of a red-haired woman of astonishing beauty who had established herself as the consort of the Krai Prince Anzejarl, was unlikely to be the 'god' itself. More probably, she was a sorcerous projection, simulacrum or bound servitor of the 'god'. Nonetheless, he believed her quite capable of summoning other allies, other magics, should the circumstances demand.

Deep within the forest to the south of Enchantment's Edge, Issul, whilst held captive by a Krai raiding party, had discovered a secret underground bunker constructed by the Krai using human slaves. Within lay a mysterious thing, a manifestation of strange and powerful magic, called a Farplace Opening. From here, according to Orbus, things of Enchantment could issue forth. Orbus spoke of Edge Riders: awesome phantasmal entities, the very expression of Enchantment itself. These bringers of destruction would pave the way for Enchantment to grow, to return the world to its own condition of chaotic flux.

And there remained another abiding mystery: that of the Legendary Child. According to the teachings of the outlawed faction known as the True Sept, the Legendary Child was the spawn of a god whose advent was predicted at a time of great crisis. The child was also Queen Issul's nephew, though none but Issul, Pader Luminis, and now Orbus, knew this. The child, named Moscul, had been born in the most terrible circumstances, pushing himself from the lifeless womb of Issul's deceased younger sister, Ressa, the twin of Mawnie. Issul, only half-aware at that time of the preachings of the True Sept, and not wanting to believe, had brushed aside the facts of the unnatural birth. In accordance with Ressa's plea before her death, she had taken Moscul and hidden him with a poor peasant family in the tiny, outlying village of Lastmeadow. Inadvertently Issul had helped to nurture the Legendary Child, had allowed him to develop and grow, undiscovered and unopposed.

In one of the guest apartments within the Royal Palace of Orbia the leader of the True Sept, Grey Venger by name, waited. Fanatically opposed to the throne, and half-crazed with hatred for King Leth, Venger was the only man believed to hold the secret of the Legendary Child's purpose. So far Issul had put off speaking to him, but she knew that she could not delay much longer.

It was all too much. Issul put her hand to her brow.

'You are unwell, my Lady? You look tired and pale.'

'I am fine.' She had barely slept in days and her mind could barely take in what was happening. But she would not give Fectur the satisfaction of knowing this. 'Is your account reliable?'

'It was sent by one of my own people within Giswel Holt, and carries coded signals. I would be aware if it had been tampered with.'

'Is there anything else?'

'Soldiers returning to Giswel Holt reported seeing large grey creatures, trolls. It was these beasts that inflicted the greatest damage upon our troops and took Duke Hugo's life.'

Issul nodded to herself. Fectur's report seemed to differ little from the one she had received, though of course he might not be telling all. It was unsettling news. Hugo's death was a severe blow. Almost certainly he had blundered into a trap set by Prince Anzejarl. And with his loss came the first reliable sighting of Anzejarl's trolls within the borders of Enchantment's Edge.

All else aside, with Prince Anzejarl's army on the move and so close, was there even time to follow Orbus's plan and travel to Enchantment?

'I want an emergency assembly this afternoon in the Hall of Wise Counsel,' said Issul abruptly.

'Another?' Fectur scarcely troubled himself to disguise his sarcasm.

'Yes, another!' she snapped. 'All knights, senior military officers, security and intelligence officers, advisors and officiers will attend. I leave it to you to arrange.'

Fectur did not flinch, but she saw the flicker of suspicion and resentment in his cold carp eye. 'Very good, my Lady.' He reached into his robe and brought forth a scroll bound in crimson ribbon. 'Here is the report you requested.'

'It is late.'

'I have been very busy.'

She took the scroll, curious as to its contents. How would Fectur have accounted for his conduct during her absence, most especially his overthrow of Leth? He was too clever to incriminate himself, but in covering his tracks Issul hoped he might at least have left clues that could help her understand just how he had accomplished his feat and, perhaps more importantly, name or give credible indications as to the identities of his closest accomplices, or at least those distinguished figures who had most readily given him their support. Many of his henchmen she already knew, but to establish himself as Regent Fectur would have needed the backing of the highest ranking ministers, knights and the heads of the numerous factions. The factions were influential in the politics of Enchantment's Edge, but their greatest weakness had always been their conflicting beliefs and inability to find accord between themselves. That they had demonstrated unity now intrigued Issul; that they had done it behind Fectur's banner was a matter for tremendous concern.

II

Issul paced her chamber, racked with indecision. Outside a light drizzle fell from uniform grey skies above Enchantment's Edge. The misty rain was chill, carried from the north-east with the changing season. The vast forest that lay at the foot of the great scarp had been almost obscured, a murky ocean of denser tone merging into the low cloud. The mountains of Enchantment could not be seen.

Barely thirty-six hours had passed since Issul's return to Enchantment's Edge. She had come home to find herself obliged to don the mantle of supreme office in her husband's absence. She was twenty-two, with scarcely any practical experience in the art of government. Taking the throne, she found herself beleaguered and antagonized, a reluctant sovereign in a time of crisis like none that had gone before in the entire history of Enchantment's Edge. From outside the city-castle's high walls enemies approached. Others circled within, like raptors waiting for her to drop, not all yet announcing themselves. And now she was faced with an impossible choice.

To go or to remain? On the face of it she had little option. Ironically, she had known, even as she was making her way back to Enchantment's Edge, that she would return to the secret Krai bunker beneath the forest floor, where the Farplace Opening – the way to Enchantment – lay entombed. She had made the impossible journey, had been to Enchantment, and something of Enchantment was within her now. It called her back, a mystery that could not suffer abandonment. But she had never imagined she would be returning there this soon, nor under circumstances as desperate as these.

'Orbus . . . Orbus, speak to me.'

Issul ceased her pacing and focused her gaze upon the blue casket that rested with other precious ornaments and items of finery upon an open shelf of an ornately carved oak chiffonier to one side of the room. Orbus would not be far away. By his own account, prevented from re-entering his world, he could also not leave it. He, the world, and the casket were somehow one and the same – a concept which Issul was not fully able to grasp.

Issul had agonized over the problem of concealing the casket. With Pader Luminis, she had decided upon open display, where it would in fact draw the least attention. No one knew of the casket. Her apartments were private, and more closely guarded now than ever before. Fectur was always a risk, but he had no direct access to Issul's private rooms, and he had already failed to note the casket when it lay conspicuously upon Leth's workdesk. To hide it now might actually be to risk exposing it in the event of calamity or clandestine search. Consulted about this, Orbus, after brief consideration, had agreed.

'Orbus, are you there?' Issul peered about the chamber, seeking out the vague figure of the god, filled with unease. She knew so little about him, nothing more than he had told her, in fact. He professed himself benign, but how could she be sure? Leth had left instructions with Pader Luminis that the casket must be protected at all costs, had hinted that the fate of Enchantment's Edge might somehow be bound up with the casket. And when Issul had taken the casket, then had come Orbus with his claim that within him, within the world that he had somehow become, Issul's children and husband were alive. What could she do but trust him, and hope?

'Orbus, I have to talk to you.'

The silence unnerved her, set her fearing the worst. 'Orbus!'

At last there came a voice, dry, aged, laboured, from behind her. 'Ah, Queen Issul.'

Issul turned. The stooped, bulky figure of Orbus, not wholly distinct, waited beside the window, surrounded by the faintest corona of pale blue.

'I apologize,' he said. 'I was lost.'

'Lost?'

'Within. It is an extraordinary thing. I have yet to become accustomed to the idea, the *fact* that I am truly that which I have always denied I could be, a god in the purest interpretation of the word. Out of dormancy, out of unconsciousness and an infinity of striving, without knowing that this was what I was striving for . . .' His massive head shook slowly and he leaned heavily with both hands upon his staff, his spine bowed. '. . . I have given birth to a world. This is a wonder almost too immense to contemplate. And it pains me, renders me ecstatic, moves me . . . Ah, Queen Issul . . .' He trailed off. 'No words can possibly convey this.'

'What do you find?' enquired Issul with hope. 'Are you able to see within?'

'Sense is a closer approximation. But I am outside, an exiled god. I can see nothing.'

'But you sense life?'

'Oh yes. Absolutely yes. I have told you already, Orbus's world has life. It *is* alive. And fragile.' He peered towards the blue casket on the chiffonier. 'So vulnerable and easily shattered. Take care, Queen Issul. Cherish it like a babe in your hands, for it is upon you that its future depends.'

Issul bit her lip. 'What do you sense of this life?'

'That it *is*, that is all. I told you before, I cannot identify the creatures that dwell here. And I know your real question. I am sorry, if I could find Leth and your children I would, but I do not know how. Should I discover something, anything, I will tell you.'

Issul was silent for some moments, rocked by waves of emotion. When she could speak without her voice betraying her she said, 'Orbus, tell me there is an alternative.'

'An alternative to what?'

'To going with you to Enchantment.'

Orbus hesitated. 'I cannot. There is not.'

'There has to be.'

'I am sorry. I wish it could be otherwise.'

'I cannot leave.'

'You do not have a choice.'

'I will be giving Enchantment's Edge into the hands of my enemies.'

'Remain here and you give it both to your enemies and mine. It is utterly certain that all will perish, and Leth and your children . . . we will never know. But go with me and there is at least a hope.'

'Hardly. You have said it yourself.'

'I am your only hope. But here, deprived of the Soul of the Orb, I am scarcely better than helpless.'

'But you admit that the Orb's Soul may lie anywhere within Enchantment, or even beyond.'

'But if you can take me to Triune . . .'

'Yes?'

'We have certain things in common, Triune and I. A mutuality of interests, if Triune can only be induced to see it as such.'

Issul stared at him, torn. His figure was vague; he seemed composed of little more than shadow – a bulking, uncertain mass of shadow thrown from no discernible objects. She shook her head, forcing back tears. 'I cannot leave.'

In her mind an image formed, of Leth and her two small children wandering, lost, in a hostile, alien world. She stifled a sob that threatened to break her in two, and turned away so Orbus might not see her face.

'You are noble,' said Orbus, 'and brave, so brave. But you are tragically mistaken. You believe that by staying here you are helping your people and the kingdom, and that this is your duty over and above your devotion to your own family. You have it wrong. Yes, your duty is to do all you can to save your people. But stay here and you will be sacrificing them and your family too.'

Issul shook her head. Her voice quavered. 'I need evidence.'

'Am I not evidence enough?'

'All I have is your word. You say you want to help me, but Fectur would say the same thing. I know nothing of you, yet I am expected to follow your bidding, and in doing so entrust the kingdom to Fectur. I need more, Orbus.'

She almost choked on her tears. *My babies, Leth, am I forced to abandon you?*

'This is taking a terrible toll on you, child,' said Orbus softly. 'I can give you nothing more than I already have, but I can only reiterate: there is no alternative. And we must go now, for the

Krai are almost upon us. Soon there will be no way out of Enchantment's Edge.'

III

Until now Issul had felt that a meeting with the man known as Grey Venger would be more than she could bear. He was reckoned to be dangerously insane, and Pader Luminis had attested to the unnerving power of his mental state and the effect it had had on Leth during their meetings. But with Leth no longer here, and Fectur desperate to have Venger in his grasp once more, Issul knew that she could avoid him no longer.

Pader Luminis had brought her up to date on everything that, to his knowledge, had passed between Venger and King Leth before Leth's disappearance. Much defied comprehension, verging on deranged babble. Yet, as Pader carefully pointed out, there were in Venger's pronouncements uncanny correspondences to the circumstances that embroiled Enchantment's Edge, particularly in regard to the True Sept's prophecy concerning the coming of the Legendary Child. And Pader knew nothing of Orbus or the Orb's soul. Issul, like her husband before her, thought she descried a particular possible connection which set a question clamouring in her mind: *Is it possible that Venger holds the key to everything that is happening here?*

She knew she could avoid Grey Venger no longer.

With some trepidation she approached the door to the chamber where Venger was held. A male voice rang out loudly, 'The Queen!'

Sentries stiffened to attention. The sergeant-of-the-guard, breast-plate and helmet gleaming, marched forward to meet her. He tilted his head smartly and saluted. 'Your Majesty!'

'I wish to enter.'

The sergeant swivelled and beckoned to a pair of guards further along the corridor. They came at the run and stood rigid behind him.

'No,' said Issul. 'I am going in alone.'

The sergeant's jaw went slack. 'Your Majesty?'

'I do not require a guard. Simply remain on station outside the door.'

'But, Your Majesty, the prisoner —'

'Please unlock the door, sergeant.'

The blood had drained from the unhappy guardsman's cheeks. He hesitated, swallowed, found the courage to speak again. 'Your Majesty, I beg you to forgive me, but I would be negligent in my duties if I failed to point out to you that the prisoner is not restrained in any way. He is considered unpredictable and highly dangerous.'

'Thank you, sergeant.' Issul gave a wan smile of reassurance. 'Your concern is right and proper. I will call for you if I require assistance. Now, unlock the door, please.'

The sergeant hesitated, then gave a stiff nod and moved to comply. Inside the apartment Issul could at first see no sign of the man she had come to interview. The main chamber was silent and still; from outside she could hear the gentle hiss of drizzle upon rooftiles and stone. She wondered if Grey Venger was asleep in the bedchamber beyond. She stepped towards the door of the bedchamber, then stopped, spying a lean-limbed figure crouched upon a chair before one window.

'Grey Venger.'

The figure did not move. She could not make out much of his features due to the light at his back. She took three steps in order to position herself where she might view him better.

'Who are you?' Venger's voice was harsh and, even in such a blunt question, tinted with mockery.

'I wish to talk to you.'

'Talk? Talk?' He gave a derisive chuckle, tugging at his grey beard. 'What would the Grey Venger want with talk with a miltpot? Are you not sent to give comfort to the Grey Venger?'

Issul stood calm. 'I am not. I come only to talk, to share knowledge, which is the reason you agreed to come to Orbia.'

'What new trick is this?' Grey Venger uncurled his legs, placing his feet upon the floor, and leaned forward from the waist. 'Leth sends me one of his splashers, to *talk*? To *"exchange knowledge"*?' He snorted, then his face became still and he peered suspiciously at Issul. 'Or is it the High Lord Spectre who has sent you?'

'Neither. I am the Queen.'

'The Queen?' Venger sprang out of his seat and thrust himself at her. Surprised, Issul drew back. Grey Venger pushed his agonized features close to hers, inspecting her as though she were no more than a whore, a slave or workbeast up for sale. 'The Queen! Issul! Godless spouse of the godless mouse! Yes, yes, it truly is! I did not recognize you, but then why should I? I make no apology for you are of no consequence. Am I required to bow?'

'I will not insist upon formality if it displeases you.'

'Displeases!' Venger laughed briefly and mirthlessly, stroking his chin and appraising her with haughty insolence. 'What do you want?'

'You came to Orbia, I am informed, to talk with King Leth, one to one, as equals. I ask only the same.'

'Equals? *Hah!*' With a guttural bark Grey Venger threw himself from her. He crossed the chamber with long bounds, stabbing at the air with bony hands. 'Leth! Low, skulking Leth! He still thinks himself my equal? Bah! He is nothing. *Nothing!* He is less than a beetle's droppings which I am not even aware that I crush beneath my feet. And you, *Queen* Issul—' Grey Venger spun around and bounded back. He thrust his hooked nose almost against hers, his hands poised as if to seize her. Issul readied herself for defence, but his fingers did not make contact. '– Lesser men deem you beautiful, but they see with the eyes of the Unclean. Grey Venger's eyes have been opened by the One Truth. The Grey Venger sees what is real. He stands before "beauty" such as yours and sees only the sputum of a louse that he plucks from the crotch of a dog!'

Venger's breath was sour, the reek of his sweat pungent and foul. Issul did not flinch. 'I trust you are being treated well, Master Venger. I passed orders that you were to be accorded every hospitality.'

Venger's upper lip curled into an ugly smirk.

'Have you eaten and drunk your fill? King Leth was anxious that you be made to feel welcome. Is the apartment to your liking? Certainly more comfortable than the dungeon you have recently left, I would think.'

''Tis all one to me.' To Issul's relief Venger moved away again, head forward, scowling. 'What subterfuge is this, Issul?'

'There is no subterfuge.'

'I never doubted that Leth would break his word. That is the way of the godless. Has he understood now that he cannot break me? Not even the Spectre, the scourge and terror of ordinary mortals, can instil fear into the heart of the Grey Venger.'

'Leth did not break his word, Venger. The Lord High Invigilate acted without authority. He has been severely reprimanded. Did he harm you?'

'I have already said, he cannot.' Venger stood squarely facing the Queen, bitter contempt etched into his face.

Issul was hard put to withstand his gaze. This man she could not fathom. By Pader's account he had permitted the execution of his two sons, in the full knowledge that with a word he could have saved them. They had been implicated in Venger's and the True Sept's plot to assassinate King Leth – a plot which was never meant to succeed. Venger had known this; Venger had engineered it. He had deliberately faked a murder attempt on Leth in order to promote the True Sept's beliefs regarding the coming of the Legendary Child. Ignorant of the deception, Leth had outlawed Venger and the True Sept and granted orders for the arrest of the Sept's leading members. Venger's sons were located and taken into custody. Under intense pressure from the other major factions and prominent persons in certain sections of government Leth had pronounced the death sentence upon Venger's sons, to be commuted to imprisonment upon Venger's giving himself into custody. Venger did not show and Leth found himself with little choice but to sign the death warrant of his two sons.

Issul felt a sudden, overwhelming sense of desolation. *What hatred you must feel, Venger, for Leth and everything he holds dear. And, oh! I see so clearly now, over and above all else, how you must loathe yourself. I pity you, Venger. Truly. How you must crave oblivion.*

'Where is Leth?' demanded Venger, his gaze wavering for an instant, as though disconcerted by her thoughts. 'What does he hope to gain by sending his miltpot to me? I am of the Righteous and Faithful, immune to the temptations to which lesser men succumb. The charms of the King's harlot will not move the Grey Venger.'

'Leth has sent no one. I have come, as I have said, in the hope that we might talk, that is all. That we might profitably exchange information.'

'No information you possess can be of interest to me.'

'Then I shall trouble you no further.' She turned briskly, her head high, and made for the door. Her fingers closed around the handle and she closed her eyes. Was all lost? Her heart was in her mouth. She twisted the handle and drew the door towards her. Had she failed to judge him correctly?

'Wait!'

Issul almost slumped with relief. She half-turned, her hands still on the open door.

Grey Venger had not moved. His eyes burned. 'I will hear what you have to say.'

Slowly Issul eased the door closed, noting the solicitude on the faces of the soldiers in the corridor outside. 'First you will answer some questions.'

'You spoke of information.'

'Yes.'

A peevish note crept into Venger's voice. 'Yes. Then speak.'

She concealed her anger. *Enjoy your arrogance, Venger, for the tables are about to turn.* She stepped slowly towards him, pensive as she considered her words. Then, deliberately, she raised her eyes and met his gaze. 'I have spoken with the Legendary Child.'

The effect was extraordinary. Issul savoured the moment, brief though it was. The muscles in Grey Venger's taut face twitched in a sudden spasm, all virtually at once. His wiry body gave a jerk and he could not prevent a sudden, audible intake of breath. Momentarily all self-control deserted him. His face flushed, and he grew stock still, his eyes wary, boring into Issul.

'It is a lie!'

'Would your Queen feed you falsehoods?'

His thin lips quivered. It seemed he came close to showing a grim smile as he acknowledged the irony of her challenge. Some of the tension slipped from between Issul's shoulderblades. *This man is arrogant and remote beyond belief, but he is not untouchable, much as he would have me believe otherwise.*

'You must give me proof,' Venger said.

'There is no proof. You have only my word, but I think it will convince you. And I will tell you something more: I was present at his birth.'

Again, pure shock on Venger's face, and resentment in his pale grey eyes. Denial, then outrage and envy, and denial again. Then he shook his head. 'No. That cannot be.'

'Oh yes. I did not fully realize then, for I had scant knowledge of the secret the True Sept holds. More than that—' Issul halted, rendered mute by the terrible image of her younger sister, Ressa, Mawnie's twin, outstretched upon the grass on Sentinel's Peak, bloodied and all but lifeless, mounted by the vile monster that was Moscul's sire.

'Yes?' demanded Venger hungrily.

Issul shook her head. 'Before I tell you anything more I have questions for you.'

Grey Venger smirked, folding his arms across his chest. 'Do you think I am so foolish? Leth tried the same trick, luring me here with empty promises, then telling me only that the Child had been found then lost again. And now you try to beguile me with more spurious claims.'

'Are you so certain that you can disregard them?'

Venger pursed his mouth into shrewd grimace. 'You said your word could convince me. So far it has not.'

Issul nodded to herself. 'What do you seek?'

'You were present at the birth, you say? So, tell me, that I may know whether we have more to discuss.'

The memory pained her, but Venger's demand could not be considered unreasonable under the circumstances. She said, wincing, 'The Child was born out of Death.'

Grey Venger's shoulders and head jutted forward, his mouth hanging open. He nodded, urging her on.

Issul glanced beyond, seeking solace from the awful image her mind's eye beheld. 'It gave birth to itself, out of the womb of a mother who had been dead for three days.'

Grey Venger appraised her venomously for several moments, then stretched his lips tightly across decaying teeth in a bestial grimace. He gave a single nod. 'We will talk.'

He reseated himself in the chair, folding his legs beneath his buttocks, his hands gripping the carved chair arms with whitened knuckles. Issul could barely see, so affected was she by the memory of sister's body being ravaged by the unnatural child that fought its way free of her womb. She pushed back the tears and nausea, and remained standing though she was faint and would have preferred to sit. Gathering her thoughts she said, 'Tell me about the King Without A Soul, Venger.'

'I have told Leth.'

'I seek to know more.'

'Where *is* Leth?'

'Engaged in vital matters of state. You know there is a great crisis upon us. He considers, due to my experience with the Child, that I am better equipped to speak with you at this juncture.'

Grey Venger mulled this over but made no comment.

'Your teachings tell of the coming of the King Without A Soul,' Issul continued. 'And you have declared Leth to be that King and that he is to be overthrown by the Legendary Child, who will establish a new faith and a new domain.'

'That is so.'

'You say also that the Soulless King cannot be killed, at least not by any mortal. That he must live to witness the extirpation of his people and his kind, and then be destroyed by one qualified to perform that act. Whom do you deem to be that one? The Legendary Child, or some other?'

'It is written but is for the eyes only of the most trusted of the True Believers.'

'The Soul that has been cast away, where might it be found?'

'Sealed within a crucible of shining adamant inside the high fortress sanctum of the One True God, within Enchantment.'

'Does the True Sept know the location of the fortress sanctum?'

Venger looked at her with mocking eyes, but said nothing.

'If the King were reunited with his Soul . . . ? What then?'

'That cannot be.'

'Why not?'

'Ha!'

'Can you be so sure, Venger?'

Grey Venger held her gaze but the taunting smile that adorned his face began to waver. He glanced away. She nodded inwardly. *Something here disquiets him. I have penetrated his armour again!*

'Remember,' she said, 'I have spoken with the Legendary Child.'

'Then ask the Child about the Lost Soul.'

'I have. And now I am asking the leader of the True Sept.'

A measured tone crept into Venger's voice. 'Why?'

She sensed that the idea of her having actually had contact with the Legendary Child was almost intolerable to him. He did not want it to be true, probably doubted that it was true, but could not be sure. 'To compare your answers,' she said.

Venger shifted in his seat, stretching the muscles and sinews of his neck and flexing his fingers. 'I am the Grey Venger, a mere servant who prepares the way. I know secrets, many secrets, and The One and True Sept has custody of many more. But you are of the Soulless, not worthy or deserving. I tell you only as much as I tell.'

'You have said that the Legendary Child is the scion of the One True God and that they are to rule, as one, in Unity?'

'That is so.'

'How is this to come about?'

'Ha!'

Again contempt, and such defiance, such godly superiority in his eyes. Issul grew angry.

'Venger, you say you are a servant of the Legendary Child and the One True God, and that you and the True Sept have prepared the way.'

'That is so.'

'What will be your reward for this service?'

'Righteous peace,' he sneered. 'When the last of the Unbelievers and Corrupted have been wiped from the world.'

'Intriguing.' She smiled blandly at him and saw the wariness creep back into his gaze. 'Are you truly certain that the Child will know its followers? Are you certain that it even knows itself?'

She was gambling. She had gained so little from her conversation with Moscul at Lastmeadow, in part because she had hardly known what questions to ask. Her priority then had been to bring him back to Enchantment's Edge, where he could be observed, questioned further, if necessary . . . if necessary, yes, she would have had him killed. She had been in no doubt that Moscul was an extraordinary child, and that he knew himself to be extraordinary. But she had not been sure that he knew precisely what he was.

'What do you mean?' Grey Venger said, a muscle twitching high on his left cheek.

She watched him closely to try and gauge how her statement affected him. 'The Child made no reference to you or the True Sept, nor to the One God who is his father. When I left him it was with a feeling that he does not know you. In fact I do not believe he knows his purpose at all.'

Venger glowered at her with murderous eyes, grinding his teeth, but she thought, for an instant, that a flicker of . . . could it have been fear? . . . showed behind the terrible glare. Before he could

speak she followed up. 'How is he to find you, Venger? Can it be
that he does not know his true role, that he has to be told?'

The thought came to her even as she voiced it. But its effect
upon Grey Venger was illuminating. He leapt from his seat again
and stood before her, arms outstretched, tortured face turned to the
ceiling. In a voice that rang with emotion he proclaimed, 'It is the
time of the godless, known by the Righteous Powers which will
range themselves against the Unbelievers and their foul King Who
Is Without A Soul. And at this time the Child of Legend shall be
born and will seek out its followers, the Righteous Believers of
the One And True Sept who have paved His Way! He shall come
among them and restore the True Faith, for he will know them just
as he will know the Unbelievers: he will know them *by their ways!*
And he shall join with his Father, the One True God, and together
with the faithful they will restore the world to the wholeness that
went before.'

The wholeness that went before! Even as Grey Venger stood
before her with a crazed triumphal grimace, breathing hard, daring
her to challenge his words, the veins standing out on his temples
and neck, Issul struggled to extract and make sense of the essence
of his words, behind the bombast and rhetoric. *Restore the world to
the wholeness that went before.* Orbus had said that the Higher Ones,
the gods of Enchantment, hardly knowing what they did, warred
endlessly in order to survive, and that their conflict maintained the
energies that Enchantment itself needed to survive. The world had
once been all as Enchantment was now, and the ultimate aim of the
beings known as gods was to reclaim the world, to return it to the
flux that was Enchantment.

*Is this what is happening here? Can the True Sept itself be,
unwittingly, a pawn of the forces of Enchantment?*

The thought threw a new fear into her which she was not yet
able to assimilate fully.

'Thus is it written,' Grey Venger declared, lowering his arms
and standing, teeth bared, before her. 'The Child is here, just as
we predicted. And that is the proof. He knows us. Now, enough of
your questions, *Issul.* Tell me now about the Legendary Child.'

TWO

I

When she came from Grey Venger's chamber Issul was unable to prevent herself trembling. As Pader had warned, Grey Venger's personality was extreme, exuding a rancour and hatred that was almost palpable. The tension of dealing with him had been almost unbearable. She felt that he had somehow got inside her. Her head throbbed, the muscles of her chest had tensed, constricting her lungs so that she breathed in short, shallow gasps.

The sergeant-of-the-guard in the corridor outside came forward with a strained look and enquired whether she needed assistance. She replied in the negative and went on her way, in a daze. Her mind was abuzz with the possible ramifications of what she had gleaned. Venger, largely unwittingly, had given her much to think about. In the latter stages of their meeting, when Issul had recounted elements of her encounter with Moscul, his agitation had mounted. She had left him with the conviction growing ever more forcefully upon her that the True Sept might be being manipulated by forces it had no real knowledge of.

She turned a corner. A side-portal opened a short distance ahead of her and the slight, aged figure of Pader Luminis stepped into the passage. He waited, dressed in a loose grey robe bound at the waist with a cincture of soft, tasselled cord. His thin hands were clasped at his chest, a small affectionate smile upon his lips as he peered over a pair of glass discs balanced low upon his nose. When Issul came alongside him he took pace with her.

'Did you see and hear all, Pader?' Issul asked.

'I heard, certainly,' the little Murinean replied. 'Vision was not as clear. The plug in the wall panel allows a very restricted view. You handled him well, dear Issul. In fact, I do believe you unsettled him. The results may be interesting to witness.'

'Do you think so?'

'I believe you planted a seed of doubt deep within his psyche. That is remarkable in itself. He will do everything in his power to suppress and eliminate it. But the mere possibility of the Legendary Child's being something other than he has spent his life believing . . . well, it threatens the very foundations of his creed. And you have met the Child. This he cannot ignore. Now he is alone, and must mull over his thoughts without the support of his brethren to reinforce him. Whether the outcome will benefit us in any way is, of course, another matter entirely.'

'He is . . . *terrifying*,' seethed Issul through clenched teeth.

'If terror was your experience you concealed it admirably. I think you even gained his respect – as far as is possible for the sputum of a louse plucked from the crotch of a dog, that is.'

Issul laughed briefly. 'He has a remarkable ability to charm.'

'I have heard that he selects his wives by gathering together half a dozen young women in a ritual setting. They are subjected to various abuses, commencing with verbal and graduating to more violent forms. The process can last for many hours, even days, without let-up. The woman who withstands his attentions the longest without breaking gains the honour of bearing his child.'

'It must make her very proud.' They arrived at an intersection of passages, and Issul halted. 'Pader, apply yourself to the minutiae of what you have just witnessed. Later we will discuss it in detail in the hope that something useful may come of it. For now though, I must clear my thoughts of that man.'

She departed, filled now with self-reproach. She trusted Pader implicitly; she was reliant upon his wisdom and insight. But she had not confided everything to him. Pader knew of the existence of the blue casket, knew too that it was of incalculable value and importance. But he did not know about Orbus, nor that Leth and the children were trapped within the casket. Orbus had forbidden her to reveal these things, and she was not yet ready to go against his wishes. She knew too little about him, and the consequences could be far too high. But to exclude Pader Luminis from vital information seemed self-defeating, placing restrictions upon the invaluable assistance his expertise could provide, as well as being a betrayal of an old friend.

Issul carried on through the elaborate maze of Orbia's corridors, through fabulous marbled galleries lined with statues and tapestries of inconceivable value, along arcades opening upon flowering courtyards and pleasant gardens. Eventually she entered the military sections. In due course she stepped through an open portal onto the first level of a two-tier gallery that overlooked a hall commonly used for weapons-training by officers of the Palace Guard. Below, her eyes fell upon Shenwolf, who was engaged in swordplay with Master Meles, one of Orbia's most eminent weapons-masters. Among his many other duties, Meles was arms-tutor to Prince Galry, Issul's son. Issul had trained with him herself on many occasions: she knew him to be formidably skilled and a devoted and demanding taskmaster. So it interested her to observe that, facing Shenwolf, Master Meles was not having an easy time.

Seated upon a bench to one side of the hall were Kol and Phisusandra, the two companions who, with Shenwolf, had helped Issul escape the secret Krai camp in which she had been held prisoner. They sat with intent expressions, engrossed in the combat. Issul moved silently into the lee of a graceful fluted stone column supporting the upper tier, and watched unseen.

The two fighters wore hauberks of stuffed leather, leather shin-guards and hardened leather bascinets. Master Meles fought with a longsword, a slim dagger gripped in his left hand. Shenwolf, somewhat to Issul's surprise, used his own smallsword, notable for its unusual down-curving quillons. He too held a slender dagger in his left hand. The fact that they were his own weapons suggested that the edges were not dulled, as was the norm in practice.

The two men seemed not to have been duelling for long. Neither of them was breathing hard or had worked up a sweat. They moved cautiously across the floor, circling one another, sizing each other up. Occasionally one would make a feint, but neither seemed ready yet to press the attack seriously. Then Master Meles lunged. Shenwolf slanted his torso to the side, stepping backwards at the same time. Meles's blade pushed past his breastbone, missing him by a finger's breadth. Shenwolf's shorter blade came up and caught Meles's sword with the curved tine of his quillon. Shenwolf twisted deftly and thrust away, pushing Meles momentarily off balance. Meles swivelled, quickly recovering his guard, and parried a thrust from Shenwolf. He leapt in and sent Shenwolf back with a series of blindingly fast thrusts.

The combat was earnest now. Both men had the measure of their opponent, and each had gained the other's respect. They sparred back and forth. Issul found her eyes more frequently on Shenwolf. There was a grin upon his face; he was plainly enjoying the sport. A slight glow had begun to colour his cheeks and sweat could be seen gleaming on his brow below the rim of his leather bascinet. Likewise Master Meles was breathing harder, a sheen of perspiration upon his face.

Shenwolf was the taller and more slightly built of the two. His movements were fluid and graceful, extremely fast and perfectly controlled. It was almost like watching a skilled dancer. His attacks came from unusual angles. He would lean his body to one side and strike upwards to Meles's flank, forcing Meles to an awkward back-handed defence. He would raise his blade high and stab downwards over Meles's attack. At times he would appear to leave himself open, but when Meles moved to take advantage, Shenwolf would dart or twist or bend his body and Meles would strike only air, or clash against Shenwolf's blade.

It was true that Meles was Shenwolf's senior by well over a decade, and might therefore want for the speed and stamina of the younger man, but he was superbly fit and powerful. His superior strength and experience, by Issul's calculations, should have out-weighed any advantages that Shenwolf had. But as the combat proceeded it became obvious that Meles was being forced onto the defensive far more frequently than was to his liking.

Quite suddenly it was over. Meles was being pushed back, step by remorseless step, until he was close up against the wall opposite the gallery from where Issul watched. Each blow, had it struck home, would have impaled him. But he fended with quick, expert parries and deflections and further backward steps. Abruptly he stepped in with a powerful counterstrike. Shenwolf dodged, caught the blade with his quillon and twisted hard, this time with a sharp downward motion. Meles grunted; his sword flew from his hand and clattered across the floor. He straightened with an expression of rueful resignation, Shenwolf's swordtip at his throat.

Issul clapped. All four men looked up. Kol and Phisusandra rose immediately from the bench where they sat, and they each bowed their heads.

'Do not stand on ceremony,' said Issul. 'That was impressive to observe. An excellent display!'

Master Meles, nursing his wrist, said, 'Master Shenwolf tried hard to convince me verbally of the merits of the shortsword over the long. I was not persuaded and invited him to prove his case.' He wiped his forearm across his brow. 'I confess, I did not anticipate quite so much exercise.'

'And are you persuaded now?' asked the Queen.

'I have been well bested, on this occasion at least. He is a master of his craft. Even so, I cannot say that I am persuaded to recommend a wholesale change of weaponry for the entire army of Enchantment's Edge.'

'Nor was that my aim,' smiled Shenwolf. 'But I hope I have successfully demonstrated that in certain situations, most notably when fighting in a confined space, the smallsword is the superior weapon. Musclebound soldiers will scoff and declare it to be suitable only for women and children, but I have seen more than one 'expert' bladesman pay the price for such an arrogant assumption.'

'This is hardly a confined space,' Kol pointed out.

Shenwolf gave a shrug, almost apologetically. He looked at Meles and grinned sheepishly. Meles slapped his shoulder. 'You beat me, lad, and there's nothing more to be said. I hope you will teach me some of those moves when an opportunity arises.'

'Gladly.'

'Your technique is unorthodox,' Issul observed.

'Where I come from the smallsword is more commonly the weapon of choice. Such techniques are the norm.'

'Still, I suspect you have devoted much time and effort to their mastery.' Issul stepped back from the balustrade and descended to the floor of the hall via a winding staircase at one end of the gallery. 'Shenwolf, would it be too much to request another demonstration, or are you fatigued?'

'I would be pleased to do so.' Shenwolf turned. 'Master Meles?'

'No,' said Issul. She stepped across the hall to a weapons rack which stood before one wall. 'You will fight me.'

'My lady, Shenwolf uses his own weapon. The blades are keen,' protested Master Meles.

'So I noted,' replied the Queen. 'It should add an edge of excitement, and I am in need of the exercise. It will help to focus my mind.'

She selected a smallsword from the rack, tested its weight and balance and took a few swift swipes at the air, then nodded to herself. 'Meles, would you help me into a combat suit, please.'

'You employ your quillons to good effect,' she said to Shenwolf as Master Meles adjusted the straps of her leather hauberk. 'Our smallswords lack such refinement. It is clearly something our weaponsmiths should look at in future. For now, I must be wary.' She pulled a helmet onto her head and stepped to the middle of the hall and faced Shenwolf. 'Do you think to show quarter because I am the Queen, or simply a woman?'

Shenwolf grinned wryly. 'I have fought beside you, and know that to do so would be unwise.'

'Good. Then let us engage.'

She drove forward with a yell, her blade flashing, a blur of motion. Shenwolf was pushed back. The clash of their swords reverberated around the hall as he deflected her flurry of moves. He dodged, drove in with a slashing blow to her middle. Issul blocked him, but was forced to step back to avoid the dagger in his left hand. Now it was Shenwolf who advanced, Issul defending against a rain of blows that came hard and fast, vibrating along the length of her arm, almost numbing her. Shenwolf's eyes were bright, his lips parted, smiling with sheer exhilaration.

The combat continued, back and forth, neither gaining the upper hand. Issul changed her tactics, switching suddenly from deflective moves to an attack. Shenwolf blocked her, she retreated again. Suddenly she was against the wall. Shenwolf stepped in quickly and pushed aside her blade-arm. He was suddenly up against her. His sweat was strong in her nostrils; she felt the heat of his body almost touching hers. Shenwolf's hands were pressed against the wall behind her. He breathed hard, their faces separated by less than a hand's breadth.

'No quarter?' breathed Issul.

'Neither expected nor given.'

She pushed him off, ducked beneath his arm, and stepped back, panting. Shenwolf faced her, lowering his body, his weapon held towards her. Issul sprang, stabbing. Shenwolf drew back. They circled, then Shenwolf lunged forward, aiming a blow at her middle. In an instant Issul dropped to the floor, raising her sword to block his and at the same time sweeping his advancing foot away with her own. Shenwolf fell, and Issul rolled and came up over him, her leg pressing his to the floor, her blade at his windpipe.

'Your death, I think.'

'Ah, but I do not go alone to my grave.'

He glanced down between them. She looked down and saw his dagger blade held firm, its tip a mere finger's breadth from her ribcage. Had he thrust forward, or had she pushed towards him, she would have been impaled.

Shenwolf threw off his leather helmet and let his head fall back upon the floor, closing his eyes for a moment, breathing hard. For a moment Issul gazed at him. His damp hair clung to his forehead. He opened his eyes and met her gaze. She rolled away and rose to her feet.

Master Meles approached, clapping. 'Superb! Most instructive to watch.'

He began to help Issul unfasten the straps of her hauberk as Shenwolf stood. Shenwolf looked with irony at Issul. 'And you called my technique unorthodox? That last move with the feet is something I have never encountered before.'

Issul smiled. 'But I don't think you will be caught by it again.'

Shenwolf gave a sigh, sheathing his blade. 'Ah well, it was an enjoyable tussle.'

Issul shrugged off the hauberk. Her face became pensive. 'I have given much thought to your station here within Enchantment's Edge. You have demonstrated loyalty and service over and above the call of duty. I learn, too, that you earned King Leth's personal commendation before you rode from Enchantment's Edge in search of me. I am grateful, Shenwolf.'

'I did only what was required in the circumstances.'

'No. You did far more. Will you accept promotion? I would have you raised to the office of captain. Furthermore, I wish you transferred from the King's Cavalry to the Royal Orbia Guard, where you will serve in my personal guard. You will be quartered here, within the Palace, in your own private apartment. Is this agreeable to you?'

Shenwolf bowed his head. 'This is a great privilege. I have served such a short time.'

'But exceptionally, with courage, initiative and signal devotion to the Crown. You have shown yourself again and again to be more than worthy. It would please me immensely if you would accept.'

'Then I accept gladly.'

Issul turned to Kol and Phisusandra. 'And you two, who are also my brave and loyal companions. I promised financial reward to those who returned with me to Enchantment's Edge, and this will be forthcoming. Furthermore, it is my hope that you will choose to stay here with us. On the face of it the prospect may not appear too enticing, given the conflict that is upon us. But the struggle will not end here unless we of Enchantment's Edge can bring about its end. It will spread in ways we cannot yet imagine, for it is no natural conflict that we face. All the known lands will be engulfed, and those that lie beyond, too. So, if you choose to leave you will depart with my fond and grateful good wishes. I will provide you with the best mounts, and your purses will bulge. With fortune on your side you may yet somehow escape the terrible war that embroils us. On the other hand, I need loyal and responsible men around me at this time more than ever. Out of gratitude I will provide good homes for you both, with money enough to establish yourselves in whatever business you may choose, without further commitment on your part. If you have a taste for the soldier's life, however, I would also have you both drafted into my personal guard, to serve directly under Shenwolf's command.'

Without hesitation Kol replied, 'I would consider it the greatest honour.'

Phisusandra stepped forward and bowed. 'You pay me a great compliment, Majesty. I will be proud to remain here and serve you.'

'Excellent!' declared Issul, smiling broadly at each of them. 'Excellent! Already I feel that my enemies have taken a step back!'

'Perhaps we could –' Shenwolf began, then broke off, the smile leaving his face. He was looking upwards at something beyond Issul's shoulder.

Issul turned, following the direction of his gaze. At the balcony of the upper gallery a figure stood silent and motionless, clad in a loose black robe.

Issul stiffened. Her features grew cold. 'Lord Fectur.'

Fectur inclined his head slightly, his face impassive.

'What is it you want?' asked the Queen.

'I was passing, that is all, and found myself drawn to observe the activities here,' the Lord High Invigilate replied. 'It was a magnificent display, my lady. My congratulations to you.'

'I was not truly the victor,' Issul said.

'I meant for your choice of partner.'

She caught the inflection in his voice, and bristled. Fectur's eyes travelled briefly over Shenwolf, then back, expressionlessly, to the Queen. 'Ah yes, the emergency assembly you requested has been convened for two hours hence.'

'Very good.' Issul turned away, a hundred emotions warring in her head. Fectur glanced again at Shenwolf, then, flickeringly, at Kol and Phisusandra, and withdrew.

II

In her apartment once more, Issul undressed as her maids filled a porcelain bath with warm water scented with crushed leaves of lemon verbena. She lathered herself all over with sandalwood soap, washing away the exertions of the morning, and rested for mere moments as the water soothed her tired muscles. Then she climbed from the bath and donned fresh garments. She chose a long, loose blouse of pale gold satin, sashed at the waist, and baggy blue pantaloons gathered at the ankles, with soft doeskin ankleboots upon her feet. Such attire, like that which she had worn earlier, was better suited to present circumstances than the more formal and cumbersome vestments of office, which restricted movement and made every breath an effort.

She thought about Leth and the children. What perils were they facing in Orbus's world? Leth's sword rested in its rack; during his confinement it and all other weapons had been removed, by Fectur's command, 'for his own protection'. Leth, almost certainly, was defenceless.

Issul almost choked. *It was I who allowed the Legendary Child to live! I have brought all this about!*

She shook her head, dispelling the thought. She had allowed her nephew to live. Could she have known?

She cast her mind back yet again to the terrible moments of Moscul's unnatural birth. Yes, she had known something. She had suspected, even though she did not wholly believe. She had hidden her nephew with Ohirbe's family at Lastmeadow, hoping against desperate hope that her fears were unfounded. How could she have been so foolish?

Beyond her window the roofs of Enchantment's Edge shone in a dazzling golden light. The earlier drizzle had ceased and the sun had burned through much of the mist. Enchantment's Edge presented an unworldly spectacle, cloaked as it was now in the defences erected at King Leth's orders to deter slooth attacks. Netting, rope, sheets of metal mesh, lines of cord, cloth, anything at all that could be slung from window to bastion, merlon to finial, were draped from roofs, towers, turrets. Pikes, spears and sharpened poles jutted skywards everywhere at bizarre angles – any device or contrivance that might conceivably hinder the slooths should they choose to descend once more upon the capital.

The great city-castle appeared wrapped in a colossal web, a web ragged, bristling and spiny, as though cast by some unknown gigantean arachnid. And still so much remained unprotected. Labourers toiled day and night to produce more net, more rope, more mesh, but it was an impossible task. The vastness of Enchantment's Edge forestalled any hope of covering it in its entirety.

Arbalestiers and bowmen were stationed at alert at battlements and windows, their eyes upon the skies. Great water-butts and pails had been installed at regular intervals on parapets and in the city streets, for use in the event of a repeat of the fire-bombing that the slooths had brought against Giswel Holt. Far off, beyond the ocean of mist-wreathed forest far below, the rain and clouds still obscured the fiery peaks of Enchantment's mountains. Issul felt a strange conflict of emotion as she gazed there towards the unseen.

I have been there, and returned!

She recalled the words of the strange tripartite child-god, Triune: 'Welcome to the true world, the many-named domain, where all things are possible.'

All things? Can you return my children to me? Can you save my husband and King? Are you able or willing to act to prevent your world claiming mine?

'The unstill air. Something always becomes. Or strives to become. This is *Creation*.'

Creation? Which you strive to suspend?

'The formed can be unformed, the unformed formed. Here is raw power. Here is dream. Here is magic.'

For what end?

40 *PHILIP G. WILLIAMSON*

'Here is Enchantment'.

She recalled her fear, her confusion as she faced those three identical children with their brilliant, peering blue eyes, as she floundered helplessly in their globe of blue vapour.

'Be aware when you dream, for you take something of the true world with you now. Something of Enchantment is yours.'

But what? What happened there? What does this all mean?

Issul grew conscious of someone knocking upon the door of her chamber. She smoothed her blouse, gathered her thoughts. 'Come.'

A high seneschal entered. 'My lady, I an informed by the captain of the guard upon the Palace Gate that someone wishes to see you.'

'Who?'

'A lady – A woman. From the country.'

Ohirbe? With a pang Issul recalled that the last time she had seen Ohirbe, Moscul's foster-mother, had been on the road to Crosswood. Issul had been bringing Moscul to Enchantment's Edge; Ohirbe and her husband, Arrin, had been in the party. They had been ambushed by the Krai. Moscul escaped, Arrin was killed, Issul had been taken prisoner. She had barely given a thought to poor Ohirbe since. Her last sight had been of Ohirbe frantically climbing from the cart in pursuit of the fleeing Moscul. Had she survived? Returned to her home in Lastmeadow? Or come on as planned to Enchantment's Edge?

'Does she have a name?'

'The captain says she gives no name,' replied the seneschal. 'She has been in custody for some hours, apparently. She is insistent that she must speak to you, only to you.'

It would not be Ohirbe, then. She would not have failed to give her name, or to have made her identity plain in some other manner. 'I do not have time for this.'

'As we thought, my lady. However, the woman sends a message which she claims you will find meaningful. She says that you and she met in the forest near Crosswood, and that she comes to talk of the Foulborn. The captain says to mention that she bears a recent wound upon her left cheek.'

Issul's heart kicked. She recalled the moment, as she struggled through the undergrowth in search of Moscul, when she had emerged into a small clearing. Facing her was an old woman on hands and knees, bulky of build, clambering to her feet. Blood streamed down her cheek. There had been no sign of Moscul, but the woman had pointed a shaking finger at Issul and cried out in portentous tones, 'It has begun! It's too late now. I tried, but it is too late!'

There had been a blinding pain, and darkness. Issul's next memory had been of waking to find herself a prisoner of the Krai.

Is a crucial element in this great mystery about to be solved?

'I will be there immediately,' she told the seneschal.

'Tell the captain that on no account must anybody be allowed to speak to this woman until I get there. And summon Shenwolf. Have him attend me at the guardroom where this woman is held.'

III

The captain of the guard of the Palace Gate informed Issul that the woman had entered the city-castle the previous evening. One among hundreds of refugees seeking sanctuary from the advancing Krai. Upon gaining access she had separated from her group and made for the gates of Orbia Palace where she had loudly demanded an audience with the Queen.

'The men thought her mad, a harridan in her cups, or a witch. They paid her little heed, other than as the butt of their jokes. In time they were on the verge of having her removed, were even considering tossing her back out through the city gates, so I understand.'

'So what changed their minds?'

'Her persistence, perhaps. It is not clear. But apparently she had seated herself before the Palace Gate and refused to budge. She was crying out over and over again, something about a lost child in the woods and the Queen being taken by the Krai.'

Issul drew in a breath. How much had this woman revealed in the presence of so many?

'These things were reported to me, my lady,' the captain continued. 'Her words made little sense, but knowing of the ambush beyond Crosswood in which you were involved, I was intrigued. I elected to speak to the woman. She is a strange creature. A witch? Yes, perhaps she is that. She certainly has an unfathomable quality. But I got little out of her, other than her insistence upon an audience with you. I would have dismissed her, but when she told me that she had met with you at the site of the Krai ambush, I felt I must refer the matter directly to you.'

'You did well, captain. Does the Lord High Invigilate know of this woman?'

'I have not informed him. Her hubbub was loud and protracted, though. Someone may have thought it significant enough to bring to Lord Fectur's attention; I cannot say.'

'I prefer that he knows nothing of this. Should he turn up here refer him to me. He is not to be permitted to see or speak to this woman without my express permission.'

'Very good, my lady.'

'Now, show me to her.'

The old woman did not rise when Issul entered. She was seated upon a rough pallet beside one wall, her legs stretched before her. 'Forgive me. I mean no disrespect, but I am old and my limbs ache, my joints are stiff. I have walked a long way to find you, and now my old body is admonishing me in no uncertain terms.'

Issul stared at her. She was the same woman she had come upon in the woods. The deep scratches upon her cheek had darkened into unsightly scabs. Issul felt herself growing angry. 'What is it you want? Do you have a name? Who are you?'

The old woman did not rush to reply. 'I wondered,' she said at length, 'when we met in the forest, but I did not know it was you. Not that it would have made a difference. The Krai warriors took you. I did not think we would ever meet again.'

'But they did not take you?'

'What good was a hag like me? No, they pushed me to the ground and made off with a younger, more comely prize.'

'But they let you live.'

'I fully believe I am alive, yes. Had there not been fighting all around perhaps they would have killed me. But the element of surprise, which had been theirs, had now been taken from them. They were more interested in getting away.'

'My soldiers scoured the woods. There was no report of you.'

'Why would there be? The forest is dense, and I did not wish to be found. And who, in such a fray, would take notice of an old peasant woman in the woods?'

Issul weighed this. 'I say again, have you a name? And why have you come here?'

The old woman gave a gummy smile. 'Aye, I've a name, though it'll mean nothing to you. I am called Arene. As for what I want . . .' She sighed, and stared ruefully at an uncertain point low upon the opposite wall. 'I have come from afar. Initially, Queen Issul, I came to save you.'

A chill slid the length of Issul's spine. 'Save me? From what?'

Arene's eyes moved back to her. 'There is a destiny upon you, and upon your world. I could have prevented it. That is why I was sent. I could have done it so easily, but it is too late now. I have been foiled. Twice. Twice the Foulborn has been in my grasp, and twice he has escaped. Fate played a hand, I am sure of it. Now all I can hope to do is instruct you.'

'Foulborn?' Issul shuddered.

'The Child who came from Death.'

She knows! 'How – What do you know about him?'

Arene raised her arm and lightly touched her wounded cheek with the back of her hand. 'He is strong, that little boy. I had him in my hands. He tore half my cheek away. I had not expected such furious zest.'

'What did you want with him?'

'To kill him.' A harsh edge of emotion tinged Arene's voice. 'To end his brief life before –' she waved her heavy hands '– all this and everything that will now ensue.'

'It was you beside the pond, was it not?'

'You know of that? Of course, you would. Aye, that was me.'

'Were you planning to kill him then?'

'His guardian slept. It could have been an accident. An infant left alone beside a pool . . . Who would have thought anything?'

'Then what stopped you?'

'The presence of another person. A young man who came unexpectedly out of the forest –' She paused, her eyes narrowing. 'Almost as if he were sent.'

She laid a peculiar inflection upon these last words. Issul reflected uneasily for a moment, then said, 'Did you not know the young man?'

'I had never seen him before, nor since.'

Issul nodded to herself. It was as Moscul had told her. The assumption, from Ohirbe's and Julion's accounts, had been that Arene and the mysterious stranger were together. Issul reached into the sash at her waist and drew forth a small pouch of blue leather, gathered at the neck with a slim thong. She untied it and emptied the contents into the palm of her hand. 'Have you ever seen this before?'

After a moment Arene nodded. 'I think it is the gift given to the Foulborn by that young man beside the pool. May I examine it?'

Issul hesitated, then nodded. Arene took the small ivory carving which Julion had illicitly taken from Moscul, and which Fectur's man, Gordallith, had subsequently brought back to Orbia. She inspected it closely, holding it circumspectly between finger and thumb. 'Often have I wondered about this thing.' She closed her hands around it and shut her eyes in concentration. When she opened them she said, 'There is magic here. This thing – what is it, a tooth, a tusk? – it has come out of Enchantment or its environs, almost certainly.'

The hairs at the nape of Issul's neck prickled. Pader Luminis had said as much. *What can it contain?* She took the carving back. 'Can you tell me anything more?

'Of that? No. How did you come by it?'

Issul ignored the question. 'The young man – he prevented you committing murder? Did he see what you were doing?'

'If so, he gave no indication. And I would use the word "murder" with caution, lady. I hesitated, for I had no heart to kill an innocent babe. But that babe is no innocent, as you surely know. Now he is free, with who can say what consequences?'

'Do you think the young man knew the Child?'

'He seemed not to, but it was a strange meeting. I do not know.'

'Did he speak his name?'

'He did. But understand, the moment was filled with tension. I was discomposed, caught almost in the act of infanticide, as it would have been viewed. He spoke with the Child's guardian at the same time. His name . . . it was not a common name. At the time that marked it, so I thought. Ah, but I am old. I curse my failing powers. So much was on my mind. By the following day, in my confusion, the name had escaped me. He was coming here, though. I know that.'

'Here?'

'To enlist in the King's army and vanquish the Krai, so he said.'

'If he spoke the truth.'

'Aye, if he spoke the truth.'

Issul rolled the ivory carving pensively between her fingers, her brow knitted in perplexity. 'You were sent, you say, to kill this child you call Foulborn? Who by? And how do you know of him?'

'Be seated, young Queen,' Arene replied, and nodded towards a chair in the corner of the cell. 'I will tell you what I know. And when I have done, well, you will perhaps be a little better informed, even a little more prepared for what you must face, truly even a touch wiser. But the world, alas, will not have changed.'

She waited while Issul lowered herself onto the chair, then resumed, 'I am of the *Hir'n Esh*, a term which you will not have heard before. An approximate translation into your tongue renders it as "Witnesses of the Unfolding". We are a community, few in number, united by a common experience, a common activity. Our home is a secret location hard upon the border of Enchantment, but at a great distance from here, upon the other side. In that location there manifests an unusual concentration of energy, a magical coalescence, known to us as the Well of Immaculate Vision. Ages past our forebears constructed a protective fortress about the Well, and we have devoted our existence to its study. We are able to attune with its extraordinary energy, and in so doing the events that have befallen this world are revealed to us, as, in many cases, are events which have still to occur.'

'You see the future?' asked Issul.

'Futures among possible futures would be a more accurate summation. We see what has been, what is, what is predicted or intended to be, and then some of the many possible futures that such events may engender. Hence we foresaw the coming of the Foulborn and all that its birth might entail. We did not know exactly where or even when its coming would fall. That is why I was sent here, to search him out and end his existence before he could bring catastrophe upon the world. But I failed. Perhaps Fate – one possible, unforeseen future – intervened to prevent me carrying out my task. I know only that I did not accomplish it, hence another train of events has been set in motion, and you, beautiful Queen Issul, are at its centre.'

'I?'

The old woman nodded. 'You allowed the Foulborn to live, secreted him where he might not be found, told no one the terrible secret of his birth. Is that not so?'

Issul held her gaze but said nothing.

'And later you realized the awful truth, and sought him out – to do what? Would you have killed him? No matter, you lost him, as did I once again. He is free now, dwelling in the wild, preparing his way. He knows something of what he is, and that he is sought by those who would end his life and others who will follow him and do his bidding. He knows he can command great powers. And he is of Enchantment, at least in part, and so he must war. And others must war with him. So it unfolds.'

'And I have a part in this?'

'If you will save your kingdom, and your husband and children.'

Issul drew in a sharp breath. Arene nodded, half-smiling to herself. 'Yes, I see that it is true. They are gone, are they not?'

'How do you know of this?'

'Its potential was manifest in the Well, as were others. Now that you have confirmed this particular strand, I can instruct you if you so wish. Of course, I can guarantee you nothing. We are limited when it comes to predicting accurately events which have yet to come to be. We see only possibilities within the uncertain flux. We see a myriad paths, yet myriads more exist. So I cannot say that my guidance will bring you what you desire, only that your failure to heed it will certainly bring you what you do not. Now tell me, have you yet found the way to Enchantment?'

Issul stared at her, speechless for some moments.

'Speak, child!' demanded Arene.

'There – there is an opening, yes.'

'Good. That is one less task, then. So, what else? Another world, yes? A world that was a prison, is still a prison; a world that is a god? Tell me, for these things are vague.'

'Yes, what you are saying makes sense to me.'

'Then heed the god. You have no choice.'

'And leave Enchantment's Edge to my enemies?'

'You have many perils ahead of you, that is the one absolute certainty. All of this could have been avoided had I slain the Foulborn, or indeed had *you* slain him at birth – for that was one other potential that was revealed by the Well. Such a path lies ahead of you, Issul, and I would not be you for anything. But if you do not take it you face the certain knowledge of defeat, total and irreversible. That much the Unfolding revealed without ambiguity.'

Issul's heart was too full for words. In her mind's eye an image of her children formed. Alone in an alien world, they cried out for her. She heard their frightened voices. A sob escaped her lips; she turned her head away.

'Oh, child, I know your anguish and I do not wish you harm,' said

Arene softly. 'If there were a means of avoiding this, I would choose it. But there is none. I am sorry.'

Issul rose, holding herself stiffly. 'We will speak again later,' she said, her voice betraying her. 'In the meantime I will have you moved to somewhere less oppressive.'

She departed quickly, and outside took a moment to recover her thoughts. From the far end of the passage Shenwolf strode towards her. In the fingers of her right hand she still clasped the little ivory carving. Again she looked at it, wondering, then dropped it back into its pouch and slipped it inside her sash.

'I am sorry, I was delayed,' said Shenwolf, arriving at her side. He was garbed in the crimson-and-blue livery of the élite Palace Guard, the bar of rank at his throat. 'Moving from my former barracks. The messenger took time to find me. What has happened? Are you distraught?'

She shook her head, her voice still faltering. 'Nothing.' She turned back to regard the door of Arene's cell. 'I had . . . there is a woman in there. I thought perhaps to have you join me when I interviewed her. It is no matter. I will see her again.'

She passed instructions to the captain of the guard for Arene's removal to a more comfortable chamber, and moved on, absorbed in a thousand agonies.

IV

'Orbus.' Issul stood alone in her chamber, staring at the blue casket, her face a mask.

'Orbus.'

She turned at a penumbral movement to her side, and saw him at the edge of the room, half-shadow, the wall behind him visible through his form.

'Child?'

'I have come to a new decision.'

'You have?'

'I am given no choice. We will go, Orbus. To Enchantment. We *must* go.'

THREE

I

'I'm hungry. Daddy, I'm *hungry!*' Little Jace, fractious now and beyond comforting, beat her father's shoulder with one small fist. Galry, mercifully, was asleep on Leth's other shoulder.

Leth, too, was not impervious to the gnawing hunger in his belly. He walked on, carrying both children as he had for some time now, weary and with a growing sense of futility. His anger was mounting. He raged inwardly at Orbus for having abandoned him here, at the ceaseless blue world, at his own hunger – all of these things, which he had no power to remedy. And he feared, as he waded on, clinging to his two children, he feared the path along which hunger might draw him, for a famished man is a creature stripped of moral-conscience and humanity, capable of anything. Leth forcefully shifted his thoughts elsewhere.

Nothing had changed, except . . . just once or twice, Leth was not clear in his mind but he thought he had glimpsed, or just sensed . . . something. He couldn't say what. It might have been hallucination, but he thought he had perceived a movement, the inkling of disturbance in the air, a briefest flicker, just ahead of him and off to one side. He had turned towards it, glimpsed it, or sensed it, again. Something ghostly had brushed against him, just whispering past his ear.

He had almost dismissed it, then Galry had said, 'What's that?'

Galry had pointed, but there was nothing to be seen, and his young brow had furrowed in puzzlement.

'What?' Leth had asked. 'What did you see?'

Prince Galry had shaken his head. 'I thought something was there.'

Now it happened again, as Galry slept and Jace demanded food. Jace grasped the flesh of Leth's neck between fingers and thumb and pinched with all her strength. *'I'm hungry!'* Fighting his temper, Leth took her hand away. 'I know, I know. Soon. We will eat soon.'

A cool breath passed across Leth's face. Briefly, hardly perceived, yet it was sufficient change in this changeless place to have aroused his senses. In the same moment the air a little way in front of him seemed to flux. He had the impression that an unseen wing or wings had stirred.

Leth screwed up his eyes, peering intently. 'Is there something there? Come forth and speak.'

Nothing happened. Fearful of alarming his children, Leth said nothing more. He passed the tip of his tongue across his dry lips. His throat was parched; he had grown hoarse from his earlier shouting for Orbus. Jace whimpered and he stroked her hair, pressing her to him and kissing her head.

'I want to go home now. Daddy, why can't we go home?'

Leth ceased walking. He shook his head in despair. The cessation of movement roused Galry from his sleep. He peered around him, bleary-eyed. When he saw the emptiness before him again, a look of terrible desolation appeared on the boy's wan features. He turned to his father with an expression of pained reproach which cut Leth to the core, then Galry buried his face in the crook of Leth's neck and clung to him.

Leth stood, breathing hard. He turned around, wanting something to blame, something palpable to rage at. He lifted his face to the great vault so high above, then back to the misted blue and the endless wall. And then he saw it.

His heart thumped. He squinted into the distance. Again he was not certain that he had actually seen anything. An obscure shape had seemed to materialize in the mist. A darkening – was it? – then a glint, a glimmer, something flickering brightly just for an instant, then gone, and the dark again.

He watched for several seconds, his pulse quickening. The thing appeared to be fixed in place. It was definitely *something*, a feature, unidentified, which for the first time broke the mind-numbing monotony of the blue domain. Leth took a few steps towards it, wary, casting his eyes around, then focusing back on the thing ahead. Jace had seen it too. Her complaints ceased, turned to small sobs and sniffs as she stared at the curious manifestation.

'What's that?'

Her enquiry roused Galry, who turned and craned his neck.

Leth shook his head. 'I do not know.'

He could make out a little more detail now. It had the form of an arch, featureless but of a much darker hue than its surroundings. And every few moments its silhouette became outlined in light, just for an instant throwing out slender shards of luminescence, dazzling argent and sapphire blue, purest white and shades of pale yellow through to amber. They glimmered through the mist, then rapidly faded to leave only the darker form, then glimmered again.

Leth stared for long moments then, suddenly, gasped. He blinked, stared again, past the glimmering arch.

'The wall, Daddy!' Galry had also torn his eyes from the arch and was staring upwards, pointing.

Leth was without words. The great encircling wall which had never been closer, never further away, had changed. Without being aware of it, his attention fixed upon the glimmering arch, he had failed to notice that the wall was no longer retreating with every step he took. Suddenly it was looming close, suddenly there before them, towering high, its surface smooth-looking and unreflecting. And the arch standing at its base appeared to be – and Leth's hopes soared – appeared to be a portal of some description set within the wall itself!

He set the two children down and took their hands, feeling ever more vulnerable without a sword or weapon of any kind. He moved towards the portal, still wary, and at length stood directly before it. The portal, if that was what it was, seemed to be formed of something extremely dense, featureless as the great wall, of deep indigo colouring. But the glimmering light, pulsing on and off, sending out sharp lucent beams from around the edges of the portal, appeared to originate on its other side. From beyond the wall.

Leth released Prince Galry's hand and extended his own to touch the portal. His fingers made no contact. They sank into the blue, vanishing.

'Dadda!' Galry clung fearfully to his leg. Leth withdrew his hand. He stroked Galry's head.

'Don't be afraid, child. I am here. I am always here.'

He felt little of the confidence he was trying to instil. He moved aside and pressed his hand to the wall. It was utterly smooth and quite cool to the touch, diorite-hard, thought he could not precisely identify the substance of which it was made. He moved back to the portal, pushed his face close. To his surprise he saw people on the other side. Blurred figures – he thought they were human. They appeared to be crowded in some number just a little way beyond the portal. He could not make out their faces or any detail other than their dim forms. The glimmering light pulsed, just for an instant, and dazzled him.

Leth drew back, thoughtful. He turned, stared again into the hopeless blue void over which they had travelled. he cast his eyes over the wall, which extended still without perceivable end to either side of him, curving slightly inwards in the distance. He looked up again at the great vault, and back to the mysterious portal. Then he gripped his childrens' hands, took a breath, and stepped through.

The people on the other side of the portal drew back with a collective gasp. There were perhaps eighteen or twenty of them, women and men of varying ages, three or four children. They were white-skinned, brown-haired, clothed in garments of linen and cloth that were generally unadorned and functional rather than ostentatious. They carried no visible weapons but stood in a wide semicircle before Leth and his children, their hands linked. Leth had the impression that they had been rocking slowly from side to side. He thought he had heard a low, rhythmic chanting, though they were silent now, all staring at him and his two children, apprehensive, their faces reflecting acute astonishment.

At the centre of the semicircle of chanters, between them and Leth, was a man, kneeling. His head was bowed. In contrast to the others he was garbed in a long flowing robe of carmine-hued silk-like material, richly embroidered in gold with complex designs. He was spare of build and his hair was a dense grey cloud that billowed in unruly tufts about a narrow head. His hands were raised before him, palms upwards, and upon them rested a sword in a fabulously jewelled scabbard.

At the sudden gasp from his companions the man glanced up. His eyes fell upon Leth, and widened, his jaw falling agape. Leth looked from him to the other people, to their surroundings. They stood in an open, rocky place. The sun was pale in a brittle blue sky, a cool breeze touched Leth's cheeks. There were scrubby trees and bushes a short distance away, and beyond them low bare hills.

The kneeling man was struggling for words. 'Y-you – You have come!'

He climbed to his feet, still bearing the sword before him, still gaping at Leth. Then he turned to cry back over his shoulder, 'He has come! See! At last! At last! It was as I said!'

The others seemed struck dumb. They clung to one another's hands, their eyes round and fearful. The man with the sword came towards Leth, proffering the weapon. 'Take it, Lord. We have not forgotten our covenant. We have held it for you all this time.'

Leth frowned in puzzlement and surveyed the sword, then the man, then the others. 'I do not understand. What is this? Where is this place?'

'Please, my Lord. The Sword of the Orb. It is yours. From before.'

He almost pressed the weapon to Leth's chest.

'The Sword of the Orb?' Leth's frown deepened. Releasing his children's hands he grasped the sword by hilt and scabbard. There came a hushed murmur from the assembled group. The man in the robe smiled, then bent from the waist in an attitude of obeisance. 'Now, now we will be saved! You have returned. Go forth, oh Great Lord. Strike down our tormentress! Let her bestride this land no more!'

He backed away, his head bowed, then edged to one side and picked up a cloth bundle from the ground. This he laid upon the earth before Leth. 'This, too, is for you. We know how great has been your ordeal, Lord. This will give you strength.'

He retreated again. Leth glanced at the bundle upon the ground, then passed his eyes over the sword-hilt and scabbard. Both were of exceedingly fine workmanship, set with glittering gems and figured with precious metals, their value incalculable. He grasped the hilt-grip firmly in his right hand and drew forth the blade. There came another gasp; all those before him drew back further. Then, almost as one, they turned and scattered. Only the robed man remained.

Leth stared after them but briefly as they fled, for his attention was on the sword's blade. It was metallic, though the metal was of a type he could not identify for it was of a fiery roseate hue and gave forth a bright halo of rose light.

The robed man blinked and heaved a great sigh. He clasped his hands before him, moist-eyed and smiling. 'It is as it should be. The Sword is at last returned to its rightful master.'

'The Sword of the Orb?' queried Leth.

'No other has seen the blade, for no other could draw it free. Lord, I have devoted my life to this, and at last I am rewarded.' He gazed adoringly at the roseate blade, then at Leth. 'At last! At last!'

The robed man backed away.

Leth shook his head in perplexity. 'I do not understand what is happening here. I fear this is a mistake.'

The robed man backed further away, bowing his head. Then, quickly, he turned and walked off.

'Wait!' Leth called. 'Stop! I command you! Stop!'

But his words were not heeded, and quite suddenly there was no one to be seen. Muttering to himself he sheathed the blade and strapped it around his waist. 'Curious. Still, I am no longer naked, but I would give much to know where we are and exactly who or what these people believe me to be.'

He crouched and undid the outer wrapping of the cloth bundle the robe man had left. Inside he found hard yellow cheese, a haunch of cured meat, some dried fruit, bread, a leather flask and a knife.

'Aah, we can staunch our hunger at last.' He reached back for his childrens' hands. 'Come, my brave little ones. Let's eat now, then we will be better set to seek out these strange nervous folk and learn more about them and their land.'

Neither Galry nor Jace took his hand. He swivelled, suddenly conscious of their silence these past few moments. The children were nowhere in sight. Leth sprang to his feet, a cold hammer of fear almost paralyzing him. 'Jace! Galry!'

They were nowhere to be seen. Leth looked back to the portal through which they had stepped. To his shock there was nothing before him but a sheer cliff face. A symbol or rune, consisting of two spheres divided by a single, angled shaft, had been chiselled into the rock and coloured deep carmine.

With an anguished cry Leth threw himself at the rock and rune, but it did not give. There was no indication of the portal through which he had stepped. He beat at the rock with his fists and threw his entire weight against it, but it did not give.

Leth turned around with an agonized roar. 'Galry! Jace!'

Some kind of bird cried harshly high in the sky. There was no other indication of life. Leth stood alone.

II

Leth ate sparingly of the food, his hunger largely banished by the turmoil and shock of the sudden loss of his children. He knew he must eat, but his mouth was dry and he could barely chew or swallow. He drank from the flask, which contained sweet water laced with a subtle hint of fruit and spice.

Again and again Leth turned back to the rune upon the cliff. Solid and impenetrable now, he knew that this was the portal through which he and the children had come. And the children *had* stepped through with him. Their little hands had been in his, he recalled that much with total clarity. Though he had been too stunned at the time to speak to them, or even to glance down and confirm their presence, he knew that they had been there. He had felt them. It was only when he had taken the roseate sword that he had released their hands.

So what had happened?

Many times he walked back to the cliff and examined in minute detail the area around the rune. There was nothing to be found, no indication of a doorway or anything irregular in the rock. They could not have gone back through, so where were they? Could they have been taken by the chanting people assembled before the portal? It was possible. Leth had not taken note of everyone around him. Some might have been out of his field of view, to his rear. At the instant that he released the children someone – two persons – could have crept up behind and snatched them.

Without a sound?

Leth's attention had been wholly directed away from Jace and Galry. It was quite possible that, stunned as he was, any brief scuffle would have escaped his notice. The children lifted from the ground, their mouths covered . . . they would have made so little noise.

'Gah!' Leth struck the rock once more. He looked impotently around him. Where had they been taken? There was no settlement in view, and the landscape was virtually bare, offering scarcely any opportunity for concealment. When he had first realized that the children were gone he had, after finding no way through the portal in the cliff, rushed out into the wilderness in pursuit of the strange assembly and the robed man. They had all vanished, as though into the air, for the land was almost flat until it met the hills in the distance, and he could see no feature that might have concealed them. The cliff behind him towered higher than he could see. It was almost too sheer to offer purchase to any but the most experienced climber. Its face was blank, without visible crevice, fissure or cavern. There was nowhere that any climber might have gone to hide from view, least of all climbers carrying two small, struggling children.

There was magic here, then.

Leth wrapped the food once more, mindful that his children would still be hungry. He secured it over one shoulder with the cord that bound it. The leather flask he strapped to his belt, then set off in the direction that the robed man had taken.

It did not take him long to determine where the robed man and his companions or followers had gone. Leth had walked barely one hundred paces when a shallow declivity, discernible only when he was virtually at its lip, revealed itself in the bare land. At its base was a cluster of small dome-like structures, the colour of the earth, each with two elongated oval openings for door and window. Leth cursed. He stared at the buildings for some moments. Nothing moved; he descended. He drew the roseate sword and approached the first building.

Through the window opening of the dome he saw the robed man kneeling inside. His back was obliquely to Leth and he had his forehead pressed to the wall. The chamber he occupied was small and round with little in the way of furnishings. He appeared to be alone.

Leth strode to the door and with one blow kicked it open. The robed man jumped and spun upon his knees, half-falling, then lurched quickly to his feet. His face registered total dismay. 'Lord! Wha —'

Leth threw himself across the chamber, seized the man's scrawny throat with one hand and slammed him against the wall. 'Where are my children?'

The robed man made strangled noises, his eyes bulging, face swelling and turning purple. Leth relaxed his grip enough to let him speak. 'Where are they?'

'Y-y-your ch-children?' the man stammered.

'Tell me, or you will feel the rosy glow of this strange blade you have given me penetrating your worthless bowels.'

'L – Lord, do you not know?'

'Know what? I know nothing, save that I stepped through a door to find you grovelling before me, and moments later discovered my children gone. Who are you? Where is this place, and what is happening here?'

The robed man lifted his hands in a placatory gesture. 'Wait. Wait. Release me. I will tell you all.'

Leth took his hand from his throat and stood back. The man recovered his breath, massaging his throat. 'Your children . . .' he began, then fell silent.

'My patience is limited,' Leth growled. 'And by all the forces of Enchantment, if they have come to harm . . .'

The man grimaced. He could not meet Leth's eye. 'Lord, I do not know where to begin.'

'You call me Lord, and act as though expecting me. Whom do you believe me to be?'

'Why, you are the Swordbearer, are you not? He who will deliver us from our pain. No other could draw the Sword of the Orb. You have returned after long ages, to slay the Kancanitrix.'

Leth scowled. 'I know nothing of this. I want my children, that is all. Where are they?'

'Why . . . ? You truly do not know?' The robed man stared at him for long moments. He seemed lost for words. '*She* has taken them.'

'*What?*' Leth advanced upon him again. 'Taken them where?'

The man shrank back. 'Lord, please! Do not wreak your anger upon me! I have done nothing except call you forth. That was my task, for I am Summoner, nothing more. My life has been lived only for this. It has taken so long!'

Leth drew back his lips across his teeth. 'Riddles and obscurantisms! I will have no more of it! Tell me in plain words, or the life which you have lived for this one purpose will end now and you will sizzle on this scorching blade!'

The man called Summoner paused, then raised a forefinger. 'Wait. Wait, Lord. I will show you something.'

He slid along the wall, his eyes on Leth, smoothing his crumpled robe with the flats of his nervous hands, until he came to a blue curtain which hung to the floor. 'Give me a few moments, Lord. I am not sure where I put it.'

He drew aside the curtain and began rummaging behind, muttering to himself. 'Ah! Where is it now? Is this it? No. Be patient, Lord, please. Bear with me. I will have it in a moment.'

A wooden crate came out, then a large jute sack stuffed to bulging with unknowns. 'Ah! No. Curse it! I think it is further in.'

Leth drummed his fingers in agitation upon his sword-hilt. Summoner was wholly behind the curtain now. It convulsed and billowed wildly as he searched. His voice sounded again, somewhat muffled, 'I see it now. Just a moment more.'

There was a creaking sound; the curtain grew still. Sensing the worst, Leth sprang. He wrenched the curtain aside. A grim gulf was before him, wholly dark but for the uncertain outlines of stacked crates, sacks and sundry objects. He heard a muted thud at floor level further in as an unseen door was closed, then a heavy bolt slid home.

'Craven varlet!' Leth threw himself towards the sound. He stumbled over something on the floor, and fell, crashing into a solid wall. Beneath him was wood, a trapdoor. On its other side he heard faint, hurried footsteps receding.

'Knave! Reprobate! Come back now!' Leth's fingers groped in the dark, found an iron loop set into the wood. He pulled, twisted, but the trapdoor was fast and did not give.

Leth stormed back into the main chamber, furious with himself for having been so easily tricked. He looked intently about the round chamber, seeking something with which to prise or smash open the trapdoor, but nothing was to hand. He went outside, ran to the nearest of the other dome-dwellings and peered through its single oval window. It appeared untenanted. Leth tried the door, found it unlocked, and stepped inside. The room he entered was virtually identical to that within Summoner's dome. To one side a curtain hung upon the wall. This Leth tore aside. The sight that met him was, again, similar in all respects to that in Summoner's abode. Leth tried the inner trapdoor, and found it bolted from the other side.

In the third dome the tale was the same, but as he stepped outside again Leth spied a small wooden outhouse at the rear of the neighbouring dome. Here he found tools: scythe, hammers, pincers, various irons, hooks and spades. And in one corner – at last – a heavy tree-felling axe and an iron crowbar. These he seized and returned to Summoner's dwelling and the trapdoor through which Summoner had made his escape.

The axe was superfluous; with the crowbar Leth was able to wrest the trapdoor free of the bolt that held it underneath. It came free with loud cracks and a shriek of protest. Leth raised it and let it fall back, away from the opening. A flight of steep wooden stairs led down. Leth, streaked with sweat, lowered himself through, to find himself in utter dark.

He listened: there was no sound. He took a single cautious step forward and found his foot upon the lip of a drop. He could not gauge its depth in the dark, but recognized that to a less circumspect intruder it could have proven injurious, even lethal. Sufficient time had passed for Summoner to have made good his escape, and there was nothing to be gained now by recklessness. Leth climbed the wooden stairs, returning to Summoner's dwelling, and sought out an oil-lamp which he quickly lit with flint and tinder. Then he returned to the dark below.

He found himself in a downward-sloping passage hewn into rock and earth, its walls and roof shored with sturdy tarred timbers. The drop over which he had come close to falling was almost as deep as an average man was tall – had he blundered over it he could indeed have suffered severely. But to a person aware of its existence it was simply a matter of scrambling over and then making off down the steps beyond.

Leth did just this, and with his lamp held before him began his walk into the unknown.

The tunnel was cold, damp and earthy. But it was well-constructed and seemed in no danger of collapse. Leth passed a series of side-passages angling off the main tunnel. All seemed to lead roughly back the way he had come. Investigating one, he found that it took him back to one of the dome-dwellings, with a rear trapdoor letting into a curtained vestibule or storage cupboard just as in Summoner's home. At the foot of the steep wooden stairs, again, a deep and sudden drop had been dug to catch the unwary or unwelcome. Leth returned to the main tunnel and continued on his way.

The tunnel levelled out and then began to ascend. In due course, warm from the exertion, Leth found himself approaching what appeared to be the end of the tunnel. A door of proud ancient timber barred his way. Upon the ground to one side of it was a lamp similar to the one he carried. Leth drew his sword from its scabbard; only then did he discover that the glowing blade cast a pale rose light sufficient to see by. He doused his lamp and put it beside the other, then tentatively tried the door.

It opened without resistance. He looked into a small unlit chamber lined with blocks of stone, straw scattered upon the floor. An iron door was set into the opposite wall. Cautiously he stepped into the chamber.

There was a scuffling sound above his head. Instinctively Leth threw himself back. Something dark bulked in the swordlight, leaping from a recess or shelf high upon the chamber wall. It landed solidly in front of Leth, a hideously deformed man-like thing with huge pale eyes, small arms and formidably muscled, clawed legs. Its head was small and bony, almost perfectly flat on top, its skin thick and calloused, slightly glistening, the colour of dirty grey clay. A long, strong prehensile tail lashed the air before it. At its tip a three-fingered hand grasped a weapon resembling a heavy, cruelly spiked mace. The creature drew back its wide lips, revealing fangs like small daggers, and hissed at Leth. Strange chatterings came from above.

Another of the creatures leapt down, and another. The first swung at Leth with its mace. Leth dodged the blow and struck out with his sword, aiming a swinging blow at the tail where the 'wrist' joined the hand that held the weapon. To his surprise the roseate blade bit clean through the creature's tail, so cleanly that Leth barely felt its contact. He was momentarily thrown off balance, having anticipated far greater resistance. The creature vented a dismal howl as its tail-hand fell to the floor and a pale ichor pumped from the truncated limb. It quickly bent and picked up hand and weapon in its little forelimbs then sprang high and disappeared.

Six of the creatures now menaced Leth from the crowded chamber. Leth had retreated through the door to a position just within the tunnel, so they could attack him only singly. They gibbered incessantly; one made a feint, then drew back as Leth's sword stabbed. Another followed suit. Leth lunged, taking a single long step forward. His blade entered the creature's eye, surprising it before it could draw back. It screamed and leapt away.

The din from their gibberings was deafening now, and Leth realized that many more of the creatures must be lying in wait beyond his sight. He was relatively safe where he stood, for whilst powerful, the creatures were not particularly skilled fighters. But if he advanced he would almost certainly be overpowered, for he could not hope to kill them all.

How had Summoner got past? Leth would surely have heard them had they been roused by his passage. Had Summoner power over the creatures, or could he have taken another route? Leth had seen no other way in the tunnel, but that did not mean no concealed passage existed. Or might Summoner simply have taken one of the early side-passages back to the dome-dwellings? Leth had explored only one of the passages. Did all of them lead only to the dwellings?

Leth was seized with sudden alarm, the hairs rising at the back of his neck. He spun around, sword at guard, for he was half-expecting to see Summoner bearing down on him. But the tunnel was empty. Leth swung back. A creature had instantly seized the advantage, leaping through the door. Leth took a half-step to the side and dropped to one knee as a mace sang past his head. He drew his blade up and across in a reversed scything motion, opening the creature's belly wide. As its entrails spilled onto the dark earth the creature writhed, throwing back its head with an ear-splitting shriek. In a reflexive movement it leapt skywards, seeking the security of its overhead lair. It smashed hard into the tunnel roof and fell back to the floor, dying.

Leth was up, driving back another of the creatures which had ventured to the door. It retreated, yammering and glaring malevolently at him, its great mace held low before it, swinging rapidly back and forth. The strength of tail-muscles that could wield such a weapon so effortlessly could only be guessed at.

Leth again glanced quickly behind him, fearful that Summoner or some other assailant was at his back, but still the tunnel gaped black and empty. It seemed that he had no choice but to go back that way now, but this in itself presented difficulties. On this side of the door the tunnel was wide enough to enable the creatures to menace him in pairs. He would be forced to fight them as he retreated, and could not hope to best so many in such conditions. If he turned and ran he had little doubt that, with such formidably muscled legs, they would quickly outpace him.

He stood, eyeing the creatures but making no move, conserving his strength, seeking another way. The things milled in the chamber, monstrous phantom-like forms in the pink half-light, spitting and striking from within. They eyed him balefully but made nothing more than feints towards him. *I can move neither forward nor back*, came the dismal thought. *Must I wait here helplessly until I perish?*

Such inaction was unthinkable. He flexed his grip upon the glowing sword. He thought of Galry and Jace – where? – needing him, crying for him. And Issul, lost, he knew not where. The pain was too great to bear.

And then, to his surprise, a voice rang out. A woman's voice, strong and potently pitched, cutting through the noise of the monsters. 'Put away your sword!'

The sound came from within the chamber where the creatures milled. Now Leth saw her, pushing her way calmly through them, one arm extended, her forefinger pointing at him. 'Your blade! That is what they fear. Put it away!'

'It is my intention that they should fear it!' Leth called back incredulously. 'Do you think me mad?'

'You don't understand.' The woman, totally fearless, shouldered her way forward to stand in the door. She was tall and quite young, garbed in red half-armour, her hair confined beneath a moulded, ridged helmet. She was not beautiful by any means, yet her features were handsome, even striking, the bones well-formed. She stood confidently, feet firmly planted and hands upon her hips, and to Leth's eyes it seemed there was something distantly familiar about her. 'It is the light. The *ools* cannot bear it.' Her glance took in the corpse of the creature Leth had slain, and her features fell. 'Oh, you have killed one.'

She lowered herself onto one knee beside the body and touched its head almost tenderly with the tips of her fingers.

'And injured others. They did not seek to barter,' said Leth.

'Put away the blade!' she repeated, rising abruptly, a note of impatient command in her voice.

'And be blind and helpless?'

The woman shook her head, sighing. 'Here. Here is my own sword.' She drew a slim blade from the scabbard at her hip and tossed it to Leth, who caught it in his left hand. 'The *ools* do not attack while I am here. See. Now, retreat a distance, as far as you wish, until you feel you can stand unharassed. Then sheathe the Orbsword, but keep mine on guard before you. If the *ools* advance you will hear them and can draw the Orbsword and see again.'

And face them in two's or more, thought Leth, but he backed away, for he could do little else. As he withdrew the noise of the *ools* diminished; they seemed less agitated. At fifty paces he paused.

'It is all right,' called the woman. 'They will not harm you now.'

Tentatively Leth sheathed the Sword of the Orb, and was engulfed in blackness. In almost the same moment the yammering of the *ools* fell to little more than a murmur.

The sweat ran cold between Leth's shoulder blades. 'I can see nothing!' he called, though this was not strictly true. From the chamber of the *ools* there came the faintest greenish glow, enough to show the shape of the tall woman in outline and the dim figures, now quite still, of the *ools* behind her.

'Do not be afraid,' came the reply. 'As long as you do not draw the Orbsword you are safe. Listen, already the *ools* are leaping back to their lairs above.'

Leth heard queer whisperings and pipings, then grunts and scratching as immense muscles launched the creatures from the chamber-floor and they scrabbled to their unseen lairs somewhere overhead.

'That is all it was: the light.' The woman's voice was closer now, though he could no longer see her. 'Nothing else will rouse them so, unless they are deliberately provoked.'

'I could not have known.'

'No, you could not.' She was in the blackness beside him now; he felt her breath warm upon his cheek. 'Will you take my hand and let me lead you? Do you see there is a dim light ahead? We will pass through the chamber. Keep my sword, but on no account draw the other.'

Leth found her hand in the dark, and was grateful for its touch. 'Does not that light offend them?'

'Were it any brighter it would. Come.'

She led him forward. As they entered the chamber where he had so nearly died, Leth hesitated. He could still see barely a thing, but could hear the *ools* breathing and scuffling in the black above him.

'It is all right.' The woman drew him on. His muscles tightened and he hardly dared breathe. He gripped her sword tensely.

And then they were through and standing in a passage on the other side. A lantern fixed to a bracket upon the wall, draped in a thin, dark green square of cloth, shed the illumination that barely permeated the *ools*' chamber. The woman released Leth's hand and stepped back past him. She pushed against the heavy iron door, which swung slowly shut with a sepulchral boom, then she turned and smiled. 'Will you return my sword now?'

Leth did so. He felt suddenly self-conscious at having revealed his helplessness to her, having allowed her to lead him like a frightened child through the chamber. She sheathed her weapon as Leth sucked in a deep draught of air, feeding welcome oxygen to lungs which tenseness and fear had drawn tight within his chest.

'These malformed creatures . . . what are they?' he asked. 'They appear part-human, but are abominations.'

She shrugged. 'They are *ools*, that is all. Cavern-dwellers. Generally docile, despite their fearsome appearance, and with only rudimentary intelligence. Now, I am called Lakewander. Come, we should not delay. Master Protector is most eager to meet you.'

III

The woman called Lakewander led Leth to a steep, narrow stone stairway which spiralled dizzyingly upwards until they emerged through a door into a chill corridor paved with flagstones. From his surroundings Leth gathered that they were inside a castle, large villa, keep or manor of some description. They passed along the corridor and up a flight of sweeping stone stairs, then Lakewander led him through a double door into a spacious chamber where an old man sat before a large table. At his back a fire blazed in a cavernous hearth. Beside him, bent as if in conference, stood Summoner.

'Ah, welcome, Lord. Welcome,' said the old man, smiling broadly and raising inflamed, shaking hands to beckon Leth forward. 'Come, please. Be seated. Forgive me if I do not rise to greet you. It is infirmity, not discourtesy, that obliges me to remain in my chair.'

From his general demeanour Leth took him once to have been a stout and probably vigorous man. But the years had withered his flesh, which hung slackly about him, grey and maculate, and his head was given to nodding slightly upon his shoulders. A few wisps of white hair hovered about his skull, and no more than half a dozen crooked teeth still remained in his gums. His eyes, however, though smoky, were alert and intelligent and lit with a glint of humour. He was garbed in a robe of dark umber relieved with gold braiding at collar and sleeve-hems. He beckoned again, 'Come, please. Do not be concerned. We are friends.' He was seized abruptly with a fit of wheezing. He leaned forward and coughed and spat into a tin spittoon at his side, then, recovering, smiled again. 'Allow me to introduce myself. I am Master Protector. My two companions, Lakewander and Summoner, you have already met. Be welcome, Lord. We are privileged. I especially, for I had come to believe that I would live out my entire span and not witness your coming. Ah, this is a day to be recorded. We have waited such a long time.'

A score of questions clamoured in Leth's head, but for the moment he held his silence. He accepted the proffered seat opposite the old man at the table, perceiving himself to be in no immediate danger. Lakewander moved to the end of the table and perched herself upon its edge. She took up an apple from a glazed earthenware platter and took a bite.

'Eat, sir, if you will,' urged Master Protector. 'Here are nuts and fruit, and I can have meat, fish, bread brought if you so wish. And drink. Will you have wine? Ale? A cordial?'

Leth patted the cloth package given to him by Summoner. 'I have lately eaten, thank you. A little ale will serve me well, though.'

As Summoner poured dark ale from a jug Leth spoke again. 'Perhaps you would answer some questions, to help clarify my position here.'

Master Protector inclined his head. 'Please, ask what you will.'

'You – all three of you – refer to me repeatedly as if I am known and expected, yet to me you are all strangers, and this is a strange and unknown land.'

'Yes, Summoner has conveyed something of this to me.'

'Summoner ran from me when I questioned him.'

'Ah, Summoner . . .' Master Protector glanced up at the man beside him, weakly fluttering a hand and chuckling to himself: a deep, chesty chuckle that spoke of pulmonary obstructions and shortness of breath. 'I apologize. He is young and callow. The shock of your arrival . . . it quite put him out.'

Leth, shifting his gaze to Summoner, was not struck by his youthful demeanour. Indeed, Summoner was more than old enough to have been Leth's father.

'But Summoner did say that you proffered him violence,' Master Protector added.

Leth shifted uncomfortably and reached for his ale. Then he paused, his anger returning. 'Understand, my children have been stolen from me. Seen in this light my actions surely cannot be judged so extreme? I will stop at nothing to get them back.'

Master Protector nodded ruminatively at this. 'Good. That is good.'

'For my part I find nothing good in it,' said Leth heatedly.

'I meant, it is good that your devotion to your offspring should outweigh all other concerns, not good that you should be suffering such wretched frowns of fortune. No, Lord, not that at all. Not at all.'

'Summoner implied knowledge of their whereabouts.'

'Did he? Did he? That was rash, indeed. Summoner, what is this foolishness?'

'I said only what is known: that *She* has taken them,' protested Summoner. 'Nothing more. I was alarmed at the Lord's manner.'

'You tricked me and fled,' accused Leth.

'To preserve my life, Lord, as anyone would do!'

Leth spoke between clenched teeth. 'If you know of their whereabouts, tell me, now!'

'No, no,' old Master Protector's head moved from side to side. 'We know – or certainly believe – that they have been taken by her. Their precise whereabouts . . . that is another matter entirely.'

'Who is this woman to whom you refer? And whom do you consider me to be?'

The old man began to laugh. It was a pained, suppressed laugh, full of wheezes and strange poppings of an almost musical quality. For a moment Leth thought to hear the honking of distant geese carried on a wind. Master Protector's shoulders were racked; his eyes streamed. He raised one hand, bidding forbearance until in due course he could say, 'The question seems more pertinently to be: whom do you consider yourself to be?'

Leth weighed his reply. Knowing so little of these people and their land he judged it inadvisable at present to disclose his full title. 'I am Leth . . . of Enchantment's Edge.'

'Enchantment's Edge?' Master Protector looked to Summoner, who shrugged.

'It is plainly of the other world, Master,' Summoner said. 'The Lord came, like the others, through the Sign. But so great has been the passage of time, it is conceivable that he has forgotten us and our covenant.'

'Others?' queried Leth.

'Others have answered the summons,' said Summoner. 'Two in my lifetime, others before. But they were not you.'

Lakewander spoke. 'He means, Lord, that they could not bear the Sword. They came in error, or perhaps in vain hope, but it is the Swordbearer and no other who can help us.'

Leth shook his head. 'I know nothing of this.'

'Do you not even recall the Sword?' Lakewander asked. 'Does it not feel familiar?'

'Recall? *Recall?* I have not been here before. Nothing is familiar.'

A silence fell. The three exchanged glances. Leth, growing apprehensive, stood.

'Truly, it has been such a long time,' Master Protector said.

'His memories will return, I think, as the days pass,' said Summoner.

Lakewander nodded pensively. 'Essentially it makes little difference, other than to him.'

'Enough!' flared Leth. 'Have I not made myself plain? I am a stranger to your land, and I seek nothing except to return, with my children, to my own.'

'Just so' Master Protector seemed both sympathetic and resigned. 'And perhaps you shall, Lord. Perhaps you shall, if you succeed.'

'No. You plan for me to slay some putative enemy of yours, a woman of whom I have no knowledge! This I cannot – will not – do. I know nothing of the problems of this realm, its politics and intrigues. I cannot interfere. But at home I am needed. Find some other to perform your assassinations, I entreat you, and show me how I might return, with my children.'

'Lord, Lord, is it still not clear?' Master Protector looked pained. 'There is no other; no other can draw the Sword.'

'Then here!' Leth roared. He swept the bright rose blade free of its scabbard, causing the others to draw back in alarm. Lakewander's hand flew to the hilt of her own sword, but Leth thrust the Sword of the Orb down hard so that its point bit deep into the table top. He released it and it stood, oscillating rapidly back and forth, its aura casting a pale, agitated fuchsia lambence across the chamber, lamplight reflecting in the blade. '*Here!* Take your cursed weapon and give it to another. Instruct *him* never to sheathe it, then burden *him* with the task of murder that you enjoin upon me!'

'Lord, Lord, we understand your anguish, but we cannot do as you ask,' cried Master Protector. 'For such long ages we have waited, and we have known that the Godworld might cast forth others, but they can only fail us or try to lead us false. Only he who can bear the Sword of the Orb can be the true god.'

'I am no god!' Leth's eyes blazed. He slammed his fist down on the table, causing cups, plates and cutlery to leap and rattle. 'I am a man, a mere man, who has been drawn here – I do not know how – and seeks nothing but to return.'

Master Protector nodded sombrely. 'That will be your reward . . . when your task is complete. You see, we know of no way back, save that which lies within the temple of our oppressor, the Kancanitrix, Ascaria, the Dark Flame of the Orb. It is she who holds your children. Find her, for your own sake and ours, slay her, and you may leave our world. There is truly no other way.'

Leth grew still, fighting his rage and frustration, sensing no way out. Eventually, in a voice that shook with emotion, he said, 'What is the name of this land? What is its extent? Who are your neighbours?'

'It is Orb,' said Master Senior. 'That is all. We are ignorant of its extent. As for neighbours, there are folk of many kinds resident here, though far fewer than in the past. Ascaria has seen to that. Do you wish to know the names of them all?'

'I referred to neighbouring lands. The nations, races, domains that lie beyond your own.'

'Beyond?' Master Protector seemed mystified. 'Beyond the Orb there is only the Godworld, of which we know nothing.'

Leth heaved a heavy sigh. He turned away. But through his exasperation he felt a measure of intrigue. These repeated references to the Orb . . . As far as Leth was aware he remained still somehow within Orbus's world, the world within the blue casket which rested upon his desk in the Palace of Orbia – the world that Orbus himself, by his own account, had been trapped inside; the world he had unknowingly created. Orbus had never professed knowledge of anything other than the empty blue domain which Leth had so recently left. Could it be that this land and its strange people were also held within the blue casket? Or could he have been cast back into some remote corner of his own world, or even to another universe entirely?

'How comes it by its name?' he asked.

'Orb? Ah, Lord, now you speak of unfathomable mystery. We will show you – Lakewander will show you if you will rest awhile with us. Will you do that, Lord? Night approaches and it will gain you nothing to leave now. Chambers have already been prepared.'

'My children –' Leth began.

'– may be of greater value to Ascaria as hostages than corpses,' cut in Lakewander. 'Though we do not know that. But even if not, you cannot travel until you know the way. Pass this night here, beneath our roof, and you will be more ably equipped to commence your journey tomorrow. There are things you should see, things you should know. And perhaps, even, things you may begin to remember.'

Leth stared at her uncomfortably. Again he thought she seemed faintly familiar. Something . . . something was not right. Here . . . here in this place . . .

'Will you stay, Lord?'

He glanced back to Master Protector, who had posed the question. He hesitated, then nodded resignedly. 'Aye, I will stay, for I see no alternative. But this one night only.'

'And will you take back your sword?'

Leth regarded the glowing blade, which rose proud and pulsing from the table. He reached out and grasped its hilt, levered it free. 'For now.' He slid the Sword of the Orb into its jewelled scabbard. 'But when this night is done, and I have seen and learned, I may yet return it to you.'

FOUR

I

Leth waited in a state of some agitation in the modest suite of chambers that had been provided for him by Master Protector and his companions. The chambers were situated on the ground floor and were windowless, which did nothing to set Leth's mind at rest. But the door was not locked, nor had a guard been placed outside. Should the desire so take him, it seemed to Leth that he was free to wander more or less as he pleased.

After he had been shown to the apartment by Lakewander, who then departed, Leth had decided to test this. He left the chambers and began to explore the corridor outside. No one moved to prevent him; more to the point, no one was around to do so. Apart from the three persons to whom he had already been introduced, and the hideous *ools* below, Leth had seen no one. Not servants, nor guards, nor staff of any description. The castle, or whatever the building was, carried a strange and lonely aura, an underlying feeling of desertion, the sense that little existed here other than, perhaps, fading echoes of the past, and, among the living, a glimmer of a hoped-for future. Such was Leth's impression as he stole from the silent chamber.

The corridor, like the chambers, was windowless. Statues and carved stone reliefs did little to ease its chill and austere character. He passed along it to a towering double-door, which opened without complaint. Another passage led away, and Leth saw, some distance down, an arched window. To this he walked, his shadow multiplied, distorted and shaken by the flames from torches mounted on brackets upon the walls. He looked out.

Little was visible at ground level, bar an empty service yard bordered by a high stone wall, the massed black silhouettes of trees outside looming above its parapet. Dusk had closed in, but in those windows that Leth was able to see no candle or torchglow was evident. The sense of emptiness was amplified. He looked upwards. The firmament was starless indigo. He stared, seeking stars, seeking the familiar, and finding neither. As he stared it seemed he descried irregularities within the indigo: deep folds and canyons revealed themselves to his questing eyes; raised features, and scars and depressions, bringing to mind desolate blue highlands, dark gorges and shadowed empty vales. To Leth it seemed he gazed impossibly upon a far landscape, vast, mountainous and barren, formed of the evening sky itself.

A voice spoke, close in Leth's ear, making him start and spin around.

'Swordbearer!'

There was no one beside him.

'Who speaks?' demanded Leth, stepping away from the window.

'I, who am beside you.'

'I see no one.' A chill ran down Leth's spine. He stepped back again, then cast his eyes up and down the corridor, his hand upon his sword-hilt.

'You see me, but know it not.' The voice was remote and ghostly, yet so close at hand: a penetrating whisper.

Leth took two more steps back.

'Do not draw your blade, Swordbearer. It is unnecessary, and will avail you nothing.'

'Where are you? What do you want with me?'

'I am here, within the stone. And I want nothing, save to ask you what you seek.'

'Within . . . ?' Leth focused upon the bare stone wall beside the window where he had stood. 'What manner of creature are you?'

'I am simply one who has lived, and who passed. My being now helps sustain this edifice in which you presently reside. I was once a Protector. Now, like all who have gone before me, I am a part of that which I lived to protect.'

'This is strange to me.'

'No matter,' said the voice. 'Many ages have passed. If you have forgotten, that is perhaps to be expected. But I sensed your confusion. That is why I asked, What do you seek?'

Again the insinuation that this had all once been familiar. Leth was guarded. 'I seek . . . I seek to know and to understand. This place, this world, is alien.'

'But you are the Swordbearer, the True God with whom our covenant was made so long ago. This is your Transformation, is that not plain?'

'Nothing is plain.'

'Be patient, then. All will become known to you, as is proper.'

'I am not a god!'

'Be patient, Swordbearer. Be patient.'

'I want only to find my children,' protested Leth. 'And then to return with them to our home.'

There was no reply. Leth spoke again, but if his voice was heard it was ignored. He grew angry, though anger was futile. In a state of heightened distraction he made his way back to his apartment. A platter of roasted fowl in rich, dark gravy, with vegetables and bread, had been set upon a table. Also a pewter pitcher of ruby wine, and a bowl of various fruits. He wondered as to the hands that had placed them, for the food and drink had not been there moments earlier. The food's aroma teased his nostrils; he discovered he was hungry again, and sat down to eat.

He pondered his encounter as he ate. The entity that had spoken to him – was it confined to that one area of stone, or could it pass at will from location to location? There were others; it had said as much. Leth cast his eyes about the walls of the chamber. Were they all pregnant with the souls or shades of those who had lived and died here?

'Do you watch me now?' he asked loudly, and was answered by silence. 'Is there someone here?'

The thought lingered uneasily that every corridor and stairway, every chamber, every niche, nook and cranny, could be haunted by the ghosts of those long gone, that his every movement was observed, and nowhere might he find privacy.

The roast fowl was very good, and despite himself Leth ate heartily. The wine, too, was of the finest quality, though not surprisingly of a source and vintage he could not identify. He mopped the last of the gravy from his plate with the bread, then sat back, cradling his head in his hands, contemplating his circumstances. He felt warm now, yet though the wine blunted the edges of his thoughts he found scarcely any comfort. His belly was filled, but his mind raced and would not be stilled. Did the walls observe him? Did they harken to his very thoughts?

He thought of Issul. Had she perished? In his final hours in Enchantment's Edge he had all but given up hope of seeing her again. And now, all this . . . Enchantment's Edge and everything he held dear . . . so far away, another world, almost another existence. Perhaps the wine muddled his thoughts, for it seemed for a moment such a distant memory. He felt a sudden spasm of alarm. It was not so long since he had left; he recalled it all clearly. But this place where he now found himself, so strange and dreamlike . . . the disquieting insistence of all he met that he had been here before . . .

Do I dream?

The notion unsettled him, but another one, speeding hard upon its heels, made him stiffen in horror, numbing him to the bone: *Have I died?*

Fectur! Had Fectur done what he had plainly intended to do, the one thing he had to do to fully secure control of Enchantment's Edge? Leth's blood ran suddenly cold in his veins. He stood slowly, staring at his pale hands. He cast his gaze around the chamber again. No, he could see. He could hear. He had full sensation. And yet he knew that even in a dream, many times, he had felt the same things. He had dreamed that he dreamed, and knew it too. He had pinched his flesh to feel pain, and yet still he dreamed on.

But this had another quality, similar yet strangely, disorientatingly different. Something not experienced. As though his mind was not quite his own.

Can this be my death?

Could death possess the quality of dream? How could he discover? Was there a means, a foolproof way, of knowing?

Why should there be? My death has waited for me, as it waits for all men, inexorable and pitiless. Now it waits no more.

His guts churned suddenly, trying to reject the food they had just welcomed. Would a dead man's guts rebel like this? Why not? In the deathdream, if the deluded soul is still attached to the embedded memories of life, clinging to the familiar, or what remains of it, at least for a time . . . If the soul does not know that life has gone, still believes that nothing has changed, is in limbo but not yet in oblivion . . . Would death be so merciful, allowing memory, sensation and consciousness to dissipate slowly in the dream?

Leth shook his head, trying to dispel these thoughts, fighting. He tried to think back. He recalled, clearly, the events at Enchantment's

Edge, how Jace's childlike curiosity had cast them all into the void of Orbus's world.

The children! Had Fectur murdered them all? Why did he not recall that? Where were they now? Had death separated them all, casting each into this solitary dreaming state? No. No. It *was* as he recalled it. It had to be. It *had* to be!

Leth felt light-headed and nauseous. He sat down again at the table. A dead man, deathdreaming lightheadedness, deathdreaming nausea and fear, deathdreaming that he sat? Was it possible? He stared at the remains of his meal, at the wine cup beside his plate. Had he been drugged?

How can I know what is happening here?

He considered Orbus, the god who was not a god. The irony of it! Orbus professed himself and those against whom he had fought and been defeated to be something less than gods. Yet Orbus existed within a world that was, essentially, within himself. And now Leth, who had struggled for so long with his own people to persuade them against putting their faith in gods they knew nothing of, was within that world, and welcomed as a long-awaited god.

And Orbus has abandoned me here!

He recalled words spoken by Orbus – it seemed long, long ago now – as they faced one another in the blue domain: 'You, who have lived your entire life on the Edge, have you not always known, somewhere deep inside you, that one day you might have to step over? You have surely wondered what might lie on the Other Side? We are entering Mystery, Leth. Do you not wish to travel? Truly, this is only the beginning'.

The beginning? Leth wrenched his head from side to side. *I did not wish to travel alone. Orbus, what is happening here? Why have you forsaken me?*

The chamber door opened. Lakewander entered. She stopped short upon seeing Leth's face. 'What is wrong, Lord? Are you ill?'

Leth rose again, his limbs weak and liquid. He stared hard at her. 'How did I get here?'

'Here? To us?'

He nodded.

'You were borne, Lord, through the Sign.'

'From where have I come?'

'From the Godworld. Your own world.'

'And what was I there?'

Lakewander looked nonplussed. 'You would have been . . . I do not know. A god among gods?'

Leth shook his head heavily. 'A man, among men. That is all.'

'But a leader of men? Is that not so?'

Leth heaved a sigh. 'Aye, I was – *I am* – a leader of men.'

'And you wish to return.'

'That is all I wish.'

'We have told you the one known way.'

Leth nodded to himself. *Perhaps there lies the sole means by which I might discover the truth, for a man who has died may not be restored to life.*

But a man who has stepped over?

'Lord, I have come to show you something,' said Lakewander. 'Will you accompany me?'

Leth did so. He was grateful for her company, the chance it offered, so he hoped, to relieve his mind of its morbidity.

'What is the name of this place?' Leth asked as they passed from his chamber.

'This place?'

'This castle, or whatever it is, in which you reside.'

'It is Orbia.'

Leth stopped dead in his tracks. Lakewander continued a few paces before realizing he was not with her. She turned, a quizzical look upon her face. 'Lord?'

'How came it by this name?'

'Why, you named it yourself.'

Leth was incredulous. 'I?'

'In ages past, before you abandoned us. Before you passed to the Godworld.'

Leth could only stare, though he did not see her now. Lakewander gave a consoling smile. 'You are still convinced otherwise.'

'I have not been here before. I am a man, not a god. I am mortal flesh and blood and bone.'

'Lord, you come among us as one of us, this we know. But you are the Swordbearer, Ascaria's doom.' She watched him for a moment, then added, 'No other could have slain the *ools*.'

'How is that?'

'Their hide is thick and resistant to steel. A normal blade, even a two-handed sword wielded by one twice your size, would have caused hardly more than a flesh-wound.'

'The Orbsword has magical properties, I do not deny that,' said Leth. 'But I have none.'

Lakewander made no comment. They walked on, Leth in a daze, hardly aware of where he went. The passed along further passages then into a round tower, up a long winding stairway until they arrived at length before a door which Lakewander opened to admit them into a high circular chamber with a domed ceiling made almost entirely of glass.

'The observatory,' announced Lakewander.

Leth was gazing upwards, through the glass, which was almost flawless and clearer than any that could have been manufactured in his own land. He gazed in wonder at the night sky.

Lakewander stood close beside him. 'From here we observe and note the movements of the Godworld.'

Leth's eyes had been drawn to the single celestial body visible. It hung low above the – as he judged it – western horizon, a brilliantly radiant object, oval in form, which resembled a colossal and fabulously lustred blue-white gem. He was transfixed for some moments, for it was a beautiful and mysterious sight.

'Our world is Orb,' Lakewander said, 'and we are guided by the great Orb of the Godworld. It sustains us, it gives us its light, and from time to time, if our need is so great, it sends one of its own to walk among us.'

Leth glanced aside at her. She was observing him closely. He turned back to the great star. Something else caught his eye. There was another starlike thing, he now saw, far smaller, emitting a bright golden light, lying below and somewhat south of the Orb of the Godworld. 'What is that?'

'That is the World's Pain,' said Lakewander. 'It appears only occasionally, and without herald. But when it comes we know something momentous will occur.' She was silent for some moments, but when no question came she said, 'This time it brought us you.'

Leth swallowed. He looked at the twin stars, if stars they were, and he knew anguish, though he was not quite sure from whence it came.

'Gaze as long as you wish, Swordbearer,' Lakewander said. 'I will await you outside and escort you back to your chambers when you have done. And tomorrow I will show you the End of the World.'

II

The night was well advanced. Leth lay upon his back in the bed provided for him within his modest apartment. Sleep eluded him; his mind threw itself from one set of memories, one concern, one experience, to another. He had lingered long in the observatory high above, staring at the unworldly night sky and the two strange and beautiful bodies it held. He had asked no further questions of Lakewander, though his brain teemed with enquiry. It seemed that anything he asked of Lakewander or her two companions was answered only in terms of perplexing conundrums, ellipses or evasions, vexing him further and setting more distance between him and the answers he sought. So he had come from the observatory in a state of deep reverie and abstraction. When Lakewander left him at his door, bidding him goodnight, he hardly noticed her departure.

He lay alone in darkness, darkness so complete in this soundless, windowless place that Leth could well imagine himself to be adrift in some unearthly void, deprived of all sensation save that of thought. And again the notion came to him that he was no longer among the living. This was night without end. His thoughts were those of the disembodied, the recently dead. They filtered from him as his soul, accustomed to flesh, gradually grew to accept its new – or former – state, and when all conscious thought had gone he would be absorbed into . . . what? Non-existence; the mystery of whatever lay beyond life.

No! Again he cast off these notions. *I am a living man! I am Leth, King of Enchantment's Edge! I have not died! I am in another world, and I will return!*

There was a sound, and Leth was instantly alert. The handle of the door to his apartment grated lightly as it was turned from outside. Leth reached for the Orbsword which lay in its scabbard beside the bed.

He could see, through the open portal that let into the main chamber, that the door had now opened. The deep yellow glow of a lamp illumined a tall figure which entered silently, closing the door behind it. It approached the bedchamber, clad in a robe of some dark material that fell almost to the floor. Long fair hair framed the face, falling past the shoulders. Leth recognized Lakewander.

'Lord Swordbearer, are you awake?' She came to his bedside and looked down at him, smiling. 'Don't be alarmed. You do not need the Orbsword.'

Lakewander placed the lamp upon a table beside the bed, then straightened, unfastened the cord that bound her robe at the waist and shrugged the garment from her shoulders. She stood naked before him. Leth gazed up at her. Her body, pale and shadowed, was magnificent, lit by the warm lampglow in tones ranging from deepest umber to saffron. Tiny downy hairs upon her flat belly glimmered in the light, her belly and breasts rose and fell in rhythm with her breathing. Her limbs were long, supple and well-toned. The breasts, though not large, were full and perfectly round, the areolae dark circles, the nipples proudly erect. She bent to draw back the bedclothes and climbed in beside him. Leth smelt her fragrance, a blend of musk, the soft tang of orange blossom and woodland grass.

'Lakewander –' Leth began, but her lips were on his, warm and searching, her long body pressed against his, deeply stimulating. Leth almost succumbed, so great was his need, so profound his anguish, his desire almost overriding all else. But he twisted his head away.

'What is the matter, Lord?'

'I do not wish this.'

'Do I displease you?'

'No.'

Her hand slid between his legs and she took him in her fingers. 'And you desire me, that much is evident.'

'You do not understand.'

'Will you not love me?'

He thought: *Through the act of love we affirm that we are alive.* And how desperately he needed such affirmation just now. He looked into her face, wanting her, drawn towards her lips, pulsing, yearning in her tender grasp. Her face was close again, her breast brushing his arm, her lips parted.

But this is not love! Issul! Issul!

He turned away.

'Lord?'

'Lakewander, I do not want to offend you, but this cannot be. Please understand.'

'But why? If you desire me, as I desire you?'

'Is it not obvious? There is another. My wife, my greatest friend, the mother of my children. The woman I love.'

Issul, Issul, I do not even know if you are alive!

'Lord, I think it is you who do not understand.'

'Please. This cannot be.'

Lakewander removed her hand. He let out a breath, not wanting her to stop.

'Your words tell me one thing, your body something quite different,' Lakewander said.

Leth stayed silent. He was so close to reaching for her. Moments passed, filled with uncertainty, then he felt her climb from the bed. He turned towards her as she slipped back into her robe. 'I am sorry, Lakewander.'

'I too, Lord,' she said, but her tone was not cold or terse. Rather, she seemed wistful, a little preoccupied. 'I do not know what will happen now.'

'What do you mean?'

'This is not what was expected.'

'Expected?'

Her words suggested she had come here with the knowledge of others, even at their bidding. Leth was curious, and indignant. Had he been the subject of an experiment or test of some kind?

'Now we may have to reconsider,' she said. 'Goodnight, Lord. We will meet on the morrow.'

She took her lamp and left him.

III

In the morning Leth discovered a bowl, a large pitcher of warm, scented water and a cake of soap in his chamber. Again, he did not know who had left it. He washed and dressed, then left his chambers and made his way back to the room where he had spoken with old Master Protector the previous day.

Master Protector sat alone at the table, a spread of various foods before him: oatflakes and warm milk, hot white bread rolls, butter, preserves of quince and blueberry, pancakes steeped in honey. 'Lord Swordbearer, greetings. I trust you slept well and find yourself refreshed.'

'My sleep was broken by uneasy dreams, many questions and more,' said Leth. 'Still, in the end, I did sleep, and feel better for it.'

'Well, then, I am both sorry and gladdened – sorry that beneath my humble roof you should find sleep hard to come by, but glad that you found it in the end. Will you take breakfast with me?'

Leth nodded his thanks and seated himself at the table.

'You saw, last night, and you learned, did you not?' enquired Master Protector.

'I saw a sky that was furrowed and valleyed like an unworldly landscape. I saw a massive jewel in the sky, the Orb of the Godworld, and the World's Pain at its side. I learned that this place is known by you as Orbia, and that it was so named long ago by the one you believe me to be. I learned also that this place is haunted by beings who dwell within the very stone that forms it.' Leth glanced about the chamber walls, wondering how many ghostly entities listened in to this conversation. 'In short, I saw wonders and mysteries, but learned little to enlighten me. It all seems much like a dream, and perhaps that is all it is.'

'All?' Master Protector smiled to himself, dabbing his thin blood-less lips with a napkin. 'If so, it is a dream from which there is no escape, except death, and who can say whether death is truly an escape?'

His words chilled Leth, who glanced again at the walls. 'Death in your domain appears to be an experience unlike death in my own world. Do all of you become part of this when you pass on?'

'All who are Protectors.'

'Then you are immortal.'

'Orbia is immortal, Swordbearer. You more than anyone should understand that. But it is immortal only as long as no one knows how it may be destroyed. Ascaria, the Kancanitrix, is seeking to do that, and we know that she may be close upon her goal.'

'Hence you would have me slay her first.'

Master Protector sipped from a mug of steaming spiced pos-
set. 'I see that the Orbsword remains buckled at your waist. I am
thankful.'

'You are premature. I have made no compact.'

'Quite so. Yet you have not returned the Sword to us.
Swordbearer, this is the only weapon that can slay Ascaria, and
you are the only one who can bear it.'

'No. Perhaps no other may draw the Sword, but as I said last night,
that need not preclude another's wielding it.'

Master Protector shook his head. 'The energy of the Orbsword
would rapidly deplete the strength of any ordinary man who bore
it. But not you. No, indeed, I see by your very bearing and the light
that shines in your eyes that the Sword empowers you. Do you not
feel it?'

'I feel only anger and mistrust, and the desire to be away from
here with my children, to our own home,' declared Leth with vehe-
mence. 'You brought us here against our will; you allowed us to be
separated; and now you blackmail me with their lives. I want nothing
of this!'

'No, Swordbearer, we did not bring you,' said Master Protector.
'You were dying and we offered you life. We showed you a way
but you came of your own free will. Is that not so?'

Leth hesitated. Strictly speaking, Master Protector was right. Yet
there was more to it than that. 'You have said yourself that you
summoned me!'

'We call it the Summoning, but you yourself know it was not.
It was more an opening of the way, and an offering of life. We
knew from the conjunction of the World's Pain with the Orb of the
Godworld that a being from the Godworld was trapped beyond the
Sign. We opened the way to you, praying that it would be you, the
Swordbearer, who came this time, and not some other, lesser being,
as before. But it was not we who put you in the limbo in which you
wandered. We do not possess that power.'

'Then how –' Leth began.

Master Protector was seized by a fit of coughing. For some
moments he was unable to speak. Leth waited, and eventually
the old man sat back, wheezing as he struggled to draw air, his
frail, thin hands gripping the armrests of his chair. He shook his
head, his watering eyes turned upwards, and spoke in a thin voice.
'Surely you know more than we of the how and why you came to be

there? If you did not choose to come, then you were sent in response to our need. Your children, too. Nothing is by chance or hazard.'

Sent! Leth thought of Enchantment's Edge, of Lord Fectur, Orbus, Grey Venger. *Sent!* No, it had been hazard that had cast him into Orbus's world. Nothing was premeditated. But why was Orbus not present? Why had he abandoned him?

'You seem troubled, Swordbearer. I am sorry if my words bring you disquiet.'

There are no answers, Leth thought. Every question just extends the mystery and the paradox. He thought of the furrowed night sky, deepest indigo, like a surrounding shell high above, enclosing this strange world. And he recalled the blue casket and reminded himself that somehow he and all of this world were contained within it, and he shook his head. In circumstances such as these how might he expect logic or rationality?

'Did Lakewander tell you of the End of the World?' Master Protector asked.

'She did.' Leth watched him. 'What did she mean?'

'Wait. Go with her. Then you will see. Now, if you will forgive me, I must leave you. Please eat and drink as much as you wish.'

Shakily Master Protector began to rise. A servant entered, a broad-shouldered, stocky fellow in a long off-white garment, who crossed the chamber in short brisk strides and took the old man's arm. Together they departed. Left alone, Leth musingly completed his early repast, and a short while later was joined by Lakewander. She was clad in the red-toned half armour in which Leth had first seen her in the *ools*' lair the previous day. Yet again it seemed to Leth that she was not entirely a stranger, though if ever he had seen her before he could not recall it. She cradled her helmet in the crook of her arm. 'If you are ready, Lord Swordbearer.'

She took him to a yard outside where a pair of grooms waited with horses. 'This is your mount,' Lakewander indicated a magnificent black stallion. 'His name is Swiftwind. He is a fine, brave beast who will serve you obediently and well. And here is your armour.'

She gestured towards a wooden frame standing to one side, upon which was borne a suit of fabulous shining ribbed plate armour, its metal tinged with brilliant sapphire blue. 'It has been kept for you. No other has worn it.'

Leth admired the suit, which was clearly of the finest craftman-ship. 'I am to wear this now?'

'You may have need of it, Lord.'

'I was not aware that we were riding into battle.'

'It is a precaution, that is all. I cannot say exactly what we will meet.'

Somewhat reluctantly Leth allowed Lakewander and one of the grooms to help him don the armour. It fitted perfectly – almost as if it had been moulded upon his body. And to his surprise, once on, the armour felt both flexible and light. He found it allowed him almost complete freedom of movement; he might have been clad in nothing more than light mail. An ornate visored helm with comb, plume and stylized horns complemented the body-armour assemblage, but Leth elected to take a less elaborate secondary helmet, with peak and cheek – and neck-guards instead. This he donned, curious as to the kinds of perils Lakewander anticipated meeting.

Lakewander stood before him, her hands upon her hips, appraising him with a smile of approbation. 'You are as the artists of yore have portrayed you, Lord. I feel proud and stirred. That you should be with us now gives me such hope.'

Leth made no comment. They mounted their steeds and rode from the place called Orbia, out to find the End of the World.

IV

A dirt track led them through a narrow belt of trees onto a wider way that plied out across a landscape of scrub and low swells. Leth's intention was to look back and determine the character and extent of the building from which they rode, but as they came from beneath the trees his eyes were taken by an arresting sight. In the sky before him, midway to its zenith, hung the great jewel that Lakewander had described the night before as the Orb of the Godworld.

Its brilliance pained his eyes as he stared, yet he could not for some moments take his attention away. He squinted, shielding his eyes with one hand raised to the peak of his helmet. He realized now that yesterday, when he had stepped through the portal out of Orbus's empty blue domain and confronted Summoner and his followers for the first time, he had been mistaken. He had glanced briefly skyward and seen what he had taken without question to be the sun's familiar disc. But it was not. It was this, this extraordinary manifestation, the Orb of the Godworld, brilliant and pale, glorious and strange, a sun yet not a sun, a gem that could not be fully described, as mysterious and unreachable as any sun or star, casting pure and unfathomable light upon its own world as it travelled across an unnatural firmament.

Eventually Leth could bear its light no longer. He lowered his eyes but the after-image persisted for some time, impressed upon his vision. When he recalled his intention to look back he turned in the saddle, but the place called Orbia, which he had just ridden from, was wholly concealed behind the trees.

He raised his face again to the skies, searching this time not for the blinding Orb of the Godworld but for that other, lesser body which Lakewander had called the World's Pain. It was not, as last night, close below and to the south of the great Orb. But Leth scanned every inch of the unclouded blue and eventually was rewarded by the discovery of a pinpoint of light, pale golden and low in the sky, almost directly ahead. To the casual observer it was easily missed, for the brightness of the day veiled its radiance, in contrast to the Orb of the Godworld which blazed with almost solar magnificence. Leth's gaze shifted from one to the other, then to the wide blue sky which in daylight appeared perfectly smooth and unmarked. He shook his head. The wonders of this world seemed to acknowledge no physical logic: what he saw could not be explained, nor assimilated in the familiar – if also inexplicable – terms of the celestial wonders of his own world.

Lakewander led him onward, across a desolate plain relieved only by low grassy swells, and in the furthest distance a high ridge which burst stark and strangely gleaming from the raw earth. Leth studied its distant formation as they rode. It was reddish in colour, and to his eyes it appeared curiously moulded, almost visceral.

The ridge passed from view as they began a long descent into green woodland. They came to a shaded dell specked with flowers, where a clear spring bubbled between moss-clad boulders. Lakewander suggested stopping to eat and rest the horses. From her pack she produced meat, cheese, fruit, hard biscuits and a flask of watered wine. Leth ate in near silence, finding himself in no mood for conversation, no matter that his mind remained aflood with questions. Lakewander, perhaps intuiting something of his state of mind, made little effort to engage him.

They rode on. A little way down the road they came upon a man crouched at the wayside. Lakewander trotted past, paying him no heed, but Leth reined in his horse, concerned at what he was seeing. The man was naked but for a few soiled, rotting rags. He was huddled upon one knee, his spine curved forward, chest pressed to thigh and his head bowed towards the ground and held close against the inner side of the upright knee. His body, what Leth could see of it, was filthy, thin and bony. One spindly arm was thrown across the back of his head, the other hugged his forward shin. He was held in this position, almost wholly immobile, by a series of rigid, interconnected clamps and straps forged of black iron, which were affixed to various parts of his body. A clamp upon his head was linked by a metal strap to one around his left wrist. This also connected to a band around his right thigh, which was similarly clamped to his right lower leg and, in a separate grip, to his left ankle. The left arm was also clamped fast to the inclining left leg. The right arm which was thrown over his head was likewise bound to his neck and left forearm. He could not stretch or twist any of his limbs other than in the most infinitesimal degree.

Leth dismounted and approached the figure. He lowered himself beside him, unable to see his face. The man's head was covered in a mass of filthy, louse-ridden black hair, and a smell rose from him of excreta and unwashed flesh.

'Who has done this?' enquired Leth, outraged. He cast his eyes over the monstrous contrivance which held the man, seeking a means to release him. When the man did not respond he touched his shoulder. 'Friend, I wish to help you.'

'Go away,' came the short reply.

Surprised, Leth said, 'Do not be afraid. I am here to help you if I can. Tell me first what crime you have committed to be punished thus? Such a sentence is inhuman.'

'Go away,' the man repeated. His voice was gruff, strained and part-throttled due to his unnatural posture. Leth could see no way of releasing him; the contraption had been formed with perverse ingenuity, virtually as one piece. What joints and links there were had been expertly bolted and melded.

Leth scratched his head. 'It will take a smithy to release you from this.'

'Leave me!' growled the man. 'This is my place! Begone!'

'I cannot leave you thus,' declared Leth, astonished. 'I will not.'

'This is my place!' the man flared, his chin forced against his chest. The metal device shook and rattled. 'Begone, interferer! Leave me! Leave me!'

Lakewander had turned her horse around. She addressed Leth from the saddle. 'Do as he says, Swordbearer. This is his choice.'

Leth straightened. 'His choice? Who has put him here?'

'He has – that is, he has employed some person to bind him thus and transport him to the roadside. But it is his choice, free and without pressure or coercion from any other. He is a Sufferer, and this is his place.'

Leth stared at her, uncomprehending, then turned and knelt once again beside the confined man. 'Sir, tell me what she says is not true. Tell me that you desire to be freed and you have my word that I will give you liberty, without expectation of reward.'

'This is my place!' declared the man, and his voice now was impatient and imploring. 'Leave me! Leave me!'

'Do you fear her?' said Leth, suddenly suspicious. 'Do you think that she commands me, that I am deceiving you? If so, you are mistaken, be sure of that.'

'Fool!' spat the man, jerking his rigid shackle hard, the veins standing out on his neck and arms. 'Beef-wit! Dolt! Do you not understand the common tongue? Your proximity offends me! Your words rankle in my ears! Get gone now, brainless maggot, before I piss upon you! Get gone!'

Leth rose, dismayed, and backed away a couple of steps. Lake-wander gave him a consoling look. 'Do as he says, Swordbearer.'

'Why will he not accept help?'

'It is his choice.'

As they rode off Leth said, 'He will die there.'

'Eventually, yes. He is able to shuffle very slowly, and his one hand has sufficient mobility to enable him to pluck tall stalks of grass and other plants and some insects. Hence his body is provided with basic sustenance and moisture, enough that he does not starve.'

'And he has chosen this? Why?'

'He is a Sufferer. That is the short answer. It is his devotion. No doubt in the Godworld perfection reigns. None feel guilt. None suffer without knowing why. None seek answers to the mysteries and agonies of existence, nor feel the need to petition higher deities for mercy and understanding. Here it is not like that. Here some are utterly borne down by the burden of living, the privations that have been thrust upon them. Some find only misery in life. Some weep and some seek solace through pain, as if it will purge them of imagined sins. Some, so brutalized, elect to exhibit themselves as he does. They perceive themselves as worthless and undeserving, save as receptacles or embodiments, in some form, of the World's Pain. It is all they know, and it is perhaps a kind of affirmation of their existence.'

Leth absorbed this sombrely, then said, after a pause, 'You are wrong. Where I come from it is not so different.'

'Then can you understand how one might be devoured by one's yearning and the bitter knowledge that your dreams can never be realized?'

'Aye, but . . .' Leth fell silent, contemplating this. It seemed hardly an answer, but he expected nothing more.

'Slay Ascaria,' Lakewander said, 'and perhaps he and those like him will suffer no more.'

'Ascaria? She is responsible for all you have described?'

'She is the Kancanitrix, the Dark Flame of the Orb. If her flame can be extinguished the true light of the Orb may once again enter the darkened souls of our kind.'

Leth looked back at the solitary huddled figure beside the road, diminishing slowly into the distance. Then they rounded a bend and the Sufferer was lost to sight.

Throughout their journey Leth had seen no human settlements nor, with the exception of the Sufferer, any indication of human life at all. No fields nor farm beasts. The terrain they traversed was predominantly bare, almost a wasteland. Wild beasts and birds were evident in some small number, and were indistinguishable in most respects from the common creatures of his homeland. But his overall impression was of uncanny emptiness.

Now things began to change slightly, though not in ways he might have anticipated. He became aware of metal statues at the roadside: one on its own, initially unremarkable, then a little way further another, and another. Now a cluster of three in close proximity to one another, with more visible in the distance.

In size they were more or less uniform: bald, almost featureless leaden or iron figures cast in human form, but somewhat more massive than a man. In the first few that Leth passed their postures were similarly without variation. They simply stood, their legs melded together, their arms at their sides, likewise melded to the torsos. But now he came upon one kneeling, its metal hands upon its metal thighs, blank face turned towards the sky. Another stood with arms outstretched to either side; another knelt with spine curved, chest upon the tops of its thighs, elbows hugging calves and thighs, fingers clutching knees and face almost in the soil. Some of the figures appeared to have been set in place quite recently, others bore marks of weathering and rust, suggesting they had stood for a long time, perhaps years or even decades.

As Leth and Lakewander rode on they passed more and more of the metal statues. The variations in posture became the norm. A handful were mounted upon plinths or pedestals; one had been affixed high atop a tree trunk which had been shorn of leaves, branches and bark, and sawn clean through at its top. The statue stood perhaps forty ells above the ground, sentinel-still, a metallic stylite gazing blindly into infinity.

Leth assumed the figures to be solid until he noticed that one feature common to them all was a mouth orifice, which suggested that they might in part be hollow. He eyed them somewhat uncomfortably. Their silence and number gave them an eerie presence, and he was bemused as to their purpose in so desolate a place.

The woodland had begun to thin. Leth and Lakewater emerged now onto a dusty plain, and were confronted by scores of the metal statues spread across the landscape all around. Many were high on up-ended tree-trunks or pinnacles of rock, others stood, sat, knelt, squatted, sprawled upon the earth. Leth pulled up his horse. He had never seen a sight like it. And as he gazed around him, to his shock, the nearest statue spoke.

Or rather, it uttered a series of sounds.

The hairs at the nape of Leth's neck stood on end. He wrenched himself around in the saddle. His horse shied and he struggled for a moment to control it. He peered at the statue, which stood less than five paces away. The sound came again, a voice so close to human as to be almost a mockery. It moaned, shaping words of a sort, but he could not make them out for they were faint and oddly distorted.

'She is asking for water,' Lakewander said. She had halted her horse and walked it back to stand beside him.

'What? She?'

'She is a Soul.' Lakewander gestured out across the plain, and back to the woodland from which they had ridden. 'All of them are Souls.'

The voice spoke again, sibilant and hoarse through the metal mouth orifice, and this time Leth made out the words. 'Waa-terrr. Pllleease, sir. If you ha-ave a hea-arrtt. Waa-terrr.'

Shaken, he reached reflexively for the flask strapped to his saddle-pack. He dismounted, then hesitated. He knew nothing of these strange metal beings. Was he being tricked?

He turned to Lakewander. 'Should I?'

'You will come to no harm, if that is what you are asking, Lord,' she said, then added with unexpected sarcasm, 'and no doubt it will salve your conscience. But in all truth it will do little else except prolong her suffering.'

Leth felt his temper rise. 'Listen, what is going on here? Am I to help her or not?'

'It is as I say. You will relieve her suffering in the short term, but prolong it in the long term.'

'What is she? She, and all these others? Souls? What do you mean?'

'They are women, like I, and men—' she hesitated, looking at Leth, then away, '—like other men, whose faith, belief, conviction or, as some would conceive it, madness, has driven them to the extreme of having themselves encased forever inside these metal shells.'

The voice came again, entreating him from within the figure.

'You mean –' Leth looked about him in stark horror '– these are not fabulous living statues, or some other form of creature? They are human beings? All of them? Trapped?'

'Voluntarily,' said Lakewander. She looked around, her face suddenly haggard. 'And not all of these figures contain people. Not any more. Many have long since perished. You see, they are wholly dependent upon the goodwill of passers-by for sustenance, and there are few passers-by hereabouts.' Lakewander lifted a hand to her face, and Leth realized she was brushing away a tear. 'This is not a good place to be, Swordbearer. We should move on.'

'Not until I have done what any decent man would do.' Leth strode to the statue that had spoken and put the neck of his flask to the lipless mouth.

'Are you truly so merciful, Swordbearer?' asked Lakewander.

'This is how the Souls inflict their suffering upon us. They are martyrs, making us pay the price of their devotion, and they know that whatever we do – help them or ignore them – we are wrong. And we are right also. It is we who are trapped, as much as they.'

From within the hollow figure there came a faint scrabbling sound. A straw of rolled grass appeared through the mouth orifice, probing for the life-giving liquid. Pale bluish lips, cracked and scabbed, were pressed against the inner surface of the mouth, and began to draw greedily upon the straw. Leth recoiled, despite himself.

'Do you feel better now, Lord,' Lakewander asked, her voice high and laden with sorrow. She passed her arm out again across the plain. 'Where will you stop? *How* will you stop?'

Even as she spoke there came, from a kneeling statue close by, a voice, this time a man's, similarly pleading. Others joined in: one, then another, then more, until the air was alive with their terrible pleading.

Leth calculated that his flask was now less than one third full. He pulled it away from the Soul's desperate mouth. She gave a dismal wail of distress and begged him for more. Ignoring her he ran to the next metal figure, pressed the flask to the mouth. As before a straw emerged and withered lips began to suck.

'Help me!' shouted Leth. 'Lakewander, bring your flask!'

Lakewander was weeping openly. She slid from her horse, her shoulders and head bowed, and took her flask and walked across to a nearby Soul. The awful cacophony continued, tearing into Leth's heart. He yanked his flask from the Soul he was succouring, ran to another, then another. He realized his flask was empty, and dashed it to the floor. He ran to Lakewander, frantic, almost maddened. 'What can we do?'

Lakewander turned to him. She was shaking, her face gaunt, the tears streaming down her cheeks. 'We can do nothing. Nothing!'

She fell against him, her body racked with sobs. Leth threw his arms around her and held her close. He cried out, his voice almost lost beneath the screams of the dying Souls. He knew that she was right. There was nothing they could do. As with the Sufferer back in the woods, they required the skills and workshop of a smithy – of many smithies – to release these people from their metal shells.

'Why did you bring me here?' he cried.

'I had no choice. It is the only way. Please, Swordbearer, take me away from here!'

He helped her back to her mount. She was still shaking, as, he realized, was he. He climbed onto Swiftwind's back, pressing his hands to his ears. Lakewander turned a stricken face to him, pointing along the road between the Souls. Then she spurred her horse to a gallop and rode, her face pressed to the mount's neck. Leth, the tears streaming from his own eyes, bent his back and rode after her, the howls and moans of those he was leaving behind seeming to grow even louder.

V

'Can we do nothing? Is there no one in this region who could help us to free them?'

Free of the plain of imprisoned Souls, both Leth and Lakewander remained deeply affected by their experience. They rode along a stony path, winding upwards into the ridge that Leth had spied earlier, which seemed to have curved around to lie directly in their path.

'To what end?' asked Lakewander. 'Do you not understand that they *choose* to subject themselves to this? Free them and they would not thank you. They would drink and eat and have themselves sealed up once more. And they might even charge you with the cost of creating another shell, for they do not come cheaply.'

'But why? Why do they do this to themselves?'

Lakewander gave a pallid smile, her expression one of resignation and cynicism. 'They are fanatics and religious zealots.'

'No! That is insufficient!'

'They experience themselves as souls incarcerated within flesh, extant and conscious but not knowing why. They seal themselves inside bodies of iron as a physical demonstration of this. They are literally imprisoned within bodies which, paradoxically, will long outlast their own, and which will stand as reminders for all to witness. The Souls consider themselves living works of art, and examples both to others and to their creator. Their suffering becomes both their art and the physical embodiment of their belief, which are perhaps one and the same thing. Ultimately they believe that at some point, when enough have suffered and perished, their Creator will show mercy and will come and set them free, both of their metal prison and the prison of their flesh. Is that sufficient for you, Swordbearer?'

Leth pondered this. 'They await their god?'

She looked askance at him.

'Is it not possible,' Leth said, 'that with the Sword of the Orb I might cleave their prisons from them?'

Lakewander gave a sigh. 'You tell us – you insist – that you are not a god.'

'That is not what I asked.'

She shook her head. 'No, Lord Swordbearer, you are not the one they wait for. Believe me, you are not. And neither can the Orbsword release them. Even if it could they would, as I have already said, only build themselves new prisons.'

'You do not like them, do you?'

'They are a menace. They force upon us a terrible moral dilemma – as you have just experienced. We wish to help them, yet whatever action we take will only increase their agony. We must live with ourselves in the full knowledge of this. The Souls are martyrs, and through their suffering they needlessly cause others to suffer. Do you see? Such people are a corrosive influence on our society and the individual. They do not deserve respect.'

'That is a harsh judgement.'

'You have not had to live your entire life knowing and passing among these people.'

'This is wilderness, far from society!' exclaimed Leth. 'The Souls have hardly placed themselves in your midst. No one is forced to look upon them or be witness to their pleas day in and day out.'

Lakewander bowed her head, shaking it leadenly from side to side. When she looked up again Leth saw that her eyes were wet once more. 'Lord Swordbearer, you know so little. But we are almost at the End of the World. Perhaps then you will see. I will say this, though. I pity the Souls. They are a menace, but they cannot help what they do. It is Ascaria's baneful influence that makes them torture themselves the way they do. Hence she torments us. When the Orb is rid of her, then, perhaps, will all suffering be done.'

They had come to the lip of a narrow gorge at the bottom of which a fast-flowing river raced foaming and leaping to more level ground far below. Before them was a bridge formed of a single colossal slab of red-toned rock laid longwise across the gorge. On the other side a cavernous opening let into the towering rock face. Leth let his eyes travel upwards, over the sheer face of the ridge, noting the smooth, glistening surface of the rock and its queer, almost fleshlike form.

Lakewander dismounted from her horse and indicated to Leth to do likewise. They tethered both mounts to a nearby tree. Lakewander stepped forward to place herself before the bridge. In a loud voice she called out, 'Bridgekeeper, are you here? We wish to cross.'

She waited a few moments, then called out the same words again. Then once more. 'Bridgekeeper, for the third time I hail you. Two persons wish to cross. If you hear me show yourself now, for I will not speak again and we will cross without toll.'

Something stirred in the cavern's dark maw. A shadow shifted and a huge figure trundled from the gloom to confront them. His arms were long and massively sinewed, his legs squat and wide. A great paunch bulged beneath hirsute and fleshy ribs and wide, high shoulders supporting a head as large as a bull's. Small, dark, deeply sunken eyes were squeezed into a narrow slit between a low, beetling brow and high, prominent wedges of cheekbone. The nose was a huge purple bulb that flopped over a wide mouth with thrusting jaw and large crooked teeth. He wore only a soiled leather codpiece, and dragged an enormous knobbled wood cudgel behind him. He stood before the bridge, blinking at the two.

'So, you are here, as I thought you would be,' declared Lakewander. 'Did you think to trick me by lying low? You should know I would not forget.'

'Lakewander, is it you?' The huge Bridgekeeper, peering across the chasm, raised a long heavy arm and scratched his head. 'It has been such a long time.'

'It has.'

'You look so different. Where do you go? To the Shore?'

Lakewander nodded. 'To the Shore.'

'And who is this who accompanies you?'

'A warrior, fearless and strong, so do not think to cheat us, Bridgekeeper. Here. Here are two pieces of copper for our passage.' She strode forward and pressed two coins into the Bridgekeeper's vast palm. 'Now, let us pass.'

The Bridgekeeper stared for a moment at the coins. He lowered his head and sniffed them with his great purple nose, then shuffled aside. Lakewander beckoned to Leth to come forward.

'How is business, Bridgekeeper?' she asked as she stepped to the other side of the bridge.

The Bridgekeeper shook his head lugubriously. 'Not good. Not good at all. Few pass this way. After all, the only thing to see in this place is Nothing.'

'So travellers no longer come from near and far to gawp in awe at Nothing? Could it be that your reputation has frightened them away? After all, for the uninformed your toll can be excessive, to say the least.'

'Oh no, I am sure that is not the reason,' replied the Bridgekeeper. 'No, I am very fair. I think rather that the wonder of experiencing Nothing has worn thin.'

'Perhaps,' said Lakewander sceptically.

The Bridgekeeper trailed behind Lakewander and Leth as they moved to the cavern mouth. 'You know, I think I may have seen no one since you last came, Lakewander.'

'That is indeed a long time. Have you not grown bored, leading such a solitary existence for so long?'

'Yes, it is. And I have. Still, I have my amusements. And you are here now. Will you not stop now and sup with me, you and your heroic warrior friend? I have a tasty stew warming in the pot. I will tell you marvellous stories.'

'I regret, Bridgekeeper, we cannot. We are pressed.' Lakewander replied. Aside to Leth she whispered, 'You will pass this way again. Accept nothing from him. Always announce yourself three times and pay his toll. Do not attempt to sneak past; the Bridgekeeper is wilier than he looks. He will catch you out and you will wish he had not. Do not eat his stew, and never listen to his stories. If you do you will never leave.'

'Ah, that is regrettable,' said the Bridgekeeper. 'And surprising, for after all, where you are going, there is Nothing to keep you entertained.'

He seemed to find something highly amusing in this, for he began to laugh, a rumbling sepulchral sound that emerged from deep in his swollen gut and reverberated heavily off the cavern walls. His laughter accompanied them as they passed down a dim flight of steep, deeply cut steps towards a shaft of pale grey light some one hundred feet below.

At the bottom they faced an opening; brilliant daylight from out-side dazzled and failed to reveal what lay before them. Lakewander laid a cautioning hand upon Leth's arm. 'When you step out, stand until your eyes clear. Do not go any further.'

He did as she said. When his eyes adjusted to the unnatural brightness of the day he found he was standing at one end of a long narrow beach at the foot of a high headland stretching into the distance. But it was unlike any beach he had ever seen. It extended as far as his eyes could see and was composed of sand and broad streaks of shingle. But both sand and shingle were imbued with soft, hazy colours. It seemed that a blurred iridescence clothed their surface, reflecting an extraordinary light.

But this was not the most remarkable feature. For what Leth saw now made him gasp. He stood transfixed, his mind barely able to take it in. The beach sloped gently towards the waterline, but where the ocean should have begun there was no lapping water, nor continuation of sand, shingle or anything else. There was, simply and most awfully, utter emptiness; a phenomenon wholly resistant to emotional or intellectual grasp, for there was nothing, quite literally no thing, there to be grasped.

'It is the Shore of Nothing,' Lakewander said.

Leth was reeling, giddy at the sight, gaping wide-mouthed, shak-ing his head from side to side. He tried to form words but nothing came. When Lakewander put her hand to his arm to support him he drew in a great, strangled breath. In his mind a scream had been trying to manifest, an involuntary expression of the sudden numbing terror he felt at the sight of this . . . this utter absence of being, which he could find no reference for. Her touch, human and real, brought him back from the brink of the abyss.

Orbus, I do not want to travel alone!

'Swordbearer, it is the End of the World,' Lakewander said.

Struggling for breath, Leth turned his face to hers. His entire body was trembling and he knew his face revealed everything that was passing through him at that moment, but he could do nothing to conceal his shock. Lakewander gave a small smile of sympathy. 'It is all right, Lord. It affects everyone like that the first time.' She looked out into the dreadful emptiness. 'Had I been able I would have warned you, but how can you prepare anyone for a sight, a phenomenon such as this?'

'H – How –' Leth began, but he could still not form the words.

Lakewander turned back to him. He saw, without understanding, that her face had been transformed. She looked at him with an expression that told of profound personal tragedy. Her eyes swam with tears and her voice shook. 'Ascaria.' She swallowed, inhaled deeply. 'This was once my home. There were lakes and forests here where I played. A town where I was born and grew to adulthood. My family lived here, and many others. But she took it all away.'

Leth only half heard her. His eyes were back upon the shore and the Nothing that lay beyond, so close to where he stood. He thought momentarily of the blue void he had wandered across with Jace and Galry. The loneliness of that place had been oppressive, yet its emptiness could not be compared to this. He looked up. The Orb of the Godworld was obscured by the high cliff, but the blue sky extended . . . and then ended, directly overhead, on a line with the shore. Beyond the shore there was no horizon, no feature of any kind, not even direction, up or down. His brain still struggled to qualify what he was witnessing. He felt nauseous. He could make no sense of what lay before him, for it was Nothing, and his mind rebelled.

And then, unbidden, the thought came: *the End of the World!*

He was rocked with a sudden racing spasm of wild hope, a swelling rush of joy. He stepped down from the rock he and Lakewander occupied, and stood upon the beach. The sand was soft beneath his feet, its colours a mist. He stared wild-eyed into the Nothing.

Was it possible? His heart hammered. Could he step from here and find himself back at Enchantment's Edge?

'Will you abandon your children, Swordbearer?'

Her voice broke the spell. Leth let loose a long, painful breath. His shoulders sagged; he felt himself slump, and wondered for a moment if he had become insane.

'That is what you were thinking, was it not?' Lakewander stepped down onto the beach and stood beside him. 'That this might be escape?'

She bent and scooped up a handful of small pebbles.

'You may be correct,' she said. 'Nobody has ever discovered. But look.'

She tossed the pebbles into the Nothing beyond the shore. They disappeared, without sound or shimmer. 'I have seen someone – several people – step from the beach. They have never been seen again. Will you risk it? Even if your children were here. Would you?'

Leth said nothing, knowing, as did she, that he would not.

'Earlier,' said Lakewander after a pause, 'you said that the Souls did not place themselves in our midst, where we must witness them always and be torn by the burden they place upon our consciences. Now you have seen the End of the World I will tell you: upon the plain where the Souls are now there was once a city. The Souls put themselves among the people, on the streets, in the squares and parks. That was their intention, to force us to be aware of them at all times. And then, one day, Ascaria took our city. It simply crumbled without a sound and was gone, and everyone and everything in it, except for the Souls. They remained. And unlike here, where the land and even the sky were taken, the land was untouched. We do not know why. But we fear her, Swordbearer. We cannot comprehend her power, we just see what she is capable of.'

Leth thought of Orbus. This was his world. Did he know that others existed here? He had always spoken as though alone. Was he aware of Ascaria, the Kancanitrix, the Dark Flame? Did she threaten him?

'We should go now,' said Lakewander, stepping back up to the entrance to the stairway. She paused. 'Soon you will return here, but you will be prepared.'

'Here?' Leth frowned. 'Why?'

Lakewander raised her hand and pointed along the line of the shore. Far off, in the sky above the point where the headland met the beach at the limit of their vision, Leth spied the glimmer of the World's Pain. It appeared slightly larger now than when he had observed it that morning. Slightly closer. Or might that be illusion?

'That is your guide. Follow it always. It will lead you to her.'

'And what else lies along that route, beyond the far limit of the Shore?'

She shook her head. 'No one has succeeded in walking the length of the beach. There is something . . . We do not know what. It robs people of their minds.' She met his eyes, and forestalled his protest. 'But not you, Swordbearer. Not you.'

'How do you know this?'

Her face was filled with sorrow. 'We believe.'

VI

They made their way back up the long dark steps. The huge form of Bridgekeeper was slumped near the entrance. He was sleeping, his back propped against the stone wall of the tunnel, his legs stretched across its maw. He was snoring loudly, almost as loudly as he had laughed during their descent. They slipped by him, squeezing past his enormous feet, and crossed the bridge to where their horses waited.

The journey back to the place of the haunted walls, which Lakewander and her people called Orbia, passed without incident. Leth and Lakewander sped across the Plain of Imprisoned Souls, neither pausing nor turning their heads to look at the terrible figures. No Soul cried out to them, or if they did they did not hear. In the wood they came upon the Sufferer at the wayside. He was in approximately the same place as before, and this time they did not stop. Nor did they pause to rest or eat again.

As dusk began to close in they approached Orbia. Leth turned in his saddle to look back at the two celestial bodies. The Orb of the Godworld was low above the hills, and more clearly defined in the fading light than it had been in the brightness of morning. It blazed brilliant blue-white, like a fabulous gem, cooler than in its daylight phase. It appeared to have moved only slightly since the morning. Certainly it did not seem to rise and set as did the sun over Enchantment's Edge, and Leth could not determine if it followed a regular, set path across the sky.

In contrast to the Orb of the Godworld, the World's Pain shone more brightly with the decreasing light. As he watched it Leth felt again the sudden anguish that he had experienced when he first laid eyes on it from the observatory the previous night. He turned back, remembering his intention to view Orbia's exterior as he drew close, but once again he was foiled, for it was invisible behind the trees, and then, quite suddenly, they were beneath the trees and within its walls.

At Lakewander's insistence they went directly to Master Protector's chamber, where the old man awaited them, Summoner at his side. Master Protector seemed in good spirits, greeting them with raised arms and a broad smile. 'You have seen everything, Lord Swordbearer?'

Leth nodded soberly. 'Enough. And more.'

'And do you understand now and accept what must be done? There is no other can do this, only the Swordbearer armed with the Sword of the Orb.'

'I have not seen evidence of that.'

'Then will you take our word?'

Leth looked at Lakewander. Her eyes were upon him, grey and still. She was pale, tense, plainly fatigued from the journey and the experiences they had shared, as too was he. But he saw the hope in her eyes, and he remembered her tears. He swallowed, and nodded. 'There is no question that I will go wherever my children are, and do whatever must be done to return them to their home. And if, in the process, I can help you, I will.'

Master Protector brought his hands together and sat back, beaming. 'We are so grateful that you came, Swordbearer. So, so glad. You cannot know.'

'You lay so much store by me. I wish I could share your certainty.'

'Nothing is certain, Lord. But until yesterday we hardly even had hope.'

'Still, you are sure enough to allow me to stride the Shore of Nothing where, I am told, men are routinely driven to madness.'

'But not gods!' Master Protector's eyes glittered. 'Believe me, many perils lie before you, and no one can accurately foresee how you will fare. But you are the Swordbearer. You have come, and you carry the Sword, and we believe in you!'

Leth was tired. He saw no point in arguing his case further. He felt that, whatever his own wishes, he was being driven by forces he could barely comprehend, and certainly could not command. His one desire was to find Galry and Jace and return with them to Enchantment's Edge. Nothing else mattered.

So he held his protests and made ready to excuse himself and retire. But Summoner was whispering into Master Protector's ear, and the old man nodded with an inward look, then addressed Leth once again. 'There is another matter, which good Summoner has just recalled to my attention.' He cleared his throat, seemed a little uncomfortable. He took a deep, wheezing breath. 'This is, er, delicate. I hope you will not consider it an affront, Swordbearer, but I would be remiss in my duties if I were to fail to mention it.' He coughed slightly into his frail hand. 'Last night you declined to lie with Lakewander. We wonder, do you find fault with her?'

Taken by surprise, Leth was initially at a loss for an appropriate response. He crooked a forefinger beneath his nose, allowing his mind to settle. Such a direct, personal interrogation *was* an affront, but to respond as an outraged monarch – or deity incarnate – seemed unlikely to serve him well.

'Not at all,' he said, as evenly as he could. 'I explained as much to Lakewander. In my own land there is a woman whom I cherish. She is the mother of my children. I love her dearly and absolutely. I will not betray our love.'

Master Protector seemed to breathe with some difficulty. 'Then will you not lie with Lakewander if she comes to you tonight?'

'Have I not made myself plain? In just a short time I have come to admire and respect and feel affection for Lakewander. She is a remarkable, courageous young woman, and I am far from unconscious of her feminine charms.' He turned and bowed his head to Lakewander, who stood at the end of the table, her eyes lowered. 'But I hope truly that she will not be hurt or offended when I say that I will not lie with her, nor with any woman other than she whom I love.'

Master Protector nodded to himself, his brow furrowed, lips puckered in shrewd reflection. 'This is unexpected, I will say, and it presents us with a problem we had not foreseen.'

'How so?'

'Swordbearer, tomorrow you must leave us. We cannot delay your journey. You must seek out and slay the Kancanitrix. This is beyond further question. Yet, if you are to leave us and will not lie with Lakewander, or indeed with any other woman we may send to you, how are we to have your child?'

'My child?'

'Your offspring, Lord. You must leave us something of yourself. When you depart the Orb we do not want to be left alone and helpless again.'

Leth was stunned, and for some moments once again lost for words. Master Protector began to cough. He doubled over, wheezing and gasping. Summoner rubbed his back and held the spittoon at the ready. When the old man recovered he leaned back, his eyes closed, pale lashes and cheeks wet. Breathing heavily, his mouth hanging open, he said finally, 'She must accompany you.'

Lakewander gasped and stared at him. Summoner dropped his gaze to the tabletop.

'Child, it is the only way,' the old man said.

Leth sensed that Master Protector was close to weeping. He felt himself in a turmoil of emotion. 'It will do no good. I'm sorry, but I will not change my mind.'

Master Protector was looking searchingly at Lakewander. 'Will you go, Child? Will you accompany the Swordbearer, knowing all that we know?'

Lakewander, clearly torn, gnawed her upper lip, then nodded. 'Of course, Father.'

Father! Leth looked from one to the other, and knew the pain of them both. Yet it could make no difference. He would not go back on his word. He would not betray Issul, even if she were – He stopped himself. *I do not know that! She is alive! Issul, Issul! Be alive! Be alive!*

'You should retire now and rest, Lord,' Master Protector was saying. 'Your journey must commence at the rise of the Orb.'

FIVE

I

'Something has happened!' Issul suddenly froze, clutching her hands to her breastbone. 'My children! Something has happened to my children!'

She stared about her, stricken, seeing none of the faces that surrounded her. She knew it as certainly as if Jace and Galry had been in the same room. She had heard them cry out; she knew their distress.

Shouldering through the others, pushing past Shenwolf, she made off hurriedly up the passage, then broke into a run.

'My lady!'

'Majesty!'

Issul heard no one. She rushed on through the Palace of Orbia's fabulous, airy corridors, ignoring palace staff, courtiers, sentries, everyone she passed, until she came at last to her own apartments. She entered her bedchamber, breathless, and bolted the door behind her. 'Orbus! I must speak with you! Orbus!'

The ragged god, at first an unseen shape, shuffled forward from the shadows of a corner of the room and placed himself before her, the muted blue aura that surrounded him lit with pale coruscations. 'I am here.'

'Something has happened to my children!' Issul cried. 'I feel it. I know it. They are in danger. Orbus, can you feel it? What has happened to them?'

Orbus heaved a deep sigh, nodding his great rag-swathed head heavily back and forth in some kind of acknowledgement. 'I have been feeling . . . oh, there is such conflict within me. Like I have never known. It preys upon me, yet I am blind within and cannot identify its source. All is a dense and dark jungled shroud.'

'But my children, Orbus! And Leth! Have they been harmed? Are they alive?'

Orbus's voice was like a parched rush of distant wind across the mouth of a faraway tunnel. 'I have already told you I cannot be that precise. I am sorry.'

'You feel nothing?'

'Nothing? Do you mock? I feel too much. Too much!' Pushing his staff aside, Orbus raised his hands to the sides of his bound head, rocking and turning slowly from side to side, his robes swishing upon the floor. 'I am aware of change – the beginnings of change. And of turmoil. I have not had this clarity before. Perhaps that is a positive sign; I try to see it as such, though it pains me. But these things, they come so close upon the heels of Leth's entry with your children into my world. I do not think it is coincidence. But . . . it is so difficult. Oh Leth, Leth, why did you enter my world unbidden?'

'They think I have abandoned them,' said Issul, her voice breaking. *Leth! Leth! Keep them safe!*

Orbus had lowered his hands and grasped his staff again. From within the mass of rags he seemed to be observing her. He stood for some moments, then asked, 'Queen Issul, how is it that you are so certain of these things?'

'It is a woman's instinct, a mother's union with the children that have grown within her womb. I know it, that is all. They cried out for me.'

'Do you feel it still?'

'I am not sure. I think so, yes.'

'Then at least you know they are alive.'

Issul put her fingers to her brow and turned away. She did not feel so sure, not of anything. Except . . . they had cried for her and she had not been there to help them.

'Child, do not torture yourself so.'

'They need me.'

'And you are doing all that is within your power to find them.'

'I went away. I left them here. I should never have done that. No true mother would have done that.'

'You have already made it plain that you had no choice.'

'I had a choice. I could have told Leth what I knew about the Legendary Child. If I had only spoken up when Moscul was born.'

'Issul, child, you are destroying yourself with these thoughts. You did what you thought was right at the time.'

'It was not enough!'

Orbus moved away. He came to a halt beside the window, took a moment to consider, then turned and faced her. His next words came as a shock. 'Issul, have I misjudged you?'

Issul looked up sharply. 'What – what do you mean?'

He spoke in severe tones. 'I thought you up to this task. I believed you possessed the courage, the will, the resolve to see this through. Yet you bring me only your fears and laments. You are pathetic, threatening to collapse before we have even begun. Are you truly to bear me? I had not foreseen that you would be prone to such indulgence. You make me feel that all is lost.'

It came, as he had plainly intended, like a swingeing slap upon the cheek. Issul straightened – she had unwittingly slumped forward, folding in upon herself and clutching her middle. Ashamed, and angry at herself, she gulped several breaths, her cheeks burning. 'I am sorry.'

'Don't be sorry! I want no more of "sorry"! I want to know whether you are able and committed – to the possibility of life, or the certainty of surrender and death. We go to Enchantment to seek out the Orb's Soul, but I will not allow myself to be borne by a ditherer or a faintheart.'

Issul winced. 'You need have no fear of that.'

'Then enough of this. Tell me of our plans. When do we leave Enchantment's Edge?'

'In the morning.'

'Why not today?'

'I know there is little time, Orbus, but I cannot simply take a horse and ride away. I have to prepare. And we cannot go alone.'

Orbus stiffened – if a ghost can be said to stiffen. 'Whom else do you intend to accompany us?'

'The place where the Farplace Opening is hidden was a secret Krai camp. We destroyed it, but by now Anzejarl will be aware at the very least that all is not well there. He will almost certainly have dispatched a force to secure it. Hence I will take fifty mounted soldiers. Ideally I would have more, with a catapult or two, but I dare not deplete the garrison here.'

'Will these soldiers know of me?'

'No. But listen, I must take steps to ensure, as far as I can, that Enchantment's Edge does not fall to enemies within its own walls the moment my back is turned.'

'You refer to the Lord High Invigilate.'

'Fectur, yes. Predominantly. Orbus, this is important. There are others I must speak to about you. Men I trust. One already knows of the casket, though not what it is. Leth trusted him with that information, and he served us well, as Leth knew he would. Without him I would not have found the casket, or you.'

'And who else?'

'One who rescued me from certain death and saw me safely back to Enchantment's Edge. He is unusually skilled and will accompany us, at least as far as the Farplace Opening, and maybe into Enchantment itself.'

Orbus bowed his head, considering her words. 'Child, you know how vulnerable I am.'

'Yes, and I want to be certain that, should I perish, there will be one other at least who will take the casket, knowing fully what it will mean to lose it.'

'You are sure of these men?'

'As sure – *more* sure than I am of myself.'

He nodded his head with slow gravity. 'Then you should bring them here.'

Issul hesitated. There was more she wished to say, more ideas and ghosts of ideas circulating in her mind. But now was perhaps not the time. 'I have convened an Emergency Assembly which I must attend in less than an hour. I will inform the government then of my intention to depart.'

'You will face opposition, will you not?'

'From some quarters, and for differing reasons. Fectur, and those who support him, will be unlikely to oppose me, for there is nothing he desires more than my absence, except of course my death. But it is going to be very hard. Orbus, I must leave you now. There is someone I must speak to, and preparations I must make. I will return later, and bring the two of whom I spoke.'

She turned and departed, and Orbus stood for a long time watching the door, deep in contemplation.

II

The Assembly was, as Issul had anticipated, a difficult affair, but when it was over and she walked from the Hall of Wise Counsel, the subdued murmurs of her members of government behind her, it was with a sense of triumph. Fectur remained in the Hall, silently gnashing his teeth, and no doubt formulating in his mind the first dark and certain steps along a path to total revenge. Issul had out-guiled him. The memory of his face when he cognized the manner in which he had been led was something she would long cherish. She glanced aside at Pader Luminis who had accompanied her from the Hall. The little Murinean's eyes met hers; his lips quivered and his eyes shone. Simultaneously they both broke into wide grins. They walked together with light steps and heads held high, quietly and joyfully celebrating their shared achievement, and for the present putting from their minds any thoughts of Fectur's inevitable response.

Fectur had been effective in broadcasting notice of this latest in a series of unscheduled meetings. As many awaited Issul as when, at midnight the previous night, following her return to Enchantment's Edge, she had called all ministers, knights, grandees, notables and faction heads together to declare herself sovereign during King Leth's 'incapacitation', and to relieve Lord Fectur of his self-appointed Regentship. Leth had convened other emergency assemblies in recent days, she knew. She anticipated apathy and weary cynicism, half-expected to find many seats unoccupied. Yet they were there in virtually full number, and she sensed their expectation.

Issul had wasted no time in stating the purpose of the Assembly. Firstly she announced the death of her brother-in-law, King Leth's cousin, Duke Hugo of Giswel. Some were already informed; most were not.

'This is a most painful tragedy on both a personal and national level,' Issul said, when the first cries of shock and sorrow had died down. 'The full consequences have still to make themselves known. Most immediately, though, there is a lesson to be learned. Duke Hugo was a great and beloved warrior and leader, yet in the end he was foolhardy. Yes, foolhardy! I do not say it lightly, nor is my love and respect for him diminished. But in his eagerness to lock horns with the foe he made two fundamental errors, for which he has paid the ultimate price. He acted in direct contravention of King Leth's orders. Note that. My husband, the King, is wise to the guiles of the Krai, and gave specific orders. Had Hugo heeded them, he and his valiant soldiers would be alive today. But he thought he saw a weakness in the Krai ranks, an opportunity. And therein lay his second mistake: he underestimated his enemy. Instead of opportunity he found a deadly trap set by Prince Anzejarl.'

Issul paused, only now coming to a full awareness of the anger she felt at Hugo's impetuousness and the needless losses it had brought. She took a deep breath. 'Now we are informed that the Krai army marches directly against Enchantment's Edge itself.'

'Has Giswel Holt fallen?' asked one of her senior knights.

'No. The Krai still surround it, but the bulk of their army, with Anzejarl at its head, comes here. What is most important now is that we do not give way to fear or perform any rash actions. The Krai will almost certainly be visible within three days. We know their reputation, we know their conquests. But they cannot enter Enchantment's Edge, no matter what they bring against us. And King Leth has made sure that we are secure here. We can survive within these walls for a long time.'

'How long?' called Chandiston, head of the Golden Thought sect. 'It is the wrath of the Highest Ones that falls upon us now, for we have been forced to deny them. The gods will take Enchantment's Edge in retribution for our failure to acknowledge them. Our resistance is futile.'

'I will hear no more of such talk!' declared Issul angrily. 'No one has been forced to deny the gods. Rather, we have admitted our ignorance of them, which is something of a wholly different order. That admission has enabled us to vanquish superstition and blind unquestioning belief, and to begin the process that will lead eventually to true knowledge and perhaps wisdom.' She hesitated, carefully considering her next words. 'But, as it happens, there is an element of truth in what you have said. I have learned that the

Krai have indeed secured the patronage of one of Enchantment's most powerful beings.'

There were cries now of astonishment and outrage. Several persons rose from their seats and began shouting. She waited for the hubbub to die down, carefully pondering her next statement. What she was about to say was not wholly the truth, but more important than absolute truth just now was the need to instil within her people a feeling of hope and a belief in themselves, a sense that the dreadful threat that faced them could be overcome.

'Yes,' she said, rising, 'and there is more. I have learned also that there is a way of meeting the Krai on even ground, and perhaps more importantly of nullifying the threat presented by their supernatural patron. To this end I am undertaking a journey. The details must necessarily remain secret, but within hours I shall be leaving Enchantment's Edge again.'

As she spoke these words Issul's eyes shifted to Lord Fectur. He had been sitting hunched forward in his chair, his forearms over his thighs, hands bunched before him. His eyes were slits, focusing on nothing in particular. At Issul's mention of the Krai god his head turned half-way towards her. But at her announcement of her imminent departure his body gave a small jerk and his thin eyebrows lifted in reflex.

Issul met his gaze. There was uproar now, more animated than before. A hubbub of questions was being thrown her way, demands for more information on how she intended to foil the Krai and their ally, and of course, imputations and slurs couched less vocally, accusations that she was abandoning them now in their hour of greatest need, that she was interested only in saving her own neck. Issul half-closed her ears. She had anticipated every step. She concentrated solely on Lord Fectur.

His eyes had, momentarily, a faraway look. Issul knew he was absorbing the full implications of her words. He was doubtless piqued that this information should have been declared in Assembly, without prior consultation with him. He was especially intrigued as to the nature of her business. But most importantly, he surely could not fail to grasp what must now follow.

Fectur's eyes flicked back to her. Her lips compressed, almost in a tight, compact smile. She gave him the smallest nod. At once Fectur rose. He lifted his hands, bidding calm. 'Silence, please! Be silent! Let the Queen be heard!'

Issul hid a smile; her heart beat fast. Fectur called again for silence, more sternly. The Assembly quickly grew quiet.

'Our Queen acts as she must, with the interests of the Realm at heart,' Fectur said, with a small, steely, ingratiating twist of the lips to Issul. 'Please, let us hear her out and support her as best we may. Let us not forget that these are desperate times, calling for desperate measures.'

He passed his eyes around the Hall, daring anyone to challenge him. When no one did he sat again and gestured with the flat of his hand to the Queen.

'I truly regret that there is no other way,' Issul said. 'And because of circumstances that I am not at liberty to explain, there is no other who can go in my stead. King Leth is unable. You know that, of course, for many of you helped vote him temporarily out of office.' She paused, letting that sink in. 'The onus then falls upon me. But I say again, if all is well then upon my return the Krai threat will be significantly reduced, possibly even removed entirely.'

Again she hesitated. This was economy of truth applied with a sweeping hand. She did not know what she would find in Enchantment, nor what she might achieve or return with – if she did return. But she had to persuade them, by virtually any means. She had to gain their support, and give them heart and hope and the strength to hold on to the very last. 'I may be absent a week, a month, I do not know. But we have the resources and the manpower to withstand whatever the Krai throw at us in that time. I will discuss particular strategies and contingencies with the senior knights, officers and military advisors before I leave. But the message is, remain within our walls. They will protect you.'

Now she allowed the floor of the Assembly to rise again. A barrage of yelled questions came at her, most notably from the faction leaders. Military leaders, ministers and advisors of the government and Crown seemed in the main to be consulting between themselves. As the din continued she glanced to Fectur again. He was watching her intently, a glint both covetous and circumspect in his narrowed eyes. The tip of his tongue flickered briefly, lizard-like, as he wet his lips, and a quiver of a half-smile momentarily lifted a corner of his mouth. He stood once more, and raised his arms and appealed for silence. 'Please, let us listen respectfully to our Queen's words. You have heard what she has said: she is without choice in this courageous action. There is no other course.'

The commotion began to diminish. Issul saw that numerous heads were turned to regard Fectur with curiosity. Fectur inclined his head and shoulders towards her unctuously. 'Your Majesty.'

'There remains the appointment of a regent, a Protector of the Realm, during my absence,' Issul said. She kept Fectur in the edge of her vision, and saw his shoulders go back, his hands link behind him and his chin lift a fraction. 'I have given a great deal of thought to this, and have consulted long and hard. Those who can be seriously considered for such a vital and trusted role are obviously few in number. Under the conditions of such emergency as we now face the natural course is that the office be bestowed upon the Lord High Invigilate and Master of Security.'

Her audience was silent. Fectur's chest swelled. He held back his elation, the muscles around his mouth slackening and his lips puckering slightly.

Issul continued. 'Due to the particularly difficult circumstances now pertaining, inordinate demands are being made upon the Lord High Invigilate's time. His expertise and finesse, never in question, are required in a multitude of areas and situations as he applies himself with unwaning diligence to the security of our Realm. Under such circumstances I have come to see that to burden him further with such a taxing office would be unreasonable and not conducive to the greater welfare of the Realm. The Lord High Invigilate must be permitted to carry out his duties without further complication or demands that might distract him from his so-essential task.'

The first flicker of doubt glazed Fectur's eyes now. His head came slowly down and his broad shoulders began to tense and rise. Slowly he turned towards her.

'I have therefore made the decision to entrust the office of Regent and Protector pro tem to another; someone known to us all as a loyal, trustworthy and devoted officer of the Crown, someone who, like the Lord High Invigilate, has the highest qualifications and who has also given a lifetime of service to the Crown and our beloved country. I refer to the revered Imperator of the Arcane College of Enchantment's Edge, Grand Master Pader Luminis.'

It was as though a rapture had been cast upon the Hall. No one moved or made a sound. Fectur's eyes were gimlets, his features suddenly tumescent with suppressed rage. His arms had stiffened; Issul suspected he was gripping his hands tightly behind his back, lest they assume a volition of their own and reach out to encircle her throat and throttle the life from her, which was surely what he desired more than anything at that moment. She permitted herself no outward display of the satisfaction his displeasure gave her. She took her gaze from him and smiled at Pader Luminis.

Pader was on his feet as his astonished audience began to break into polite and then enthusiastic applause. Issul nodded to herself: Pader was well-liked and greatly respected. Not a natural or aspiring statesman, he was nevertheless a popular, esteemed figure. Though his status as Imperator of the Arcane College set him somewhat at odds with the factions, he had been careful at all times to distance himself from the political hagglings and in-fighting that character-ized the relationship between factions and Crown. It could be said, then, that while Pader had opponents, he had no serious enemies – until now. Issul knew he would have support, at least in the short term. And the short term was all they had.

Earlier, just minutes before the Assembly had convened, Issul had gone to Pader's apartment high in the White Eaglet's Tower. In as few words as possible she had told him about Orbus and the blue casket, about the Soul of the Orb, and her need to travel now to Enchantment in the hope of saving Leth, the children and Enchantment's Edge. She told him about Arene, the *Hir'n Esh* and the fortress of the Well of Immaculate Vision. She became almost distraught as she spoke; so much depended on so slender a thread. Finally she had asked him if he would take the office of Regent pro tem in her absence.

'Pader, it is dangerous. Be in no doubt of that. Were there an alternative I would not ask this of you. But there is no one else, no one I can trust.'

Pader was at first taken aback and flustered. 'My child, I am honoured, deeply honoured. But are you certain of what you do? I truly do not consider myself either equipped for or deserving of the office.'

'Oh, I am certain, Pader. I am certain. And I know too that Fectur will do everything in his power to undo you. But if I announce you before the entire Assembly he will find himself with very little space to manoeuvre. I will assign my Élite Guard to protect you at all times. You must go nowhere without them. Your food will be sampled before your eyes. Every possible precaution will be taken to ensure your safety. I fully believe you will have the support of the majority of the government. But it will not be a comfortable existence, nor an easy one. Should you feel that it is too much to ask of you, I will understand.'

'And do what?'

'I must go, so I can only legitimize Fectur's desire and appoint him Protector.'

Pader Luminis drew in a sharp breath, and shook his head vigorously, as if to dislodge something upon it. 'Oh no. No, no. No, no, no, we cannot have that. Not ever again.' He adjusted his spectacles, sat in thought for a few moments, then looked up and beamed at her. 'You know, it will give me great pleasure to look upon the Spectre's face when he learns that he has been passed over for a petty conjuror such as I.'

'Then you will do it?'

'Well of course! For you I would do anything. But hurry back, dear Issul, that is all I ask. And bring your family with you. All of them. Orbia is not the same without them.'

She had thrown her arms around him and hugged him and kissed him then, and Pader had beamed happily to himself, his face flushing with delight and embarrassment.

Next they had put their heads together to determine how best to deliver the news to Fectur. Upon learning of Issul's imminent departure he would be all but adrool at the prospect of seizing power once more. Pader agreed that Issul's plan to make the announcement at the Emergency Assembly was the best. No one of importance would be ignorant of the appointment or its implications. It was Pader's suggestion that Fectur should be seen apparently to give his support to the arrangement. Fectur's humiliation would be the greater, and his ability to rally support should he seek to oppose the decision would be significantly restricted.

'It will make of him an ever more implacable enemy, Pader.'

'Child, how implacable can implacable be? We know him, we know what he is and what he desires. Nothing has changed.'

Now, in the Hall of Wise Counsel, Issul addressed the Assembly for the final time. 'I have discussed immediate policy with Pader Luminis, as had King Leth before me. You may consider any orders he gives to be fully in accordance with the wishes of the Crown. I know I can trust you all to give him your unreserved and unqualified support. Now, I am to leave on the morrow. Those of you who need to speak to me to discuss anything in greater detail, apply to me now in my office.'

She stood, taking no visible heed of the seething Fectur, and departed the Hall, Pader Luminis beside her.

III

The morning came, bringing with it a chill drizzle and bitter blasts of wind from the north, harbingers of a cruel winter not so far away. The wind sliced pitilessly across the great scarp and the city-castle perched upon its lip, penetrating every street and alleyway, every crack and crevice. The city seemed to roar as the multiform defences erected as protection against the slooths rattled, hammered, clanked, shook, swayed, creaked and groaned under the battering squalls. From her chamber window Issul looked out at the iron skies and swathes of slanting rain and wondered what effect an early onset of winter might have upon the Krai.

Little, she thought. The Krai were a hardy race, not given to complaint. They had battled through the previous winter, conquering a major city in one of the Mondane Kingdoms with, if reports were to be believed, no great difficulty. If anything, the worsening weather might spur them to greater efforts. On the other hand, a day or a week might see a period of calm and even balmy weather, and the Krai approaching almost at their leisure. Nothing was predictable in this late season.

Could they take Enchantment's Edge? Issul felt the weight of it upon her. They could. She knew they could, in time. How much time she could not begin to estimate, for she was still far from certain of the forces they would pit against her.

And if they had help from within . . . It was a notion that terrified her. The True Sept had made overtures – could they, from their burrows deep within Overlip, be aiding the Krai, preparing to rise up at a given signal and cause chaos and diversion within the city? Not only the True Sept. Any one or more of the most hostile factions might have seen an opportunity for gain by extreme measures, most especially if they believed a god rode at Prince Anzejarl's side.

And what of Fectur? The thought had crossed her mind more than once that he, too, might seek to form some kind of allegiance with Anzejarl. To what end? To secure survival and power for himself after the conquering was done, even if it meant serving Krai masters. He was capable of that. Yes, Fectur was capable of anything.

And Issul shuddered, her anger growing, and her fear for Pader Luminis. No matter the steps she had taken to try and keep him safe, was he really capable of standing against both Fectur and the Krai?

'Are we ready?' Orbus asked.

Issul came from her grim reverie and gathered up her cape and swung it about her shoulders. 'Aye, we are.' She took up a small, sturdy wooden chest bound with studded iron straps, and carried it across to the oak chiffonier upon which the blue casket stood. 'Are you sure this is the best way?'

Orbus slowly nodded. 'There is no other. But remember, it is me whom you carry. It is also my world, and your husband and children. If the casket is shattered, we are all gone. Forever. Now, if you need to speak to me you have only to call, as before. But be certain you are not observed. And be strong, brave young Queen. As I know you can be. Be strong.'

He faded slowly from her sight. Issul stared blankly into the space he had occupied. She could still not fully assimilate it all – that the casket was, somehow, Orbus; that it was also an entire world, an entire universe, as was he; and that within it, within him, Leth, Galry and Jace roamed, lost and believing themselves abandoned.

She unlocked and eased open the lid of the chest. Inside it was deeply padded with soft grey velvet stuffed with densely packed wool. With infinite care she took up the blue casket in both hands and placed it inside the chest. It slotted neatly into the centre, the padding cushioning it on all sides, its base and, when she closed the chest's lid, the top also. Issul locked the chest, filled with a sensation of strange disquiet, anticipation, nervous hope. She pocketed the key in her tunic, then took up the chest and strode from her apartment. Outside Shenwolf waited with Phisusandra and a squad of six Palace guards. Shenwolf stiffened, clicking his heels, and smartly bowed his head. 'Are you ready, my lady?'

Issul gave a nod. At Shenwolf's command the soldiers formed a guard around her. They marched through the corridors of Orbia, descending to ground level and passing from the royal household to the military wing, and thence to a barracks yard set off the main parade-ground. Here Issul's full company awaited her – five knights and fifty proud men-at-arms, all mounted and clad in breastplates and mail, with waxed, hooded capes shielding them from the rain.

Issul strode to her horse and strapped the chest containing the blue casket onto a special pad mounted afore the pommel of the saddle, on the horse's withers. Here she could keep the chest in view at all times when in the saddle. Then she turned to Shenwolf, and Phisusandra who stood beside him. 'Remember, if I should fall, this is to be protected at all costs. Shenwolf, you know what it means, and what you must do if I am prevented for any reason from carrying on. Phis, it is better that you do not know all at this point. But be in no doubt that your task is to protect this. I have instructed Shenwolf to reveal all to you in the event of my incapacitation, captivity or death. It is vital that at least one other knows what must be done.'

'Do not doubt me,' said Shenwolf.

'Nor I,' said Phisusandra.

To one side of the yard Issul spotted Pader Luminis sheltering from the rain beneath a wooden awning, his eyes upon her. Half a dozen guards were ranged at his back, and Kol stood in uniform at his side, his feet planted firmly apart and his arms folded across his broad chest. She smiled, tears stinging her eyes, and walked over to embrace the little Murinean. 'Pader, you should not be here.'

Pader clung to her for a moment, almost childlike. 'Did you think I would not come to see you off?' He wiped his eyes, as emotional as she was. 'Travel safely now, do you hear me, child? Travel safely.'

Issul released him and turned to Kol, but could not trust herself to speak.

'Do not concern yourself, my lady,' said Kol softly. 'I will not let him out of my sight.'

She nodded, forcing back her tears. Kol had at first been unhappy at the news that he was not to accompany the Queen and his two companions. But Issul had stressed that it was vital he remain behind to guard Pader. 'It is as crucial to the success of this operation that I know that everything possible has been done to safeguard him,' she had said, 'and that he is protected by someone I know I can trust without reservation. I am taking Phis because of his sensitivity to magic, which may be of great service again. But you, Kol, I am entrusting with a role of no less importance.'

Understanding this, Kol had assented gladly and, as now, had assured her that he would not leave Pader's side until she returned.

Issul embraced him, then turned away, one hand to her cheek. She climbed onto her horse; Shenwolf and Phisusandra did likewise. Issul raised her face to the rain and cast her eyes once more around the yard, to the walls, the roofs and towers beyond, and back to Pader Luminis once more. Then she signalled to the leading knight, who raised his hand and urged his steed forward. Slowly the entire company filed out of the barracks' yard and on towards the palace's main gate.

From a narrow window on the third level of one of the palace's myriad marbled towers a pair of cold grey eyes watched unseen as the cavalcade departed. The Spectre's thin lips twisted into an expression that could have been part-smile, part-sneer, or anything in between. He looked down into the yard and watched Pader Luminis re-enter the Palace with his armed escort. Then he looked to the heavy grey skies, his eyes reflecting their hue and their anger, and slowly nodded to himself.

PART TWO

SIX

I

The winds and rain that battered Enchantment's Edge on the fateful morning that Queen Issul and her company rode out towards far Enchantment had also driven southwards during the night. They had raged across the forest-clad lowlands to descend with barely diminished ferocity upon the heads of the soldiers of the mighty Krai army which plied its way with grim and determined purpose towards the capital.

The night had hardly passed; the camp was rousing itself in preparation for the next leg of the journey. Prince Anzejarl stood in the centre of his field pavilion, listening as the rain drummed in wind-driven blasts upon the canvas over his head, the sides of the tent shuddering and billowing with the sudden gusts. In one hand he clutched a tight fistful of bruised *ghinz* leaves. From time to time he tore free several leaves, spat out the bright green residue of what remained in his mouth, and thrust the new leaves between his teeth. He chewed and drained their bitter sap, inhaling deeply, his gemlike eyes, searing cobalt-blue with slit-pupils of fevered jade, half-closed as he let the narcotic numb him and bring order to his thoughts.

Olmana was before him, instructing a Krai maid who packed her belongings in preparation for the day's continued march northwards. Olmana turned and faced the Krai prince. She was clad in a long ermine robe, with nothing beneath. The clasps that held the robe were unfastened, so that it fell partially open, revealing her fine pale body, the full inner curves of her breasts, the inside of one long slender thigh, and the near-perfect triangle of flaming red hair at the base of her smooth belly. Her weight was on one leg, her thighs slightly parted, one knee swaying loosely back and forth. Though they had loved many times, passionately and even violently, during the night, Anzejarl felt his blood stir again at the sight of her standing so brazen before him.

Olmana's red lips parted in a knowing half-smile, and her eyes half-mocked him. She dismissed the maid with a flick of her hand, then moved close to Anzejarl and caressed his cheek. 'Ah, Prince of the Krai, my brave and handsome Champion, how is it that I can so easily read the thoughts that pass through your mind?'

Anzejarl bent his head to kiss her. Their lips touched, just lightly, then Olmana pulled back. 'The greatest prize, Anzejarl. Before you now.'

Anzejarl's eyes were almost aglow. At this moment he had no thoughts of Enchantment's Edge. One arm encircled Olmana's waist and he pulled her against him. She laughed, leaning back, and drew aside the soft ermine, wholly exposing one naked breast. Anzejarl emitted a grunt of ardent approval. His head came down, his lips brushing against the smooth white flesh before closing upon her nipple. She bent her knees and let him lower her onto the cushions beneath her.

'What are you, Olmana?' Anzejarl hissed between breathless kisses, his lips upon her neck, her shoulder, her mouth. 'That you can bewitch me so. What are you?'

Olmana wriggled backwards and drew her legs up, parting her thighs wide. Anzejarl caught his breath, his eyes feasting. Had he been capable of analyzing the smile that curled her lips and the fire that burned in her eyes at that moment, he might have wondered about the nature of the thoughts that passed through her mind, for they did not entirely match his. But he hardly noted her smile. And to herself she thought: *That is something you will never know, Krai Prince!*

'You ask too many questions,' she whispered, and reached down, her fingers tugging free his loincloth and curling around his hardness. She eased her hips upwards and guided him into her. She gasped, arching her back in pleasure as Anzejarl slid forward. Her fingers dug into his back; she pressed her heels into his buttocks and drew him deeper. 'Just remember . . . ohh, yesss . . . the greatest . . . prize.'

When their passion was spent Anzejarl lay still, thinking.

The Greatest Prize. With Enchantment's Edge his he would have forged the greatest Krai empire known in more than twenty centuries. And in so short a time. Yet it was not enough. Not any more. Not since Olmana had come, bringing him her strange and potent gift, her Awakening, as she called it. She had roused him from the torpor that beset the Krai and kept them uncomplaining within the borders of their homelands on the vast ocean's edge in the south-west. She had launched him and his army upon this great and bloody campaign. And she had lit within him fires that might never be doused, so he was beginning to suspect. Olmana had made him powerful and strong; and she had made him want, she had made him *need.*

Here was the key. Within himself he had discovered something which, as a Krai, he had never truly known before.

Need.

But need for what?

At Olmana's bidding he had roused his people and set forth on a campaign of conquest. With Enchantment's creatures within his ranks he had overrun the Southern Mondane Kingdoms. Now the most difficult challenge, King Leth's domain, awaited him. Difficult, yes, but it could not withstand him.

So close!

And then? The Northern Mondanes? Anzejarl closed his eyes. Would anything ever be enough?

The satisfaction of victory had begun to pale. Anzejarl's newly awakened mind craved new stimuli, new kinds of excitements. His lust for Olmana grew with every day, yet he was sated only briefly, then the need was upon him again. He took men, women, children who had been foolish enough to remain behind in the villages through which the Krai passed. He played with them; he burned and mutilated them, hung them slowly or impaled them on sharpened stakes, yet their writhing agonies hardly gave him satisfaction now. Everything, everything had begun to pale.

Within him, a void, and this restless unease, this tyrannical desire that could not be fulfilled, that only the *ghinz* or some other intensity of pleasure could hold at bay. Olmana had told him that what he sensed was that part of him that yet remained to be Awakened, that soon he would no longer need the *ghinz.* He had gained so much, yet he knew such doubt, so many questions, a dark and teeming jungle of emotions, such untameable wanting. As a Krai this was something he could not fathom.

He wondered, as he had wondered so often before, about Olmana. What was she? No ordinary woman, he had known that from the beginning. A creature of the mysterious. She controlled him utterly, and though he could not resist her, did not even wish to, he resented that. Yet she was giving him everything. She had no interest in the lands he conquered, the peoples he subdued. Her single goal was a mysterious child, she had confessed that much, but without elaboration. She sensed the child was close now. What she would do when she found it – *if* she found it – Anzejarl could not guess. He sensed that his role would be complete. Would she cast him from her? Could he bear it if she did? Emperor of the Krai, the mightiest warrior, a legend. Would it have meaning without her?

Olmana!

In his dreams Anzejarl had envisaged her transformed into some other creature, something dreadful and repulsive. Did his dreams tell him something? He knew that in his sleep she performed esoteric rites of some unknown form. She said she was renewing the Gift, the Awakening, bestowing upon him the power to continue to command the trolls and slooths which were so vital to his army's success. And in the mornings he felt strong. Yet he wondered what it was that she could do only when he was unconscious. He wondered —

Anzejarl stopped. In truth, what point in wondering? Olmana had him in her palm. He could never resist her, and he could know only what she chose to reveal.

He sat up suddenly and reached for the *ghinz*. Olmana watched him and her fingers traced a slow, sensual pattern over his back. 'The greatest prize, my Prince,' she whispered again. 'It lies just before you.'

Anzejarl felt a burning anger rise. He stood, a fire in his eyes. 'Aye.'

'Just an arm's reach away. And the Child will be there.'

'Do you know this?'

'I know that in whatever land the Child resides, its presence will be known. So go now, Anzejarl. Take Enchantment's Edge for me, for you. Slay Leth and all his kin.'

Anzejarl nodded fiercely as the wind and rain buffeted his tent. At a word from her he knew the passion again, the insuperable lust for battle, for the lives of those who opposed him; the warrior's charged, irrepressible impulse toward victory and glory. 'Aye, I am here now, Leth. I am upon you. For the glory of Krai, you are mine at last. I will obliterate you and all who follow you.'

And then? he thought to himself.

And then . . .?

II

Prior to and immediately following Queen Issul's departure from Enchantment's Edge, Lord Fectur applied intense concentration to the manner in which he would proceed once she was gone. His fury at having been so simply and almost effortlessly fooled by Issul, particularly before so many important personages in the Emergency Assembly, had impelled him to immediate and vengeful action. With the Assembly dissolved he had quickly descended to the warren of grim passages, cells and lightless chambers that comprised the dungeons of the Ministry of Realm Security, and there exacted terrible punishment upon a trio of prisoners hauled randomly before him. Even then, with their corpses spread in bloody ruin at his feet, he found himself barely relieved.

His dudgeon was only moderately tempered by the knowledge that, even with Issul gone, he must now act with a certain degree of prudence. Not that he was not by nature a prudent man. He was. That is, he planned carefully, was methodical in application, allowed for every conceivable contingency, and made sure at all times that his tracks were covered. He was never given to impulse or caprice. But the situation now was prickly and volatile in ways it had not previously been. He had been caught unawares; things were escalating at such a breakneck pace.

Too many uncertainties; too many unknowns. The situation had no precedent. Fectur told himself again that this was a time for cool deliberation and careful, considered decision-making, yet his rage festered. He thought back, recalling that it was he who had taught Issul so much of what she knew. That she should use it now against him! Her ingratitude was amazing.

Under different circumstances he would have been proud of her.

Not least on Fectur's mind was the spine-stiffening shock of discovering himself so ill-informed in so many areas. Something of incalculable importance was afoot, and he had somehow been kept almost entirely in the dark. How was this possible? And how now to take best advantage of her absence? She would no doubt have made careful plans herself.

He sat and brooded, and carefully took stock.

Firstly he considered Issul's journey. Where might she be going and what knowledge did she possess that could send her forth at a time like this? He could hardly doubt that it had something to do with her recent absence, but did she really believe she had an answer to the Krai threat?

What of her announcement that one of the Highest Ones, the gods of Enchantment or whatever they were, had joined forces with the Krai? Her words and attitude echoed King Leth's, when he had implied extraordinary knowledge of Enchantment. This chafed deeply, like grains of dust rubbed upon a lidless eye. How could she know such things, if Fectur himself had no such confirmation? True, his own intelligence-gathering sources had disclosed that the Krai had creatures of Enchantment in their ranks, and he had since come virtually to accept that the Krai must enjoy the patronage of one of those most powerful beings, a so-called god. But both Leth, and now Issul, had spoken with total conviction, as if with uncommon knowledge – knowledge that he, Fectur, was mortifyingly not party to.

Could the young Queen be bluffing?

Somehow, he felt not. For to bluff over an issue such as this . . . what end would it serve her? She would return to Enchantment's Edge if she could; Fectur knew her too well to question that. And if she did, she would have to bring with her the proof of her assertions. So, definitely, she knew something. Definitely she believed the words she had spoken in the Hall of Wise Counsel.

And Leth! Here chafed another mystery. Fectur broiled at the memory. How could the King and his sickeningly delightful brats have vanished? Where could they be? And of equal import, for how long could their absence be expected to remain a secret? The men of the Security Cadre who had discovered their disappearance and subsequently searched the King's apartments were well-apprised as to the consequences of loose talk, and Fectur knew that nothing would leak from that source but even so . . . it could be but a matter of time before questions were asked.

Fectur had read Issul with an expert eye, and was sure she knew nothing of Leth's whereabouts. At least, he was sure she had known nothing when she had returned to Enchantment's Edge two days ago. Since then her manner and demeanour had undergone a subtle change.

What could she have learned?

And how?

That meddling magician Pader Luminis held at least one key, Fectur more than suspected. The Murinean conjuror had spent a lifetime worming his way into the royal family's favour, but this latest outrage! It galled Fectur to admit it, but it had come as a complete surprise. He had never suspected Pader Luminis of harbouring political ambition.

Fectur's mind sped back to the late afternoon of Issul's return. He had come upon the two of them, Queen and conjuror, in breathless exchange in Leth's private study. He had caught only a few hushed and hurried words:–

The Queen: '. . . *no one must know of this.*'

Pader Luminis: '*I swore as much to Leth. He bade me warn you, or whomsoever I passed it on to: its existence must always remain a secret.*'

Issul had glanced around then, and caught sight of Fectur at the door. Fectur cursed silently now. Ordinarily, had he not wished it his presence would never have been detected. But so distracted had he been, so thrown by events – Leth's disappearance, Issul's sudden, unexpected return and the removal of Grey Venger from his dungeon cell – that he had all but announced himself to them. In doing so he had forfeited privity to their secret.

The Queen had been clutching something. Something precious bundled in her shawl. The way she held it to herself, her edginess, the shock on her face, had spoken volumes. And this something could only be linked to the journey she had now undertaken. He had not failed to note, as she rode away in the wet, early morn, the small wooden chest which she had personally affixed with such care to the saddle of her horse, then covered with a water-resistant shroud.

Fectur drew back his lips in a grimace of bestial malevolence. He lived and grew mighty through information. The Spectre's eyes penetrated all corners, all nooks and niches. That there existed now a shadowed secret that he had not pierced was intolerable to him. To this end he had dispatched Commander Gordallith, one of his most highly regarded and senior security officers, in the Queen's wake. Gordallith had with him a small band of skilled men, highly trained, black-hearted members of the Spectre's security cadre. They were ruthless fighters, accomplished spies, deft, silent thieves and deadly assassins. And their first loyalty, like Gordallith's, was to the Spectre, not the King or Queen.

Gordallith's orders were complex, but specific, and covered a variety of contingencies. Broadly, he was to put himself or at least one of his agents in close proximity to the Queen or those in whom she confided. By such means he was to determine her destination and whether she truly held a secret that might save Enchantment's Edge. If, in his judgement, she did, Gordallith was to make it his absolute priority to find out what it was. The mysterious chest upon her saddle was, of course, to be investigated as a priority.

Gordallith was then to apply himself to the question of whether the Queen was the only person capable of achieving her stated objective. That is to say, might some other person, armed with the relevant knowledge and equipment which Issul currently – and presumably solely – held, be as effective as she in this extraordinary and urgent business?

Two possibilities might then present themselves. One: no person other than Queen Issul was capable of accomplishing what she had set out to accomplish. Or two: Queen Issul was one among any number of persons who could do it.

If the former was the case, Gordallith was to use his judgement to determine the most favourable path. He could abduct the Queen – a task fraught with obstacles but, with such skilled assistants, conceivable nonetheless – and thence proceed with her to her objective; or he could allow her to achieve her objective without interference, and then abduct her as she returned to Enchantment's Edge.

But if the latter was the case, he should by any means at his disposal relieve her of any vital knowledge and/or apparatus she possessed, and proceed without her. In any instance Gordallith was made clearly to understand that Queen Issul's safe return to Enchantment's Edge was not essential, nor was it even desirable.

Additional instructions concerned the young soldier, Shenwolf, who was so clearly in Issul's favour. Fectur was bemused by his so-rapid rise from raw recruit to personal bodyguard of the Queen. If, through unforeseeable or unavoidable circumstance, Queen Issul did return to Enchantment's Edge alive, Fectur would be pleased to have confirmation that she and Shenwolf were lovers.

Should Gordallith uncover no evidence of that, well, the suggestion, properly deployed, could be almost as damaging. But this, Fectur had quietly emphasized, was not the result he most hoped to see. Conceivably, he had suggested, almost as if to himself, Shenwolf himself might perish. Even better, he might perish after having been witnessed to have, for some perhaps undetermined reason, taken the life of the beloved Queen.

Hence Gordallith had departed with no doubt whatsoever in his mind of what was expected of him. And while his task was a demanding one, Gordallith was a resourceful fellow. Fectur did not doubt that he would be effective, one way or the other.

In the meantime Fectur formulated strategies to cover the situation at home. Any attempt to seize power again was, of course, out of the question. That which had so recently, under unusual and quite specific circumstances, been conducive to his ends, could now only serve him ill. Pader Luminis could not be convincingly overthrown. Not now. His leadership could be called into question, however; he might, with tact and careful planning, be fully discredited. He was no soldier, after all, and it was a soldier's mind that would best serve Enchantment's Edge now.

But such tactics would take time, and there was little of that, with the Krai so close.

The Krai. Truly, so much depended upon the Queen. Even so, there were other avenues still to be explored.

With this in mind Fectur rose from his desk and took leave of his office. Head inclined in brooding thought, he passed from the Ministry of Realm Security and strode through the Palace of Orbia to the guest apartments set off the royal wing. He approached the entrance to the chambers in which Issul had lodged Grey Venger, the leader of the True Sept. The sentries at the door snapped to attention.

Just the two guards? Fectur was curious. 'Open the door. I want to speak with the prisoner.'

The nearest sentry spoke with evident reluctance. 'My lord, we have precise instructions. I regret, most respectfully, we are forbidden to allow any person to enter without the express permission of the Queen or her designated Regent, the Imperator-Protector.'

Fectur's head drew back, his eyes like bolts of ice. 'Do you know who I am?'

'My lord, of course. With great respect, our orders are exact. We were made to understand that they apply to all persons bar the Queen and Imperator. I am sorry, my lord.'

Fectur fixed them with his most minatory glare. Elite or not, he could have disarmed and disabled the pair of them with almost no effort. He could have snapped both their necks before they had even moved. But he saw them starting to sweat, and that was enough. It would advance his aims not at all to commit violence upon Issul's appointed guards. He spun upon his heel and made off down the corridor.

III

Pader Luminis had been appointed temporary administrative offices on the ground floor of the royal wing of the palace, just along the corridor from Issul's. Such an appointment, central and easily accessed and guarded, was far preferable to his remote and dusty chambers in the White Eaglet's tower, where he preferred to pass his time, or the libraries, sanctums and laboratories of the Arcane College, where he was otherwise generally to be found. The offices consisted of two quite small chambers, previously used for the storage of old ledgers and files and, more latterly, general lumber. They had been hurriedly emptied, swept and spruced up, and desks, shelves and seating were installed.

Pader was at his desk, poring over a chart of mysterious symbols when there was an abrupt knock upon his door. Kol entered. 'The Lord High Invigilate wishes to see you, sir.'

Fectur strode in, his lips compressed and downturned at the corners.

'Ah, my lord Fectur,' the Murinean beamed. 'How may I be of service to you?'

Fectur eyed him with cold appraisal, then turned to Kol. 'You may leave us.'

'My orders are to remain, my lord.'

Fectur's features set, his stare gelid. 'Do you think I am going to do him harm?'

'My lord, my orders are clear, regardless; unless the Imperator-Protector indicates otherwise.'

Fectur narrowed his eyes. 'I could kill you with barely a thought,' he said quietly.

'Oh but tut!, my lord, why would you want to do that?' said Pader Luminis, rising and stepping around his desk. 'Why indeed? And the answer of course is that you would not, and you speak in jest. Ha-ha! Now, Kol is doing his duty, quite properly, and I wish him to remain. You may speak freely before him. And I am sure you have not come with ill intent.'

Fectur became utterly still. Through clenched teeth he said, 'I wish access to the chambers where the prisoner has been lodged.'

'The prisoner?'

'The leader of the True Sept, whom the Queen had taken from my custody and moved to guest's quarters. Soldiers guard the door—' A small, emerald-green moth fluttered up suddenly from somewhere among the books and charts on Pader's desk. It flew close before the blunt tip of Fectur's nose, obliging him to incline himself backwards and flick at it with one hand. '—and like this person here,' he continued with a chill side glance at Kol, 'they follow to irrational extremes orders that have been passed by yourself or the Queen.'

'Are you saying they did not permit you entrance?' queried Pader.

'That is what I am saying.'

'Oh, my! Oh, my my!' Pader's brow furrowed and he assumed a pensive expression, the finger and thumb of one hand lightly gripping his bony chin. 'Of course, their conduct cannot be faulted, my lord, for they are doing precisely as they have been ordered. Still, if you desire entrance to those chambers I see absolutely no reason why you should be denied.'

A second moth had appeared; the two performed darting orbits about Fectur's head. He flicked at them in irritation. They fluttered away and seemed to vanish in the shadows.

Pader Luminis smiled. 'These offices have been hurriedly refitted after a long period of disuse, my lord. Must and dust has escaped the attentions of the cleaners, it seems, despite their best efforts. Such is the way of things under such urgency. Now, Kol, if you would mind summoning the sergeant outside, I will have him escort His Lordship to the relevant chambers and permit him entrance.'

The sergeant entered, was instructed accordingly, and departed with Lord Fectur. Pader Luminis blew a series of small breaths between puffed cheeks, then returned to his seat and sat with his chin thrust forward. A small pensive grin hovered about his lips. He stretched his arms over the desktop, his eyes staring unseeingly at the charts laid before him. He drummed his fingers on the desktop. Then he looked over his spectacles at Kol, a mischievous glint in his eye. 'How long, Kol?'

'I would say three minutes at the most, Master Pader.'

'Yes, that would be my estimate also.' Pader drummed his fingers again. 'Ah, well.'

They waited, each held upon the delicate edge of nervousness and amusement. At length Fectur returned. His expression left no doubt as to his humour.

'Where is he?'

Pader returned him a look of mystification. 'Where is who, my lord?'

Fectur fixed him with his most baleful glare. 'You know who, *Imperator*. I speak of the prisoner, Grey Venger.'

'Ah, the Grey Venger! I regret, I am unable to say.'

'Do you play games with me?'

'Be assured, my lord, I do not.'

'Then why did you send me on a wild goose chase, knowing all the while that Venger is no longer in his chambers?'

'My lord, you said you wished to enter the chambers, to which I was pleased to comply. You did not declare an intention to speak to Grey Venger.'

'You think I went to consort with empty rooms?' Fectur leaned forward, pale as putty, and placed his fists knuckles down upon Pader's desktop. His head and shoulders inclined bullishly towards the little Murinean, his grey eyes bulging with insensate rage. At that moment a green moth rose from somewhere and brushed against his nose. He twitched his head back, slapping at the creature, which dodged his hand, flew behind his head, and as he turned, vanished.

Fectur looked daggers at Kol, who stood with feet apart, hands behind his back, his eyes upon the rafters somewhere above Fectur's head. Fectur glowered back at Pader. 'Where is he?'

'Grey Venger? The Queen had him moved.'

'To where?'

'I was not made party to that information, my lord.'

Fectur remained motionless, his eyes glistening. The muscles of his jaw rippled spasmodically. It seemed for a moment that he might have burst out of himself. Then he straightened, swivelled slowly upon his heel and strode from the room, the chill gravity of his exit marred by the trio of little emerald-green moths that seemed to emerge from somewhere within his very clothing and flit about his head, causing him to twitch, flap and swat as he departed.

SEVEN

I

Shenwolf, his head bowed to ward off the rain, walked his horse back along the line of mounted soldiers to join Issul. His waxed cape was drawn close about him, the hood up over his head, but darkened hanks of wet, fair hair clung to his forehead and his face was gaunt from the chill wind and rain. He raised his voice above the lashing of the trees all around and the hammering of the rain on the wet ground and the bowed backs of the troopers. 'The fore-riders report a quagmire upon the road at Cally Pond about a league hence. They say it is almost impassable, at least for the wagons.'

Issul muttered a resigned curse. The weather had worsened considerably since they had set out. The sky was foul, a mottled grey mass, driven low upon the forest, emptying its guts relentlessly upon the cavalcade. It was as though the very elements conspired against her. They had been on the move for five hours, but their progress was slow, far slower than she had hoped. There was no possibility now of reaching Crosswood by duskfall. She shivered, and looked back along the line of soldiers. Half-obscured in the rain she could just make out the bulk of the wagons near the rear of the column – two lumbering, tarpaulin-covered cargo carriers, and a pair of smaller, open carts, all laden with the sundry goods necessary to sustain more than fifty fighting men and their steeds for a period of many days. It was these vehicles that slowed the company the most, and almost certainly they would cause the greatest problems ahead. But she was unwilling to abandon them. It was not only the supplies they carried for the knights and men-at-arms and horses, but in the wagons, travelling separately, each unaware of the other's presence, were two auxiliary members of her company.

Issul had vacillated at first, in two minds over the advisability of bringing these two. Yet in the end she had accepted, just as she had known when she first accepted the inevitability of this journey, that she could not risk leaving them behind.

Grey Venger, in particular, had to be removed beyond Fectur's grasp. To further burden Pader Luminis with the task of Venger's protection would have been unfair and unjustifiable. Pader had more than he could comfortably cope with as it was. And besides, Issul needed to speak further with Grey Venger, to delve into the furthest recesses of his splintered, vicious mind, for she was convinced that she had not yet bled him of all he might disclose about the Legendary Child.

She had sent Sir Hespero, a knight of her Guard, to remove Venger from his chambers the previous night and spirit him from the city-castle, to join her company secretly on the road near the base of the scarp. She had ordered that Venger be given no explanation, and that he be bound, gagged and hooded. It would give him something to think about, and she was anxious to avoid the risk of his calling out or by some other means drawing attention to himself.

This morning Sir Hespero and his men had ridden forward from beneath the trees to meet the Queen. Issul had gone straight to Grey Venger and removed his hood and gag. He glared at her with blazing eyes and bared teeth. 'So, Issul-whore, what treachery is this?'

'No treachery, Venger. I thought you might enjoy both the change and the adventure.'

Venger glared about him, blinking at the dense oaks and elms and the misty, wet scarp rising at their backs. He seemed, just momentarily, disconcerted, which pleased Issul. It struck her that, incredibly, this might be the first time in Venger's life that he had been outside the city-castle's walls. Then the indurate glare and sneer of cold contempt had returned to his features. 'It matters nothing. I have already said, my task is done.'

'Even so, we might have pleasant conversations together still.'

'They will be pleasant inasmuch as they will be very short-lived.'

'Why so?'

'I have told you, your doom is close upon you. You and all your kind.'

He twisted his torso, his arms straining against the rope that bound his wrists. Issul sensed he had been about to raise his arms reflexively in righteous, hate-filled declamation. She said, 'Can you really be so sure, Venger?'

Venger quivered wrathfully against his bonds. 'I am the Grey Venger, and you are the Godless and Unrighteous! You are the Deceived! And you will perish. I know it as surely as I spit in your eye.'

And he had spat. Issul shifted her head to the side. A gobbet of orange-brown sputum lodged itself upon her ear, deep inside her hood. She fought back her fury. Sir Hespero raised a hand as though to cuff Grey Venger hard, but Issul stayed him with a gesture. She put a gloved hand to her ear and wiped it clean of his spittle. Then she leaned close to him and hissed in a bitter undertone, 'That was not my eye, Venger.'

Grey Venger hawked as if to spit again. Issul stepped back. 'Gag him and put him in the wagon!'

She turned away.

'Where do we go?' Venger managed to call before the gag was applied.

Through her disgust Issul felt a glimmer of satisfaction: she had his curiosity; he was not so impermeable. She turned back and stood close before him again and said, in level tones, 'We go to change the way things are.'

She saw it then, the smallest flicker deep in his blazing grey eyes, an infinitesimal suggestion of his quandary, which even he could not hide. He did not know whether she spoke the truth.

Issul had left him then. She silently berated herself, for though she had gained a small triumph over Venger, she had not acquitted herself favourably. In that brief exchange she had mentally jousted with him, played mind games, even succumbed to the desire to taunt him. In doing so she realized she had been manipulated by him, though he might not even have been aware of it. She had come uppermost, yet he had somehow left her with the clear and galling impression that she had done so on his terms.

Issul tried to shake him from her mind, but he would not be so easily dislodged. He was under her skin; he was *inside* her. *This is a man who wilfully sacrificed his own children!* To sport with a mind such as his was hazardous and obscene.

The truth was that she did not know what to do with Grey Venger.

He could not be left behind, but how far could she allow him to accompany her? As far as Enchantment?

If not, what was she to do with him?

The other extra traveller, Arene, had posed less of a problem. Again, Issul had been wary of leaving her at Enchantment's Edge where Fectur might discover her presence. So she had gone to the guest-chamber in the early hours to tell Arene that she wished to have her company on at least part of the journey.

'But why, young Queen?' had been Arene's first response. 'I can do no more for you than I have already done, and I will surely be a hindrance.'

In simple terms Issul had explained something of the difficulties of leaving her behind.

'Then I will leave Enchantment's Edge forthwith, which is what I had planned to do anyway. I will make my way home.'

'You are mistaken when you say you can do no more for us,' Issul replied. 'I think I have more to learn from you – of the Fortress of the *Hir'n Esh* and the Well of Immaculate Vision, perhaps even of Enchantment itself and your journey through it. But you know that I cannot tarry now. So I ask that you travel with me, at least part of the way.'

'I did not travel through Enchantment,' the old woman said. 'I came here via the Edge Lands.'

'Then you have travelled through lands of which I know little. Now, you know I have no choice but to undertake this journey. Will you accompany me?'

Arene nodded. 'Aye, then, I will.'

Issul then had her escorted secretly to one of the covered wagons, just before it was time to depart. She warned her to remain within and give no indication of her presence until they were well clear of Enchantment's Edge.

Now, as the driven rain fell upon and all around her, Issul looked at Shenwolf and said, 'If we have to we will leave the wagons behind. We will even take to the forest if we must.'

'What of Venger and the old woman?'

Issul turned her face again to the lowering, saturated skies. 'Venger can ride, or walk. That is not a problem. I am not so sure about Arene.'

'Do you wish me to speak to her?'

Issul shook her head. 'I will. You go to Sir Cors at the fore. Ask him if men can be sent forward with a view to felling trees or shifting earth or something, to make a way across the quagmire.'

Shenwolf gave a curt nod, then said, 'May I ask a question?'

'Of course.'

'Are both these two so vital to this journey?'

'The situation is complex,' Issul said. 'It becomes more complex almost by the hour. So, if by your question you mean, can we not leave these two behind now that they are free of Enchantment's Edge, the answer is no. Fectur may well send men in our wake. He knows how important Venger may be. Of Arene he knows less, possibly nothing. But she, too, has shown herself to be a crucial component in a deepening mystery.' Issul hesitated, aware that Shenwolf had not yet met Arene. 'Do you recall, after we escaped from the Krai camp, I asked you if you had seen an old woman at the site where I was ambushed by the Krai, on the road beyond Crosswood?'

'Aye, I recall.'

'Arene is the woman I spoke of, and she has come to me with an extraordinary tale. She comes from afar, but knows much of what is happening here. I will not willingly part with her now.'

She wheeled her horse around and walked it back along the sodden road to the wagon carrying Arene. Passing the rein to an aide, she slid from her mount and hopped onto the back of the wagon and over the tailboard. Inside Arene sat half-dozing on sacks of meal. Issul threw back her hood and shook free the excess water from her cape, then clambered forward and sat beside her.

'The weather is against us. We may be forced to leave the wagons. Will it burden you to ride?'

'Burden me?' said Arene, rocking from side to side with the uneven motion of the wagon. 'I am old, but more hale and hearty than you might think. I walked for many weeks before I came to Enchantment's Edge. I confess, I was weary when I arrived, and my ankles were swollen and my back ached. But I am much better now. I would prefer the comfort of a carriage with padded upholstery and plump, soft, velvet cushions, but if such is not available, well, I can tolerate an old mare, if she is sturdy, not given to sudden changes of temperament, and can tolerate me.'

Issul smiled. Arene had begun to rouse herself from her half-reclining position. Issul motioned her back. 'Not yet. A league or so down the road the way is flooded. That is when we may have to take to the horses.'

Arene settled herself once more. The wagon creaked and groaned as it rolled forward, the rain battering its canvas. It pitched violently to one side as a front wheel sank suddenly into a deep rut. Arene clung to the sacks to steady herself; Issul likewise. The wagon was hauled slowly on. They braced themselves for the lurch of the rear wheel sinking. As it was dragged free Arene said, 'What of the young fellow in the forest? Have you found any sign of him among your new recruits?'

Issul shook her head. 'There has been no time to initiate a proper search. Recruits have flooded in from all over in recent weeks. It would take days to locate them all. His words may also have been intended to lead you astray.' She hesitated a moment. 'Arene, when you viewed the Unfolding, did you see anything of what might now happen, as I undertake this journey?'

'No more than I have told you, child. Our concern as Witnesses was with the path that led to the death of the Foulborn. We saw the strands of other possibilities, but they were many, and none stood forth with clarity, other than the consequences of your failure to leave Enchantment's Edge. Of course, weeks have passed since I stepped forth to seek out the Foulborn. More may have been revealed in that time.'

'If that is so, do the others of the *Hir'n Esh* have a way of contacting you?' Issul asked, rising to this small beat of hope.

The old woman gave a solemn shake of her head. 'Only by sending another forth, and this they will not do.'

'Why not?'

'We are but seven in number.'

'Seven?'

'Aye, and we are all old and failing. Has it not struck you as queer that one such as I should be sent out upon this mission? A hag, ancient and infirm, with swollen veins, no teeth and a wandering and forgetful mind, dispatched on such a quest? In your eyes, am I the embodiment of a heroic and single-minded assassin, even if my prey is but a small child?'

Issul was bemused. 'I had not considered it before.'

'We are the last of our kind, Queen Issul. The seven are all who remain. And we are barren – there will be no more when we have gone. It is the energy of the Well of the Immaculate Vision, so we believe. Over generations it has reduced our capacity to reproduce. The last fourteen children were stillborn, many others were slipped long before their time. And now, well, we are too old.'

'Have you no novices or apprentices?'

'Others cannot be brought from outside to take our place; the energy is too strong. It enervates normal folk; they cannot bear it.'

'But not you?'

'We, it seems, have grown resistant, though not immune.'

Issul was silent. Arene gave a sigh. 'So no other will hobble forth to seek me out, young Queen. No matter what the Well may have revealed in my absence.'

'Then perhaps we should go there,' said Issul.

'And prolong your journey by several weeks? I do not think so.'

After a silence Arene said, 'Do you have the carving with you? The tusk? May I see it again?'

From inside her tunic Issul brought forth the blue leather pouch containing the little ivory carving, and passed it to her. Arene studied it, then clasped it in one fleshy, calloused fist. She shook her head. 'It is a mystery. Have you considered breaking it open?'

'I fear to do so.'

'You are probably wise.' She opened her fist and stared hard at the object again, musing, 'What can it be?'

Issul took back the carving, pondered it for a moment, then asked, 'Arene, do you know much of Enchantment?'

'More than you, I would warrant.'

'Do you have it mapped?'

Arene gave a short bark of laughter. 'Enchantment cannot be mapped, child. It is ever-becoming, never still.'

'Then how is it possible to find anything? Those who dwell there must have means of locating one another.'

'Aye, they know of one another's whereabouts, more or less. The land may be stable for weeks or even months at a time, but that is of little use to a cartographer.'

'Have you heard of the Soul of the Orb? Or of a crucible of shining adamant in which it is sealed, in a fortress sanctum? Have you heard of the One God?' Issul's heart beat fast as she spoke these words. This was information that had come partly through

Grey Venger in his heated conversations with Leth. Pader had told her about it.

'There is a legend concerning an artefact called the Soul of the Orb,' Arene said. 'It tells how a being who falsely believed himself to be a god was defeated in battle by other similar beings. As punishment they deprived him of his soul and secreted it where it might never be found, sealed within an impenetrable crucible of adamant. The false god they banished from the world, imprisoning him in a bubble of unconscious stuff from which he might never wake or escape. But after countless eons the false god did awaken, and somehow he created out of the unconscious bubble in which he was held a world, of which he was both separate and a part. The legend goes on to tell of certain adventures, but concludes by saying that in time the false god who was now a true god, a true creator of his own world, broke free of his creation. He searched without end for his lost soul, and sought revenge upon those against whom he had fought so long ago, and who had taken his soul and imprisoned him.'

Issul listened intently, spellbound. At the same time a sudden, creeping unease stole over her. *A false god who was now a true god* . . . That fateful phrase: *a True God.* It echoed words ranted by Grey Venger when he had declared the coming of the One True God who would vanquish all unbelievers; namely, herself, Leth, their family and virtually all of Enchantment's Edge.

She felt as though she was falling. *Can Orbus, whom I lead in a quest to find his soul, supposedly to liberate us all, be the One True God of the True Sept?*

'Is there something the matter, child?'

Issul barely heard Arene's question. She stared at the old woman uncomprehendingly. Then she shook her head, though her face betrayed her inner turmoil. In a subdued voice she asked, 'Does the legend tell whether he finds his soul and defeats his enemies?'

'There is more than one ending,' replied Arene. 'as is commonly the case with ancient tales. No one knows which is the original, or even if it matters. Suffice to say that there are versions which tell of his victory and the vanquishing of evil, and versions which relate how he was again defeated and this time destroyed utterly. And let us not be in any doubt, the legend has come alive. You know that now, don't you? And whatever the truth may be, you and I and all who are with or against us are part of it.'

It seemed again that there was too much happening here for one mind to grasp. Issul sat stone still, a chill hand compressing her innards.

'Where is the god, Queen Issul?' Arene asked.

'He . . . he travels with us, hidden.'

'And you trust and believe in him?'

'I do. I think I do. He has my children, and Leth. He has our future, if a future is possible. I have little choice but to believe in him.'

'That is the way of it, yes. In this intricate matter, none of us is given a choice.'

'You said . . . you told me I must heed the god.'

'Aye, I did.'

'Do you still stand by that?'

'It is what you stand by that matters, child. You have said, you have little choice. And it is true that if the god can find his soul he may bring the salvation you seek. But I think, if you will permit me, I should meet this god.'

'I will talk to him. It will be difficult under these circumstances, but if he is agreeable I will do what I can.'

Issul rose and made her way unsteadily to the back of the wagon, eased herself over the tailboard and climbed back onto her horse. Shenwolf was riding down the column of soldiers towards her. Above the seething hiss of the rain and the rattle and creak of the wagon, he called, 'Sir Darly has ridden forward with eight men to try and find or construct a way over the quagmire.'

Issul urged her mount forward along the sodden road, to take a place close to the head of the column. Her head seemed to spin; again she was overwhelmed by uncertainty and doubt. She would have to speak to Orbus as soon as possible. It would not be before they made camp at nightfall; even then it might not be possible for her to find somewhere private enough to safely summon him. But what would she say to him now? Was she right to trust him?

She peered into the drenched dark forest all around her, and wondered whether, beyond her sight, a small boy watched and quietly mocked.

II

Despite all efforts Sir Darly and his men had been thwarted in their efforts to forge a passable route over or around the flooded road. The quagmire, formed in a shallow declivity by a freshet from a swollen wayside pond, covered an area about fifteen yards long. Several men had managed, with some difficulty, to wade through on horseback, so when the main company arrived a decision was taken to try to lead one wagon across.

About five yards into the sludge the wagon listed heavily to its right side. It sank slowly to its belly. Efforts to haul it free resulted in it settling more firmly into the black mud. A team of six horses hauled from the far side of the quagmire, with men up to their thighs in mud pushing the wagon from behind, but they failed to shift it. Plainly, to cross safely, each wagon and cart would have to be unloaded and its cargo carried, article by article, via the forest to the further side of the quagmire. The empty vehicles could then be hauled, pushed and levered through, and re-loaded on the other side. Even with all hands put to the task, it would require at least a couple of hours, quite probably longer. And there was still no guarantee that the operation would be successful.

After quick consultation Issul reluctantly gave the order to abandon the wagons and continue on horseback. Wagon- and cart-drivers and assistants remained behind, along with Sir Darly and half a dozen men-at-arms. Their job was to free the stricken wagon and get all four vehicles across, then proceed in the company's wake.

Issul instructed Shenwolf to take charge of Grey Venger, specifying that he should be strapped securely upon a horse, with his hands bound behind his back, and placed in the middle of the column where he might not make a break for freedom. Venger remained gagged – even so, he strained to make his protests heard for some time, with stifled roars and queer, bestial growls and honks of outrage.

For good measure Issul ordered a cloth hood replaced over his head, from which he might see nothing bar the colourful internal images of his own fury. She worried not about the indignities she was serving upon him. No matter Leth's earlier assurances to Venger, the time for courtesies and privileges had passed. Issul wanted to break this madman down. She had seen the flicker of uncertainty in his eyes when he realized he was outside the city-castle. If further disorientation would serve to permit her a greater insight into his tortured psyche and the information it held, she had few qualms about employing it now with the situation so critical.

With Phisusandra, Issul took charge of Arene. The old woman was bulky and did not sit gracefully in the saddle. By her own admission she had little experience with horses. But neither was she particularly nervous, and with Phis and another guard riding close on either side of her, she was able to take a place near the rear of the column and proceed slowly on.

As dusk approached the rain at last began to ease off, and finally ceased altogether. A red-brown scum coloured the sky, darkening rapidly, with streaks of violent bright light lining the clouds. There was no moon, and soon they were obliged to stop and make the night's camp. They pitched tents in a clearing set off the road at the foot of a tall cliff used for quarrying stone. Others were there before them: refugees fleeing the advancing Krai, making for the already overcrowded sanctuary of Enchantment's Edge. They sat huddled in small knots around glimmering campfires, and watched with curiosity and some suspicion as the soldiers trooped in. Issul sent men to join them and talk with them, reassure them, offer them food and drink if they had none, and learn what they could of the Krai advance.

Issul considered the risks of bringing Orbus forth to consult him and, if he was willing, to arrange the meeting Arene had requested. Things had moved at such breakneck speed that Issul had had only the briefest opportunity to tell Orbus about Arene before they left Enchantment's Edge. She had not brought Arene to meet him, nor had he requested she do so. He had been intrigued, though, and perhaps a little perturbed by Issul's news that his coming and predicament had been foreseen, at least in part, by the *Hir'n Esh*; that Arene had advised Issul to heed him, and that he was somehow a living, enigmatic component within a greater web of Unfolding revealed by the Well of Immaculate Vision.

These factors, Issul reasoned, would surely weigh in her favour if she chose to ask Orbus to meet with Arene. But did she want to now? Such doubts assailed her after Arene's recounting of the legend earlier, and the references to the true god. She was cast back onto her deepest fears, and a dreadful sensation of being alone and toyed with for ends that could only culminate in her loss and the downfall of Enchantment's Edge.

It was only this afternoon that she had realized she had omitted all mention of the ivory carving to Orbus. It had been unintentional, with so much else occupying her mind. But it seemed quite possible that Orbus might be able to enlighten her in some way as to its provenance and purpose, if purpose it had. He might even be able to identify it. But now . . . should she reveal it to him?

Issul summoned Shenwolf to her tent. With Orbus's agreement she had, briefly, brought both Shenwolf and Pader Luminis to her chambers before parting. There she had called forth the god from the blue casket. As the two gaped in astonishment she had explained to them the most essential details concerning the quest she was involved in, and revealed the truth – as revealed to her by Orbus – about King Leth's and the children's disappearance. Now, in matters concerning Orbus, Shenwolf was the one person she could confide in, though she was not yet ready to express her newest fears.

'Here in the camp it is not secure; I cannot risk Orbus being detected, even by my own men, yet I must speak to him urgently,' she said.

'I suggest you let me escort you into the woods,' Shenwolf replied, 'with Phis and sufficient men to throw a protective cordon around you. You can be in cover, beyond the men's sight and hearing, yet secure from any intrusions. Take a lantern with you, so that I can see your position. I shall stay far enough away so as not to overhear your conversation, if you so wish.'

'Excellent. I think that will work.'

'Then let me scour the nearby forest now for a suitable location. I will take ten men and place them in secure positions, then return for you.'

Shenwolf departed. Issul sat alone, staring at the wooden chest that held the blue casket of Orbus's world. From somewhere outside there came a cry, shrill and brief, as of some wild animal in distress. Issul sat up straight, her spine tingling. Had the sound come from without? She felt a welling of grief and guilt. It was not the cry of a wild creature; it was an inner sound, a plaint that had touched her again, wounding her to the core. It was a child's cry, and the child was her own, little Galry, her son, calling out for her.

When Shenwolf re-entered he found the Queen in tears. He quickly knelt on one knee beside her and took one of her hands in his.

'We will save them,' he whispered. 'Be sure of that. We *will*.'

Issul squeezed her eyes shut and could not speak. Shenwolf lifted the back of one hand to her cheek and gently brushed away a tear. 'Jace,' he began, then faltered. 'I am sorry, I knew you first by your daughter's name, and have not yet grown accustomed to calling you by any other title.'

'That is all right.' Issul cleared her throat. Her hand was still in his.

'I think, in my h—, in my *mind*, you will always be Jace. I hope that does not offend you.'

Issul shook her head and managed a small smile. 'Of course not. Why should it?' She understood that he had been on the verge of saying 'in my heart'. She recalled a time when they had been together in the woods outside the Krai camp, and again after the Krai had been successfully overcome, when he had also come close to professing such feelings for her. There had been other moments, when she had felt a closeness to him – a closeness she could never admit to. Even in her own mind she shied away from such notions.

In the castle of the traitor, Ombo, where she, Shenwolf, Phis, Kol and others had been imprisoned and almost lost their lives she had, out of sheer exhaustion and horror, wept upon Shenwolf's shoulder. She had been so glad of his presence then, and had sensed how pleased he had been that she had turned to him, so frank and open, in her time of distress. But now, as on those occasions, she also felt uncomfortable. She knew that something had passed between them, something undeniable, and she was confused. She averted her eyes.

Shenwolf released her hand, but remained kneeling. 'I hope you will not consider me over-bold when I say that, though you are Queen and I a commoner, I feel that we have become friends, and that, if it is so, I am glad of it.'

'I too,' said Issul, standing and smoothing her tunic with the flats of her hands. 'I rely upon you, for advice and companionship also, as well as for your skills as a soldier and bodyguard.'

'Then I am a man fulfilled!'

She smiled. She buckled her swordbelt about her waist. 'When we are alone I am pleased for you to call me by my name. My own name. But at other times you must refer to me as "Majesty" or "my Lady".'

'Of course. I understand that anything else would be inappropriate.' Shenwolf rose. 'Now, the men are in position. Shall I take the chest?'

'No, I will carry it.'

Outside Phisusandra waited with two others of the Royal Guard. With Shenwolf leading they marched across the camp and entered the forest on the further side of the road. Taking a short detour so that Shenwolf could check upon the positions and state of readiness of three of the guards he had placed, they then climbed to the crest of a small wooded knoll.

'This is the place,' Shenwolf said. 'If you are happy with it, I will leave you now. Neither man nor beast could climb this slope, even now in darkness, without our knowledge.' He pointed down the incline. 'I will be just over there.'

'Good.' Issul set the chest upon the wet ground. She took the lantern which Shenwolf proffered her.

When she was alone she gave herself a moment to take stock. Below, through the trees, the campfires of her company glowed, the nearest no more than fifty yards away. Close upon them were the fires of the refugees. Issul moved behind a high shoulder of rock, where her lantern-glow might not be seen, placed the lantern at the base of a stunted hackberry tree, then knelt before the wooden chest, unfastened its lock and raised the lid. She set the blue casket upon the ground before her.

'Orbus.'

There was a pause, a breathless silence in which she felt her fears mount, then the god materialized before her, seeming somehow more solid in the near dark. 'Issul. Is it wise to summon me here? Is it safe?'

'We are not observed.'

'Can you be sure of that?'

'As sure as it is possible to be.'

'Where are we?'

'In the forest, a day's ride from Enchantment's Edge. The weather has been against us. We have not made good progress.'

'I see.'

'And you? What have you been doing in these passing hours?'

'I? Ah well, that is interesting. I have been meditating. Deeply.'

'Meditating?'

'Just so.'

'What have your meditations brought you?'

'In concrete terms that is not easy to quantify. I have been attempting to communicate with Leth, to make him somehow aware of my presence, to reassure him that I have not abandoned him.'

Issul had caught her breath as he said this. 'Have you had any luck?'

'Luck? Luck is not something I had considered a factor. But results . . . well, it is difficult to say, since I am still not able to determine Leth's whereabouts, or to realize him, or your two children, in any way that impinges directly upon my senses.'

'Then you still do not know if they are alive?'

'It is as I said before: I sense conflict, which I believe has arisen as a consequence of their arrival within me. But Issul, what is wrong? I sense a change in you. A remoteness that was not present before.'

Issul did not know how to go about expressing her fears. To question him about his allegiance, suggest that he had other, unrevealed reasons for returning to this world, would alert him, might even turn him against her if he was something other than he claimed to be. Yet she wanted desperately to believe in him. Without Orbus she knew that she had no hope.

'The old woman of the *Hir'n Esh*, Arene, whom I told you of – she wants to talk to you. She believes it could be fruitful.'

'What, here? Now?' Orbus twisted his bulk from side to side, looking for Arene.

'No. I have come to seek your permission to bring her.'

'What benefit can a meeting have, in circumstances so fraught with the risk of discovery?'

'She knows much about Enchantment. She speaks of an ancient legend which has come alive. The tale revolves specifically around you.'

'Aha. Well, that is not entirely a surprise. So . . . very well, perhaps a meeting with her may be illuminating. But take care that we are secure.'

'Of course.'

Issul stared at him, still unsure of how, or even whether, to voice her doubts. She thought of the ivory carving, and reached into her tunic to bring forth the leather pouch containing the carving. She tugged at the string securing its neck. 'Orbus, I want to show you something.'

There came a curtailed shout from somewhere near the foot of the knoll. Then another, followed by a crashing in the undergrowth, as of a large body moving at sudden desperate speed.

'Orbus, begone!'

Orbus faded. As he did so Issul heard his last, whispered words: 'If you no longer trust me, remember, I am fragile in your hands. I am destroyed at any time.'

She had no time to heed, or even consider how he had suspected her of mistrust. There were renewed cries from below. She grabbed the casket and withdrew with it into the darkness between bushes and rock, leaving the lantern where it was. Silence now, then the sound of footsteps on the slippery earth. Issul laid the casket carefully upon the ground and drew her sword.

A dark shape moved, revealed in part-silhouette in the lantern-glow.

'Majesty! It is I, Shenwolf.'

Issul came forward. She saw the relief on Shenwolf's lean young face. Just beyond him was Phisusandra, and three other members of her Guard, peering into the enclosing dark, their blades drawn.

'What has happened?'

'Someone – or something – was seen stealing towards the knoll. One of the men surprised him, but he escaped into the woods.'

'It was a man?'

'Most probably. I could not allow a full pursuit lest others lie in wait. We would be leaving you vulnerable. I fear we have lost him. Come, we must get you away from here.'

Issul quickly took the blue casket and replaced it in its chest, sealed the lid and gathered the chest to her. 'You gained no inkling of who it might be?'

'Most probably some over-curious body from one of the groups camped in the quarry. I will have them questioned.'

'No, leave them be. They are, for the most part at least, innocent folk who have lost their homes and perhaps kin. They have suffered enough. If there is a subversive element among them, we are unlikely to uncover it now.' She watched his face. 'It was not Krai?'

In her mind was the memory of her ambush and capture by a Krai forward unit upon the road not far beyond Crosswood. Were the outriders of Anzejarl's army here again, already? Shenwolf gave a shrug. 'I could not say. I will question the guard.'

They made their way back down the slope to the camp. The forest was silent now, but for the eerie rustle of leaves as the wind, far lighter than before, passed easily through the trees.

III

With the morning came brittle blue skies laced with thin tails of dirty white cloud which stretched hazily towards the south. A chill, strong breeze had chased away the last of the stormclouds and the sun climbed sure and unencumbered, quickly dispelling the nightshadow and gilding the low forest with diverse shades of rippling gold and green. Issul's company moved on with the first light, and arrived at the township of Crosswood a little after midway through the morning.

As on the day before, the road to Crosswood was marked by an almost ceaseless straggling trail of people labouring towards Enchantment's Edge. More than once Issul wondered how the capital was going to cope with such an influx. She had learned last night that Anzejarl had been torching villages and towns indiscriminately as he advanced. No doubt it was a component of his overall strategy to place as many pressures as he could upon the city-castle, and flooding it with a terrified mass of dispossessed citizens would stretch its resources and tolerance to the limit.

Crosswood itself had, in just a few days, been turned almost into a ghost town. Homes and businesses were for the most part boarded up and shuttered; the inn of the Green Ram, where Issul had previously stayed, was likewise closed and appeared deserted. Desperation and panic were in the air, almost tangible. Few but the most stout-hearted or reckless harboured any hope that the Krai onslaught would be stemmed or diverted.

The company rode on through, aloof to the stares and occasional jeers of the people at the roadsides.

They came to the place where, only days earlier, Issul, Shenwolf, Kol and Phisusandra had bidden farewell to their young comrade Herbin. With a feeling of sadness Issul wondered how brave Herbin had fared. He had lost his brother to the Krai, and then his elderly father, Miseon, in the most terrible circumstances. Once free, Herbin had returned to his home, the hamlet of Glux, to care for his mother. But Glux almost certainly lay in Prince Anzejarl's path. Almost certainly, then, Herbin and his mother and fellow villagers would be making their way towards Enchantment's Edge, if not now then within the next day or so.

In due course the company left the road, striking off through the forest towards the village of Ghismile, upon the shore of Ghismile's Tarn. There the traitor, brigand and self-titled baron, Ombo, with a band of armed thugs, had enslaved the village and subjected its inhabitants to the most appalling depredations. Issul shuddered as she recalled her betrayal at Ombo's hands, how he had thrown her and her fellow travellers – his former companions – into the dungeon beneath his keep. He had taken Issul to his chambers on the upper level and there tried to blackmail and rape her. She had killed him; she closed her eyes as she remembered. And then the nightmare journey back through the keep to free her companions. Five more of Ombo's men died on her sword before she reached the dungeon. They were beasts – worse than beasts – guilty of the most unforgivable crimes against innocents. They would have raped and murdered her too, given the chance, and she had little compunction in ending their lives. But that day had changed her, forever. Never again would she look upon the world with innocent eyes.

She shuddered. It had happened only a week ago. The side of her face was still tender and faintly discoloured from the force of the blow Ombo had struck her.

At his own suggestion Shenwolf made off ahead of the company, to reconnoitre the area and spy out Ghismile. Two hours into the forest Issul called a halt in a small clearing to rest the horses and allow the men to eat. When Shenwolf returned his customary good-humoured expression was absent. Instead he was pale and grim-faced. Issul took him aside.

'Ghismile is occupied,' he said.

Issul gave an exasperated sigh. 'The Krai are here already?'

He shook his head. 'Not Krai. Forest things. Grullags.'

'Grullags?' Issul was stupefied. She stared at him as if waiting for him to break into a grin and confess to a joke, albeit one in extremely bad taste. His face, though, told her there was no joke. 'But they are beasts. Ferocious, yes, but they would never invade a village.'

'I can tell you only what I saw,' said Shenwolf. 'There are at least a dozen within the village and keep. They are organized, acting as if with intelligence. And I saw no sign of any villagers.'

Issul blinked several times, trying to grasp the concept. 'Then they are controlled, somehow,' she said in a low breath. 'Anzejarl . . . It can only be that he has learned how to command these monsters also.'

At that moment there was a sharp, hoarse shriek from behind her. She wheeled around. Arene stood a few yards away, stricken-faced. The old woman was pointing, her eyes wide with alarm, her arm and gnarled finger shaking, screaming, 'That is him! That is him! Queen Issul, you are betrayed! That is the one! The one I met beside the pond!'

EIGHT

I

The image of Nothing remained, a keenly perplexing question, a paradox of profoundly distressing intensity in Leth's mind. He could not free himself of it. More than anything else that he had experienced on his journey with Lakewander – the horror of the Plain of Imprisoned Souls, the numbing shock of the Sufferer and his self-inflicted agonies – more than either of these, the Nothing held him spellbound. It was ungraspable. Even to himself he could not explain what he had witnessed – or more precisely, what he had *not* witnessed – when he had emerged onto the end of the long, hazily-coloured beach and found himself staring into the End of the World.

Eternity? Infinity? These words each defined a phenomenon, albeit one in the abstract, but he had gazed upon no phenomenon. What he had seen could not be defined – to attempt any form of definition implied the existence of something, a place or thing to which a label might be attached. But what he had gazed upon . . .

In his memory Orbus's dry, distant voice drifted, talking of Mystery and madness, of defining principles and the mind's inability to comprehend. But Leth could not hear him. He shook his head. Even the word Nothing served inadequately to explain what he had witnessed, for equally, in application, the word quantified some kind of phenomenon: the absence or lack of something. But he had gazed into complete and absolute vacancy. Not absence or lack, but something which no intellect or emotion could embrace. It had waged war upon him now, broken through his resistance and entered him. He was giddy and sick at the recollection of it, at the awareness of it inside him. It was as though he, as a mere human, was thwarted by a sensorium and faculties too limited to assimilate it. He felt he was on the edge of insanity, that this unwelcome non-*thing* had lodged itself deep within him and was growing, becoming to big for his mind to contain.

So went his thoughts as he lay upon his bed that night, his last night in the haunted place called Orbia. He could not sleep, and more than once in his torment he remembered Lakewander's nakedness and her warm, lithe body against his, her hands, her lips, and he wondered whether he could reject her now if she came to him again offering solace and passionate diversion.

But she did not come; Leth remained alone and acutely wakeful. At one point, in frustration, he stole from his chamber and sought to engage once more with the ghostly presence in the chill stone walls. But his efforts were fruitless, for no voice responded to his petitions, neither in the corridor nor, subsequently, back in the chamber.

The first tones of early morning light touched the alien sky. Leth sat resplendent upon his sleek black stallion, Swiftwind. He was clad in the ribbed sapphire blue armour and fabulous helm of the god he had never been. The helm, like the armour, fitted lightly and comfortably, seeming to mould itself to the contours of his face like a second skin. The Sword of the Orb, another legacy of a past he knew nothing of, slanted back from his waist. Swiftwind was clad in barding of the same lightweight, flexible, ribbed sapphire plate. To the side of the yard stood Master Protector, supported by a servant, and Summoner, waiting to see Leth off.

The morning was becoming mild and bright, the strange sky clear, as it always seemed to be. Leth could not see the Orb of the Godworld, nor the World's Pain; both were obscured by the high screen of dark trees which massed beyond the outer wall of this other Orbia.

As he sat, absorbed in troubled musings, awaiting the arrival of Lakewander from within, Leth slowly became aware of a curious, almost subliminal distraction. He glanced up and thought to half-see a brief blur of motion in the air close before him. It was gone before he could focus upon it, so that he wondered whether he had seen anything at all. But then it recurred, slightly off to one side, and elsewhere.

It was the merest inkling of a disturbance. The air seemed to have shifted momentarily, in the way the surface of a pool of water might show the faintest stirring as something unseen flickered or twisted suddenly below.

He thought of invisible wings. There was a shadow of movement against his cheek, and yet he could not be certain that he had felt anything. He was reminded of the last hours in Orbus's blue domain, before he and Jace and Galry had stepped through the glimmering arch and found themselves before Summoner and his nervy followers. He had been famished, weak and angry, and had seen, or had thought he had seen, a similar brief motion, an instant of flux in the air before him. Galry had noticed it too, though it was gone before either could focus on it. He had thought then, as now, of the stirring of unseen wings, without knowing precisely why that image came to mind.

Quite suddenly the air was filled with such movements. Leth blinked to clear his vision and gazed around him in some bewilderment. Swiftwind shied slightly and tossed his head, but otherwise showed no alarm. Master Protector and Summoner remained as they were, watching Leth, both smiling slightly, almost blithely, as though nothing at all were amiss.

'What – What is happening here?' queried Leth. The air was roiling all around. He sensed a flow; the motion issued from within or about Orbia or beyond and converged upon the yard where he waited. In fact, he felt that he or somewhere close upon him was its focus. The hairs at the back of his neck prickled. He was within a sea of silent flutterings, whose touch was more gentle than the kiss of a butterfly's wing. And then all was still once more, and Leth could not be sure that anything had happened at all.

Lakewander appeared from within. She strode purposefully to her horse and mounted. She looked at Leth, smiled, then regarded him quizzically. 'Swordbearer, are you ready?'

Leth gazed about him. Master Protector and Summoner still smiled at him, slightly vacuously, seemingly aware of nothing out of the ordinary.

'Is something wrong?' Lakewander enquired.

Leth began to speak. 'I saw something. I think . . .'

Two vertical furrows appeared upon her brow. 'Something?'

'Phantom forms in the air. Ghosts, or things that dwell beyond the normal ken of man.'

Her brow cleared. She smiled, as if pleased with what she heard. 'Do not be alarmed.'

'Did my imagination or perception play me false?'

'I think not. I certainly hope not. Some things we can never be certain of. They reach us through perceptions not yet wholly realized.' She looked away, to Master Protector, and Leth saw her eyes mist over and her proud face grow sorrowful. 'Father, we are ready now.'

The old man nodded. His jaw trembled and he seemed to have difficulty finding words. Finally he said simply, 'Go well.'

Lakewander turned her horse about. Her features were strained. She headed towards the gate. Leth followed, unclear as to his goal, his purpose here. He could think only that everything had the character of an unending dream in which he had become trapped.

He glanced at the two men as he passed. Summoner gazed at him, no longer smiling, but transfixed, as though with wonder or awe. And old Master Protector trembled, his eyes ancient and sorrowful, filled with tears he would not permit himself to shed.

Dream or not, as he rode through the gate Leth told himself, as he had told himself over and over, that this was not his land. No matter what others might claim, he had not been here before. He would fight for them if he had to, but with the unbreachable certainty that his true striving was to be reunited with his children, by whatever means, and then to find the way back to Enchantment's Edge.

II .

'If we are parted, that is the direction you must go, always,' said Lakewander. 'Remember that. It is the one constant.'

She gazed towards the World's Pain which gleamed in the low sky in front of them, a tiny bright golden pinpoint.

Her words held a weight of premonition, it seemed to Leth. 'Is it likely that we will be parted?'

Lakewander gave a quick smile. 'Who knows what will happen?'

'You should not have accompanied me.'

'Lord, you will not lie with me.'

'That is no answer.'

'Without me, how do you propose finding your way?'

He shook his head. 'You and Master Protector were perfectly happy to let me proceed alone. You could have provided me with a map, or sent someone else with me. Your decision to come was based solely upon my refusal to take you to my bed.'

'There is no other way.'

'But it will change nothing. I have told you, I love another.'

'I understand.'

'Then why . . . ?'

Lakewander turned her eyes from him, back to the World's Pain. Her lower lip drooped in soulful contemplation. 'Because this is how it must be.'

Leth felt a spasm of irritation. Every conversation he engaged in here, with Lakewander, her father, Summoner or any other, seemed replete with evasion and mystery, every question was answered obliquely. Acutely conscious of this, he asked, 'What of the Shore of Nothing, which I may walk upon but which robs others of their minds? How will you survive?'

'I will have your protection, Lord. That is my hope.'

'How? How am I to protect you?'

'We must see.' Lakewander urged her mount into a trot, obliging him to give Swiftwind rein to keep pace with her.

Later they rested in the same dell where they had paused the previous day. Lakewander brought forth dried meat, cheese and bread from her saddlepack, with a flask of watered wine. She spread a cloth upon the grass and laid these out.

Leth sat with his back against a fallen tree, watching her. Was she all that she seemed, or was she keeping something from him? He stabbed at a strip of meat with his dagger. 'This world, Orb, seems a wild and unnaturally empty place.'

'Is your own so different?'

'In some ways. There are vast, unpopulated expanses, yet even they contain a greater diversity of life than I find here. Many species of birds in the air, perched in trees or upon lofty crags; creatures large and small inhabiting the undergrowth.'

'There are birds and wild beasts here.'

'In some small number, so it seems to me.'

'Perhaps.'

'For my own part I live in a bustling, crowded citadel. I am accustomed to seeing many people at all times, from many different walks of life.'

'And it does not oppress you?'

'There are times when one needs solitude or recreation, yes. But there are opportunities for such. Here your lives seem almost monastic. I see little in the way of diversion. Your own lifestyle is frugal, from what I have witnessed. Others here live only to inflict suffering upon themselves, and to have that suffering impress itself upon the consciences of their fellow folk. Overall, a pervasive melancholy and sense of loneliness imbues the air.'

Lakewander cast her eyes down. 'I have told you, it was not always like this. There was once a city. I remember so much, when I was a child. It was very different. Everything was different. We laughed, we played. But now . . . it is a long time since I have done either of those things.'

'But the Sufferers and the Souls, they have always been with you.'

'For many generations, yes. Though in greater number these days, as the end approaches.'

'Do they think that by their actions they can avert the end?'

'They believe, or desperately hope, that through being aware of their suffering the Creator will be moved to act. If they establish and communicate enough pain, the Creator will be conscience-bound to respond. And if they atone for their sins in suffcent manner, the Creator will consider us worth saving, and hence move to prevent Ascaria from taking any more of our world.'

'You – or they – are attributing human qualities to your Creator. By what criteria do you make such a judgement?' Leth felt some confusion as he said this, for he knew that in essence the creator of this world was Orbus.

Lakewander shrugged. 'It is not I who have judged.'

'But your words imply that if I succeed in slaying Ascaria, the Sufferers will cast off their bonds, the Imprisoned Souls will step free from their metal prisons.'

'It may be so.'

'That places an even greater burden upon me. Do you consider me some kind of representative of your Creator?'

'You came from beyond the Sign, Swordbearer, in answer to our call.'

'I heard no call.'

Lakewander concentrated upon her food. The topic seemed to discomfit her. Leth wondered whether to pursue it, to probe more deeply, then opted for another approach. 'Lakewander, I know so little about you or your family. I have met your father, if briefly, but what of your mother? Does she dwell with you in Orbia? Have you siblings? What of suitors? Surely you cannot lack for them?'

Lakewander grew troubled and distant. 'My mother . . . my mother was very beautiful, and a renowned artist. Her paintings were displayed in municipal galleries and private businesses and homes throughout the city. But she was given to fits of depression, alternating with periods of frenzied activity wherein she might become obsessed with some received idea or sudden illumination, which she would usually integrate with great success into her work. Some years ago she fell under the influence of the Souls. Quickly they became, more and then more, the predominant focus of her life. She ceased working, and one day gathered all her available artworks together and set them ablaze. She told us that such works were frivolous, that her life to date had been without meaning. No matter our remonstrations, after the city was destroyed by Ascaria she had herself encased in lead and placed out upon the Plain of Imprisoned Souls. She said that her life had to become her art, and vice versa. She believed she had been the recipient of a message from our Creator, who had told her in a vision that her suffering and eventual death would help cleanse us all of sin. Such, as I have said, is the reasoning of the Souls.'

Lakewander paused, her eyes upon the ground. Her voice came again as a hollow whisper. 'It took her almost two years to die, Swordbearer. Every day I or my two brothers or our father would take food and drink to her. Every day we pleaded with her to change her mind. But she was resolute, and would not be swayed. One day . . . one day my brothers could bear no more. My mother had ceased speaking, either because she had lost her voice through weakness or because she no longer wished to acknowledge us when we came. My brothers elected to cut her free. This they did, though she screamed at them to leave her be. When she emerged she was hardly more than a cadaver. Her limbs had wasted, she could barely stand. But she was angry, oh so angry.'

Lakewander emitted a sob. She put her hand to her mouth, then to her brow. 'As we were bringing her home she took a knife and stabbed my youngest brother – her own son! The blade pierced his heart. He died instantly. She turned upon my other brother – truly she would have murdered us all had she been able. We overpowered her, but she screamed incessantly and begged us to let her return. Eventually we did. We were faced with the choice of convicting her for infanticide, in which case she would have been executed, or letting her go back to the Plain of Imprisoned Souls, where she would eventually die anyway. She went back, had herself encased in metal once more and put back upon the Plain. None of us visited her again. She remains there still. That is, what is left of her remains sealed within its metal armature.'

'I am sorry,' said Leth in a murmur.

'I can never forgive her,' Lakewander asserted, her voice quavering. 'That is perhaps the worst part of it. Not only for the death of my brother, but for the terrible agonies she inflicted upon us all through her martyrdom. She declared that what she did was for our eventual good, yet the truth is she had no real thought for anyone. Not us, not herself. She was consumed by a belief, seduced by those who promulgated it. Like all such believers she became incapable of questioning or looking beyond it. She is gone now, but we must live with the memory of what she did: her own appalling suffering, and ours. I have tried, but I cannot find it within me to forgive her.' Lakewander turned her face to Leth. 'What kind of Creator can allow its people to suffer so?'

Perhaps a Creator who does not even know that he has created you, thought Leth, but he said nothing. He glanced up at the Orb of the Godworld which blazed with a fabulous intensity high overhead. He shook his head slowly, then looked back at Lakewander. 'What of your other brother, the one who survived?'

She smiled distantly, sorrowfully. 'He left us and became a wanderer and vagabond. He had been a great and noble spirit, a superb warrior, a young man greatly loved and who could inspire men and women alike effortlessly. He was to have been the next Protector, after the transition of our father. But the events with our mother and younger brother changed him. His mood grew dark, he drank and brawled and shut himself away – things formerly alien to his nature. And then he left us, without notice or farewell. From time to time we hear reports of him. He has travelled widely, if aimlessly. The last we heard was that he had taken up with a Noeticist named Urch-Malmain, who is said to have penetrated all the secrets of the workings of the mind. He claims the ability to rid the mind of its store of painful experiences and to replace them with more palatable memories.'

'An enviable talent,' commented Leth, and in his mind was the thought that he had heard the name of Urch-Malmain somewhere before.

'And a sinister one. Urch-Malmain takes away one's pain and substitutes for it fabrications of his own devising. Knowing what little I do of him, I see little to rejoice in there.'

'How does he achieve this?'

'Only he can tell you that, and I suspect he will not, even if you should find him. His methods are a closely guarded secret. It may be that he is a charlatan – many consider him so. Others deem him a diabolist of the blackest kind. I do not think my brother has fallen into good company.'

Leth was pensive; his thoughts shifted. From considering Urch-Malmain and his manipulation of memory, he found himself thinking suddenly of Orbus and the blue casket, of the mystery of Enchantment and its strange flickering lights in the night, of the Krai and their so-called gods, of the monstrous slooths that had attacked Enchantment's Edge, of Mawnie in her madness, of Grey Venger and the mysterious Legendary Child, of Fectur's betrayal and of his, Leth's, feeling that the ground had been wrenched from beneath him and that he was being pitched into madness.

And he thought of Issul.

'Lord?' Lakewander's voice penetrated his haze. She had moved to kneel close before him. 'Now it is *your* face that is filled with sorrow.'

He realized suddenly how afraid he was. For himself, for Issul, for the children. And for Enchantment's Edge. He did not know if it existed any more. He thought with horror of the feeling that had overcome him two nights before: *I do not even know if I am still alive!*

Leth gazed down into Lakewander's eyes. They were wide and limpid and pale blue-grey; her hand – he had not realized, but she had taken his in hers – her hand was warm, her touch soothing and tender. Her face was upturned to his, the lips slightly parted, and a look of such concern . . . How he wanted to take her in his arms, to feel her consoling lips upon his, her warm body against him, making him forget. How he wanted her, needed her, as she must need him also. To love

each other here, in delirious oblivion upon the soft grass. To
forget . . .

Lakewander whispered, 'I am here, Lord.'

Leth put his hand to her cheek. He recalled her naked in his
bedchamber, her sinuous warmth against him, her lips, the way
she had held him. He moved, to lower his lips to hers.

He hesitated – and tore his gaze away.

Issul, I will not forget! Not even for an instant!

He stood, abruptly, releasing Lakewander's hand, and walked to
the side of the road.

'I wish only to help you,' Lakewander said.

Leth turned around. She was kneeling upon the grass, watching
him, her look both reproachful and consoling.

'I know. I am sorry.'

'There is a storm raging within you.'

'I am not alone in that,' Leth said. He was uncomfortable with
himself, knowing both that he had spurned her when she, as much
as he, was in need of the warmth and comfort that only another
human being could provide, and that he had also been barely a
breath away from succumbing to her. 'Come, let us eat now and
be on our way.'

III

A short time later they came upon the Sufferer at the side of the road.
This time Leth paid him little heed, apart from wrinkling his nostrils
slightly as the smell of the man reached him. Then he stopped and
looked back. Was he becoming so hardened and cynical? He slid
from Swiftwind's back and approached the crouched and bound
man. 'Sir, just say the word and I will release you now from this
bondage.'

The man had grown still and tense at Leth's approach. His head
was cocked slightly, though he could not look up into Leth's face.
He spat, but such was his posture that the spittle merely caught in a
long liquid filament upon one of his knees. 'Scoundrel! Begone!'

Leth returned to his horse. Lakewander made no comment as he came alongside her and for some time they rode in silence. Eventually Leth said, 'There are ghostly creatures in the walls of your home. Two nights ago one of them spoke to me.'

'The Protectors. Yes.'

'How many dwell there?'

'I don't know. Many. Since the first days. They *are* Orbia, Swordbearer. Without them Orbia could not be. You should know that.'

'I know nothing. I am not who you believe me to be.'

Lakewander gave no reply. Leth said, 'In my own domain I have devoted much of my life to trying to understand the nature of gods. I have argued that belief must never become a permanent substitute for true knowledge. I have declared, as my illustrious forebears have declared before me, that those beings which many of our kind worship as gods are not gods; that we truly know nothing of them, not even that they exist in any real form, yet we have attributed to them the characteristics and personalities of deities. And now I find myself here, awaited by you and your people, a deity in your eyes. You believe me so, and I know I am not, yet I possess the qualities and abilities that you expect your god to possess. Which of us, then, is right?'

'Can it be only one or the other?' Lakewander asked.

'Oh yes. I know what I am. But I know, too, that if I so chose, I could masquerade among your kind as the god you believe and wish me to be. I could demand tribute, all the privileges of a deity. I would be false, but it would not matter to you.'

'Were you false, we would know.'

'Because I could not bear the Orbsword?' Leth shook his head in vehement dismissal. 'That is not enough. I bear it, and do not know how. But I say to you again, I am no god.'

Lakewander pursed her lips in contemplation. 'The end will be the same, no matter what. You bear the sword, therefore you are able to slay Ascaria.'

'And if I fail?'

'If you fail, Ascaria wins. The end comes upon us.'

A sudden thought struck Leth. 'You spoke earlier of your Creator. Do you know Orbus?'

'Orbus? What is that?'

'Beyond the rune through which I stepped there is a domain formerly occupied by . . . a god. I can find no other word for him. I spoke with him many times. He –' he hesitated, almost stricken by what he was about to reveal, then changed tack. 'Have you, any of you, been there?'

Lakewander was curious. 'Beyond the Sign? Of course not. How could we?' She waited, and when Leth said nothing, prompted him. 'Tell me of it.'

'Without Orbus it is a terrible, silent place,' Leth said. 'The only sound is the rush of your own blood through your veins, the storm of your breathing, the rhythmic deafening thunder of your own heart.'

'And Orbus? What of he?'

'Orbus is the place he occupies,' said Leth, and looked slowly around him. 'Do not ask me to explain it. He is this place also. And yet he has gone.'

'How can I leave myself?'

It had been Orbus's question to him at their last meeting. But he had also said that, had Leth come a few moments later, he would not have found him. And it had truly been only minutes later that Jace had inadvertently opened the casket lid and cast them all into the blue domain.

And Orbus had not been there.

Where had he gone?

A few nights earlier, Leth recalled vividly, he had lain alone and sleepless upon his bed – the bed he normally shared with Issul – in their chamber in the Palace of Orbia. And he had seen, he was *sure* he had seen Orbus, standing in a shadowed corner of the room. It had been only for an instant, and then Orbus's voice, husky and half-whispered, *'Ah, so close . . .'*

But if Orbus had put himself outside the casket, outside the Orb, outside *himself*, in that moment, could he not have done it again? Was that where he was now, in Enchantment's Edge? To what end? And why did he not return? He must surely know that Leth was not there.

Leth was unaware of how closely Lakewander had been observing him.

'The storm rages unchecked,' she said in a soft voice.

He turned to her with a fraught expression, his eyes wide and feverish. 'Has Orbus been here? Does he know of you?'

'We have not seen him, but perhaps we would not know. Is he our Creator?'

'He would deny that he is. And yet, in a sense, he must be. Yet he has abandoned this world, and he has left me here and I do not know why.'

'To help us,' said Lakewander. 'That is why you have come, Lord Swordbearer. You are his representative.'

Leth felt cast down, shaking his head. 'No. No. There is too much here that I cannot comprehend.'

'We need you. Is that not reason enough to be here?'

'My people need me; my children.'

'More than we, who will be destroyed without you?'

'As greatly. It is Orbus who should be here, not I.'

'Our Creator should be able to intervene directly on our behalf? Why should that be? Is that not an assumption based on belief, or hope, or desperation, rather than knowledge, which you profess to seek?'

Leth recalled how Orbus had claimed to have inklings of life or consciousness within himself, but knew nothing of its form or nature, nor of the scope or limits of his world. It had grown as he had grown, as he himself had become more than the prison in which he had been incarcerated.

'Is it not so?' enquired Lakewander again.

'You are right, yes. You have exposed the flaw in my reasoning. Yet only a short while ago you were asking what kind of Creator could allow such suffering in those he had created?'

'Yes, I asked, but it was not in expectation of an answer. But tell me, Swordbearer, if you have indeed met with our Creator, this Orbus, what kind of creature is he? Is he truly so indifferent to our plight?'

'He is a being,' said Leth after long moments of thought, 'who finds himself almost as mystified by his existence as you are by yours. Or indeed, as I am by mine. And he is not indifferent. The truth is, he simply is not aware that you exist.'

Lakewander gave a bitter smile. 'Ah well, much is thus explained. And he has sent you, even if he is unaware of it.'

Leth was about to protest again, but something caught his attention. He sat up abruptly in the saddle. 'What is that sound?'

'I hear nothing.'

'Nothing?'

She shook her head.

Leth glanced about him, then shrugged. 'The breeze passing through the trees.'

'There is no breeze, Lord.'

'Then it was my imagination.'

'Or a sound intended for your ears alone?'

Leth said nothing. There was silence now, but for the clump of their horses' hooves upon the way, and the low creak and jingle of harness. But he had heard something that had sounded like a voice calling from far away. An ethereal sound, that had repeated his name twice: 'Leth! Leth!'

And he had thought then that the voice sounded within him. It had faded, and then he had heard: *'Be strong, Leth. I am seeking you.'*

Whether it had come from within him or from somewhere beyond was of little account. But Leth had recognized the voice. It was that of Orbus.

IV

Soon they began to pass the metal statues that housed the imprisoned Souls, living and dead. Lakewander rode slowly between them, her head bowed. Leth eyed them uneasily, and felt relief that their occupants emitted no sound. He and Lakewander broke out upon the dust-covered plain. He cast his gaze far and wide, taking in the multitude of blank, faceless metal figures, wondering morbidly which one housed the bones of Lakewander's mother.

In due course they left the plain and began the laborious ascent of the winding stony path towards the crest of the gleaming ridge. Leth turned and looked back from time to time, seeing the panorama of the eerie plain and the distant forest spread beneath him, the red-toned ridge arcing away for as far as he could see. Well beyond the forest misty blue mountains rose in dramatic tiers and a silver ribbon of distant water glittered in the bright Orblight.

At length they halted before the stone slab-bridge. Below them the river foamed and thrashed, silent at the foot of the gorge. The entrance to the cavern which led down to the Shore of Nothing gaped darkly on the other side of the bridge.

Lakewander took a breath and hailed the Bridgekeeper, who was nowhere in evidence. Her voice cracked the silence of the place, then was gone. She called again, then for the third time, more loudly: 'Bridgekeeper, this is tiresome. It is I, Lakewander, wishing to cross with my companion of yesterday. Surely you know my voice, even if you cannot see me; and you know that I am alert to your wiles. So show yourself now if you wish to collect your toll, otherwise I have declared my presence the statutory three times and will cross accordingly without payment. So states the Law!'

Nothing moved; there was no sound.

Lakewander frowned and looked about her. 'This is curious. I do not like it.'

She made to dismount. 'Remain here, Swordbearer. Be alert. Something is not right.'

Drawing her sword she moved with cautious steps to the stone bridge. 'Bridgekeeper!'

Still no response. Lakewander stepped onto the great stone slab high above the rushing water. Leth scanned the surrounding slopes. To his right the ascent was almost sheer fissured rock, with stunted pines sprouting wherever they could find a foothold in the thin dark soil that clung between the crags. On the other side the land fell away steeply, with more pines thrusting from shale and loose, rotten earth. Leth could see short lengths of the stony path winding down between the trees, and the Plain of Imprisoned Souls below. Beyond the bridge the red-toned cliff reared towards the sky; a narrow curving ledge ran off to either side of the cavern mouth. On the right it vanished around the shoulder of the bluff; to the left it climbed into a deep cleft in the rock.

Leth listened: all was totally silent. In his own land such silence would have alerted him, for it was unnatural, as though all of nature held its breath, awaiting something. But here it signalled nothing out of the ordinary.

Lakewander crossed the bridge. She moved up to the cavern maw and peered in. 'Bridgekeeper?'

Her voice was hollow in the gloom. She stepped inside, was swallowed by the darkness. Leth waited, growing tense. Lakewander reappeared, shaking her head, mystified. 'He has gone.'

From around the bluff a few yards to Lakewander's left two men appeared.

'Lakewander!' Leth called, and nodded towards the newcomers. Lakewander swung around to face them, her sword held before her.

The two men wore makeshift shirts of dark mail and leather trews and undershirts. Upon their heads were dented iron helmets with leather ear- and neck-flaps. One gripped a huge two-handed sword before him. He was a big, burly fellow, aged perhaps twenty-five years, with mean, glittering eyes and a coarse dark beard. His companion, only marginally smaller of build, and of a no less menacing aspect, was older by about five years, bushily bearded, and toted a stained and battered battle-axe.

As Lakewander adopted a defensive stance a sound behind her caused her to glance over her shoulder. Two more men approached, similarly garbed and accoutred. From their postures and expressions she was in no doubt that their intentions fell short of honourable.

From Leth's rear came the sound of hooves upon the stony path. He twisted in the saddle. Six more men approached up the track. Four of them were on horseback; three held crossbows aimed his way.

He calculated swiftly that he might wheel and charge, and stand a chance of smashing through them. He would be dependent upon his armour to deflect, or at least stop their bolts, but the advantage of height was his. But against such odds he had little chance of sustaining a fight – he could possibly strike down two, and then flee. But Lakewander would be left at their mercy.

He turned his head back to Lakewander. She was half-crouched before the cavern mouth, swinging her blade from side to side. Her eyes were bright and wild. No one had spoken a word, but she was in no doubt that she faced the fight of her life.

In a loud, clear voice Leth said, 'Gentlemen, greetings. Can we be of assistance to you?'

The men at Leth's back smirked and grinned and muttered amongst themselves, their eyes going for the most part beyond Leth to the sight of Lakewander before the cave mouth. Then one of them – a tall, long-haired fellow, aged perhaps thirty, with a clean-shaven jaw, thin dark moustache, notably pale skin and piercing blue eyes – spoke. He was better-garbed than the others, in a dusty red shirt, leather trousers and boots, long leather gauntlets, and a long damask cloak over a mail hauberk and jupon. His voice was surprisingly rich and plummy, the words clearly enunciated and resonant. 'Yes, you may, sir. You can lay down your arms and thus spare us the inconvenience of having to take them from you.'

Leth had not yet drawn the Orbsword. His hand slid now to its jewelled hilt. 'I think, under the circumstances, we might be ill-advised to comply with that request.'

'Ah,' said the pale man in a tone of regret, 'that is a pity. Still, if that is your choice, so be it.'

His eyes went beyond Leth and he gave a single nod. Leth turned. A movement on the cliff above Lakewander caught his eye.

He cried out a warning – too late. A slender loop of rope snaked down, dropping over Lakewander's head and draping itself about her shoulders. Then it was jerked taut, snapping tight around Lakewander's neck. Two burly men hauled from the rocks overhead, hoisting her from her feet. Her sword fell from her grasp. She swung before the cavern entrance, kicking and twisting, her hands grasping frantically at the murderous noose about her throat.

'Throw down your sword, warrior,' came a politely couched command from behind Leth, 'and she will be spared. At least for now.'

If he spurred Swiftwind hard across the bridge, Leth could cut Lakewander down quickly. But he lacked space to manoeuvre the stallion on the other side. He would be overcome with no great effort, and a single slip of the stallion's hooves could have him pitched headlong into the gorge.

Grinding his teeth, Leth slid from the saddle and drew free the Orbsword from its scabbard. The sight of the glowing blade drew gasps and murmurs from the men before him.

'I say, that *is* impressive!' said the pale fellow, who was plainly the leader of this brigand band. Then he shook his head, tutting with tongue against teeth. 'But I'm sorry, it'll do you no good whatsoever. If you don't lay it down immediately, then I don't tell my dear friends over there to lower your comely companion. And I'm afraid she will be strangled. So sad; and unnecessary. Truly.'

'Lower her now, and I will lay it down,' declared Leth.

'Oh, I see, it's haggling time,' drawled the pale man. He took in an exaggerated breath between his teeth. 'Well now, let me see. There is, quite plainly, limited time in which to haggle. And I think there is little doubt that I have the upper hand. Still, if it entertains you, I see no reason to refuse. But mark you, if you fail to put down your blade immediately she will be hauled high once more, and this time she will not touch earth again as long as a single breath remains in her body. Is that clearly understood?'

Leth nodded once, his gall rising, knowing that he was trapped. The outlaw leader gestured with a gauntletted finger to the men over the cavern. They paid out the rope.

Lakewander fell heavily to her knees, tearing at the rope that throttled her and gulping in great draughts of air. The outlaw inclined his head toward Leth and wagged one finger towards the ground. Reluctantly Leth laid the Orbsword at his feet.

'Daggers also, and any other weapon you carry. And then step back.'

Leth complied. Two of the outlaws, one rotund and unnaturally short, the other a gangling, surly youth with a pockmarked face, ran forward. The youth held Leth's arms behind him while his companion bound his wrists roughly. At the cave entrance Lakewander was likewise trussed.

The leader had dismounted meanwhile and sauntered forward to stare Leth in the eye. 'So, what have we here? An unusual catch, so it strikes me.' His gaze passed appraisingly over Leth's armour, then flicked to the Orbsword lying naked at his feet. He spoke over his shoulder. 'Take them both into the cave until I have decided what to do with them.'

Leth was hustled across the bridge and made to sit with his back against the cavern wall. Lakewander was placed opposite him. The outlaws were going through their saddlepacks. The rotund fellow who had bound Leth's wrists bent to lift the Orbsword. To Leth's surprise the man, though plainly no weakling, had difficulty raising the weapon from the ground. He swore and stood back, scratching his head and scowling, then set to again. His companions laughed and taunted him as he struggled red-faced to carry the blade.

'Tag, you are getting feeble in your old age!'

'Like an old woman!'

'Ha-ha! Your muscle has all turned to fat!'

The man called Tag set the sword down again. 'By my father's balls, I have never known anything like this. You try, Derman, if you think you can do better.'

A tall, heavily-built barbarian of a man stepped forward with a swagger. He bent and grasped the sword-hilt in one hand. His sarcastic sneer vanished as he made to lift it. Evidently it was far heavier than he had thought. He bent, braced himself and tried again. Two-handed he managed to raise the sword from the ground, but was visibly borne down by its weight.

The brigand leader looked on with interest. In one gauntleted hand he held the ornate sapphire helm that Leth had attached behind his saddle. He studied it carefully. His gaze flickered across the gorge to Leth. He ordered Derman to bring the sword, and crossed the bridge, swinging the helm at his side. Derman staggered behind him, cradling the Orbsword in his arm-crooks, his legs bent, taking little steps, his cheeks puffing and eyes bulging as if he was carrying a load twice his own weight. He let the blade fall with a clang before the cavern entrance.

The outlaws were silent now, all eyeing the glowing rose blade doubtfully. The leader squatted before Leth. 'Now this is interesting. Your helm, and I'll warrant this too –' he leaned forward and flicked Leth's gorget with the back of his middle finger, bringing forth an almost musical metallic sound '– are far less weighty than they appear. Yet your sword weighs as much as ten of its normal kind. And you carried it without effort. So . . . what do we have here?'

'I am Leth,' said Leth. 'My companion is Lakewander. We are travellers, nothing more. The sword and armour I came upon more or less by chance. I can tell you nothing more about them.'

The brigand leader leaned away from Leth and casually let fly with one forearm, smashing the back of his fist hard into Lakewander's face. Her head jerked back and hammered against the rock behind her. Her eyes rolled; blood dribbled from her mouth. She was knocked almost senseless.

'Bastard!' yelled Leth, straining against his bonds.

'Now, let's start again, shall we?' said the brigand leader. 'I'll warrant that you and your pretty companion will fetch a handsome price in the slave-market. Your armour and this sword may well be worth more, to the right buyer. But first I need to be sure that I know all I need to know about you. Do you understand?'

'Hey, Harg, we're going to get to sample her before we sell her, aren't we?' demanded one of the men. 'Ascertain the quality of the goods, so to speak?'

'You will all get your rewards,' replied the leader, Harg, without taking his eyes from Leth.

'Well, don't mess her up too much, then,' said Derman, with a smirk. 'I like my women in good condition.'

The others sniggered. Through clenched teeth Leth said, 'Have you no honour?'

Harg eyed him mockingly. 'Honour? Why, of course not. Perish the concept.'

'I yielded to you that she might be saved.'

'How chivalrous. How foolish.' Harg rose to his feet. 'Now, we are going to remove your armour. To do so we must untie your hands. Do not try anything foolish. There will be blades at your companion's throat as well as your own.'

Harg stepped back, folding his arms upon his chest. Two men dragged Leth roughly to his feet. They unbound his hands, then began to work upon the straps of his armour. Leth stood helplessly, racking his brains for a way out.

His gorget, breasplate, vambraces and shoulder-guards were removed. Lakewander, slumped against the rock, opened her eyes. Seeing Leth with his hands free, she cried out, 'Swordbearer, call the sword! Summon it to you!'

Leth stared at her, half-stupefied.

'Call it!' she cried. 'It will come!'

Something – could it have been a memory? – stirred within Leth. He pushed away one of the brigands working at his armour, and simultaneously reached out a hand. 'Orbsword, *to me!*'

The glowing blade, lying in the bright Orb-light outside the cave entrance, suddenly rose as if lifted by an invisible hand. The outlaws gasped; the sword flew at an arrow's speed straight into Leth's open grasp.

The outlaws fell back, reaching for their own weapons.

Leth stepped towards Lakewander. Two men knelt with blades at her throat; most of the others had formed a semi-circle around Leth, out of reach of his sword.

'The sword is enchanted!' Leth warned, aware of their reluctance to approach its eldritch light, and wondering whether he had any chance at all of fighting his way free, even with the Sword of the Orb. 'Let her go!'

The two brigands holding Lakewander looked with some lack of certainty to Harg. He stood near the entrance, seemingly unperturbed, the fingers and thumb of one hand stroking his jaw.

'Most impressive,' he said. 'But wait.'

He turned and strode without hurry from the cavern, disappearing momentarily from Leth's view. He came back with two of his men. All three carried loaded crossbows. The two thugs knelt and took aim at Lakewander. Harg stood a few paces in front of Leth, the crossbow braced against his hip, aimed at Leth's middle.

'You wear only a linen shirt. I'll wager that neither that nor your magic sword will stop this bolt. And should they do so, can you move swiftly enough to prevent these other deadly bolts piercing your lovely companion's fair breast? Well, let us see. I will count to three. If on the third count your pretty pink longsword is not lying upon the ground again, beyond your reach, bolts, I'm afraid, will speed towards their destinations. And, oh, what a mess will be left when their work is done.' He smiled, almost charmingly, and lazily scratched his nose. 'Are we ready, then? One . . .'

Leth knew he could not defy the bolts. Nor, indeed, was he swift or skilled enough to deal with so many foes. Yet what was his and Lakewander's fate if he did not act now? She to be raped by these fiends; both of them to be sold into slavery. Was it not preferable to die now, taking as many brigands as he could with him?

And abandon Galry and Jace to their unknown fate?

'Two . . .'

'Do not yield, Swordbearer!'

Leth glanced across at Lakewander. She was glaring at him, her eyes like bright steel. 'Do not give in!'

He looked back at Harg, who met his gaze and was plainly deriving amusement from the conflict.

If I am alive at least I have hope, thought Leth. *But if I fight even life will be taken from me. My children will be alone.*

'Three. Time's up, I'm afraid.'

Leth bent and quickly laid the Sword of the Orb upon the cavern floor. He stepped back. Lakewander sagged back against the rock wall and closed her eyes.

'Good. I think that was the right decision,' Harg said. 'Now, stay well back, and please do not attempt to call it back to you. Your blade may be well-trained and obedient, but I will waste no more time on such charades.' He signalled to the surly youth. 'Bind his wrists again.'

The youth leapt forward to comply. A dark shape loomed at the cavern mouth, blocking the light from outside. Two massive hands reached into the cave and grasped a pair of brigands by the backs of their mail shirts, lifted them, crushed their heads against the stone ceiling, and let them drop. Then the Bridgekeeper bent and punched hard into the pack of astonished men, catching one full in the chest.

Leth reacted. He dived for his sword, grabbed it and rolled towards Lakewander. The man the Bridgekeeper had punched flew past him, travelling backwards, and disappeared with a cry over the lip of the steps leading down to the Shore of Nothing.

Leth swung with the Orbsword, slicing into the neck of the first of Lakewander's guards. Without pausing he struck at the other. The man deflected his first blow. Leth lunged again. The brigand made to parry his blow, but Lakewander kicked upwards, knocking his sword-arm high and leaving him wide open. The Orbsword passed through his throat. He staggered back, sucking hopelessly for air, his hands going to the bloody wound, his legs folding beneath him.

The remaining outlaws were in total disarray as they struggled to deal with their new assailant. The Bridgekeeper reached in, scooped Tag from the cavern and tossed him over his massive shoulder into the river gorge. Leth's sword pierced another's back. The remaining men fled, out of the cave and across the stone bridge, with the Bridgekeeper stomping along behind them, loudly castigating the ground with his cudgel.

Leth freed Lakewander of her bonds. She stood before him, and to his surprise her bloodied lips were drawn back in anger, her eyes ablaze. She brought back her arm and struck him across the face with her open palm, so hard that he staggered. He reeled back, his cheek exploding with pain, tears starting involuntarily to his eyes.

'You yielded!' accused Lakewander, radiating her fury. 'Twice you yielded to them!'

'To save you!'

'Save me? Swordbearer, I am not important! You could have broken through and ridden away, while you were still on Swiftwind. Their crossbow-bolts would scarcely have dented your armour. Instead you stayed, and almost died.'

'I reasoned that while we lived we had hope. I was not prepared to leave you to swing upon that rope.'

'Are you sure that is your reason?'

'What do you mean?'

'Were you, rather, not hoping that they would kill you? That by such means you might fly free of our world and return to your own?'

'That is absurd.'

'Is it?'

Leth stared at her. Her gaze faltered. He wondered, had she just revealed something that she would rather have not? 'Lakewander, is this how it is? Will death return me to my own land?'

Lakewander ran her hands through her long fair hair. 'Would you go, without having found what you are seeking here?'

She turned and walked back into the cavern. She picked up her sword and scabbard from the floor and buckled them about her waist again. Leth was angry and confused. He still gripped the Orbsword in one hand. He looked at it, disquieted. Though Lakewander had prompted him to call the blade, he had known instantly, somewhere deep within himself, that he *could* summon it. And when it flew to him it had been the most natural thing, comfortable, reassuring and familiar in his grasp.

I have been here before!

Lakewander was at his side again. 'It is coming back, isn't it, Lord?'

He met her gaze, but would not answer.

The Bridgekeeper's great shadow fell across them both. 'Well, that is a pity,' he said, a trifle breathless. 'Some of them got away.'

He surveyed the bodies around him with a doleful gaze, then scratched his belly, sniffed, and wiped his fleshy bulb of a nose with the back of one thick, hirsute wrist. He peered blinking into the cave, then turned and tramped to the lip of the gorge and stared down. 'Hmmm. I think I rather got carried away. I wasted one. Still, no matter. There are plenty here.'

'What of Harg?' enquired Lakewander.

Leth sheathed the Orbsword. 'He was the first to make himself scarce.'

'Yes, I should have guessed.'

'He is no run-of-the-mill brigand, this Harg. He speaks and bears himself like a man both educated and refined.'

Lakewander gave a nod, testing the inside of her bruised lip with her tongue. 'Count Drurwan Harg was a notable of our community before Ascaria took the city. He was absent when the city fell – it is not known where. But when he returned he was a changed man, black-hearted and iniquitous. He took to a life of banditry and has sustained himself by such means ever since.'

'He did not seem to know you.'

'He does not, though both my parents were known to him.'

From within the cave the Bridgekeeper's stentorian voice boomed contentedly, 'Oh yes, there's plenty here. They left two of their horses, too.'

He re-emerged and stood over Lakewander and Leth, weighing them with a reproachful eye. 'Now, Lakewander, I think there is something to be settled here, is there not? What of you and your warrior friend? I think you crossed my bridge without paying the toll.'

'Indeed we did, Bridgekeeper. But I hailed you loudly the statutory three times.'

'I did not hear you.'

'You were elsewhere. That is not my fault. The Law states that —'

'I did not hear you,' repeated the Bridgekeeper crisply.

Lakewander stood defiant before him. 'Just where were you, Bridgekeeper?'

'I was hiding. I saw these ruffians approaching from some distance away. I sensed they were up to no good, and concealed myself in the rocks yonder.'

'I see. And presumably they made no attempt to hail you, or announce themselves in any way?'

'They came across the bridge as if they owned it. They entered my cave. I was about to rush out and seize them when one, still upon the path, spotted you at the foot of the ridge. Their leader declared that they would wait here in ambush. So I thought I would remain where I was and see what transpired.'

Lakewander nodded to herself. 'You hid yourself where? Just there?'

She pointed.

'No. In that clump of boulders, over there. You see, it provides good cover, but there is a gap between two of the rocks which gives a view directly onto the bridge, the path before it and the area around my cave.'

'And what did you have around your head, Bridgekeeper?'

'Around my head? Why, nothing? Why do you ask?'

'You must have had something. Something thick and tightly

bound, covering your ears. Otherwise, how could you possibly have failed to hear my call?'

'Ah. I see what you mean.' The Bridgekeeper glanced at Leth, suddenly sheepish, and then at his own large toes. 'Yes . . . umm . . .'

'And you have already stated that you heard Count Harg declaring his intentions.'

The Bridgekeeper found something to interest him upon the wooded slopes beyond the gorge.

'Bridgekeeper, I think you have done well today. Certainly you have saved our lives, and we are grateful. The Law allows that you may take those who fail to announce themselves or pay the toll in the prescribed manner. The Law allocates to you their belongings also. It does not permit that you supplement your gains through subterfuge or prevarication. Is that not so?'

'Of course, Lakewander,' said the Bridgekeeper. 'Do forgive me. It is the excitement. I did hear you; of course I did. But it had slipped my mind, with all the thunderous goings on!'

He eased his bulk past Leth and Lakewander and began dragging bodies towards the back of his cave. 'It's quite a nice catch, actually. The best I've had in many a year, if the truth be known.'

Lakewander nodded. 'I don't doubt it.'

'Ooh, look at this! I think these two are still alive. Marvellous! I'll have someone to listen to my stories!'

Leth peered into the gloom. 'What does he do with them?'

'Don't ask,' replied Lakewander sharply. 'And do not try to intervene.'

The Bridgekeeper's low voice sounded again from the depths. 'Lakewander, will you and your brave warrior friend not stay and sup with me awhile? I can make a delicious fricassee, or perhaps a broth or potage with a rather splendid numbles, or pasty with black sauce. It will be such fun, and I have some wonderful stories to tell you.'

'You are kind, but I regret that we cannot. We have delayed too much already.'

'Ah, that is a pity.' He came forward again. 'Are you descending to the Shore again?'

'We are. Oh, Bridgekeeper, I must check amongst the baggage. Harg's men took our saddlepacks and emptied our pockets.'

'Very well, Lakewander.'

She turned to Leth. 'Don your armour, Swordbearer. I am sending the horses back, as they cannot accompany us any further. They will return to Orbia.'

The Bridgekeeper watched her with a lugubrious eye. 'Are you sure you cannot stay? Just for a little while?'

'Not a moment longer. I will check the baggage and we will be gone.'

NINE

I

'From here on nothing is known,' Lakewander said, her voice low and edged with dour intensity.

Leth looked out along the line of the beach but could make out little of what lay before him; the strangely coloured shingle and sand threw up a distorting haze. It glimmered and teased, and perplexed his vision. He stepped down onto the beach, his face – and pride – still stinging from the harsh slap Lakewander had landed him across his cheek, and began to walk.

As far as possible he kept his gaze straight ahead, or to the right and the gleaming fleshlike cliff that stretched to the horizon. To his left lay the Nothing, detestable, implacable, the End of the World. He could not bear to look upon it. To his mind seeing it again was to bestow it with ever greater power, unleashing the beast of the void that struggled and swelled within him. The temptation was present, even so, to look again, just to try and be sure, to grasp the impossible.

Lakewander, behind him, had put one hand upon his shoulder as he started off. 'How do you feel?' she asked.

'So far I believe I am unaffected. And you?'

'I am all right.'

'Lakewander, what are we likely to find beyond the beach?'

'I have told you, I do not know.'

'Yet you know that Ascaria dwells there.'

'Somewhere. I know only that the World's Pain is our guide.'

Leth felt a twinge of irritation. He was reluctant to admit to the trepidation that gripped him, but what he was experiencing here – and had been experiencing since the moment he became stranded in Orbus's world – was beyond his ken. Nothing in his previous life had prepared him for it. Hence he relied upon Lakewander, and found her wanting.

The way ahead of him, silent and dreadful, was becoming a blur, a wash of strangely shifting colour. He blinked and narrowed his eyes, trying to search out details, to rest his gaze upon something familiar. He could no longer see the gleaming cliff. He turned his eyes skyward: the Orb of the Godworld was a dull, filtered glow, reddish as though seen through dense bloodstained glass. But ahead in the sky was a tiny pinpoint, the sharp glitter of the World's Pain.

Lakewander's hand gripped him fiercely. 'Everything depends upon this!'

He felt suddenly an irrational surge of anger. She did not need to tell him such a thing, as though he were a fool! As though he were not aware! Glowering, he twisted his neck to look at her. To his surprise there were tears in her eyes, wet trails down her pale cheeks. He was consumed by a welter of emotion. What was wrong with her? And then his heart fell – he was filled suddenly with a sense of weariness and despair – for behind Lakewander towered the bluff and the rocks from which they had just set out. They were no more than fifteen paces away, yet to Leth it seemed that he had been trudging this terminal beach for long minutes.

'We have been nowhere!'

His disappointment bore him down, an intolerable weight. Anger, bewilderment, weariness, despair. He lacked the heart to carry on.

'Keep your eyes ahead, Swordbearer! Always, always ahead!'

He pressed his gaze to the fore again, but his feet were heavy in the soft, dragging sand, and he ached, in his muscles, in his bones, so heavy. He could not remember why he had come here, and had no inclination, no spirit, to go any further. Into his mind came an image of the Death Abyss.

'Why have you stopped?'

Leth looked down at himself, realizing that he had ceased walking. But again he felt nettled that she should ask such a question of him. He lifted an arm and twisted to break her grip upon him.

'No, Swordbearer! This is the beginning! This is how it works upon you, to rob you of your mind and destroy your will! Fight it! Fight it or we are lost!'

He did not care if they were lost. He had no desire to fight anything. He wanted perhaps to be rid of her. She irked him so, with her tears and constant cajolings, her unsightly mouth. He should have left her to Harg. That much was plain. The outlaw knew what he was about. Lakewander had told him that as long as she remained close by him, preferably in physical contact, she believed she could escape, or at least survive, the most severe of the effects of the beach. She did not explain why she thought this, and Leth no longer bothered to ask. But it amused him now that she should place such faith in him, when he had no interest in doing anything at all. And he wondered whether he should kill her.

'The sword! Draw the sword!'

There was an urgency in her voice, and Leth wondered why she was prompting him to commit the very act that would bring about her end. He thought again of the Death Abyss, without knowing what it was. His thoughts were forming in a random stream. What was happening here?

'Do it, Swordbearer! Now! Take it out!'

He was seated on his buttocks upon the sand, the colours crawling all around and over him like a plague of brilliant insects, a swarm of veils, light gems that merged and broke and clotted, swirled, exploded silently and reformed. He gasped in a great lungful of iridescent air. Lakewander was barely visible, a shifting shape among the colours, and his whole body sang with the most delicious sensation of glowing, growing, tingling, aching.

'*Swordbearer!*'

With a supreme effort of will he dragged his hand through the deliriously heavy haze, and fumbled for then found the jewelled hilt of the Orbsword. He fell back as he drew it free and its light cut through the beach-veils, the coruscating, efflorescent swarms. He heard Lakewander cry out. She was upon her knees, her lips pressed to the flat of the glowing blade, her hands upon him, the brilliant colours bursting from the moist pores of her skin, and he had known nothing like this. Poignant emotion washed over and through him, leaving sleek trails; the sky and earth vivid and blindingly bright, merging into one, merging into him. He lifted himself, his jaw dropping open as a great moan escaped him. The Orbsword was drawing him higher, part of him now, and the intensity of sensation was more pleasurable than he could ever have imagined, vermicules of pleasure silken and blissful all over him, and Lakewander, they were one, the Orb-light pulsing and penetrating, the sand no longer beneath him, her warm lips upon him and he knew what she had done and even in the ecstasy and terror of it all he felt bruised and betrayed, deeply, bitterly betrayed, and questioning, sure of nothing, trailing the Orb-light, incapable of anything but . . . the cries drifting from his throat.

'*Orbus! Orbus!*'

He had heard the god's voice, and yet now here he was. Where? A man in chains against the sky, looking down, and so far below they struggled and merged and broke free again, understanding nothing, and he knew their pain and their uncertainty, and he took it, deep into himself, transforming it, and the light so intense, so intense.

'*Orbus!*'

The Death Abyss cut through the world in a jagged tear, far, far below. And one day he could take no more and he screamed out, bursting free of the chains after so long, and, wingless, descending.

And he fell and fell and fell . . .

Three tall warriors of grim and saturnine aspect tramped forward and surveyed the body where it had fallen. They were virtually identical in face and form, clad in half-armour of gleaming black, carrying curved, wide-bladed swords at their belts, and their skin held an unusual blue-grey pallor.

A fourth warrior was seated on a horse close by. He spoke in a clipped, guttural sibilance. 'Bring him.'

Together they half-carried, half-dragged Leth's limp form. They took him along a steep trail leading up the lee of a tall, flat-topped basalt upthrust to a high tower of dun stone that rose abruptly against the sky and gazed out over the lip of the Death Abyss.

II

The twisted man limped forward with an awkward slewing gait, popping a crunchy sweetmeat into his mouth, and gazed down at Leth where he lay senseless upon a well-scrubbed tabletop. Leth's eyelids flickered. The twisted man prodded his ribs with the handle of a spoon. Leth half-opened his eyes.

The twisted man smiled a crooked smile. 'Ah, good, you are awake. Be careful how you rise, now. Don't tumble from the table and harm yourself.'

He dragged himself away and sat in a commodious carved chair, upholstered in orange velvet, set before a blazing hearth. Leth gingerly eased himself into a sitting position, his head pounding, his vision a blur. 'What happened?'

The twisted man gave a throaty chuckle. 'You had rather a nasty fall.'

He reached out with his good arm and took another sweetmeat from a silver tray beside him. His eyes on Leth, he placed it upon his tongue and began to chew.

Leth peered at him through wincing eyes. 'Where am I?'

'You are here, with myself and my beautiful spouse, in our home, the Tower of Glancing Memory. Here, let me be of assistance. Take some water.'

Leth, still slumped upon the table, propped himself against the wall at his back. He watched as his host poured clear water into a goblet and brought it over. Leth saw a man in his young middle-age, of average height, garbed in a long robe of sleek, dark purple material bound at the waist with a deep green cummerbund. His body was somewhat bent and crooked: the upper portion inclined forward and skewed to the right side, the pelvis thrust out leftwards. Leth could not see his feet, but judged from his dragging, rolling gait that he was club-footed or at least had one leg significantly shorter than the other. The twisted man's left shoulder was high and hunched, the left arm extending only as far as the waist and ending in a shrivelled fingerless hand which was clutched in a gnarled ball, by all appearances rigid. He was spare and awkward of build. His head was long, with a thin straight nose. Arsenical shadows had gathered about his eyes, supplemented by heavy sacks of drooping flesh. His gaze, no matter his solicitous manner, was distant and held little warmth. The mouth was formed of loose, fleshy red lips, the lower one slightly protruding, tight and downturned at the corners, set above a short, stubbly chin. Thin dark long hair was oiled close upon his crown.

He placed the cool goblet on the table a little way from Leth. 'This will help. And eat if you wish, though I suspect you may prefer to wait awhile.'

Leth took a sip, grateful for the cold bright water. 'I am sorry, I remember almost nothing. Can I ask who you are, and how I come to be here?'

'Aha!' replied the man, backing away. He gave a small flourish of his good hand. 'Well, it is hardly surprising that your memory fails you. You came here via the Shore of Nothing, after all. It is a rare man who can survive such a journey. As for your other question, I am Urch-Malmain.'

It seemed to Leth that the name was not wholly unfamiliar. He had heard it . . . when? Hours ago? A lifetime? For the moment, at least, it plucked no specific chord.

'And you are the Swordbearer, who calls himself Leth – or Leth, who calls himself the Swordbearer. One and the same. Is that not so?' Urch-Malmain asked.

Leth gave no answer. His eyes had alighted upon the Orbsword, which rested in its scabbard upon a bracket on one wall. It was bound tightly in a web of silver chains.

'Ah yes, your blade,' said his host, following the direction of his gaze. 'I do apologize, but rumour has it that you have trained the sword to obey your every command. Hence, until we have gained a fuller acquaintance with each other, and, we must hope, established a condition of mutual trust and understanding, I thought it advisable to have the weapon confined.'

A spasm of pain shot through Leth's head. He squeezed shut his eyes, and grimaced.

'Ah, my lovely wife!' declared Urch-Malmain.

A woman was descending via a flight of curving, rug-covered stairs into the chamber where they sat. Leth watched her through half-opened eyes. She was of medium height and aged about twenty years, slim, with a full figure, dressed in a light garment of grey silk which fell to her ankles. Her hair was dark and straight, cut just above her shapely shoulders, framing an oval face. Her lips were full and rouged, seeming to carry a knowing smile as if by habit, and her eyes, pale hazel in colour, danced with bright, gaily sardonic amusement. She bore herself gracefully; even in his pained state Leth could see that she was uncommonly beautiful.

'My sweet, the great Swordbearer has come around,' stated Urch-Malmain with a fulsome gesture towards Leth. 'Swordbearer, allow me to introduce my most beautiful spouse, the great love of my life, my cherished Hellia.'

He gave an ironic laugh. Hellia glided forward, picking a purple grape from a bunch resting in a bowl on the long table as she came. She stood before Leth, appraising him candidly, guarded humour in her eyes. Her perfume, a subtle blend of exotic spice mingled with orange-clove, was a pleasure in his nostrils. The gown she wore was almost diaphanous; Leth could see the marvellous curve of her hips, the contours of her thighs, the push and pout of her breasts against the thin material, and he felt his blood stir.

'Mmm, he is really rather handsome,' said Hellia, her voice husky and tinged with faint derision. She placed a grape upon the tip of her tongue and crushed it sensually against her palate.

'Not more handsome than your beloved husband, surely?' enquired Urch-Malmain.

Hellia whirled around. 'My darling, of course not! I meant, he is rather handsome, *for a hero!*'

She crossed to Urch-Malmain and caressed the air beside his hollow cheeks with both hands. Her lips formed to make a lingering kiss, but they made no contact with his flesh. She looked coyly back at Leth. 'Oh Swordbearer, your face!'

Urch-Malmain waved her back. 'A little too close, my dear. A little *too* close.'

Hellia backed away a pace. Leth said nothing, his brain still too fogged to make much of what was happening. Hellia giggled. 'I do hope you are not going to menace me with that magic blade of yours!'

Urch-Malmain gave a little whinny. 'Do not concern yourself on that score, my angel heart. We have his sword securely under harness.'

'But later we will return it to him, won't we?'

Urch-Malmain's thin face became set and he studied Leth thoughtfully. 'Perhaps. Later. If all is well. Yes, perhaps.'

Hellia swanned to the long table and took a sprig of grapes. She turned and held it out towards Leth. Leth declined. Hellia pouted. 'You must eat if you are to regain your heroic strength.'

'Thank you, but for the present I find I lack appetite.'

'Oh. What a pity.' She gave another little laugh, then moved to stand before the open hearth, her legs apart, one knee crooked, her back to Leth. Leth observed the rise and fall of her shoulders as she breathed, the almost luminous pallor of her back, naked to the shoulder-blades, the outline of her shapely thighs through her garment.

Urch-Malmain's eyes were bright. 'She is a sight to excite even a dead man to ardour, is she not?'

'She is most comely,' agreed Leth.

'Yes, that she is! I am so proud! But now, if you are able to walk, and if you can bear to tear your gaze from Hellia, there is something I wish you to see.'

Leth gingerly eased himself from the tabletop.

'How do you feel?'

'A little shaken.'

'You are very pale.'

'I will be all right.'

'Good. But do not strain yourself.'

Hellia spoke over her shoulder. 'You are far from menacing just now, Swordbearer.'

'That is how I would prefer it.'

'Oh, but you are our hero. You must be muscular; you must be resolute and deadly; you must wield your weapon with lusty righteousness, that all will fall down before you and worship the ground you walk upon, and maidens will line up beside your bed at night.'

'Hellia, that is enough,' scolded Urch-Malmain.

Hellia turned back to stare into the flames.

'She means no offence, Swordbearer,' Urch-Malmain said.

'She appears not to like me,' said Leth as they passed from the chamber, 'or at least to harbour distaste for what she imagines I stand for.'

'I will enlighten you in due course.'

From the hallway outside they descended via a flight of curving stairs set against the wall – from its concave form Leth judged it to be the outer wall of Urch-Malmain's tower. Leth breathed deeply, thoughts swimming in a slow fog.

Urch-Malmain! The name came back to him now, out of his inner murk. He stared at the bent back of the man preceding him, the clumsy lurching gait, deformed arm stiffly swinging.

'You are the Noeticist, the manipulator of memories.'

Urch-Malmain spoke back over his shoulder. 'Is that how I am called these days? Ah well, it could be worse. Be patient, Swordbearer. All will be explained.'

They passed along a short corridor where two of the black-armoured, pallid-skinned warriors played cards at a table. The two turned their faces away as Leth and Urch-Malmain approached, and Leth noticed that Urch-Malmain gave them a wide berth. They continued to descend. At length Urch-Malmain paused before a stout portal of solid timber plank. From within his gown he withdrew a large iron key on a chain which hung around his neck. With this he opened the portal, took a lamp from a nearby shelf and lit it from a torch set upon a sconce. He beckoned Leth through, locking the portal behind him when he had entered. He gave Leth a quick smile and continued along a short passage to another similar door. A second key opened this, and they passed through into a large chamber filled with nameless apparatus.

'Now,' he said, a little breathlessly, and indicated a bench, 'the secrets.' He passed around the chamber, lighting torches from his lamp. The chamber was without windows, and Leth suspected that they were, in fact, underground.

'I have been long ages here,' said Urch-Malmain presently, lowering himself onto another bench at some distance from Leth. 'Long, long ages. It has not been an easy time, for I do not belong in this world. I found myself in this place as a result of scheming duplicity and, with the exception of my sweet Hellia, have discovered little to comfort me here. It is a hollow place, joyless and miserable. Worse, I am deprived of many of the privileges of my nature here. So I think it can be truthfully said that we share a common goal, you and I.'

'And what is that?'

'To return to our own world. That is the end to which I have devoted myself almost exclusively since first finding myself here.

That is the primary purpose of this bizarre apparatus that you see arrayed before you.' He gestured towards the machinery. 'It is a most delicate assemblage. I have laboured long in its construction, and in the process have incurred more liabilities and obligations than I care to recall. It is in large part a living artefact, composed of essences and sentient and semi-sentient agents and entities drawn from numerous dimensions, worlds and time-flows beyond this and beyond our own.'

'Indeed, it is impressive,' commented Leth drily.

Urch-Malmain gave a nod. 'Its function is to forge a portal, opening a way between this world and our own, thus permitting me to escape this damnable existence. In my own land, with my fullest powers intact, the construction of such an artefact requires no especial effort, nor the expenditure of unreasonable amounts of time. Certainly it does not demand the construction of a monstrosity such as this. But here physical and metaphysical laws are not harmoniously aligned with those of our own domain. This has made the work arduous and fraught with disappointments. However, all my experiments and tests are done. The machine is complete and operational. There is just one problem.'

'What is that?' enquired Leth.

'It does not work.'

Leth observed him for a moment, then rose slowly and approached the strange apparatus. It consisted of a complex arrangement of large and small boxes, globes – some containing little drawers or doors – shelves, vials, bowls, bulbs and handles made from a variety of materials, not all of them familiar. These occupied a considerable area of the chamber. Strange fluids and glowing plasmas rested or bubbled within several of the globes and bulbs. Skeins and tangles of coloured wires, pipes – bulbous, thin, round, squared or flat – and tubes of similar diversity were threaded between the various articles, linking them in a manner too intricate to follow.

Central to this apparatus was an arch of silvery metallic struts and laths, more than spacious enough to contain a standing man, which supported a system of linked metallic disks and circular or looped troughs. Some of the troughs contained round beads of varying sizes. Little gates and traps within the troughs connected to other tubes and conduits, forming an intricate web of channels and conjunctions. Upon the ground directly beneath the system of troughs and discs was a set of geometric patterns drawn in several colours.

'Do not approach too closely,' warned Urch-Malmain. 'Although the machine is currently dormant, it is yet most sensitive. Your very presence can cause fluctuations within its internal weft.'

Leth turned back. 'I would say that it is hardly operational if it does not work.'

'Ah well, when I say it doesn't work, I mean it doesn't work in the way I had intended. In fact it does something else.'

'And what is that?'

'I am not entirely sure. It is a mystery to me. But I do know now why it does it, and it is not through any inherent fault in the machinery itself.' Urch-Malmain rose and performed some obscure actions around the strange array of apparatus. Something hummed, very low. Something fizzed, almost inaudibly. Leth noticed renewed motion in some of the fluids. Urch-Malmain faced Leth again. 'There, I have recalled the device to consciousness. It will awaken in a few hours; we can return then and interrogate it.'

'Awaken? Interrogate?'

'As I have said, the device is, at least in part, a living, sentient artefact. And it has a strange message to impart. Come, we will relax and talk until it is time to return.'

III

Upstairs in the main chamber again Leth partook of some sweet grapes, feeling that he could not yet stomach anything more substantial. His mind was still not clear, his memories of how he had come to be at the Tower of Glancing Memory were vague. Urch-Malmain sat opposite him, eating nuts. Hellia had departed. As if to explain her absence Urch-Malmain said, 'My preference is largely for solitude. Hellia is sensitive to this, and rarely attends me unless summoned. In fact, I do not like your being here, if the truth be told. I would far rather be rid of you; your company vexes me. But your presence is necessary just now; there is something which apparently only you can do. So, for the present . . .'

Leth was struck by a feeling of foreboding. 'Only I?'

Urch-Malmain gestured dismissively with his good hand. 'All in good time, when the machine awakens.'

He chewed another handful of nuts.

Leth thought suddenly of Lakewander. 'I came here with a companion. What has happened to her?'

'She went back. The Shore of Nothing was more than she could bear. But she used it well. She took what she needed from you and departed. You will not see her again.'

'What do you mean?' Leth recalled the bitter sense of betrayal he had experienced within the ecstatic terror on the madness of the coloured beach.

'Your essence, Swordbearer. Your seed, that she might bear your child. She and her kind require the child of a god to live among them now that their own god has departed.'

Leth shook his head, disturbed by the thought. 'They are mistaken. I am no god.'

'I know.'

'It seems you know much, Urch-Malmain.'

'The artefact below has more than one function, and in its mode of Vigilant Eye it performs almost flawlessly.'

Leth's sense of unease deepened. Had Urch-Malmain been monitoring his movements? For how long? 'It was my companion who told me of you, of your claimed ability to manipulate memory. Is it true, can you do this?'

'Indeed I can. At times with remarkable results.'

'Do you intend to perform such manipulations on me?'

With a finely tuned sense of the dramatic, Urch-Malmain paused, then leaned towards Leth with an arch grin, and said in a low voice, 'How do you know that I have not already done so?'

Leth felt himself stiffen, a chill racing down his spine. Urch-Malmain gave a knowing nod. 'I can give people complete new personalities, and have done so. Whole new trains of memories. Taken everything of them that existed before, and replaced it. How else do you think a woman such as Hellia can abide a wretch as hideous as I? She adores me, Swordbearer! Just in the particular manner in which I wish to be adored. She lives for me, only for me, and is utterly compliant to my wishes!'

'Do you have no feelings for her?'

Urch-Malmain shrugged and reached for more nuts. 'A fellow must have his diversions.'

'Yet you referred to her as your spouse.'

'She believes it. It appeals to her sense of propriety. I find that touching, if ridiculous.'

Leth eyed him with distaste, still deeply unsettled by the idea that Urch-Malmain might already have tampered with his memory. *But if so, would he permit my dislike of him? Would he allow me to question him in this manner?* To some degree this thought eased his mind, though a creeping unease lingered.

'And she dislikes you, Swordbearer,' Urch-Malmain went on, his manner becoming ever more scathing. 'I instilled within her a profound aversion to rugged, heroic types. She deems you a dullard, a fool, vainglorious and quite inadequate. Were you to attempt a seduction she would laugh in your face. There is but one man for her, and that is I, the cripple, Urch-Malmain!'

'And what was she before?'

'Before?' I hardly know. She came here from our world, via the artefact. She was terrified, until I placed her under hypnotic reverie and tinkered with her hopes and fears, redrew her thoughts and dreams. Then, when she awoke she loved me in precisely the way I wish to be loved. She neither desired nor knew anything of her former existence. Her one wish is to live out her span with me. She cannot, of course, for I grow bored very quickly.'

'This is a grotesque violation.'

'I care not.'

'Did you make no attempt to discover anything of her former life?'

'Why would I? Of what interest could it possibly be to me?'

'How many others have you performed this "tinkering" upon?'

'Oh, a goodly number. I keep no record. Some, of course, approached me, having heard of my reputation. They asked that I perform my operations upon them, for their lives were miserable beyond recounting. I did so, gladly, and they were grateful. Well, actually, they weren't, for quite obviously, upon awakening they were not aware that anything had been done. But they served me in the capacity I required.'

'But you have not done this to me, otherwise, why would you be telling me this?'

'You are perceptive. *So you hope.*'

Leth leaned back in his chair angrily. He brooded for some

moments while Urch-Malmain poured himself wine. 'You speak of "our" world, as if we hail from the same place.'

'That is so. Have you not guessed? You are Leth, King of Enchantment's Edge; and I am Urch-Malmain, of Enchantment.'

'Enchantment?'

'Quite. I am one of those whom you, against the will of your people, refuse to acknowledge as gods.'

Leth was astounded. 'Then how came you here?'

'An unfortunate accident. Caught by the hem of my robe, so to speak. When his enemies – of whom I was one – captured Orbus eons ago and banished him to this "non"-place, they sealed me with him in his Encystment of Perpetual Banishment. Agh, it pains me to recall! They are devious folk, gods. Low on morals and simple human decency.'

'That has already become plain.'

Urch-Malmain gave a humourless chuckle. Leth considered what he said. If he spoke the truth then he, a god, existed now, like Leth, within Orbus, another god – or as Orbus had once termed himself and his kind: an aberration, a conscious being of immense power, a node or uncommon concentration of energy.

Urch-Malmain knew Leth's true identity; he knew Orbus. This in itself suggested that he spoke at least partial truth. But a god? Leth looked him over.

'Yes, yes, I hardly look like a god!' Urch-Malmain declared with impatience. 'I know it. But it was a conceit, an affectation adopted at the time for reasons I have no wish to explain. And when I found myself in this dreadful domain I had been deprived of all ability to alter my form. Still and all, I am almost able to return. Almost. And in Enchantment I will be strong once more, and those who fooled with me shall know my vengeance.'

Yet again Leth was visited by the unwelcome sensation that he was dealing with irrationalities, that he trod the lonely twisting paths of some terrible dream. And he thought of Issul, whom he missed and needed so greatly; Issul, who knew instinctively how to soothe and distract him when his thoughts grew so dark and troubled.

'Do you suspect me of untruths, King Leth?' queried Urch-Malmain, observing him sidelong with one eye closed.

'I—I no longer know what I suspect. Recent days have all but stripped me of my ability to reason.'

'Well, for the sake of progress in our discussion, will you assume, at least for the present, that what I say is so?'

'For the present I perceive no advantage in attempting to gainsay you. Say on, then. You have been sealed with Orbus in his Encystment all this time?'

'I was imprisoned within his non-existence. I could not awaken until he did, and it was not intended that he should wake. Yet he did, and in that act gave birth to this world and gave liberty to me within it, misshapen and reduced though I was.'

'Is Orbus aware of you?'

'I would think not, for I still live unchallenged.'

Leth nodded. A distant memory had stirred: the name 'Urch-Malmain' mentioned by Orbus as being one of a cabal of Enchantment's 'gods' who had defeated him. Leth considered the strange tale Orbus had told him of how he had come to exist within his blue domain. For the first time since Leth had entered this world, something – the first intimation of a coherent pattern – was beginning to emerge. Something fantastical entered his mind, something which he dismissed. His eyes were on Urch-Malmain. He wondered. If a pattern could be discerned, could not a plan equally be laid? It was the beginning of a glimmer of hope, at least; a tiny candle-flame in the despairing darkness that had consumed him.

'Have you seen Orbus?' he asked Urch-Malmain.

Urch-Malmain shook his head. 'He occupies a hidden domain to which I have no access.'

'And Orbus . . . has he been within this world? Has he at any time left his domain?'

'I know not. And I tire of your questions.'

Leth shifted his position. 'Well, you have given me much information, and most obviously there is something you wish of me.'

'There you have it!' exclaimed Urch-Malmain. 'I knew from the first that you were a perspicacious fellow. Though I have already said it, there is a task for you to perform. You will be of great service to me, and to yourself also.'

'How so?'

'Your success will enable me to open the way back to our world. You, and I, will be free once more.' Grabbing a last fistful of nuts, he pushed himself up from his seat. 'Now, enough! I can bear you no longer!'

Urch-Malmain began to limp towards the upper stairway. 'I go

to dally with Hellia. The machine will awaken in due course. In
the meantime I suggest you entertain yourself in whatever fashion
you prefer. Eat and drink, and rest. A sleep will do you good.
Alternatively, my guards are available should you wish a game
of cards or chequers. However, I fear you will find them dreary
company and witless opponents. Their skills are generally limited
to slaying unwelcome intruders. Make of it what you will. I shall
come for you at the appropriate time.'

TEN

I

'Urch-Malmain, my patience is sorely tried!'

'As is mine!'

'And mine also!'

The voices issued from within the semi-sentient machine in the musty lowest level of Urch-Malmain's Tower of Glancing Memory. They were querulous and imploring, reproachful and splenetic.

'You have used us!'

'This is not part of our arrangement!'

'We demand an end to this! We demand that you release us!'

'It is surely time you let us go!'

Urch-Malmain twitched his bent body indignantly. 'Oh hssst! Cease your squabbling, all of you! It does no good! You cannot leave until I release you, and I will not release you until your function is fulfilled!' Over his shoulder he spoke sharply to Leth. 'Pay these petulant entities no heed, Swordbearer. They have entered into a compact of business, yet are bearing their travails with poor grace. The facts are simple, whatever they may claim: I employed them to a specific end, and that end is not yet achieved. Hence, they remain in my service.'

'That is not so!' came a voice from beneath the circular troughs, where a coruscating blue-green fume now curled and billowed.

'Yes, it is. You simply have a predilection for argument. Were I not here you would find fault with each other and squabble until your vapours dissipated, the plasmas were expelled and your voices became less than whispers between the stars. You do it because it is in your natures. You can do nothing else.'

'Our grievances are genuine! Your principles are called to question!'

'Ah, pah!' Urch-Malmain waved his stiff withered arm in irritation.

Leth stood by, bemused. He had entered the chamber moments earlier to find, as his dark-minded host had stated, that the machine had awoken. It hummed and burred lightly; strange lights glowed and shivered on various of its parts; fluids bubbled and spat and streamed through pipes and tubes, mingled in clear glass bulbs, became something other and coursed brightly into the machine's innards. The little beads rolled in their troughs, back and forth, and passed through gates, dropped through traps; and the whole thing gave off a disconcerting gaseous stink.

Urch-Malmain had lurched forward and taken a pinch of plum-coloured powder from within a little onyx box. This he tossed onto the coloured pattern on the floor inside the frame. There was a flash, a silent explosion and a great puff of vapour. And then the voices began.

Their babbling became an annoyance, even to Leth who was not best suited to judge whether they had justifiable cause for complaint. None of the entities were visible; their sound issued from the depths of the coloured vapour that sparkled in the space within the metallic arch.

'We cannot be blamed for what is happening here! Together we have merged to create a magnificent portal, perfect in every respect!'

'But it does not work!' Urch-Malmain stamped his foot.

'It works! It works! It is the Great Sow that has influenced its operation, not us!'

'Yes! Yes! The Sow! The monstrous Sow!'

The voice of an entity, somewhat calmer than the others, spoke out in a brief moment of silence. 'Who is this, Urch-Malmain? I see you have brought a visitor.'

'Ah, at last! One of you has perceived something beyond his own whining.' Urch-Malmain, stepping aside, beckoned to Leth. 'Come forward, Swordbearer. Here, irritating wisps, be silent and let me introduce Leth, the Swordbearer.'

'Is this another of your experiments, Urch-Malmain?' cried an entity. 'Is he to be sent through the portal? It will not work, you know. The result will be as before as long as the dreadful harridan exerts her influence.'

'No!' shouted Urch-Malmain. 'Just listen! Cease your ululations and woeful gnashings and listen! The Swordbearer is here to serve our ends.'

'How?' called an unseen entity.

'What is his power?' queried another.

'He will suffer the fate of the others. The Great Sow cannot be vanquished,' yet another brayed.

Incensed, Urch-Malmain drew his warped form to its fullest height, and filled his lungs with a great draught of air that he might deliver a roared command: *'OH, SHUSH!'*

All fell obediently quiet. He continued in a more moderate tone, addressing the entity who had first perceived Leth's presence, 'You, Aztin, you are a little less prone to foolishness than your companions. Explain all to the Swordbearer, that he might be in no doubt as to the cause of your malfunction.'

'It is not a malfunction —'

'Just explain!'

'Very well. Swordbearer, something is happening to impair our perfect function. For long ages we have striven to establish the portal between this sorry world and that of our gracious master, the here-standing Urch-Malmain, in accordance with his instructions. And yet, through no fault of ours, those whom Urch-Malmain has had pass though via our agency have travelled not quite as they should. We had no explanation for that, for we had merged precisely to form this perfect artefact. We take great pride in our work and were sorely distressed at this inexplicable failure. So we passed psychic eyes through the portal, and had them rest unseen in the inter-world drift, to monitor what went on. At first they detected nothing. And then, more recently, we discovered the subtlest waves of disturbance. A flux of instability! Further investigation revealed the source. The flux has been deliberately introduced. It is the Sow, the monstrous Kancanitrix, Ascaria. And nothing we can do will deter her or expunge her baleful influence.'

'Ascaria!' The name plunged a chill blade into Leth's innards.

'But of course, you know of her, don't you' said Urch-Malmain with a sly narrowing of the eyes.

'I have heard the name.'

'Does she not hold captive your beloved children?'

'So I was told. Though in this world I am unsure what to believe.'

'Still and all, it is a fortunate coincidence.'

Leth scowled. 'How so?'

'Why, you are on your way to find Ascaria and slay her with your magic blade and, lo and behold, you pass through here and learn that we too wish her slain.'

'What is this?' cried the entity, Aztin. 'A magic blade?'

'The Swordbearer is a mighty warrior who bears a fabulous pink sword,' said Urch-Malmain with lofty sarcasm. 'It is the only known instrument capable of taking the Great Sow's life, and he alone can wield it.'

'That is indeed excellent news,' Aztin said, and in the fume the others set up an approving chorus:

'He has come to release us!'

'Oh what marvels! We will be free again!'

'At last, we can perform our function as we always intended to do . . .'

'. . . and take leave of this drab and miserable world!'

'And good riddance!'

'Fortune and the good will of the Unity of All Dimensions is with us after all!'

Leth was less enthusiastic. He gazed mordantly into the fume. Lakewander and Master Protector had told him that Ascaria, the Kancanitrix of the Dark Flame, guarded a portal which would take him back to his world of Enchantment's Edge, and now here was Urch-Malmain and his living artefact claiming to have created another. Did Urch-Malmain know of Ascaria's portal? Did it truly exist? Leth was in two minds as to whether to speak of it now. He resolved to stay silent for the present, but something else that had just been said bothered him. He asked, 'What of those who stepped through your portal and 'travelled not quite as they should'? What become of them?'

'We do not know,' said one voice.

'Perhaps they arrived as they should, perhaps they did not,' said another.

The remaining entities added their thoughts:

'Perhaps they were transported to the back of a far star in the constellation of Hesque.'

'Or into the bowels of a blind Legfish swimming deep in the sea of Dismality.'

'Perhaps they hover still in uncharted regions of netherness, or were reduced to their constituent atoms and dispersed throughout all the planes of the cosmos.'

'Perhaps —'

'*Enough'!* shouted Urch-Malmain, almost beside himself. 'Their fate is unimportant. They were subjects to test the function of the machine, nothing more.'

'But who were they?' demanded Leth.

'I would not know who they were.' Urch-Malmain glanced towards the billowing blue-green mist. By his look and posture Leth sensed him to be uneasy. Was he afraid that the entities might reveal something he wished to keep quiet?

Leth turned to the mist within the artefact. 'Aztin, perhaps you or your companions will enlighten me?'

'Bah! You are a meddlesome fellow! Their identities are of no relevance,' Urch-Malmain expostulated.

'Nonetheless . . .'

'Time has passed. I have forgotten.'

Leth was unconvinced. 'Then let me ask you something else. If you do not know what happened to them, what evidence do you have that they did not pass through the portal and arrive safely on the other side as intended?'

Urch-Malmain drew back his lips and hissed through his teeth. 'One: they sent back no signs. And two: the reciprocity was awry.'

'The reciprocity? What is that?'

'The Law of Reciprocity. There must be a mutual transfer between domains. If I send something from this world to our own, something of similar context must be drawn here. It is a universal balance.'

'And it did not occur?'

'It occurred, but not as it should. On the first attempt it was immediately obvious that something was wrong. The old man I sent through appeared to burst into flame as he passed; in his place there materialized a leather-skinned warrior who promptly expired. Later, after various adjustments had been made, I tried again. The transfer appeared to go well, though I cannot say where the subject ended up. On that occasion I received a dazed young tinker in exchange. At another time I sent the tinker back; in his place came a savage creature, a hybrid of human barbarian warrior and some kind of blue-skinned reptilian-brute. So ferocious was it that, again, I jettisoned it immediately, before it could leap forth and tear the life from me. This time my darling Hellia came through.'

'And you did not think to ask her where she had come from?' asked Leth, incredulously.

'Oh I did, but the poor sweet was hysterical and could barely grasp what had happened to her. She was of our world, though. That much was plain.'

'Then the portal had operated as it should.'

'Perhaps, but I could not be certain. I had no proof, and for reasons which require no explanation I am not prepared to make my own attempt to return while there remains even a scintilla of doubt as to the outcome.'

'What is this proof, these signs that you refer to?' asked Leth.

Urch-Malmain smiled thinly, a nerve at the corner of his mouth twitching rapidly. 'There is no reason why I should reveal that to you.' He paused, turning again to the milling vapour, then went on: 'Most recently I sent a young man through. The entities reported that, as far as they could tell, his passage had been without untoward incident. And someone who might be of interest to you came here in his place. The omens were good, then. But the entities considered it a matter of chance and could not guarantee such success again, not as long as Ascaria continues to disrupt the harmonies of the passage.'

'Someone of interest to me?' queried Leth.

'I think so.' He turned away. 'We will discuss that at another time.'

II

An hour had passed. Leth stood alone at a window of the Tower of Glancing Memory, his brain seething with questions. In the far distance misty blue hills rose, meeting the sky at a point beyond his perception. Away to his left was the shimmering enigma of the Shore of Nothing, its strange sands a haze of colour in the Orblight. The gleaming red cliffs curved away into the distance from which he had come; before them the End of the World, the void that he could not contain or bear to look upon. And beneath him, falling away dizzyingly from the foot of the tower, was the Death Abyss, its far-off depths concealed beneath a blanket of dense, broiling grey mist.

There dwelt Ascaria, Urch-Malmain had just told him. There lay his children, and his goal. High above, directly over the Abyss, as if in corroboration of Urch-Malmain's sentiment, was the World's Pain. Closer now, it no longer shone with a piercing golden light; its lucence was the colour of blood. And the sky had darkened, not with the approach of night but more as though reflecting the sombre, unknown character of the great Abyss over which it hung.

'Have you made your decision, Swordbearer?' came Urch-Malmain's voice from behind him.

Leth felt his heart in his throat. Without turning around he said, in a solemn voice, 'I think the decision has been made without me. What choice have I? I will not rest until I have found my children.'

'A noble sentiment. But in itself it is not enough. You must slay the Great Sow and return here if you intend to find your way back to your home.'

Now Leth turned. *And you will be gone, the portal closed, its entities dispersed. Vanished, as if it had never been.*

'It is a dangerous way,' said Urch-Malmain. He stood at the far end of the chamber. 'But I will provide help. You will not travel alone.' He gestured to where four of the tall, pale, black-armoured warriors stood facing him with their backs to the wall. Their expressions were blank, though fierce. 'They are Abyss fighters. They know the way. They were once Ascaria's.'

'How is this?' asked Leth.

'From time to time she launches forays against me. That is, she did. She was quick to curtail her actions when she saw that I was . . .' Urch-Malmain pursed his lips and wriggled his fingers, seeking appropriate words, '. . . changing her troopers' minds.'

'Is it so simple?'

'To put someone into reverie? It's just like hypnotizing chickens. Somewhat against my preferences, though, for it obliges me to place my person in very close proximity to the subject in order to arrest his or her gaze with my own. Such intimacy is an affront to my nature.' He gave a shudder. 'The process of relieving a person of their entire memory store and replacing it with another takes somewhat longer, of course, but I am relieved of the necessity of touching them or gazing into their horrible eyes. Now,' he jerked a finger at the warriors, who filed quickly from the chamber, 'you will have others with you besides these grim-visaged fighters.' He nodded towards the far end of the chamber. In the shadows beneath an overhead gallery a man lounged upon the edge of a table. Leth had not been aware of him before. He swung one leg carelessly back and forth; the other was almost straight, the foot resting upon the floor, supporting much of his weight. With one hand he tossed a small white object into the air and caught it as it fell, tossed it and caught it again. He looked across at Leth, nodded and grinned nonchalantly. 'Good day, valiant hero.'

With a shock Leth recognized Count Harg, the brigand leader. He turned upon Urch-Malmain in outrage. 'I will not have this man accompany me. He is a villain of the lowest order.'

'As am I,' replied Urch-Malmain, who had moved to the foot of the stairway. 'Still, he will be useful to you, and to me also. Hence he and his company will travel with you. They are charged with your protection.' His voice had hardened. 'The matter is not being offered for debate.'

Count Harg languidly tossed the little object high and let it drop into his open palm once more. 'Regrettably my company is greatly depleted, due to a rather unfortunate incident at the other end of the Shore. We are but three in number now.'

Leth turned to him and growled, 'How did you come here?'

'Why, the same way you did, I would imagine.'

'You walked the Shore of Nothing?'

'That is so.'

'And were not driven mad?'

Harg studied the little article in his hand. 'I am perhaps not the best judge of that. But as far as I am aware I am sane. Unprincipled, yes. Irredeemably miscreant, well, perhaps. But of unsound mind? I do not think so.'

Of unsound mind! The words threw Leth back to his encounter with Fectur in the Hall of Wise Counsel, when the Master of Security for Enchantment's Edge had so deftly and deviously usurped his office. It had been . . . when? Incredibly, only days ago, unless more time had passed than he was aware of.

Was it just coincidence that had bidden Harg to use these words? He had put no particular inflection on them, nor did his expression betray any double meaning. Leth put the words from his mind.

'Why have you come?'

Count Harg made a weary gesture, and smiled sardonically. 'Oh, everyone is so *glum* back there. Have you not noticed? There is no relief. I tire of it.'

'If you came this way, did you encounter my former companion, Lakewander?'

'I did,' said Harg, brightening. 'She was making her way home.'

Leth bristled. 'Was she harmed?'

'By me? No. To be honest, I was far more interested in you and your marvellous pink sword than I was in her. And as it happened, we met near the stone bridge. She sought and gained the aegis of that simple-minded hulk who guards the way.'

'And the Bridgekeeper let you pass?'

Count Harg eased himself off the table and crossed the room. He paused before a side-table upon which rested a small vase of translucent white gypsum that held a single, vibrantly pink rose. Harg lifted the rose to his nostrils and enjoyed its perfume for a moment, then replied, 'Mmmm, yes, he did. I hailed him in the proper manner this time, so he had little option. And besides, he was busy attending to my former companions.' Harg made a grimace of distaste. 'He is a creature of strange appetites, even to someone of my hardened sensibilities.'

Urch-Malmain had ascended to the second step of the stairway. He had taken a pale blue foulard from within his robe and was applying it to his mouth and nose as if to ward off a foul odour. Leth saw that his brow gleamed with perspiration. 'So, Swordbearer, can I take it that you are ready to depart?'

Leth felt no readiness, either to travel with Harg or do Urch-Malmain's bidding. Yet somewhere his children were hidden, awaiting him, and ahead lay the possibility of escape, of a return to Enchantment's Edge.

So he nodded, his countenance dour.

'Excellent!' Urch-Malmain edged away up the stairs, delivering little staccato coughs into his foulard. 'I shall apprise you later of all that I know of the journey that lies ahead of you. For now, I must remove myself from your presence, for you offend me. Amuse yourselves!'

III

It was a bitter day, a day chill with foreboding, as Leth rode out from the Tower of Glancing Memory. He was accompanied by Count Harg, his two surviving thugs and the four lean, putty-skinned Abyss warriors who had once been soldiers of Ascaria.

Urch-Malmain had informed him of the four warriors' names. They were: Rasgul, Hurri, Dembarl and Fhurn. So similar in appearance were they that Leth could barely tell them apart, with the exception of Rasgul, their captain, who had irises of deep burnt-orange pigment, in contrast to the dull umber of the other three. He was also a little more massive than they and had a distinguishing blemish or birthmark like a faint stain or shadow upon the left side of his jaw.

None of them were prone to conversation in any form bar the exchanging of orders and necessary responses, which suited Leth. Count Harg, on the other hand, seemed keen to establish a feeling of bonhomie between Leth and himself. Leth had neither desire nor stomach for such a rapport, and gave him no encouragement. Harg was undeterred and spoke on as the mood took him, his manner smooth and light-hearted, as though they were setting out on an adventure no more perilous than a deer-hunt.

Leth was bemused by him. Harg was plainly a man of refined background, almost likeable, yet, by demonstration and his own admission, devoid of conscience, decency or feeling for others.

Harg's two men were the gangling, pockmarked youth, called Juson, who had helped to tie Leth at the stone bridge; and a smaller weasel of a man, spare and quick of build, with cadaverous features and darting black eyes, whose name was Trin.

They were heavily armed, all of them. Leth wore his sapphire armour; the Orbsword was buckled at his belt, his dagger also, and he had been provided with a bow and arrows by Urch-Malmain. Behind his saddle was the magnificent horned and visored sapphire-blue helm. This had in fact been stolen by Harg at the bridge, but he had borne it with him along the Shore of Nothing and presented it to Leth as they prepared to set out from the Tower of Glancing Memory, commenting archly that he felt it only proper that a hero be fully accoutred when setting forth upon a quest.

Count Harg himself carried a longsword and numerous knives. A repeating crossbow, capable of firing several light bolts in quick succession, was attached to his saddle, as were quarrels for it. He also carried a small silvery instrument which fitted into the palm of his hand. Leth had caught but a glimpse of this device. He was ignorant as to its precise function but assumed it to be a weapon of some kind.

Juson and Trin each carried a longsword and crossbow, with a battle-axe slung from their saddles. The four Abyss warriors had their scimitars, knives, bows and short spears.

Leth was far from easy in his mind, knowing that he rode with men in whom he could place no trust. Had he searched the furthest corners of his kingdom he could hardly have found himself a more poisonous band of travelling companions. Each one of them he knew to be either a black-hearted villain or a tutored killer. Any or all of them might slide a blade between his ribs the moment his aim was achieved; he was not blind to the likelihood of their having received orders to this effect already. And apart from his brief to slay Ascaria he knew so little of the full nature of the mission he was engaged upon.

Prior to their departure Urch-Malmain had withdrawn to his workroom with the four Abyss warriors. Hours later he had emerged to announce that the four were now subservient to Leth's command. 'They will follow your orders, Swordbearer, but only insofar as they concur with my own. Bear that in mind. These pale fellows will do all in their power to assist you in entering Ascaria's stronghold. They will deliver you to her if they can, so that you may end her vile life. But they will not then lend you a hand to return here and slay me, heh-heh-heh! No, be assured, their loyalty to me is never in question.'

A chill breeze scoured Leth's cheek. It seemed to come up from the Death Abyss, which lay just yards away to his left. Harg had said they must travel several leagues from the Tower of Glancing Memory, more or less following the lip of the great Abyss, before they came to a way that would let them descend into the chasm.

The landscape was harsh, a rutted plain of weak grey soil and rock. Here and there low hillocks relieved the overall flatness. A few stunted trees struggled for growth, small yellow flowers grew at the wayside, otherwise thistles and occasional tussocks of tall, spare grass were all that found purchase in the feeble earth. Misty hills and mountain tiers reared in the distance.

Leth brooded on a thousand concerns. Not least was the ever-present, gnawing fear that his mind might have been tampered with, that his memories and perceptions, all he believed he knew, might not be his own. He strove to reassure himself and cast such thoughts from him. But Urch-Malmain's leering grin and his question, *'How do you know that I have not already done so?'* lingered persistently at the forefront of his consciousness.

Urch-Malmain and Harg had alerted him to difficulties ahead, though neither had been specific. 'There are a number of levels to the Death Abyss, each with its own denizens and dangers. In the village of Sombren, beyond which the trail begins to descend, the folk are fearful and prone to superstition. Beyond it is the first level, where the wolfhearts dwell. We must be wary.'

Leth wondered: should he succeed in reaching Ascaria's stronghold and actually slaying her, what then? Did the Kancanitrix truly guard a portal that would return him and Galry and Jace to Enchantment's Edge? It seemed unlikely that Urch-Malmain could know nothing of it.

Still something else unsettled him. By slaying Ascaria he was opening the way for Urch-Malmain to return to Enchantment – allowing a hostile god to reclaim his former powers. What would be the cost of this?

And again, what of the innocents who, as not only Urch-Malmain but he – Leth – and the children stepped through the portal, would be randomly plucked from their own world and cast into this? Could he justify his own freedom, knowing what they must suffer?

Leth looked at the bleak landscape around him, and at the sky. Did Urch-Malmain's Vigilant Eyes lurk here somewhere unseen, observing his every move?

To distract himself he turned to Count Harg. 'I am curious. You are from my own land, are you not? Where exactly did you reside?'

Harg seemed mystified. 'I think you are mistaken, Swordbearer. This land has always been my home.'

'By Urch-Malmain's account, someone of interest to me came

through the portal from my world. I assumed, by your subsequent appearance, that it was you to whom he referred.'

Harg shook his head. 'Not me, Swordbearer.'

Leth frowned. *Then who?* Or did Harg lie? Or did he simply not know? For the first time it dawned upon Leth that Harg was one of Urch-Malmain's creations, a man whose memories had been erased, others substituted in accordance with the whims or ambitions of the Noeticist.

Might Harg be of Enchantment's Edge, but unable to know it?

Ah, but what had Lakewander said, after they had escaped Harg and his band at the stone bridge? She had spoken of Harg as a former notable of her community, who had absented himself and then returned a changed man, a cutthroat and brigand. Plainly, then, Harg had come upon Urch-Malmain during his earlier travels. Willingly or not, he had undergone the Noeticist's ministrations.

And Leth recalled his own sense of familiarity when he had summoned the Orbsword to him. As though he had done it before. As though he was recalling buried memories, the memories of a former god, which Lakewander, Summoner and Master Protector insisted he had been.

Leth shivered. *What is happening here?*

IV

Late in the morning they came upon the village of Sombren: a shabby cluster of dirty grey clay-and-wood dwellings huddled in a dusty declivity. Leth and his band rode down at an easy pace, scanning the village and its surrounds. A few peasant folk could be seen about the dwellings or in the nearby fields. All of them ceased their business and hurried indoors at the sight of such grim and unambiguously accoutred warriors.

'It would be a good idea to rest in the village for an hour or so,' said Harg, nodding towards the village's sole tavern, set to one side, its roof sagging, its signboard long since bleached by time and weather so that neither name nor emblem could be read. 'We might garner some useful information.'

Leth steered his mount towards the tavern; the others followed. They dismounted and entered. Within the common-room the landlord leaned upon his counter, in conversation with a pair of peasant men who sat at separate tables. At the arrival of Leth's band the two customers promptly took their hands from their tankards, rose and with nervous haste took their leave.

Harg addressed the landlord. 'Hail, good fellow! We are tired and hungry and our throats are caked with the foul dust of this unforgiving land. Stoke up the fire, for we are also chilled, and bring ale and good red wine – and let not either the ale or the wine be watered, or your head will dangle from the sign outside! And food! With what marvellous fare can you tease our tongues and tempt our empty bellies?'

The landlord was a short, thin man with a mass of curling cloudy grey hair. He jerked into fearful motion, putting jugs to spigots and grabbing tankards. 'Sirs, welcome! Welcome! The hospitality of my house is yours. But we are poor folk in Sombren, sirs, and can offer little to excite the palates of refined folk such as your good selves. All I have, sirs, is stew, with good coarse bread, if that will suit you.'

'Stew? Stew?' Harg dropped himself onto a wooden stool before a table near the hearth. 'It is rare indeed to find stew on offer in a tavern such as this! Very well then, stew it shall be. However, my good friends here—' – he indicated Rasgul and the other three Abyss warriors – ' – prefer their flesh fresh and uncooked. Can you oblige them?'

'I can have a goat slaughtered, if that will suit you,' replied the landlord.

Rasgul gave a curt nod.

'Most excellent!' declared Harg. 'Set about it, then, landlord. And waste no time. These four especially are impatient when famished. If their appetites are not quickly satisfied they may throw themselves upon you and your family.'

Leth flashed Harg an angry glance, which Harg failed to acknowledge.

The drinks were brought, and in short order the food too. As he ate Harg addressed the landlord once more. 'Now, good man, what news from the Abyss?'

The landlord seemed to draw in upon himself. 'Sir, we know little of the Abyss, and would wish to know even less. We do not venture there, nor question any who pass through from that direction.'

'Wise fellow. But has there been activity in recent weeks? Have its vapours risen? Have you suffered visitations? What of the wolfhearts? Have they come up over the lip?'

The landlord shook his head, wringing his hands. 'No, sir, none of those things, not recently.'

'Good. And have any of your children been taken?'

'No, sir. But there are no children in Sombren, nor have there been for a long time now.'

Leth leaned towards Harg and asked, in an undertone, 'What is this about children?'

'The Great Sow abducts the children, by physical or magical means,' Harg replied. 'It is possible she has taken too many.'

'For what purpose?'

'She needs them, to stoke her dreams.'

'I don't understand. What are you saying?'

Harg flashed him an indulgent smile, spooning stew to his mouth. 'Her own are pallid, diluted affairs. She can barely imagine. Other dreams are required to achieve her aim. She takes the dreams, the pure imagination, the wonder that children generate naturally and spontaneously, and she adds her own corruption, transforms their dreams into an energy of her own. It is with this corruption that she eats our world.'

There was a strange gleam in Harg's blue penetrating eyes. He seemed to take pleasure in the sight of Leth's face as he absorbed this revelation.

'And . . . what of the children, when she has done?'

Harg's smile was cold, almost sneering. 'They are children no more. They can barely be termed human. You will see. They are less than shells.' He hesitated, glanced at Rasgul. 'Some become warriors.'

Rasgul glowered at him momentarily, but made no other response.

The blood drained from Leth's face. For a barely controllable instant he was overcome with the urge to ram his fist hard into Harg's face, for the man was amused. *Amused* by what he was telling Leth and the impact he knew it was having upon him. But Leth controlled himself, then thrust himself out of his seat. 'Then what are we doing here, drinking and feeding our faces?' he roared. 'Up! All of you! To your feet! We go, now!'

'All in its proper time, Swordbearer,' said Count Harg evenly, as though nothing were amiss. 'Juson and Trin are vile company when their bellies are not properly filled. As am I, come to that. And these Abyss men, if they hunger, are as likely to turn upon us as they are upon our enemies. Besides, I wish to question the villagers a little more before we depart. So be seated and clean your plate.'

The others were eating with vigour and paying Leth little heed. He stood for a moment longer, in two minds. Then, knowing that he could not continue alone, he sat again. But his appetite was gone. He waited restlessly, trying to dispel the terrible images that impressed themselves relentlessly upon his mind.

When Harg had finished his meal he stood, drained his tankard, and left the tavern. A short while later he returned. He took coins from a pouch at his belt and paid the landlord. He leaned upon the counter pensively, stroking his chin, then turned and nodded to Leth. 'Now we go.'

Less than an hour later the company halted at the soaring lip of the Death Abyss. Here the trail narrowed and wound down steeply into a cleft flanked by rough walls of rock. It was necessary to proceed in single file as they commenced their descent. The four Abyss warriors went first, followed by Harg, then Leth. Juson and Trin brought up the rear.

Leth looked out across the great Abyss. Its opposite wall could be seen, bare and jagged, perhaps half a league distant. Between it and Leth was the emptiness, falling away to dense shifting cloud a long way below. The air was cold; colder than before. The chasm fell away sheer and dizzying, only inches from their horses' hooves. Their motion sent grit and small pieces of rubble skittering over the side.

As he began to descend Leth was reminded of the descent from the great city-castle that was his home and the pulsating heart of his kingdom, Enchantment's Edge. From the gates of that city the way swooped, commonly through chill mists which could freeze one to the bone, to the swelling green forest at the foot of the massive scarp. But there the comparison ended. For now he was descending into the unknown, the great Death Abyss of Orbus's world, and the sure horrors that it concealed.

ELEVEN

I

That is the one! The one I met beside the pond!'

Arene's trembling finger pointed directly at Shenwolf.

Issul gaped. She was unsure of what to make of the old woman's outburst. Had Arene taken leave of her senses?

Shenwolf stood stock-still, blinking in blank surprise, a slight frown furrowing his brow.

'It is him, Queen Issul! Believe me, I am not mistaken! It is him!'

'Shenwolf, is this true?' asked the Queen, her voice cracking. An awful hollowness was beginning to form inside her.

'I –' The young soldier seemed for a moment at a loss. 'I am unsure. What is it that is being stated here?'

Issul's voice shook. *Don't let it be so!* 'This woman claims to have met you just weeks ago, in the forest beside a pond just a few leagues from here. There was a child present also, and its warden.'

Shenwolf's brow cleared. His eyes went to Arene. 'Why, of course! I remember you now!'

Issul was aghast. Her thoughts spun in turmoil. 'Then it's true?'

Others of her Guard observed curiously.

'Yes, we met, but briefly. But what is wrong?'

Issul could barely find words. The hollowness within her had become a chasm. *Betrayed? By he whom I had come to trust so completely? By he whom I had begun to —*

She cut that thought dead in its tracks. Now blind rage threatened to consume her. And Shenwolf stood there so cool and unperturbed.

'Majesty, what is the matter?'

Issul's hand went to her tunic. She wrenched forth the blue leather pouch, all but tore it open. She thrust the ivory carving at Shenwolf. 'And this? Do you know what this is?'

Shenwolf drew back, seeming shocked at her venom. He peered at the object she held, then nodded with a quizzical expression.

'You know? Then tell me now, what is it?' Issul's voice rose in pitch. Her hand was shaking. 'And why did you give it to the Child?'

She was dimly aware of commotion away to her left. Loud cries; the sudden sharp whinnies of horses. She twisted. At the edge of the clearing where they had rested there was fighting. She stared, disbelieving. Hirsute brown forms were materializing out of the forest, dropping from the trees, falling upon her soldiers.

'To arms! We are attacked!' Issul yelled.

She reached for her sword, staring wildly about her, instantly forgetting all else. There was more shouting now. Grullags were attacking from at least three directions. Beyond Shenwolf a group of them burst roaring from the undergrowth.

Issul's Guard fell into defensive formation around her. Shenwolf was among them as the first of the creatures slammed into them. The grullags came with mindless ferocity – huge, man-shaped things with broad, flat skulls and blunt snouts. They roared and bellowed, some swinging clubs or heavy sticks, most relying upon fiercely clawed hands, teeth and brute strength.

The first creature was downed by Issul's Guard, but more were pounding down in its wake. How many? Glancing around Issul estimated at least a score. How could this be? Never in her life had she heard of grullags behaving so.

Anzejarl, where are you? Show yourself and I will slay you with my own hands!

But there were no Krai faces.

Issul had no more time to think. A grullag had broken through the ranks of her men. Two of her Guard were down. She lunged with her sword, pierced the grullag's breast and darted back beyond its reach before its swiping claws could tear her open. A soldier hacked into its flank, another stabbed from the other side. The grullag's roar became a soft sigh and it crumpled to the ground.

Issul retreated a few quick paces, trying to take stock and gauge the focus of the grullags' thrust. To her left was carnage. Half a dozen of the creatures had pushed through her men's defences;

others came behind. Several grullags lay dead or wounded, but a greater number of her men were injured or slain.

A group of grullags were close to the area where Grey Venger was being held. Issul cursed. Her men had been taken wholly by surprise. They fought valiantly but were divided and in disarray. Though sentries had been posted around the clearing, they had barely had time to cry out an alarm before the grullags were upon them. She scanned the clearing, and the forest beyond, still seeking the white, wrinkled faces of Krai, but finding none. And then a terrifying thought rocked her to her core.

Had Shenwolf brought these creatures back with him?

He had gone to reconnoitre Ghismile. He had returned with a tale of grullags occupying the village. And then this.

She searched for Shenwolf, could not see him. The fighting was too close and confused. She felt panic-stricken. Another thought slammed through her, tripling her fear.

Orbus!

She had to protect the blue casket at all costs. Her horse was tethered ten paces way, the casket in its chest on the saddle. She yelled to her Guard, 'Fall back!' and dashed for the horse.

A dark rust-brown blur loomed, blotting out the sky. She glimpsed a long, powerful arm upraised and swinging at her. Instinctively Issul ducked, threw herself to the earth, rolled, came to her feet and slashed hard with her sword. The beast's scalding blood sprayed her face; it split her ears with its shriek. Two soldiers hurled themselves upon it and hacked it to the ground.

Issul reached her horse, leaped into the saddle, swung about. A grullag rushed at her, fangs bared, arms high. From somewhere a crossbow bolt thudded into its hide, then another. The creature twisted its body and bellowed. Issul lofted her sword and brought it down, splitting the grullag's massive skull. It toppled forward, exhaling its last breath, its dead weight crashing onto her terrified horse and all but knocking it to the ground.

Her soldiers were falling back as best they could to re-establish a protective ring around her. Across the clearing as many as a dozen had reached their horses and were battling their way towards her. But more of the grullags charged from the trees, cutting into their path. Issul spotted Arene stretched motionless in a ragged heap upon the ground, whether alive or dead she could not tell.

Her horse reared suddenly, shrieking. A grullag's long arms were wrapped about its neck, fangs tearing into its throat. The grullag bore the poor creature to the ground. Issul was thrown from the saddle. Half-dazed, her one thought was for the blue casket. She scrambled forward on hands and knees, seized the handle of the chest, wrenched it free.

She rose, crouching, deafened by the cries and roars all around. A riderless horse rushed by. She ran out, grasped the saddle one-handed and leaped onto its back. She could not tell how the battle was going, but the number of fallen men alarmed her. A handful of soldiers fought desperately a few yards away, but were in danger of being overwhelmed. None had gained their horses. She realized she had become separated from the larger body of her troops.

Issul was faced with a terrible choice: to return to the fray and face the very real threat of being overcome, losing the precious casket and all it signified, and perhaps being killed; or to flee.

In reality it was no choice; everything depended upon Orbus and the blue casket. Even if it meant abandoning her men.

She scanned the clearing in a last desperate hope.

'To me!' she screamed. 'All who can!'

There was an avenue of escape to the rear, leading directly into the forest. A pair of grullags were bearing down on her from her left. If she did not go now she might not have another chance.

Issul wheeled her horse around. Bending low she spurred it forward. She swung at the first of the beasts as she charged by. She could not see if any men had succeeded in joining her.

She dodged a swinging limb, raced on. Suddenly she was free of the carnage, galloping between the trees. Her ears pricked at a strange sound: a voice, highly pitched, hailing her. 'Run, Aunt Issul! That's right! Run! Run!'

She twisted her head. On the crest of a bank rising behind a thicket of hazel bushes, two figures stood. The first, who called to her, mocking and laughing, was small of stature, just a child: Moscul, her own nephew. Tears of laughter streamed down his cheeks.

'Yes, run! Run! That's it, Aunt Issul! That's the way!'

And beside Moscul was a man. His crazed features were contorted in jubilation and contempt, his feet planted firmly apart, and his hands, free of restraining bonds, were raised high as if calling down wrath from the skies. Grey Venger's tongue flew back and forth inside his mouth, and from his throat there issued a shrill, warbling ululation of victory.

II

Issul's wild flight took her far into the forest. She weaved between the trees, took advantage of clumps of dense undergrowth where possible, spurred her horse into a shallow stream-bed and followed its course for some hundred or more yards, all the while scanning the banks to either side in case of the sudden appearance of grullags. At length a channel presented itself, cutting up from the stream through the high bank. A mass of rhododendron bushes provided further cover. She galloped on, deliberately changing course several times, and finally slowed her panting mount to a walk.

Her heart hammered. She watched the woods at her back carefully. It seemed she was not pursued. The forest was silent. How far had she ridden? Not even the sounds of fighting reached her ears.

Issul struggled to take stock. Had she acted wisely? Should she not have stayed, or at least waited until some of her men were able to ride free with her? She was alone now, and quite possibly lost.

But she had had no choice. The grullag assault had been so sudden and savage. She had been isolated. There was a real threat of being overwhelmed.

But she had deserted her soldiers!

Issul shook her head, seeking to expel the thought. Her loyalty at this time *had* to be to Orbus and the blue casket. There could be no question. It was not for her own sake, nor even for Leth's and the children's. It was for Enchantment's Edge, its future and the future of her people. She had run, though under different circumstances she would have stayed and fought. The grullags had been far too close to seizing the casket.

Had that been their intent? Specifically, had that been the intent of the force that commanded them and threw them against her? It was impossible to know whether Moscul had knowledge of the casket or of its contents, but the consequences of his having gained, or even inadvertently destroyed it, were too terrible to contemplate.

Now Moscul and Grey Venger were united: the Legendary Child brought together with its most fanatical apostle. Issul felt her blood run cold.

And Shenwolf!

An anguished sob escaped the young Queen's throat. This was perhaps the bitterest blow.

She pushed her horse on. Her immediate concern now was to speak to Orbus. She would put more distance between herself and the Legendary Child and its grullags, then find a suitable spot in which to summon forth the god.

A little while later she noticed that her horse had developed a limp which was becoming more pronounced the further it bore her. She dismounted and found a bloody lesion and swelling low on the animal's right foreleg. It must have smashed it against a boulder, or perhaps had been struck by a weapon.

With a sigh Issul led the horse into a natural grove of dense shrubbery and tethered it to a branch. Then, checking once again that she was not observed, she seated herself upon a rock and took the blue casket from its chest.

Orbus manifested almost upon the instant. 'Child, you are in turmoil, I can tell.'

Recalling the questions that Arene's tale had engendered in her mind the previous day, Issul found her words stilled upon her tongue.

'Is it that you doubt me?' Orbus enquired. 'I sensed this when we spoke last night. I tried to reassure you.'

'Yes, you said you are fragile in my hands, and I may destroy you at any time. But you know I cannot, Orbus. You know I cannot. You have my husband and children.'

'It was not by my design.'

'That is irrelevant.'

'I am not your foe. I have said it before, and there is little else I can say or do to reassure you.'

'And I can only hope that what you say is true.'

Orbus hovered in silence, seeming to observe her, then said, 'I want you to understand that it is not only myself that I am trying to save. Nor is it specifically Leth or your children.'

She stared piercingly at him. He seemed to be reflecting the very thoughts that had driven her. 'And it is not the future of Enchantment's Edge. So, then . . . what?'

'Do not speak too soon. There are still many things of which you are not aware.'

'Explain.'

'In due course. If the right time arises. But the point I wish to make is this: I love my world. Very, very deeply. I do not understand it; it is something that astonishes me, fills me with wonder. I do not know how it came to be; I am cut off from it and do not even know what it truly is. But I created it and I do not know how, but now it *is*. Somehow I have given birth to it, and I want it to have the opportunity to become, to discover itself. I want it to have a chance, just as you want your own children to grow and prosper and discover their own destinies. But it is in your hands, not mine, and all around us men make war. It could be destroyed at any time, and I exist only in the hope that that can be prevented.'

Issul pursed her lips and nodded to herself, saying nothing.

'You do not believe me?'

'You are my only hope, Orbus. I have to believe you.'

'That is hardly a declaration of trust. Still, let us continue. What was the disturbance that interrupted us last night?'

'Someone approached by stealth.'

'Were we observed?'

'No. The intruder was discovered in time, though not appre-hended.'

'Do you know who it was?'

'There are numerous possibilities. Any one is as likely as any other.'

'What of the old woman of the *Hir'n Esh*? You were to have her speak with me, yet I do not see her.'

Issul gave a disconsolate shake of her head. 'Arene is injured; she may even be dead.' In leaden tones she told Orbus of what had just occurred. When she reached the point of Arene's revelation about Shenwolf her voice cracked; she felt herself begin to tremble uncontrollably.

'Oh, this is grave news. Grave news indeed,' intoned Orbus. He moved off a little way across the grove, deeply pensive. When he returned he said, 'Issul, child, we have to cover this in detail. Are we safe here?'

'As safe as anywhere, I think. Wait a moment. I will make sure that no one approaches.'

She crept through the shrubbery to the edge of the grove, and there stopped and listened. Other than the whisper of the breeze through the forest the only sound was of birds – itself a reassuring sign. She crept a little further into the trees, mounting a rise that permitted her a view for some considerable distance through the wood. She waited, watched; the forest was still. In similar manner she scouted all around the shrub grove, halting to look and listen every fifteen paces or so. Eventually she was satisfied that she was alone, and slipped back into the bushes to Orbus.

'We are safe, at least for the present.'

'Firstly, then, tell me of this legend which the old woman of the *Hir'n Esh* related to you.'

Issul recounted the legend, sticking as closely as she could to Arene's exact words.

'Interesting indeed,' said Orbus. 'But not a cause for alarm, I think. Certainly it appears to refer in its broad detail to my own defeat and vanquishment. In itself, that is perhaps not surprising. The event was without precedent. I blush to admit it, but no other before me had been bested so. No doubt my enemies boasted mightily of how they had robbed me of my soul, and the tale spread . . . Yes, this is the very stuff of legends! That it should also refer to my return and subsequent search for my soul is perhaps more intriguing. Still, the *Hir'n Esh*, so I understand, are witnesses of the future, or of the strands of potential futures.'

'Arene explained as much.'

'Then there, surely, is the wellspring. But I do not understand. What is it in this legend that so troubles you, Issul?'

Issul swallowed. 'It is the mention of the false god who becomes a true god.'

'Ah. You think of the One True God, spoken of by your True Sept. Such a being, by their account, is destined to destroy you and your kingdom. So Leth told me. And you wonder, "Can this be Orbus?"'

'You have us in the palms of your hands, Orbus.'

'As you also have me. In this respect neither of us holds the advantage. We need each other, Issul. It is as simple as that. What more can I say to put your mind at rest? Leth was similarly troubled when I revealed my true nature to him. I said to him, as I say to you now: I mean you no harm. Eons of solitude have deeply impressed upon me the folly of my former existence, and that of my kind. I seek now only to be whole again, and for a way to bring this terrible business to an end without further conflict, though I fear conflict is unavoidable.' He paused. 'You have to accept that what I say is true, Issul.'

Issul lowered her gaze. 'I want to. But I have discovered that to be sure of anything or anyone is to invite disappointment, and more.'

Orbus swung his great bundled head from side to side. 'No. You are certain of your love for your husband and your children, and for your country and its peoples also. Hold to that love, Issul, and let it be your staff and your guide.'

Her eyes prickled wetly; she could not speak.

'Last night you were on the point of showing me something,' Orbus said, 'before our meeting was cut short.'

'Yes.' Issul delved into her tunic and brought forth the fateful leather pouch. She revealed to Orbus the little ivory carving. 'Can you tell me anything about this?'

Orbus leaned forward and studied the carving. When he straightened again his voice came from far away. 'How very strange. Where did you get this?'

'It came to me by roundabout means. Orbus, what is it? You know, don't you?'

Her pulse had quickened. Was she on the verge of discovering some vital clue in this cursed mystery?

'Many ages have passed since I last set eyes on one of these. Many ages.'

'What *is* it, Orbus? Tell me!'

'In the far and distant past before my fall, when I was active in Enchantment, articles such as this were associated with one of my adversaries, a dark-minded creature named Urch-Malmain. He was one of a cabal who put their scheming minds together to lure me into a trap and bring about my downfall. Another was Strymnia; another Bartacanes. It is most curious, but despite eons having come and dwindled away since that time, Urch-Malmain has been very much in my thoughts of late. I cannot say why, but I have scarcely been able to rid my mind of him. Even now, as we speak, I feel his presence, as though he watches me. That you should bring this object to me now is an uncanny coincidence.'

'Has this thing power, or import?'

'That is hard to say. Most commonly Urch-Malmain forged these objects as talismans. That is to say, their purpose was largely protective. He bestowed them temporarily upon servants he had brought from beyond Enchantment's borders. The talismans emit an aura which can counteract the effects of certain magics, at least to some degree. In particular, a non-denizen of Enchantment wearing this talisman would, for a time, gain immunity to Enchantment's natural energies, which would otherwise have harmful, and quite probably deadly, effects.'

Shenwolf carried this! Issul could barely think. 'These servants of Urch-Malmain,' she said, 'what would be their function?'

'That is impossible to say. What would anyone employ a lesser being for? The possibilities are endless.'

'Is Urch-Malmain alive now?'

'I have just said I sense him. It is a queer, uncomfortable feeling, unlike anything I have known. In such a span of time anything might have happened, yet I would say without a doubt that Urch-Malmain exists today, in some foul form. How did you come upon this object, Issul?'

Issul's mind was in a slow, sickening spin. Haltingly she told Orbus of the talisman's history, as it was known to her.

'Shenwolf . . . Is he the young bodyguard you brought to me before we departed Enchantment's Edge?' enquired Orbus when she had concluded. There was a sternness to his tone that she had not heard before.

She nodded, filled with self-reproach. 'I trusted him, utterly. He had proved himself so many times! Now I think, what was it for? What was he really doing?'

'What of the other man you brought to me?'

'Pader Luminis? No. Orbus, no. He is incapable of deceit. That much I do know.'

She stared imploringly at Orbus's brooding phantom form, then twisted her head from side to side, her jaws tightly clenched, fists also. Her limbs were tense and shaking; she was held in the terrible grip of anger and agony. Orbus stood over her, his arms helplessly extended. 'Oh, Issul, child. Would that I could do something to ease your pain.'

'Can you forgive me, Orbus?'

'There is nothing to forgive. You acted in what you truly believed were our best interests. If you have been shown to be mistaken, it is through the pernicious machinations of others rather than through any fault or failing of your own.'

Her tears flooded forth, quite suddenly. She stood, her head bowed, and strode to the edge of the grove, furiously wiping her eyes with her sleeves. 'I do not want to go on, Orbus. I have had enough.'

'Child, I have told you before what I think of such sentiments.'

'I no longer trust my own judgement. I am afraid.'

'Then what do you intend to do? Abandon me here in the woods?'

She turned and fixed him with an anguished stare.

Orbus's voice softened. 'Issul, dear child, listen to me. When it seems that the entire world and the gods themselves are against you, when all you see is darkness and all you feel is pain and confusion, then you must reach within. Deeply and trustingly, for there you will find a light; it only waits to be found. Hold onto your love and, with that as your staff, seek your inner light. Once found it will never be extinguished. It will illuminate your way, no matter the darkness; it will be your guide. Sometimes to find it your need must overcome all else. You must know that it is the one thing you seek, and you will be tested. Your sincerity and intent will be put to the trial. But if you are truly determined, you will never look back again. I know you are sincere, so look, look again for that light which only waits to be found. *Never give up!*'

For long moments Issul was still, her look questioning. At last she nodded. 'I cannot allow them to defeat me. Not as long as the blood still runs in my veins.'

'Exactly so. Now, tell me again – and be exact in detail – of the encounter between the old woman and Shenwolf, and the grullag attack that followed.'

Issul recounted her tale, taking care to recall every nuance to mind.

'So Shenwolf offered no account of why he had given the talisman to the Legendary Child?' Orbus queried.

'There was no time. The grullags were upon us.'

'How did he react to Arene's accusation?'

'Blankly. He was bemused.'

'But he admitted the charge readily, making no attempt to deny or cover up his guilt?'

'That is so.'

Orbus pondered a moment. 'Do you think you might have judged him too harshly?'

'What do you mean?'

'You have no firm evidence that he acted with malign intent.'

'But why else would he do it?'

Orbus shrugged. 'I do not know.'

'It makes no sense.'

'Still, I would prefer to keep an open mind. Too much is still unknown. The business is ever more perplexing. When the attack came, what happened to Shenwolf?'

Issul shook her head. 'I lost sight of him almost immediately in the mêlée.'

'So he could be alive or dead.'

'Or walking at the side of Moscul and Grey Venger!'

'Issul, you are letting your emotions rule you. I think we should defer judgement until we have a clearer picture.'

'That is a charitable approach.'

'And a pragmatic one.'

Issul drew in a great breath and released it in a long sigh. 'Orbus, I do not know where to go now. I feel lost.'

'You go on, surely? Nothing has changed in regard to your goal, after all. You have to continue to the Krai camp and the Farplace Opening beneath it.'

Issul was uncertain. Orbus said, 'Perhaps I can lift your spirits, at least a little. I have something interesting to report. I have made strenuous efforts to sensitize my awareness to Leth's presence.'

'And you have had success?' Issul was suddenly enlivened.

'Of a modest kind, I think. I have heard, or sensed, Leth's appeal, and his recrimination.'

'Recrimination?'

'My perception is that he may not know how he has come to be within my domain, or why it is that I am not there to assist him. He thinks I have forsaken him, possibly deliberately. I have tried to impinge my thoughts upon his consciousness and reassure him that he is not abandoned. I cannot tell whether my efforts have had an effect.'

'What of Jace and Galry?'

'I can say nothing with certainty, but if Leth lives then it gives me confidence that they are with him.'

'Keep trying, Orbus! You must reach them!'

Orbus half-turned, tilting his head to one side. 'Hark! What is that sound?'

Issul was still, her senses attuned to the forest. It was silent –
even the birds held their voices.

'What did you hear?' she whispered.

'Someone or something is nearby. That way!'

'Quick, begone!'

Orbus faded. Issul pushed the casket and chest deep into cover
beneath the bushes, throwing moss and leaf litter over the precious
items to further conceal them. She moved to her horse, took bow
and arrows from behind its saddle, then stole silently through the
bushes in the direction Orbus had indicated to the edge of the
little grove.

Crouching, she scanned the forest, then slipped forward and
placed herself behind a boulder. She waited, eyes and ears alert.
Nothing moved or made a sound. Satisfied that she was not observed
Issul moved again, creeping soundlessly up a rise to take cover
behind the decaying, fallen trunk of an oak clad in dense ivy and
moss. She raised herself a little to peer over the trunk, and froze.

Not ten paces away a man was crouched on one knee, his fingers
touching the rain-soaked earth. He was of middle stature, from what
Issul could see, and lean and sinewy. His skin was leathery brown,
the mouth a thin, cruel gash beneath a long curved nose and narrow,
deeply set eyes. High, prominent cheekbones, together with the skin,
suggested possible Murinean blood. He wore a dark leather doublet
and deep green pantaloons. About his head, confining long, thick,
unruly black hair was a broad green fillet, knotted at the back of the
skull, with two long ribbons hanging between his shoulderblades.
At his belt were several knives, a sword and, stuffed into his
pantaloons, the stock of a whip. He appeared to be examining
the ground.

Looking for tracks?

Her tracks?

The man lifted his gaze and peered into the forest shade. He
seemed puzzled. A sudden thought struck Issul: if her horse should
make a sound . . . Silently she drew an arrow from her quiver and
notched it to her bowstring.

The man rose slowly to his feet, poised almost like a dancer.
His eyes were still searching the forest around him; his head was
slightly cocked. His head swivelled gradually in her direction.

Challenge him, or stay hidden? The chances weighed against his
being alone. But was it her he was looking for? With benign or

wicked intent? Something in his expression suggested that goodness was not one of his dominant traits.

A movement in the undergrowth to her left, about thirty paces away, caught Issul's attention. A second man came into view. This one was taller, more massively built, with a low black fringe and a beard covering much of his face. He wore studded leather, with a peaked steel cap of good quality upon his head. He looked questioningly at the first man, who turned towards him and shook his head. The newcomer glanced quickly about the woods, then jerked his thumb across his chest, turned and disappeared back beneath the trees. The first man followed him, watching the forest as he went.

III

Issul leaned her shoulder against the fallen trunk and breathed again, thinking rapidly. Who were these two? What were they seeking? Were they in company?

She knew she could not leave without finding out more about them. If they were looking for her and she set off alone for the Farplace Opening, they might surprise her along the way. Perhaps worse, they might let her lead them directly to it.

No, she could not risk that. But could she conceivably turn the tables upon them?

Issul glanced back to the grove. The blue casket was well-concealed, but . . . the horse. She ran back down the slope and quickly stripped the horse of saddle and equipment. These she hid in the undergrowth, away from the chest. Then she led the horse from the bushes, removed its bridle, pointed its head to the south-west – the opposite direction to that in which the two strangers had gone – and slapped it hard on the rump. The mount trotted away, its injured leg troubling it less now that it was unburdened.

Issul hid the bridle, then set off in pursuit of the two men.

She moved with great caution, darting from tree to boulder to tree. She listened, slipped forward another twenty paces, listened.

At last she was rewarded: the snap of a twig, the faintest clink of something metallic. The men were almost directly ahead of her, and close.

She moved forward a few paces, listened again, utterly still. Now she heard the murmur of voices, too low to make out what was being said. And it seemed the men were stationary.

A low limestone bluff rose a short distance away to Issul's right, its crest perhaps thirty feet above her head. She slipped away and crept warily up the tree-strewn slope that would take her to the lip of the bluff. Approaching the summit she dropped to the ground and wriggled on her belly to the lip. From here she was able to look down to where five men were grouped in a sheltered glade at the foot of the bluff. One of them was the larger of the two she had followed. His companion was not in sight. Three others were of similar, rough and somewhat sinister appearance. The last, who was seated on a low boulder with his knees wide apart and facing away from Issul's position, wore a long dark blue cloak over hardened leather, and impressed her as being the leader.

Horses were tethered nearby. The five men were in hushed conversation, and though she strained her ears Issul could not hear what they said. The man in the blue cloak rose and took a few steps to the side. Something about him disturbed Issul. His face was obscured, yet there was something in the way he moved – she felt that she had seen him before somewhere.

At that moment another man ran into the glade. He spoke quickly to the others, gesturing. The leader issued a curt command and the men dispersed hurriedly in various directions.

Issul ducked back quickly from the lip. She was struck by the men's manner. Though they had the look of cutthroats their actions showed them to be trained and disciplined. She sensed that she should hide herself, and began to move away. Rising, she found herself confronting two men. One was the tracker with the green headband whom she had followed here. He stood with his whip in one hand, a knife in the other. Beside him was a younger man with a bow drawn and aimed at her.

Others came swiftly and silently up the slope. Wordlessly they surrounded her, stripped her of weapons, bound her wrists behind her back and led her down to the glade beneath the bluff.

IV

The men were unsure of what to do with her, that much Issul worked out within minutes. Did they know who she was? They had made nothing plain, and she was unwilling to reveal her identity until she knew more of what they were about. She wore no crown of office; from her clothing and light mail they might judge her to be a noble woman and warrior. An unusual combination, but it did not in itself give her away.

But if they did not know who she was, why had they been tracking her?

Or had they been looking for someone or something else?

Issul was seated upon the ground, her back against the bole of a young oak. Her ankles had been bound now, as well as her wrists. She fumed silently: that they should dare to treat her so! That she had been stupid enough to allow herself to be captured – she had virtually done their job for them!

She still did not know who they were, but she was convinced that they were not mere common criminals.

And they seemed ill at ease with her, almost embarrassed, if it was possible for such men to know such an emotion. Were they unhappy at having taken her prisoner?

Four of her captors sat a short distance away, conferring in occasional whispers and casting dark glances at her. The others, she assumed, had taken up look-out positions. Their commander, the man in the blue cloak, was not present.

So far she had been asked few questions. The burly, bearded fellow who had been in the forest with the tracker earlier had asked her why she had been watching them.

'Did you expect me to just walk up and introduce myself?' she replied scornfully.

His next question chilled her, and provided more than a clue as to their goal. 'What has happened to the chest?'

'What chest?'

'Don't be obstinate. The chest that you carried upon your horse.'

'I don't know what you are talking about.'

For a moment she had thought he might strike her. Instead he turned, scowling, and rejoined his cronies.

Minutes passed. Another of the gang arrived, spoke briefly with the rest, out of Issul's hearing, then left again. Issul continued to rail at herself. Such a fool to have followed them. She should have taken off immediately with Orbus. What had she been thinking of?

She considered: if they wanted the chest then they surely knew something of what it contained. Under such circumstances her status was perhaps not even relevant. It was Orbus they wanted – and what would they not do to her to force her to reveal his whereabouts?

Issul thought of Galry and Jace. She thought of Leth. She gritted her teeth, and vowed to herself. No horrors that animals like these might inflict could make her give up Orbus's world.

But Orbus's world was lost anyway, the casket concealed in a thicket deep within the forest. If these men took her far from this lonely place, not even she would have a hope of ever finding it again.

TWELVE

I

Lord Fectur padded the western corridors of the Palace of Orbia, his head low, his brooding gaze inward and intent.

Too many mysteries, all at once! His brain could barely contend with them all. And a newly instated, delicately tuned apparatus of government plainly established to keep him as much as possible in the dark. An infestation of curses upon the meddling magician, Pader Luminis! He dared play games with the Lord High Invigilate? Well, it was not with impunity. These were dangerous games the bespectacled little picaroon played. Master Arcanist or not, he would learn that simple fact quickly enough.

For now, though, Fectur did his best to put the new Lord-Protector out of his thoughts. Matters of even greater immediacy occupied his mind.

He continued on his way, discouraging by his very stride and bearing anyone who might have an inclination to speak with him. He entered the royal residence, passing along its many gilded passageways until he arrived at the apartments occupied by the recently deceased Duke of Giswel, his living but mentally stricken young widow Mawnie, Duchess Demawndella, sister of the Queen, and their infant daughter, Lir.

Without a glance at the guard at the entrance, who snapped erect at his approach, Fectur strode through the various anterooms, ignoring the various members of Demawndella's staff and coterie, and marched without announcement into the Duchess's bedchamber.

Mawnie lay pale and inert in her bed. Upon a table beside her pillow a china bowl was filled with steaming aromatic herbs. Springs and sprays hung from bedposts and around the window. A compress had been laid upon the Duchess's forehead. On a chair beside her sat a plump, red-headed nurse and, standing close by, the spare, stiff figure of Doctor Melropius examined a thick green paste in a mortar.

Fectur sniffed, vaguely offended by the vapours that imbued the air in the bedchamber. 'How is the Duchess today, Doctor?'

Melropius, visibly disconcerted by the arrival of the Lord High Invigilate, answered in a vexed near-whisper, 'I – there is an improvement. Sh-she is calmer than before and has sh—has shown extended periods of lucidity.'

'Good. Well, that is welcome news,' said Fectur silkily, his grey carp eyes on Mawnie's still features. 'I need to speak to her.'

'My lord, I do not think that would be advisable.'

Fectur fixed him with his most implacable stare. 'It is important, Doctor.'

Melropius balked. 'Ah, well, er, yes, of course. But please take care not to over-excite her. She is in a most fragile condition still. And remember, my lord, the Duchess knows nothing of recent events.'

'Very good.' Fectur grew still. A moment passed. 'Well?'

'My lord?'

'You may leave us, Doctor. I do not need you here.'

'My lord, I – I think —'

'Thank you, Melropius.'

Melropius swallowed. He hovered for a moment in indecision, then set down his mortar, bowed, and withdrew. As he reached the door Fectur spoke to him over his shoulder. 'Melropius?'

The doctor halted nervously. 'My lord?'

'I just wanted to thank you for your support in that terrible business with the King. Witnessing his decline and realizing the inevitability of his removal from office must have been most painful for you, as it was for us all. Rest assured, your actions will not be forgotten. Not by myself nor anyone else.'

Doctor Melropius flushed and his eyes grew suddenly moist. A small sob issued involuntarily from somewhere deep in his chest, and he backed from the chamber. Fectur turned a glacial stare to the nurse, who hastily relinquished her station and scurried from the room.

Lord Fectur took the seat she had vacated at Demawndella's head. He watched Mawnie awhile, thinking. Then he leaned forward and peeled the compress from her forehead, its medicinal odours not to his liking, and tossed it onto the floor on the other side of the bed.

'Mawnie.'

Mawnie's eyelids flickered.

'Mawnie.'

Fectur lightly smacked her cheek with the back of his hand. Mawnie blinked and opened her eyes. Fectur took her hand, which lay limp upon the coverlet. 'Hallo, Mawnie.'

Mawnie's head turned and she focused her eyes blearily upon him. Her brow knitted. 'You? What do you want?'

'I have come to talk to you, Mawnie. I was so sorry to hear of your illness.'

Clearly, the discovery of the Master of Security for Enchantment's Edge seated at her bedside had cast the young Duchess into a state of some confusion. Fectur had anticipated this; in fact it was quite desirable, as long as her mind was not too far gone. She of course had no knowledge of his recent clashes with members of her family, nor his current descent from grace, and that too was in accord with his wishes. 'I wanted to ask you about your sister.'

'Iss?'

'No, not Issul, Mawnie. Ressa.'

'Ressa?' The tiny muscles around Mawnie's eyes contracted.

Fectur nodded. He had received firsthand reports of Demawndella's illness, her dementia and the wild outpourings that issued from her mouth. His curiosity had been aroused. There had always been an element of mystery surrounding the incident on Sentinel Peak in which Mawnie's twin-sister, Ressa, had incurred the terrible injuries that led to her death. Fectur had himself been instrumental in ensuring that news of the tragedy was kept to the barest details.

A bear attack, that had been the story. But Fectur knew otherwise. He had ridden out to the promontory himself, with a platoon of his men, to hunt down the creature that had attacked the two sisters and raped Ressa. But he had found nothing. After Ressa's death Mawnie had fallen into a deep depression. She appeared also to have effectively blocked the incident from her mind; certainly she could never be drawn to speak of it. She had subsequently been courted by, and married, the King's cousin, Duke Hugo of Giswel, though everyone but Mawnie, it seemed, was aware that Hugo had merely transferred his attentions from the maiden he had loved and who was now gone from the world, to one he did not but who was her mirror-image.

The incident and its consequences had intrigued Fectur. That Mawnie should have begun ranting deliriously about it now, after keeping it buried for so long, struck him as being possibly significant. He was acting somewhat on a hunch. Was there more to be known? Perhaps, perhaps not. But he would probe delicately, just in case. He would see what he would see.

He had no great liking for Mawnie. She had been light-headed even as a child. These days he considered her little more than a souse and a trollop. Still, in her most inebriate moments she had given Fectur potentially useful information about her lovers and Hugo's, and the intrigues that passed between them. More than one had since been recruited into the ranks of the Ministry of Security's informants, the threat of scandal and subsequent reprisals being a far greater inducement than any thought of payment.

Fectur saw now that the very mention of Ressa's name caused Mawnie upset. She turned her head away. 'No.'

Fectur squeezed her hand and adopted his most avuncular tone. 'Mawnie, it is important that we bring this into the open. For your own well-being, and perhaps even for the good of the kingdom.'

Mawnie's brow furrowed again. 'What do you mean?'

'There *is* something, isn't there? Something with poor Ressa? Something you haven't told us.'

'No. There is nothing.' She pulled her hand from his. 'Go away!'

'Mawnie, I only want to help you.'

Mawnie had begun twining strands of her fine, long hair around her finger. She shook her head. 'There is nothing.'

'But you have said, Mawnie. In your sleep, you have said things.'

'What things?' Her agitation was mounting. She began to sit up, would not meet his eye.

'Here, let me help you.' Fectur stacked the pillows behind her back.

'What things?' she repeated.

'Nothing too specific,' replied Fectur, feeling his way carefully. 'But several times you have made reference to that awful incident in which you and Ressa suffered so. We wonder whether there might be something, some detail, that you have never spoken of. The King has asked me to question you about it.'

'Leth?'

Fectur nodded. 'He is very concerned about you.'

A spasm of a smile flickered on Mawnie's lips.

Fectur continued: 'You have said that it was you. In the woods, it was you that he wanted. And just nights ago you suddenly called out . . .'

'What? I called out what?' She tugged vigorously at the ends of her hair.

Fectur leaned nearer, convinced he was close to something. 'It was not easy to make out, but I was driven to infer that something might have happened, something on the promontory, or linked to that unspeakable incident. Something that, either through your own inability to remember or unwillingness to compromise those closest to you, you never disclosed.'

Was there anything? Mawnie was shaking her head adamantly. 'No. I told you everything. There's nothing more.'

Lord Fectur sat back. He could see the distress in her eyes, and did not want to push her too far. It was quite possible that she was genuinely unable to remember. Or was there nothing there after all? The creature had never been sighted again. Yet it was not a fabrication, for Issul had seen it too.

'Nothing more. Nothing more.'

Mawnie was on the edge of raving. Frustrated, Fectur resolved to come back and try again at another time. If there was something to be known, and Mawnie held it, he would draw it from her. If it meant scouring her brain and leaving her without a single lucid thought in her head, he would draw it from her.

He stood, smiling, and reached into his tunic. 'Well, give it some thought, Mawnie dear. Something might come back to you. We will talk again soon. In the meantime, here is something for you; to aid you in your recovery. But *ssh!* Not a word to the good doctor, mind. He would not approve. Put it beneath your pillow. It's a little secret, just between you and me.'

'What is it?' Mawnie examined the small metal flask he put into her hands.

'Your favourite fortified plum spirit. To be taken only in small doses, now!'

He saw her eyes light up. She would be intoxicated within minutes. As he turned to leave, a movement in a corner of the room drew his eye. Little Lir, Mawnie's infant daughter, sat in the shadows, watching him, her deep sea-green eyes almost aglow. Fectur scowled, then flashed her an affectionless smile. He found children an irritant. This one in particular he considered a brat precocious beyond reckoning, even more obnoxious than her two ghastly cousins.

He was aware of Lir's eyes following him as he left the chamber. In the room outside he paused and leaned close to speak surreptitiously into the ear of the red-headed nurse. 'The Duchess will likely become quite voluble in a little while. I want to know every word she speaks. *Every* word.'

II

Grey Venger's disappearance continued to prick and prod at Lord Fectur's consciousness. It irked mightily that the True Sept's leader, who had already caused him grave personal affront, should have slipped through his fingers now. He wondered at Queen Issul's hidden reasons for moving Venger. Obviously she had wished him put somewhere beyond Fectur's reach, but what secrets could Venger have given forth?

Venger's willingness to enter into protracted discussions with King Leth had come as a surprise to Fectur and had brought him no little chagrin. Fectur had been unable to place ears in any position to overhear what had passed between them. Hence he had found himself almost entirely reliant upon what the King chose to disclose, which was precious little. His own brief time in Grey Venger's company had proved tantalizing and exasperating in the extreme; Venger had revealed nothing of what had passed between Leth and himself. Before Fectur could interview him again the Queen had gotten to him. And now, just when he had thought to have the chance to confront Venger again, and extract what he wanted by whatever means he deemed appropriate, the man had vanished!

A thorough undercover search of the Palace had failed to reveal Venger's lurking-place. Fectur felt reasonably confident that Grey

Venger was in fact no longer in Orbia at all. Probably not even in Enchantment's Edge. Yes, that would make sense. The Queen would have smuggled him out under guard during the night. He would have been brought to join her company somewhere beyond the city walls.

Confirmation would no doubt be brought with Fectur's first report from Commander Gordallith. But that might not come for another day or two, or even longer. In the meantime Fectur could do little more than chafe and gnash and wonder.

There was the Queen's other 'guest', too. An old woman, reported to have been causing a nuisance at the Palace gate. Screeching about a child in the woods! Mysteriously admitted to an audience with the Queen, and now, like Venger, vanished!

Fectur ground his teeth. A bent figure in a shawl and cowl had been escorted to one of the Queen's company's wagons just before departure. So, who was this hag? Not the peasant woman, Ohirbe, he knew. Could she be the other one, the crone whose appearance at the forest poolside had first brought Ohirbe scurrying here and set so much in motion? If so, what secrets did she possess?

Again, he could but trust that enlightenment in some form would soon be brought in the shape of a missive from Gordallith.

In the meantime Fectur took himself to the White Eaglet's Tower. Ascending to the uppermost level, he paused before the carmine oak door that was the entrance to Pader Luminis's private apartment and workshop. A red ram's head, forged in iron, faced him, a heavy black iron ring between its jaws.

Fectur grasped the ring and hammered twice, resoundingly. By preference he would have simply burst in with a squad of good men and taken the place apart. But circumspection had to prevail now; he could not afford any overtly illicit actions against the Lord Protector pro tem. It could be construed as treason. At the least it might be an embarrassment, and used deftly against him could further diminish his courtly status. In any case, he was not quite sure what he was looking for.

Fectur waited, tapping one thumb against his hip. There was no reply from within, no sound at all. He had passed by Pader's new office on his way here and reassured himself of Pader's whereabouts. But he knocked again, for it was quite conceivable that Pader would have installed a watchman or some trusted retainer in his absence.

Still no reply. Fectur tried the handle and was mildly surprised to discover the door unlocked. Senses alert, he pushed it open, allowing it to swing back to its fullest span.

A musty, shadowed passage faced him. Stone columns lined its sides; cobwebs hung thickly from the vaulted ceiling. Beyond was an arched, murky-glassed double-window, throwing a measure of dull lavender light onto a larger room. Fectur stepped forward, slowly and quietly, his grey gaze absorbing every detail. In the dominant chamber massive leatherbound tomes burdened the sagging shelves that lined every wall. More were piled in dusty corners and strewn across a large central workbench. Also upon the bench were flasks and retorts, little lidded containers of various shapes and sizes, obscurely figured charts, writing materials and items of paraphernalia and esoterica whose precise function Fectur could only begin to guess at.

He stood beside the workbench and stared intently about the dimness of the chamber. An ancient chair and a divan were set close before an empty hearth. In a shadowed recess a huge black stove stood, its crooked iron flue disappearing into the ceiling. Pots, plates and other scullery items surrounded it. Fectur could feel the stove's warmth stealing through the chamber.

He opened the door of a nearby cupboard. More books and charts and sundry personal items faced him. He paused for thought. What was he hoping to discover?

He knew not. But Pader Luminis had enjoyed intimate contact with both the King, prior to his disappearance, and the Queen since. Surely somewhere there had to be a clue which would indicate at least the beginnings of an explanation of what had happened?

Fectur's lip curled. Such coincidence! So many disappearances! Oh yes, Grey Venger and the hag had vanished with the help of human hands. But the King and his brats?

It galled. And the fact that Pader Luminis and Issul obviously knew so much more than he galled even more.

But was the little conjuror likely to leave evidence of any kind behind? He would expect Fectur to be on the prowl, as would the Queen. Fectur acknowledged it was unlikely. Still, he would make no assumptions; nothing was lost by double-checking. This unease in his mind, this unaccustomed feeling of not knowing, unsettled him greatly. Truly, he was conspired against. Incompatible forces seemed to be working together to undo him. He, who had always thrived on information and knowledge about others, was for the first time in his life finding himself before locked doors to which others held the only keys.

In the midst of these thoughts, Fectur became suddenly still. The hairs at the back of his neck crawled; all his instincts tingled. By a sixth sense that the years had taught him to trust unfailingly, he knew that he was watched.

Slowly he let his gaze, travel the shadows and corners of Pader's chamber. It shifted past the stove – yes, the stove, embers still burning within. How could he have missed that? Someone *was* here.

Fectur took a single step backward, swivelling slightly. He allowed his weight to settle, bent his knees slightly, poised for instant defence or attack.

There! A shrinking movement! In the shadows of a recess in the wall!

Fectur moved as if casually, giving nothing away. An observer might have thought him to be approaching a small desk set against a wall at the furthest end of the chamber. As he arrived in front of the desk his hand shot out. He grasped hair, warm flesh. He pinched, twisted, wrenched. There was a shrill whimper from the dark depths of an alcove over a shelf set above the desk.

'Come forth, miscreant!'

With a sudden, cruel jerk Fectur dragged out his victim, who tumbled skull over buttocks onto the little desk. Fectur did not relinquish his grip. He yanked the creature to its feet.

'Who are you? What is your name? What are you doing here? Why do you watch me?'

He had at his mercy a boy, dishevelled and scruffy, whose face was constricted in pain. Fectur's grip was such that the boy was forced onto the very tips of his toes, his whole body rigid with pain.

Seeing that he posed no direct threat, Fectur released him and thrust him away. 'Well, answer me!'

'I—I—I—I—' The boy quaked so violently that he could not speak.

'Be easy, youth. Answer my questions. Do you know who I am?'

With chattering teeth, the boy nodded.

'Then answer me. You will not necessarily be harmed.'

'I— I— I am R-Radius, sire.'

'Radius . . . .? Radius . . . ?' The name meant nothing to him. 'What are you doing here, skulking in holes like a creepy-crawly?'

'S— sire, this is my home.'

'Your home? Ah, of course! You are the magician's assistant.' Suddenly it seemed to Fectur that the boy might be a very worthwhile find indeed. A smile warmed his customarily chill and austere features. He reached out and took the boy's shoulders. 'Come, Radius. Come and sit down. Let us have a little talk.'

He brought Radius to a stool beside Pader Luminis's workbench, then dragged another one forward and seated himself directly before the boy. 'You have worked for your master a long time?'

'Since I was very small, sire. He looked after me when my parents both died of smallpox. He— he has been very good to me.'

'How touching. I would imagine that you have come to know your master very well in the intervening years.'

Radius shifted unhappily. 'I s'pose so, sire.'

'And, of course, you are very loyal.'

'Of course, sire!'

'Loyal to your master, and to the Crown and Government also.'

The phrasing of the question seemed to dismay Radius. 'Y— yes, sire.'

'Good. That is most admirable – and to be expected, of course. Now, there are a few things I wish to ask you, Radius. They are important questions, but they shouldn't take long, provided that you are straightforward with me. I hope, that being so, that I will not have to resort to interviewing you further at the Ministry of Realm Security.'

The boy's eyes went wide in stark fear. 'I haven't done nothing, sire!'

Fectur smiled inwardly. 'I am sure you haven't. No, that would be an extreme measure that I am sure will not be necessary. Just be honest with me and you will have nothing at all to fear.'

In short order Lord Fectur had extracted from Radius all that his instincts told him the boy had to give. It cast light on some of the questions that clamoured in his mind. In one or two instances it proved a revelation. And it perturbed him no less than when he had striven and probed in ignorance. He rose stiffly from the stool.

'Very good, Radius. You have done well. Now, there is one last important matter. I have not been here. You have not seen me or spoken to me. Do you understand?'

The boy looked up at him in trembling stupefaction.

Fectur's eyes glittered icily and his voice took on a harder edge. 'If your master asks, you have not laid eyes on me. Do you understand?'

Radius nodded dumbly.

'There is great upheaval in the Realm just now. You know that, don't you?'

'Y – yes, sire.'

'There are certain investigations underway. Certain folk – some of them the last people anyone would suspect – have demonstrated themselves to be working against the better interests of our beloved kingdom. Truly, you would be surprised at some of the persons I have had to investigate.'

Radius was open-mouthed.

'But when all is done, those who are seen to have served the Realm faithfully will be rewarded,' continued Fectur. 'I do not mean only the great knights and ladies, the ministers and grandees, the doers and shakers. No, everyone who is known to have contributed to the overall welfare of the Realm will be duly rewarded. No matter their station, high or low. Do you follow me, Radius?'

Again Radius nodded.

Fectur smiled and lightly patted his head. 'Good. But in the meantime, discretion is the watchword; that is, speak to no one, *no one* about what has happened here between you and me.'

'Of c – course, sire.'

'You see, it would be a grave matter, a grave matter indeed, if I learned that you had spoken to anyone about what has passed between us. It might even give me cause to question your allegiances.'

'I— I won't say anything. N— not anything, sire. My lord.'

'That's as it should be. And I think, too, that if your master thought you had been gossiping about his private business, he might be displeased. What do you think he would do, Radius?'

'He— he would be very cross, sire.'

'Do you think he might deprive you of your station? Cast you out?'

Radius swallowed, nodded.

'Well, we wouldn't want that.' Fectur reached into his pocket and brought forth a coin, which he held out to the boy. 'My thanks, Radius. And keep your eyes and ears open. There is a chance I may have need of your services again one day, if I am sure you can be trusted. Now, about your business.'

With a last cold glance around Pader Luminis's chambers, Fectur turned and departed.

III

Evening found the Lord High Invigilate at the window of his private office high in the Ministry of Realm Security. He gazed out abstractedly over the shrouded and netted towers and rooftops of Orbia Palace and Enchantment's Edge, his wide brow knitted in concentration. Under their strange new mantle Orbia's extraordinary towers seemed somehow less, rather than more, fantastic in their form. For there was normally an inexplicable quality, an element of the fabulous and fantastic about Orbia. Its many-hued, multiformed marble towers and spires seemed at times to defy rational and physical laws in their construction. Even in the near-dark they struck the eye and mind. Fectur was reminded that Orbia's origins were unknown, the subject of centuries of speculation and debate.

And, as if the sight of the Palace was not enough in itself to strike wonder into the hearts and consciousnesses of any who beheld it, far off, beyond the dusk-clad city-castle and the great void beneath the high scarp on which it perched, the weird-lights glowed.

Many times Fectur had stood here. Many times in his life he had wondered, as so many had wondered before him, about the nature of Enchantment and the coloured lights that flitted and flickered so enticingly and eerily about its peaks. Like everyone else, Fectur had always been of the opinion that no man or woman could travel there. Such was the evidence, undisputed for generations.

And now here was the boy, Radius, telling him that the Queen was bound for Enchantment, that, fantastic as it might seem, she had been there already. And with her now, somehow hidden in a small blue casket, was a god.

It strained credibility to its uttermost limits. Yet Radius had not lied, Fectur was certain in his mind of that. The boy had simply described what he had seen and overheard passing between the

Queen and Pader Luminis. He had been too terrified to conceal anything, incredible though the truth appeared.

Hence Fectur had learned that the Queen had come to Pader Luminis in a state of some agitation just weeks earlier, to speak of matters grave and mysterious. This had followed immediately on the heels of her perilous visit, under Fectur's aegis, to Overlip where, in the Tavern of the Veiled Light, she had spoken with a man known to be an associate of Grey Venger. It was on the following morning that she had departed so suddenly and without explanation for the village of Lastmeadow.

At that meeting with Pader Luminis, Radius had, out of sheer caprice, feigned ignorance of the Queen's identity. She had demanded his dismissal from the chamber but, intrigued by what he had already heard, Radius had not actually left the apartment. Closing the outer door with deliberate emphasis, he had lingered for some moments undetected in the dark. Hence, fearful, his heart in his mouth, he had heard the Queen and his venerable master talk of Enchantment and its gods, and the True Sept's creed in respect of the so-named Legendary Child.

Eventually Radius's fear had overcome any earlier sense of derring-do. He knew he was hearing forbidden things, things that would land him in terrible trouble should he be discovered. So he had slipped silently from the apartment some time before the Queen made her departure.

Even so, in its own way much of what Radius had to say had proved illuminating.

Radius also told of a meeting between Pader Luminis and King Leth. The boy spoke as if relieved to unburden himself, as though what he had heard had seethed and churned within him ever since, building to a dangerous pressure and constantly seeking an outlet. And now Fectur had provided that outlet.

The King had come to Pader's rooms, Radius said, only days ago. He too had been gravely agitated, and seemed to think that something dreadful might happen to him. They had spoken about King Leth's talks with Grey Venger, then the King had asked a great boon of Pader. Radius was ignorant of the nature of the boon, for at that point King Leth had asked Pader to accompany him to his private apartments.

Fectur had pounced eagerly at this mention of Leth and Grey Venger, but Radius's powers of precise recall were sadly limited.

He reported snippets of information regarding the True Sept and the Legendary Child, but plainly the bulk of it had passed over his head. Still, there was something there, and quite obviously it had been kept most deliberately from Fectur's ears.

Even more recently, the very day prior to her departure, Radius had overheard further snatches of conversation between the Queen and Pader Luminis. Again he had been dismissed, but had lingered secretly as before, intrigued and terrified. And now came the thunderbolt: Queen Issul discussing with Pader the fact that that she had been to Enchantment! That she was now bound to return there!

Every time he considered this, Fectur experienced a surge of complex emotion in his breast. How could Issul have found a way into that forbidden land? Radius said she had not made this clear. But she had confided to Pader that she sought something called 'The Soul of the Orb', which resided somewhere within Enchantment. And she had spoken of a blue casket and a god-creature named Orbus who resided within it.

And as if all this were not revelation enough, it appeared that the fate of the vanished King and the darling little prince and princess were also bound up in Issul's quest, as much as was the fate of Enchantment's Edge itself.

So both Issul and Pader Luminis knew what had happened to the King, after all.

And all of it had been kept from the Spectre!

Fectur steamed silently. It galled. Oh, how it galled. He recalled again how he had caught Issul and the cursed conjuror, heads together in Leth's study. Surely then, it was this blue casket that they had been discussing, which Issul clutched hidden to her breast.

'No one must know of this!'

'I swore as much to Leth. He bade me warn you, or whomsoever I passed it on to: its existence must always remain a secret.'

Well, it was a secret no longer. Fectur itched, almost bursting from his skin as he fought the urge to ride out now in pursuit of the Queen and her precious cargo. More than a day and a half had passed since her departure; he would not find her. And so much still demanded his personal attention here in Enchantment's Edge. He could only trust that Gordallith would do his job well and that a report would soon be forthcoming.

* * *

In addition to all else, Radius had confirmed that Issul and Pader Luminis had made arrangements for Grey Venger's removal from Enchantment's Edge. The old woman too. She was called Arene. Radius took her to be a mystic or clairvoyant of some description, but could furnish nothing more about her.

Finally, at Fectur's urging, Radius, his cheeks aflame, had described how the two had planned the Lord High Invigilate's humiliation in the Special Assembly.

Fectur closed his eyes. There would be a reckoning for this. Oh yes, that much he promised himself.

But in the meantime, how was he to make the best of all he had learned?

To begin with Fectur considered the possibility that the information Radius had passed on might be dissimulation. Not on Radius's part. No, the boy had been far too scared to tell anything but the truth. But could Issul and the magician have concocted this fantastic tale deliberately to mislead, knowing that the boy would pass it on?

The more he considered this the more he was inclined to dismiss it. No, it all rang true. Looking back, everything fell into place; all – or almost all – the unanswered questions. He would proceed cautiously, but in the belief that he was not misinformed.

Next he thought of Radius. The boy's knowledge made him a serious risk. Was it wise to let him live?

For the time being, all things considered, Fectur decided that it was. The boy had privileged, trusted access to Pader Luminis. He had useful ears. He might still remember more details of what he had already reported. It would be a pity to lose such a unique and valuable source just yet. If the necessity arose he could be disposed of with little trouble.

Then Fectur gave his attention to the Queen's quest, but resolved that to mull any further over it just now would be time wasted. He had acted with foresight, after all. The machinery was in position. Until he heard from Gordallith there was little more that he could do. Except . . .

Hmmm, the bodyguard, Kol, who was now assigned to Pader Luminis, had travelled back with the Queen from wherever she had been after leaving Lastmeadow. His knowledge could prove very useful.

At this point in his musings Fectur was interrupted by a curt knock upon his door. An officer of his Security Cadre entered, halted before Fectur's desk and saluted. 'The prisoner is below, sir.'

'Any problems?' Fectur enquired.

'None. There will be some repercussions, almost certainly, but nothing we aren't prepared for.'

'No identities?'

'We carried nothing. Of course, fingers will point after an abduction like this. But our accusers will never dare to raise their voices without sure evidence.'

'Good. Let us see if those fingers can be made to point elsewhere.'

'I will attend to it.'

'His chamber has been prepared?'

'Just as you specified, my lord.'

'Then I think I will go down and pay my respects.'

Fectur descended via the numerous stairways that let into the grim, lightless bowels of the Ministry of Realm Security. Here, in the chill dungeons, he passed along narrow aisles, ignoring the cries that came to him from the honeycomb of tiny cells on either side, seeing nothing of the desperate prisoners huddled within. He came at length to a locked door outside which a sentry stood guard. At Fectur's nod the sentry unlocked the door and the Lord High Invigilate entered.

He stood in a dank, windowless cell which was illumined by a single torch on a bracket beside the door. The walls were of cold, rough stone, streaked with damp. Filthy straw littered the floor. A trestle-table had been set against one wall, a number of metal instruments arranged neatly upon its surface. Beneath the table was a three-legged wooden stool.

Against the opposite wall a man was spreadeagled, naked. His wrists and ankles were restrained by iron clamps attached by small lengths of chain, bolted to the wall. Over his mouth was a thick soiled gag, tied at the back of his neck.

Fectur stood before him and surveyed him for long moments without uttering a word. The man was aged in his late twenties, athletically built, though with signs of an incipient paunch. A mass of dark head hair complemented a thick, trimmed beard and a cloud of hair upon his broad chest. He looked up briefly and stared Fectur in the eye. A latticework of faint purple lines upon his eyes revealed indeterminate otherling origins; he was no doubt a hybrid of two or more of the various races that had made Enchantment's Edge their home over the centuries. He met Fectur's gaze long enough to make plain his contempt, then let his head hang again.

Fectur took a few moments to consider, then stepped forward and punched the man hard in the solar plexus. The air rushed from the prisoner's lungs in a loud blast, constricted by his gag. He writhed against his chains, striving against his agony to draw breath again. Fectur went to the table, and from the instruments there selected a pair of small, broad-bladed clipping-shears. He tested the action a couple of times, enjoying the clean smooth sound of the metal blades caressing. Then he stepped across to the prisoner, pulled aside his hair and snipped off the top of his left ear.

The man vented a muffled roar and yanked helplessly against his chains. Fectur stepped back to the table and replaced the shears.

'Just so that the terms of our conversation are properly understood.'

When the man's noise had subsided Fectur took up the shears again. The prisoner recoiled, straining against his chains, desperate sounds coming from behind the gag as his tormentor stepped close.

'Relax, man.' Fectur brought the shears up and sliced through the gag. 'Now, let's have a little chat, shall we?'

He pulled out the stool and sat down, his arms folded upon his chest. 'I have no taste for this, you know.'

The prisoner eyed him silently through glassy, narrowed eyes.

'Truly, I do only what is required,' Fectur continued. 'So, it is in your hands from here on. Now, do you want to start, or shall I?'

The prisoner spoke between his teeth. 'What is it that you want of me?'

'Oh, I think you know the answer to that,' said Fectur. 'And I will have the information I seek. Be sure of that, Iklar. Be very sure.'

He paused, letting his words work to their greatest effect. Iklar, naked and so vulnerable, his neck and breast slick with the blood running from his mutilated ear, dropped his gaze.

Fectur said, 'But let us proceed methodically. You will recall, a matter of less than a moon's passing ago, you were approached one evening in the Tavern of the Veiled Light in Overlip by a young woman, far from unattractive. She bade you carry a message to the outlawed leader of the True Sept, Grey Venger. This you duly did. You do not deny this, do you, Iklar?'

Iklar hesitated.

'Oh, come now,' said Fectur. 'Do not make me resort to cruder means. You *do* know where you are, don't you?'

Iklar's gaze flickered across the table and its contents. He closed his eyes and nodded. 'Aye. What you say is true.'

'Very good. Now, tell me what happened next.'

'I delivered the message as it was passed to me. But why do you ask this? It is well known that Grey Venger responded. He met, with King Leth himself, in Overlip, and later went voluntarily to the Palace.'

'Quite so. And now he is abroad, a prisoner of the Queen.'

Iklar's brow furrowed.

'It is true. Believe it or don't. I care not.'

'What of the King's promise?'

'What of it? Let us say that in regard to Grey Venger, the Crown and the Legendary Child, things have changed. Now, you will tell me how you contacted Venger.'

'I have never had access to Grey Venger. I merely delivered the message to another.'

Fectur took up the shears, stood, and approached him. 'Tell me only the truth, Iklar. If I have as much as a hint that you lie I will take off your nose, then your lips, then . . .' He traced a line down the man's neck and breast with the points of the shears, then circled the nipple. He stood back. 'Do you understand? And it would be only a beginning.'

'I do not lie!' insisted Iklar. 'I am a messenger, nothing more. The first stage in a channel, well-known to you and to the Crown. After me there would be others, three or more, before the channel touched the heart of the True Sept.'

Fectur knew it to be true. After the True Sept went quite literally underground he had expended much time and effort trying to reach its inner core. Frustratingly, the trail ended always at the Veiled Light. Surveillance teams had made Iklar their target, yet never had they discovered the moment when a message was passed, or to whom it was passed. Any of a hundred or more persons with whom Iklar mingled could have been the next link in the chain to the True Sept's heart. Fectur had wished for a purge of Overlip, but knew it to be impractical. So dense and intricate was that warren – it was another world, one which all the wiles of the Spectre could not penetrate.

'Yet the channel remains in place?'

'It did until an hour ago, when your men arrested me. That was reckless, my lord. I am nothing.'

'Do you think I am not aware of your status? But I am sure, if you were to return, the way could be opened once more. You will have passwords, codes, to cover all contingencies?'

Iklar gave a half-nod. He seemed puzzled.

'The True Sept established contact with the Krai Prince Anzejarl,' Fectur said. 'Do not deny it. I caught one of your members virtually in the act. In fact he died, confessing his crimes, here in this very chamber. The question that remains is, why? Anzejarl is not known for his love of bargaining or negotiation. What end does the True Sept seek in contacting the Krai? What do they have to offer?'

'You are asking the wrong man,' Iklar replied, his eyes pained. 'I am but a messenger.'

'Yes, I know that!' Fectur snapped. 'But the apparatus for reaching the Sept's heart remains in place, does it not? Through you I might still make contact with whichever High Priest now stands in Grey Venger's stead.'

'It might be possible. You could have done that without bringing me here first.'

Fectur glared at him. 'What do you know of "Orbus"?'

Iklar returned him a blank stare. 'What is this?'

By the look in his eyes Fectur knew him to be telling the truth. 'The "Soul of the Orb"?'

Iklar shook his head, his gaze enquiring.

'Well, let us see.' Fectur bent and picked up the fallen gag. He studied it ruminatively, then applied it to Iklar's bloody ear. Iklar flinched.

'You really should have a doctor see to that wound.'

Fectur tossed the shears onto the table and strode from the cell.

IV

Shreds.

They were all he had.

Everything came in shreds. Even now, with all he had learned today, he seemed hardly to have advanced a step. When he strung the shreds together he stared only at gaping holes in between.

For a man of Fectur's bent and temperament such a fragmented tapestry was an outrageous provocation. Moreover, it was a threat. He believed Iklar. He accepted that he might apply pain beyond imagining, take Iklar to and beyond the brink of death, and the man would yield nothing more than he had already given up. Yet the key, or *a* key, to resolving much of this intolerable mystery lay in discovering just what it was that the True Sept had that could weigh significantly in Prince Anzejarl's mind. Of this Fectur had become convinced.

But how to get to the Sept's secret heart?

He could send Iklar back, but would the Sept respond favourably?

Fectur had a single ace to play; something he had for the last two days been pondering how best to use. He did not himself understand it, but recognized that it had to be of consequence. It was something of which no one but he had knowledge.

He had not been totally truthful when reporting to King Leth the results of his interrogation of the captured agent sent by the True Sept to establish contact with the Krai. The man had not died as Fectur had claimed. Not quite. He had lingered, until only two days past.

For some time in the man's final hours Fectur had been on the point of dispatching him, yet something, an intuition, told him that the man had not quite given his all. Fectur was impressed by his resilience, by the Sept's capacity for instilling such extremes of loyalty into its members. But in the end his intuition had proved correct.

It was in his dying breath that the prisoner had finally given up his secret. He had been a man no longer; no longer knew who or what he was. And Fectur, with infinite patience, had won his confidence and prised from him those final, fateful words.

Those words, combined with everything else the Spectre had now learned, seemed laden with meaning. How it galled that he had been prevented from revealing them to Grey Venger as he had planned to do. But all was not lost. If he could just work out how best to use those words, they must surely now provide him with his longed-for access to the True Sept's hidden heart. And if he could reach the heart of the Sept, then through it he could reach Prince Anzejarl as well.

And if he could reach Anzejarl . . .

PART THREE

THIRTEEN

I

The wolfhearts milled below in a clearing bounded by a circle of obsidian standing stones.

'It is not a good time,' whispered Count Harg. 'They are assembling for a ritual of birthing.'

Leth gazed down upon the scene. He had rarely set eyes on creatures as strange as these.

They were twenty or so in number and had emerged from holes in the rock at the base of the cliff from which he and his dubious band of warriors looked down. Others were coming from rock formations beyond the stone circle. They came forward on all fours, approximately lupine in form, with long bodies clothed in sleek grey hair. They were far larger than wolves – perhaps as large as men – and their legs were accordingly large-boned and muscular. Their heads were wholly devoid of hair, bloody red in colour. The skulls were heavy and broad, crowned with thick folds of skin out of which rose short, thick cartilagenous stalks, three in number, at the tip of each of which was a bulbous eye set into a carapace of horny flesh. Their mouths were wide, gaping slits filled with a mass of fleshy tendrils which fell to a level somewhat below the wide jaws where they shivered and writhed ceaselessly, like beards of worms.

'I think we will have to attack,' whispered Harg. 'We can charge in at the gallop, take out as many as possible without pausing, and be through them and away before they properly know what has hit them.'

'Will they not permit us to pass unhindered?' queried Leth.

Harg shook his head.

'Can we not speak to them, negotiate a way through?'

Harg gave him a look of forbearance.

'I am reluctant to attack creatures who have done me no harm,' Leth said.

Harg nodded over his shoulder. 'Move back. We will talk about it.'

He signalled to Rasgul, the leader of the Abyss warriors. The three slid from their hiding-places and made their way back to the wayside where their horses were tethered, tended by the long-limbed youth, Juson.

'The Swordbearer thinks we should engage the wolfhearts in friendly badinage, and ask them if they will allow us to pass,' said Harg to Rasgul. Rasgul's frozen, scornful expression left Leth in no doubt as to the esteem in which the warrior held this opinion. Rasgul glanced away down the path and jettisoned a thin stream of saliva between his teeth into the dust.

'My point is that it seems a base, cowardly act simply to charge into them, swinging weapons, when they have done us no harm, nor even menaced us,' Leth said.

'They have done us no harm for the simple reason that they are not aware of our presence,' Harg replied. 'Were they so, we would be fighting for our lives just now. The wolfhearts are not inclined to cosy chats.'

'Then can we not wait for them to disperse?'

'Under different circumstances that is precisely what we would do. Unfortunately we have come upon them at the beginning of a birthing ritual. A new wolfheart cub is being brought into the tribe. It is an event that occurs rarely, perhaps once every three years. The rite and attendant celebrations could last for up to three days.'

'Is there no other way past?'

'You have seen for yourself that the path passes right alongside their circle. The one factor in our favour is that their attention will be focused wholly upon the centre of the circle. It is the only way.'

A weird, melancholic sound reached Leth's ears. Harg nodded to himself. 'The ritual has begun.'

Rasgul stared at Leth as though expecting something, though he spoke no word.

'Well, Swordbearer, you are our leader. What is your decision?' asked Harg, his sarcasm unconcealed.

'I am a stranger here. I can but follow your advice,' said Leth.

'But if it must be as you have said, then let it be with the minimum of bloodshed.'

'Fear not for that. Not one of us will be lingering amongst these beasts for a moment longer than is necessary.' Harg turned to Rasgul. 'It is preferable to wait for the moment of birthing, I think.'

The pallid warrior nodded and muttered something in a guttural hiss that Leth did not catch. Harg nodded pensively, and turned back. 'Rasgul is in agreement. Come, you are about to witness a phenomenon rare and strange.'

From the rocks they looked down again upon the bestial assembly. The wolfhearts had ceased milling; they sat now in orderly fashion upon their haunches around the ring of tall dark stones. Leth estimated that there were more than forty of them now. They were all focused upon the centre of the ring, and from their open mouths came the woeful howling, which rose and fell in pitch and seemed to make the very air vibrate in sympathy.

Leth watched and waited. The sound troubled him, arousing contradictory feelings and tangled emotions. Over his head the roiling chill mist through which they had descended was a mass of low, dense dark cloud, scummy brownish in hue. It cut out much of the daylight from above, stealing any sight of the Orb of the Godworld or the World's Pain, and casting an umbrageous demi-light upon the vista below.

The wolfhearts' tragic song dropped abruptly in pitch to become a near-drone. Leth felt Harg's touch upon his arm. Harg handed him a scimitar in a leather sheath. 'Use this when we attack. Do not under any circumstances draw the Orbsword. The Kancanitrix will sense it. She will know that you are near and will prepare herself. We are beneath the mantle now, fully within the Death Abyss. This is Ascaria's domain. Do not draw the Orbsword until you stand within her fortress.'

Leth buckled the scimitar beside the Orbsword. Below, the wolfhearts fell suddenly mute. The silence was uncanny, seeming to swell and take on an almost palpable form. The standing stones at the periphery of the circle had begun to glow softly. Their obsidian blackness was gradually being replaced by a dull greenish lambency. This strange light was directed into the centre of the circle, where it coalesced to form a slowly rotating globule which rested a little way above the earth. Leth stared, intrigued. Within the green globule he thought to see movement, as though something lived and struggled.

As he watched, the wolfhearts nearest to the edge of the circle rose onto all fours and padded slowly and reverently towards the green ball. Close upon it they sat again and stretched wide their jaws. From within the beards of tendrils long tongues extended to penetrate the glowing form.

Count Harg slapped Leth's arm. 'It is time!'

The seven warriors scrambled quickly back up the slope to their horses.

'Don your helm, Swordbearer,' said Harg. 'We don't want you harmed. And remember, stay upon the path if you can. Ride straight through at your best speed, and do not stop until I say.'

They set off at a canter. The path permitted them to ride in twin files. Two of the Abyss warriors, Huuri and Dembarl, took the lead, then came Rasgul and the remaining Abyss warrior, Fhurn. Next came Leth, alongside Count Harg. Harg's men, Juson and Trin, followed close behind.

One hundred yards along, the way veered sharply right and broke out onto the plateau where the wolfhearts were gathered. The warriors fanned out to ride four abreast, and spurred their mounts to a gallop. Each man drew his blade as they bore down upon the unsuspecting wolfhearts.

They were almost upon the circle of obsidian stones before the wolfhearts grew aware of them. The first of the beasts turned as they detected the thunder of hooves, then scattered as best they could with shrieks and yowls of panic. The first rank of riders ploughed into them. Leth found his path almost clear. No wolfheart menaced him closely so he gripped his scimitar at the ready and steered his horse between them, concentrating on the roadway ahead. To his right the Abyss warriors were hacking at the sleek grey beasts, and beyond, Harg and his men were charging into the centre of the circle itself, whooping with bestial delight. Harg was leaning low in the saddle, charging directly at the green globule, his sword swinging. Leth glimpsed a wriggling form in the green.

The wolfhearts were hurling themselves at their attackers, but already Leth was through, speeding on past the circle, Rasgul close at his side. He turned to look back. Several wolfhearts were racing after him, but their speed could not match his horse's, and they quickly gave up. Juson and Trin smashed into them from behind, cutting them to the ground. He heard the frantic wails of the pack behind them. A little way off to the side came Count Harg, grinning ferociously.

The path led down through a wood of tall dark leafless trees. The riders slowed their pace but cantered on for several minutes until Harg raised his hand and brought them to a halt.

'Good work!' he declared, and held up a small sack within which something struggled. 'And this may serve us well down yonder.'

'What is this?' demanded Leth.

'It is the newborn cub.'

'You have abducted it? Why?'

Rasgul spoke. 'A newborn wolfheart will command a high price further along our way. Such a prize will facilitate our passage no end.'

'In what way?'

'The giant Cerb Two-Heads guards the road ahead. He likes to sup daily on folk like us. Fresh wolfheart is even more to his taste. But a newborn cub . . . in exchange for this delicacy I wager Cerb will both permit us unhindered passage and pay a healthy supplement in gold.'

Leth shook his head angrily. 'Take it back.'

Both Rasgul and Harg returned him incredulous stares.

'Swordbearer, I think you may have taken leave of your senses,' Harg said.

'Take it back or I will do so myself.'

'We are simply trying to ease our passage to Ascaria and your children.'

'You, at least, have travelled this way before,' Leth said to the Abyss warriors. 'And if the birth of a wolfheart is so rare an event, then you did not previously carry such as an offering or a way to riches.'

Rasgul shrugged. Harg said, 'You are making a mistake, Swordbearer. They are just savage, senseless beasts.'

'As are we, if we must resort to abducting their precious offspring. This is something I will not countenance.'

'What of your children, Swordbearer?'

Leth felt a rage rising within him. 'I have said, this way has been travelled before. We will use whatever methods were found effective then. Now, give me the cub.'

He leaned across to take the sack from Harg. Harg hesitated. 'You surprise me, Swordbearer. I had not taken you for a fool.'

'Whereas I have been in no doubt of your character from the beginning.'

Harg smiled darkly. 'Touché.' He gave up the sack. 'Go then, champion of brutes. But I will not accompany you, nor, I suspect, will the others.'

'Wait here.' Leth put his heels to his horse's flanks and made off rapidly back up the way. He was racked by his decision. Was he endangering his own children? Were the wolfhearts no more than brainless, savage beasts? Yet he knew, within himself, that had this creature that he carried been a human child, there would have been no question. And if he carried on now, without returning the cub, he would be no better than the animals he rode with.

The distressed wails and whimperings of the wolfhearts reached his ears. He rounded a bend to see them rushing back and forth within the circle of tall stones, plainly distraught. A few saw him and stopped, pricking up their ears uncertainly. Their whines turned to furious growls. Leth quickly loosened the neck of the sack, then leaned low to place it carefully upon the ground. The wolfhearts rushed towards him. Turning his horse about he glimpsed a small grey form begin to emerge from the sack and feel its way about blindly in the dust. He galloped off.

Looking back he saw the wolfhearts gather as one about the tiny cub. The tone of their cries had changed once again. None pursued him.

II

Leth half-wondered whether Harg and the others might have gone on without him, but he found them where he had left them. No one spoke a word as he rejoined them and they continued on their way.

He was angered by this turn of events. It had been unnecessary and had cost him valuable minutes in returning the wolfheart cub. Why had he felt so strongly about the abduction of the cub? Had it been a calf, a kitten or the offspring of any other wild or domesticated beast known to him, he would not have been so affected. He knew virtually nothing about the wolfhearts. Plainly they lacked high intelligence, and by Harg's account were no more than brutes. Still, their society was not entirely without organization, as evidenced by the way they had gathered at the stone circle. The strange magical birth-rite was deeply intriguing, and the fact that wolfheart newborns appeared so seldom surely meant that a new birth must be an event of extraordinary consequence to the pack. Hence, Leth reasoned, to deprive them of their newborn was a cruel and wanton act, as much if not more so than with any other creature.

But he knew nothing of this land. Was he wrong?

He sighed. What was done was done! He could not change it. He resolved to put it from his mind. But his anxiety over his own children mounted.

As before, he felt he could not wholly explain nor rationalize the nighmarish quality of the journey he was engaged upon. He vowed to himself that nothing now would sway him, even for a moment, from his first concern: his two children. They waited, he desperately hoped, somewhere ahead, needing him.

And when he found them?

An impossible question. There were too many variables involved. The possibility of return to Enchantment's Edge, Leth's doubts concerning Urch-Malmain and the passage he had constructed between this world and their own, the ever-real risk of Count Harg and the others turning upon him – all these things would wait, at least until he had rescued Galry and Jace from their immediate peril.

Leth and his band found themselves crossing a wide tract of wild pasture land, the way leading ever-downwards, though more gently now than when they had first descended into the Death Abyss. They came at length to the crest of a grassy slope, slightly steeper, characterized by low swells, hummocks and ledges. In the far distance the landscape seemed to dissolve into the air, though directly across from where they stood Leth made out the sombre shadow of the far wall of the Death Abyss rising into the dull cloud. A dirty-red haze rose out of an area clad in mist far away in the depths of the Abyss.

Count Harg began discussing something with Rasgul. They spoke in undertones and Leth did not make out all that was said: He understood that they were debating the best way to proceed now, and weighing the dangers that they could expect to face. Several references to ghosts and illusions did nothing to put his mind at ease.

In due course Harg spoke to him. 'Some way ahead is Ardbire Keep, where the giant Cerb Two-Heads resides. We require his assistance if we are to proceed further. Hence delicate negotiations will be called for. Very delicate, now that we have nothing to offer him.'

'Rasgul and his warriors have passed Cerb Two-Heads before, if you have not,' replied Leth, refusing to be goaded. 'So I suggest we follow their advice, and leave any negotiations to them, as Cerb will surely know them well by now. He knows nothing of the wolfheart cub, after all, and so cannot be disappointed by its absence.'

Harg scowled. 'All well and good, but Cerb will not be pleased by the arrival of so many strangers.'

'Perhaps if you were to volunteer yourself or one of your two men as a hostage, or even sacrifice, Cerb might be appeased.'

The idea did not find favour with Harg. He sniffed and wiped his nose on the back of his gauntlet, then looked out across the slope. 'First, though, are the Meadows of Dreaming, within which manifest phantoms of innumerable descriptions. So says Rasgul. These phantoms are innocuous if accepted for what they truly are, which is to say, harmless phantoms. However, when certain conditions are fulfilled, they may become real, at least for a short period.'

'What conditions?' asked Leth.

'I have not been here before, and am reliant upon Rasgul's advice. He declares that to believe in the phantoms you see, or to indulge in intercourse of any form with them, is sufficient to permit the phantoms to establish themselves in material form. Hence, keep your wits about you. Concentrate only upon your goal, which is the far side of the meadows, and ignore all else. Be conscious that anything you perceive here will be a dream imago conjured by the elemental forces that imbue this place as they respond to whatever they detect within your imagination. If you allow yourself to be drawn into the dream you may be lost. As may we all.'

Rasgul, listening to this exchange, gave Leth an expressionless nod. He raised his arm and pointed across the sloping meadows. 'See the ruined tower?' he hissed. 'That is your first goal. Do not take your eyes from it.'

'The Abyss warriors are not as susceptible as us to the dream-inflictions of the meadows,' Harg explained. 'We must place ourselves in their hands.'

It was not a thought that gave Leth great comfort.

They began to make their way across the first meadow. With mild surprise Leth noted the clarity of the light as he walked his horse through the lush green grass. The meadow was dotted with bright flowers and, having removed his helm, he was pleased to feel the warmth of sunlight upon his face. He closed his eyes.

'No!'

He opened them abruptly to see Rasgul glaring at him, his burnt-orange eyes harsh and bright.

'Watch the tower!'

Leth focused again, thinking: sunlight! He raised his gaze to see the depressing brown cloud-cover dense overhead, and yet when he looked down again the sunlight poured upon him, inexplicably, and he understood that there was much to be wary of in this place.

The old tower was a couple of hundred yards away, a ragged greystone tumble with a single wall left erect, rotten beams stabbing horizontally into the air where floors had once been. Low green swells lay between the tower and the eight riders. Three figures stood upon one of the swells and silently watched the company pass. It seemed to Leth that the three had appeared suddenly, out of nowhere. They were human, so he perceived: a middle-aged man of exceptional height, flanked by a pair of slender young maidens. Each was garbed in a long white robe with a garland of yellow flowers around their necks. Leth watched them in fascination. He took them for phantoms, yet he was drawn to observe them.

The Abyss warrior, Dembarl, rode up alongside him, obscuring his view of the three figures. 'Eyes ahead!' he intoned sharply.

Leth blinked as though snapping out of a daydream, and fixed his gaze on the ruin again.

'Replace your helm,' said Dembarl. 'It may help.'

Leth did so. To his right the weasel-eyed Trin said suddenly, 'What is that music?'

Leth listened, and heard nothing but the slow, steady pacing of the horses and the jink and creak of harness.

'I have heard nothing like it in my life,' declared Trin.

Leth glanced around at him. Trin sat erect in the saddle, gazing into space, his eyes like small black moons and his mouth hanging open in rapture.

'There is no music!' stated Rasgul harshly.

Trin ignored him, if indeed he heard him at all. 'Oh, such a marvellous sound . . . Never have I heard melodies like these!'

Rasgul brought his horse around, rode up to Trin and slapped his face hard. Trin drew back in sudden anger, his hand going for his sword.

'There is no music!' declared Rasgul again.

Trin shook his head dazedly, swallowed, blinked several times. 'No. No music.'

'The ruin.' Rasgul pointed, and Trin nodded and peered ahead as if into a mist.

They arrived without further mishap beside the ruined tower, at which point Rasgul warned, 'Do not enter. Stay clear of the stones.'

Leth looked up at the jagged wreck, which seemed to shimmer and distort slightly in the bright light. In antiquity it had stood four levels high and seemed to have been a single, square edifice, perhaps a watchtower. A pair of large, silent black birds circled above its ragged battlements.

Rasgul pointed again, off down the sloping meadow in a slightly leftward direction. 'The belt of far trees. There is a stone wall there, with a gate set within it. That marks the end of the Meadows of Dreaming.'

He urged his horse forward and the others followed slowly. They entered a grove of small trees with low, wide-spread branches, twisted trunks with rough, dark, fissured bark, and delicate, silver-grey foliage. Strangely, Leth had not been aware of these trees until he found himself among them. He gazed about him. Suddenly, off to his left, a fearsome figure burst from between the trees: a knight clad in fabulous, gleaming armour, three times the size of a normal man, mounted upon a gigantic black charger. Both man and beast were in flames. The knight held high a huge flaming longsword and with a blood-chilling battle-cry urged his fiery horse into a gallop, bearing down upon the eight riders.

The company stopped, each man struck with awe at the sight – only the four Abyss warriors seemed unperturbed. The eight spread out, drawing weapons. The knight aflame adjusted his path, bore down directly upon Leth. Leth gripped his scimitar, his mouth suddenly dry. He knew that any defence he might offer would be useless against an adversary such as this, but there was no time to shift his mount out of the knight's path. He freed his feet from his stirrups and prepared to dive for the ground. Then, at the last instant, the knight veered away. He passed between Leth and Count Harg. Leth heard the angry sputter of flames, felt a gust of sudden heat. The blazing knight galloped on, still venting his great roar, and disappeared between the trees.

'*Leth!*'

Leth turned. He knew the voice that hailed him. The sound made his heart quicken.

'*Leth!*'

He could see no one. He urged his mount towards the sound.

'*Help me, Leth! Help me!*'

He could see someone seated in a nearby hollow.

Issul?

It had to be an hallucination. She could not be here. But she turned her head towards him and he saw that it was her. She stood as if with difficulty and came towards him. Leth saw that her hands were bound behind her. '*Leth, help me! Quickly, free me. I am in trouble.*'

She ran up the side of the hollow towards him, looking back nervously over one shoulder. Leth half-saw figures behind her: a small group of armed men.

Issul stopped suddenly and looked at him in alarm. '*Leth? No, you are not my husband! Who are you, warrior? What do you want with me?*'

'Issul, it is me! It is Leth!' He realized that she could not see his face, for he wore the sapphire helm. The men behind her were becoming more definite in form. Issul looked about her, clearly uncertain what to do, then focused back on him.

'*Leth?*'

'Wait, Issul!' He began to lift the helm from his head. There came the sound of drumming hooves. Rasgul raced past, his scimitar raised, speeding directly at Issul. He brought his blade down and around in a wide sweeping arc, the blow powerful enough to take her head from her shoulders.

'NNO-OOOOO!'

Leth screamed at him, aghast, but it was too late. Rasgul's momentum took him on into the base of the hollow. Of Issul, or her corpse, there was no sign. Nor of the men who had pursued her.

Leth sagged in his saddle, stupefied. Rasgul brought his horse around and trotted back up the slope.

'Nothing is real,' he said.

Leth could not respond. His heart was hammering against his ribcage. He was in turmoil, wanted to weep. *Issul! Issul!*

The image of his beloved Issul, alive when he had almost come to accept that she no longer lived . . .

Leadenly he turned his horse around. There came shouts from the others. Leth snapped back into awareness. Trin was galloping at full speed towards him. His face was filled with ravenous joy, his thin lips stretched wide across his teeth. Charging past Leth he cried out, 'I hear it! Yes! The music! Oh, beautiful! I am coming! I am coming!'

The others were urging their horses to the gallop in pursuit of him. Leth, perceiving by the expressions of the Abyss warriors that they deemed this serious, did likewise. Trin had a lead of forty or fifty paces on them. He stood in his stirrups, one fist raised in jubilation. His mad cries drifted back to them on the sleepy air.

Trin led them far across the meadows, weaving between trees, into hollows, over swells. His horse was swift and did not lack stamina, and they made no ground. They came up over the crest of a low rise and a terrible sight greeted them. Twenty paces away in a shallow declivity three demonic creatures were crouched over Trin's outstretched body. One gnawed upon his hand; a second at his chest. The third held his bloody head against the earth.

At the arrival of the seven horsemen two of the creatures rose and faced them. They were almost human in form. They had smooth, hairless skins of dark mottled umber, high pointed ears, short blunt snouts. They drew back their lips to show rows of tiny needle-sharp teeth. Their postures were certain and challenging.

The group had come to a halt. Trin raised his head. 'Help me!'

It was plain from the sight of him that he was beyond help. The horses stamped their feet nervously. One of the demons took a step towards them. Leth drew his sword.

'No!' Rasgul held his arm. 'We can do nothing. We must leave.'

'They are but three!' protested Leth.

Rasgul shook his head. He was backing his horse away, as were his Abyss companions. 'We can do nothing. Believe me!'

Leth saw the fear in his face. He looked back at the three demons. One of them began walking towards the group, extending a webbed paw and making a gibbering sound.

'Swordbearer, I will stay no longer,' said Rasgul. 'We can do nothing. If they touch you, you are dead.'

Trin no longer cried out. He lay motionless while one of the creatures continued to feed.

The Abyss warriors rode away. Count Harg glanced warily at Juson, then at Leth. Then he quickly turned his horse and galloped after the others, with Juson close behind.

Leth stood alone. He looked into the approaching demon's eyes. They were black and empty. The thing spread its lips and gave a yapping laugh. Suddenly Leth heard a sound: the most beautiful music he had ever heard.

For long heartbeats he was spellbound. Such a rapturous sound! It soothed him, evoking the most marvellous thoughts and feelings. He looked once more at Trin's ruined corpse. The demon took two more determined steps towards him. A sudden frisson of fear raced along Leth's spine, jerking him upright in the saddle. He yanked upon the reins, turning his mount, and galloped away. As he did so the music faded from his ears.

III

The image of Issul haunted Leth for the remainder of his journey across the Meadows of Dreams, to the extent that, had other phantoms manifested he would quite possibly have remained oblivious to them.

The company passed through the gate on the far side of the meadows and rode on for a short while before the decision was taken to rest up for the night, for many hours had passed since they had set out. They were in an area of rough, uncultivated land, the vast wall of the Death Abyss soaring high on one side, a couple of hundred paces away. On the other the wild land extended for half a league or so before falling sharply away. A small spinney with a little rill tumbling through provided basic shelter. Juson and two of the Abyss warriors began to gather wood and kindling for a fire while Dembarl prepared meat and doughbread to cook. Leth took himself off alone. He settled himself with his back against a tree, brooding deeply.

She had seemed so real. Even now he could not wholly persuade himself that what he had experienced was entirely illusory. The encounter had seemed replete with meaning. The sight of Issul had thoroughly thrown him, but had uplifted him also. It still did. As though, somehow, somewhere, she was alive, even though the evidence was stacked against this being so.

But what conclusion was he to draw from what he had witnessed? Issul had plainly been in danger. Who were the men he had seen pursuing her? Did this vision have some basis in reality, or was it, after all, nothing more than phantoms cast up out of the eerie properties of the meadows?

Leth heaved a heavy sigh, shaking his head. He wondered for his sanity, not for the first time. A profound melancholy was settling upon him, such that he found himself questioning his ability to carry on.

What is the meaning, the purpose of all this?

A twig cracked close by. Leth looked up to see Count Harg standing over him. 'Rasgul is concerned that you have placed yourself too far from us, Swordbearer. Dark things prowl the Abyss, especially after nightfall. Come. A fire blazes and meat is sizzling.'

'In a moment,' said Leth.

He watched Harg walk back to join the others around the fire. Darkness was almost complete now. The men were glimmering silhouettes, touched by the fire's orange glow. Leth felt intensely alone. These men, these warriors, no matter their capabilities, were slaves of another, and enemies to him. They might not know it, but they were each in large part the servitors and bound creatures of the Noeticist, Urch-Malmain.

What had they been before? Harg had been a noble, by station and nature. Of the others Leth knew too little to guess. But they were wholly in Urch-Malmain's grip now. They obeyed Leth's commands, even demonstrated interest in his welfare. They would to the best of their abilities escort him safely to his objective. Which was to say, to Urch-Malmain's objective.

And then?

Leth climbed wearily to his feet. He could afford no sense of comradeship, no respect or affection for these men. Nor, he reasoned, was he right to truly despise them. They did not know what they did. They knew only that they had to do it. And he wondered whether the time would come, quite soon now, when he would find himself pitched against them.

IV

With the funereal light of morning the group rose. They rekindled the fire and ate a breakfast of porridge and corn-cakes, then set off for Ardbire Keep, where dwelt the giant, Cerb Two-Heads. By Rasgul's reckoning the keep lay a matter of three leagues away.

The path continued its descent along the edge of the great Death Abyss. Sometimes it was narrow and treacherously steep, clinging to the vertical Abyss wall; elsewhere it traversed heath and woodland which spread wide before them. Always, ahead or off to the side, the Death Abyss yawned, its lowest point never quite visible. And in the furthest, lowest reach, illuminating the mists where earth seemed to dissolve into air, was a stain, a blot, a dark reddish glow which somehow Leth knew must be the place he was making for.

Sombre woodland loomed before them and the way narrowed, becoming the faintest trail which plunged into the woody fringe. Count Harg brought his horse alongside Leth's. 'Cerb Two-Heads's residence is but a short way ahead now. My advice to you is to say nothing unless you are called upon. Let Rasgul conduct all negotiations, aided by myself if required. Above all, make no mention of the wolfheart cub. Cerb will stamp and froth and worse if he learns he has been deprived of such a rare delicacy.'

The trees grew taller and more closely packed, their canopy shutting out what little daylight there was, so that the way became dim. The path grew progressively more damp, then sodden. Patches of stinking black mud and gleaming water appeared between the boles of the trees; heavy grey moss festooned the limbs. Little by little the great trees now began to thin slightly due to the wet, insecure footing. Their forms grew more stunted. Though this helped dispel the dimness to some degree, layers of still white mist now hung over the land, hindering and bedevilling the eye.

The path upon which the seven rode took on the character of a narrow, natural causeway traversing a broad tract of bogland, and quite suddenly the dour grey walls of Ardbire Keep loomed high before them out of the murk. The Keep was lodged upon a low flat hillock heaving out of the dark mass of the marsh. A gatehouse with high iron portcullis faced them, to which the path led straight. The keep's outer wall, formed of massive granite blocks, stood forty feet high, shrouded in mist; the keep itself, a huge hunched square edifice, rose another fifty feet behind it. Several smaller turrets of varying heights and dimensions clung untidily about its crown.

The seven rode along the causeway to the great portcullis. Rasgul called out in a loud voice, 'Ho! Your Honour, Mighty Lord Cerb!'

There was a clanking above them, and from the battlements of the gate-tower a lizard-like head capped with a steel helmet peered down. 'Who are you? What do you want?'

'We are seven travellers, en route for the Lower Abyss. We humbly seek admittance to the mighty Lord Cerb's keep, and his permission to exit by the second gate, that we may continue on our journey.'

'Hmm,' said the lizard-soldier, looking them over with a mistrustful eye. 'Have you brought anything with which to barter for your safe passage?'

'Nothing, save tales of our recent travels in the High Lands,' replied Rasgul with a cool sideways glance at Leth.

'Lord Cerb has heard tales before,' rasped the lizard-head dismissively.

'Ah, but none so recent as ours, I would wager.'

'That may be so, but it is of no account if your tales fail to rise above the usual ruck of travellers' reminiscences. Be warned, Lord Cerb extends no mercy to those who bring him bland and uninspiring anecdotes.'

'We believe Lord Cerb will have heard none as interesting as ours, for we are only just returning from the High Lands. Moreover, he is unlikely to have knowledge of the wonderful quest we are engaged upon.'

'Quest? What sort of quest?

'With respect, that must be for Lord Cerb's ears only. Yet you might tell him that it is a quest he might well be tempted to join us on. Indeed, we would be honoured by his company.'

'Hmph.' The lizard-head scratched his snout. 'Well, you may enter, I suppose, and wait within the ward while I inform His Grace of your arrival. But your tale had better be good. Lord Cerb's patience has grown thin.'

'Have no fear of that.'

The lizard-head withdrew and the portcullis was raised with tortured groans and rattles. The seven entered the ward before the great keep itself. The portcullis was lowered again. Leth cast his eyes around and saw more lizard-headed guards on the parapets and elsewhere within the walls. They carried spears and shortswords, and in some cases bows, and wore mail shirts and leggings with, here and there, steel breastplates. Set into an adjoining wall some eighty yards away was another portcullis and gate.

'There is our freedom,' said Rasgul, aside. 'Let us hope that Cerb is in a good mood.'

A high double-door at the head of a flight of steep stone steps opened and out strode the first lizard-soldier. 'His Gracefulness is willing to see you. Dismount, if you will, and step this way.'

Rasgul nodded to Leth and Harg. 'You two come with me. The others can remain here.'

The three followed the lizard-man through the door. They passed along a dim, high-ceiling corridor which stank of boggy damp and ages of decay mingled with a faint taint of rotten food. Turning to the right they entered an immense hall. A huge oak table and benches occupied the centre of the floor. The ceiling was lost in the shadows overhead. Several suits of rusting armour stood before two of the walls. Various over-sized ornaments and vessels were placed here and there with little sense of order. In a huge vault of a hearth a hearty log-fire blazed. Before it stood the giant, Cerb Two-Heads, staring into the flames.

The lizard-headed guard strode foward in front of Leth and his companions, then halted and hammered the stock of his spear against the stone floor. 'The visitors, Excellence.'

The nearer of Cerb's two heads turned and surveyed Leth and the other two with a lugubrious eye. The second head continued to gaze into the fire.

'So I see,' the first head boomed. Massive in size, it was the head of a fair-haired man in middle-age. Big, drooping, fleshy purple lips showed a few crooked, decaying teeth. The eyes were round and pale grey, set deeply beneath a gnarled and nobbled brow. A sallow tinge characterized the skin, which was heavy and slack and deeply seamed. A large crooked nose dominated the face, and the chin was broad and split with a deep dark cleft. The fair hair fell almost to the shoulders in lifeless greasy hanks. Leth could not make out the second head, other than as a darker brown mass of hair at the back of the skull.

Cerb himself stood twelve feet high. His body was bulky and strong, his chest like a massive barrel, arms and legs as thick as ash boughs. He wore a heavy brown linen shirt, oatmeal coloured trousers and loose leather boots.

The first head peered for some moments at Leth, Rasgul and Harg, each in turn, then said, 'Well, I understand you plan to divert me. You have a quest. Is that so?'

'Indeed it is, my lord,' replied Rasgul. 'We are engaged upon a venture which we believe will have much appeal to the great and mighty Cerb.'

'Is this venture exciting enough to divert me from my discussions with my self?' enquired the first head.

'We would think so.'

The second head jerked upright and made a scoffing sound. 'That I doubt!'

'No, don't interrupt!' the first head retorted.

Now the giant turned away from the fire to face the three full on, and Leth was able to view the second head. In contrast to the first this was the head of a creature seemingly produced from a mingling of human and ogre and possibly other things. It had small, dark fierce purple eyes and a long twisted nose. The lower jaw was thrust forward, so that the lower teeth extended beyond the upper. Dark brown hair was pressed down upon a broad, heavy skull.

'We have entertained visitors like yourselves on previous occasions, and never have you given us a quest nor anything else worth leaving Ardbire Keep for,' the second head declared angrily. It peered closely at Rasgul, 'In fact, you look familiar to me. Have you passed through here before?'

Before Rasgul could reply, the first head spoke again in a milder tone. 'No, I think not. I have never seen this fellow before.'

'You were probably asleep,' said the second head.

'No, I think it is rather that your eyes and memory play you false. I have told you before, these matters are best left to me, for those very reasons.'

'My eyes are perfectly functional, my memory intact,' spat the second head. 'And I say I have seen this fellow before. I tire of this, anyway. His quest can be of no possible interest.'

'That is what you always say, without even paying me the courtesy of hearing what the quest might entail. I believe that to join these valiant fellows on a quest that might take us far and wide would be very interesting indeed. It is a long time since we have left the Keep.'

'Not so! Not so!' fumed the second head. 'There is nothing these men can say that would interest us.'

'Now there you go again, speaking for me as though I have no opinion of my own.'

'Bah!' Cerb's second head scowled. 'Always you have to try to gainsay me. Why? Why can you never agree with anything I say?'

'Ah now, I think it is rather the other way around,' frowned Cerb's first head. 'You must surely admit that. No matter what I say or what views I hold, no matter what I even *think*, I can always rely upon you to find fault with it.'

The second head shook irritably from side to side. 'Not so! Not so at all! But I was quite happy here, gazing into the flames and thinking my quiet and beautiful thoughts. I am aggrieved at the disturbance, and I do not want to embark upon any quest or adventure.'

'Well, there you've said it!' declared the first head. 'You simply do not want to bestir yourself, no matter the reason. You are indolent, a dreamer and stay-at-home.'

'Not so! But I desire no surprises nor forays into foreign lands nor adventures of any kind beyond the gates of Ardbire Keep. You know that as well as do I.'

'And I am tired of never going out!' declared the first head peevishly.

At this point Leth witnessed something extraordinary. It seemed that Cerb, being in disagreement with himself, tried to go two ways at once. That is, the second head turned away to regard the flames, and tried to take its body back with it. But the first head was inclined to move away from the fire towards the three men, and thus resisted the second head's effort. A struggle ensued, with each neck straining to draw the colossal body in the direction it wished to go. Cerb's body, drawn simultaneously in two directions, shuffled, twisted and lumberingly danced but remained essentially in one place.

Cerb's two mouths puffed and blew, then began to curse one another. The heads turned and glared each other in the eye. The four cheeks grew red, the two pairs of eyes bulged as the body strained to go two ways at once and its mighty muscles took it nowhere but in a slow, arduous circle. The eyes flashed; spittle flew.

'Why must you always be so difficult?' demanded head one.

'Me? How dare you? You are the one who is intent upon destroying my equanimity!' riposted head two.

'I simply want to go out!'

'And I don't!'

Head one suddenly succeeded in exerting a superior effort upon the body, and dragged it two steps away from the fire. Head two responded accordingly. The giant, grunting and growling, jerked three steps in the opposite direction, tottered two steps forward, staggered back, lunged to the side, performed another small circle and finally came to a halt beside the central table. Cerb leaned forwards, his hands upon his knees, breathing hard. His twin heads were low, pouring with sweat. His single pair of lungs gasped for air like monumental tortured bellows.

Presently the first head came up, and stared at the three. It blinked once and licked its lips. 'Now, you have not yet told me, what of this quest of yours?'

'Well—' Rasgul began, but the second head had shot up in response.

'I do not want to hear it! It is of no interest to me!'

'Yes it is,' said head one.

'No it isn't! I will hear no more of it!'

There was another brief, though relatively stable tussle, with both heads straining to pull away from the body.

'My lord Cerb, perhaps I can suggest a compromise,' said Rasgul in his harsh, throaty whisper.

'A compromise?' queried head one. 'No, I will hear of no compromise.'

'Yes, I will,' declared head two. 'What is it? What do you suggest?'

'No! Be silent, or I will have you spitted and stuffed and will eat you for my supper!' threatened head one.

'You cannot! And I have as much right to voice my opinion as you!'

At this one of the giant's huge hands came up and cuffed head one hard across the back of the skull. Head one emitted a bellow of outrage. The other hand came up and struck the second head a solid blow on the cheek. The first hand then grasped the second hand. Each held the other firm and the two heads snarled and growled and bared their teeth, berating one another in no uncertain terms.

Leth stole a glance at the lizard-soldier who stood leaning upon the shaft of his spear and shaking his head from side to side in a world-weary manner. He caught Leth's eye and said, 'Oh, it is always like this. He carps and complains, and is in two minds about everything. For the most part he keeps it to himself, doing little more than muttering and sulking with occasional vitriolic outbursts. But whenever someone like you comes along, full of bright ideas, *"boom!"* He becomes uncontrollable, just as you see. He is beside himself! It will be days before he grows calm again. Why can't you stay away?'

Rasgul replied. 'Ardbire Keep commands the only way between the Lower Abyss and the High Lands.'

'That is nothing to me,' replied the lizard-soldier. 'I am just trying to keep the peace here.' He threw up his hands. 'It is a thankless task.'

Leth ventured to interpose a word. 'If we could just be allowed to continue on our way, calm might resume.'

'Oh, I see,' said the lizard-head. 'Now you are of two voices too! What is this? Are you here to torment me, and bring His Worship to ruin? Why don't you bring your other companions in, and you can all voice contrasting views and opinions so that His Worship is driven to utter distraction and tears the Keep down around our heads.'

Rasgul flashed Leth a forbidding glance. 'That is not our intention, be assured. We wish only to continue upon our quest, and if Lord Cerb wishes to accompany us, we would be only too pleased.'

Cerb had fallen quiet to listen to this exchange. His first head now said, 'Yes, I would like that.'

Second head said, 'No, I wouldn't.'

'Yes, I would.'

'No, I would like to return to the fireplace and contemplate the flames and the profound flow of my thoughts.'

'No, I would like a change, an escape. A dangerous quest is just what I need.'

Second head shook obstinately from side to side. First head assumed a disconsolate expression. 'I am in two minds, I acknowledge.'

Second head was less charitable. 'I am utterly sick of you. All my life it has been the same. No matter what I want, you want the opposite. I have had more than I can stand!'

Without warning a giant hand flew up again and punched first head a resounding blow beneath the chin. Cerb's first head snapped back. Then, recovering itself, it retaliated by butting second head so hard that its nose immediately gushed forth a torrent of blood. Second head, its eyes watering, roared. 'That is it! I can stand no more!'

'Nor I!' bellowed first head.

'I am going!' screamed second head.

'I too!'

'I will bear you no more!'

Another monstrous struggle began, this time even more violent. The giant rolled and yawed and hurled himself from side to side as the two heads strained to their utmost to take themselves in opposing directions. They screamed themselves hoarse:

'I hate you!'

'I can stand no more!'

'This is it! I have put up with all I can!'

'I will tolerate you not a moment longer!'

Leth watched in bemusement as the giant flailed and stamped around the hall, arms and legs punching and kicking while the two heads continued their torrent of abuse. Cerb crashed into ornaments, collided with furniture, toppled suits of armour. Then he lost his balance and fell to the floor. He kicked and clawed and hammered at himself, the walls reverberating to the sounds of his acrimonies.

The lizard-headed soldier cringed, and could only bear to watch through a gap between his fingers. Blood was flowing freely from various wounds on Cerb's body and both heads. Lizard-head grew distraught. 'Oh, he has never been this bad before! He bickers constantly, and sometimes refuses to speak to himself for days on end, but I have never seen this.' He ran forward. 'Lord Cerb! Lord Cerb! Please, stop!'

Cerb had scrambled to his feet again. The two heads continued to yell abuse at one another, but no more blows were thrown. Instead, paying no heed to the lizard-soldier or anyone else, they resumed their earlier posture, faces turned outward and away from each other, straining with every gram of strength to get away, one from the other. Their eyes bulged, their lips stretched, their teeth were bared; the veins at their temples pulsed, dangerously swollen, the cords in their necks stood out.

'My lord Cerb!' the lizard-soldier cried out.

The straining giant took no notice. Simultaneously both heads roared; simultaneously both applied one last, supreme effort to be away from the other. There came a horrible, wet, wrenching sound, followed by creaks, snaps, soft pops and dubious liquid noises. A huge bloody rent appeared at the point between the two necks where they joined the massive torso. It shot quickly down the centre of Cerb's great chest, through the midriff and on to the crotch. The body peeled apart, its entrails tumbling free, and toppled to the ground.

'That'll teach you!' gasped the first head with its dying breath. The second head swivelled its purple eyes furiously and made to reply, but all that emerged was a gurgle and a sigh. The four eyes blinked and froze, and the giant Cerb Two-Heads was no more.

The lizard-headed soldier stood aghast. Leth, Harg and Rasgul were obliged to step quickly aside as the colourful raft of Cerb's innards slid towards them across the floor, borne on a sudden springtide of near-black blood and steaming humours.

Rasgul said, 'That is the angriest I have ever seen him.'

Harg observed, 'I take it he will not be accompanying us on our quest, then?'

A ghastly hot stench began to pervade the air of the hall. The lizard-head cried, 'What am I to do? My master is dead! What am I to do?'

'I suggest you gather together the rest of Lord Cerb's staff and garrison and convey to them the sad news,' Rasgul advised. 'Then I suppose you had better start making new plans for the future.'

The lizard-head looked at him stupidly, then turned and rushed from the hall. Rasgul took long strides in his wake. 'Come, I think it is time we took our leave of this place.'

FOURTEEN

I

They emerged into the ward outside Cerb's massive donjon to find lizard-headed guards in disarray. As far as Leth could see they numbered about a dozen, though he imagined more to be within the donjon and outbuildings. Additionally he assumed a household staff of at least two members, most probably more. The guards were plainly stunned, their attitudes uniformly one of dazed passivity as the first lizard-head hurried among them, broadcasting the woesome tidings of Cerb's death.

Leth, Harg and Rasgul remounted. With Juson and the other three Abyss warriors they rode without hurry to the second gate. First lizard-head was there, jabbering his news to the pair of guards stationed on the ramparts above the gate.

Rasgul called to him. 'Be so good as to have the portcullis raised. We are leaving.'

The lizard-head, standing upon the higher of two steps leading into the gatehouse, hesitated, then turned and appraised him. His expression, initially dazed, was now haughty. He put his hands upon his plump hips. 'Well, that is not yet definite. I do not recall Lord Cerb granting you permission to proceed.'

'He made no statement to the contrary.'

'That is not the same thing. I am aware that he had at least half a mind to accompany you, and by that token one might say he did not intend for you to remain. But as he is now quite unable to go anywhere at all, I feel the situation calls for a review. I must regard it in the light of what has and has not occurred, rather than what might or might not have been. Most importantly, what has emphatically not occurred is Lord Cerb's giving permission for you to leave Ardbire Keep.'

Rasgul leaned his weight upon the pommel of his saddle. 'As you have correctly pointed out, Lord Cerb is no longer in a position to make arrangements one way or the other. However, we were never at any time his prisoners; we chose to come here, and now choose to go freely on our way.'

'But Lord Cerb did not say that you may.'

'Nor is he likely to. He is dead!'

'That is irrelevant. He was alive when you arrived, and graciously gave his permission for you to enter. He was still alive when debating with you, and with himself, but he came to no final decision as to what was to be done with you. Indeed, he was quite literally in two minds as to what to do. And I say again, he did not at any time grant permission for you to continue on your way.'

'You are an arrogant upstart,' said Rasgul hotly. 'And my patience is wearing thin. Do you really presume to act in Lord Cerb's stead? By whose decree have you risen in status?'

The lizard-head considered this. 'I am Lord Cerb's second-in-command, and chief of his staff. Now, in light of his sad demise, I consider my assumption of command to be natural and automatic.'

Rasgul took a deep breath. 'Very well, I am prepared to acknowledge your authority in that regard. But I would ask, do you consider us your prisoners? If so, please explain your reasons.'

'No, I don't,' said the lizard-head, clasping his hands upon his chest.

'Then may we depart?'

'Not at this time. The situation remains—' he began, then fell silent and staggered back two steps, to bump against the door jamb. He looked down in some surprise at the stub of the crossbow-bolt protruding suddenly from the back of one hand, pinning it and the hand beneath it to his sternum. Then he sagged gasping onto the step.

'I think that settles that,' said Count Harg, casually cocking the string of his repeating crossbow. He looked up at the two lizard-head guards on the parapet and said, 'Be so good as to raise the portcullis, would you?'

The lizard-heads needed no further bidding. The iron portcullis was cranked high and the seven finally rode free of Ardbire Keep.

II

'From here on the way is relatively smooth and trouble free, until we approach the Fortress of the Dark Flame,' said Rasgul. He stood looking out over a broad flat plain which extended before them, disappearing into a haze before the distant Abyss wall, and to either side for as far as the eye could see.

Leth stood less at ease at his side, Count Harg next to him. 'And then?'

'And then we will find the best way to enter the Fortress. And then you will draw free the Orbsword and together we will fight or avoid the numerous devils that are set between us and the inner sanctum where Ascaria waits. And then it will be up to you.'

'What form do these devils take?'

'They are numerous, so I believe. I am not familiar with them all. I know of cacodaems and goles, and have heard tales of more.'

'What do the tales tell you?'

'That we will be fortunate to survive.'

Evening was gathering. The cloud mantle was a lowering deep purple-brown. Across the plain the misty red luminescence that framed the hidden Fortress of the Dark Flame was a cynosure, closer than ever before and both beckoning and forbidding. Leth's nerves were taut and he felt an oppressive heaviness upon him. At the same time his blood had quickened at the knowledge that Galry and Jace, if they still lived, were now virtually within his sight.

The company had been travelling for hours since departing Ardbire Keep. Ever descending. Ever drawing nearer to the encounter he would have avoided at almost any price had he been able. For it was not only a matter of slaying Ascaria and saving Galry and Jace, it was the repercussions, the ramifications that this act would have upon his own world. To kill Ascaria, whatever she was . . . it would mean that Orbus's world could continue to evolve, but that Urch-Malmain would be free to return to Enchantment and wreak whatever mischiefs he wished upon the world. Unless Leth could find some way of preventing him, and he knew of none. Urch-Malmain was far away and safe. With Ascaria gone he would be free to do as he pleased.

Leth turned away. Tomorrow, so much to be decided. And he could only act as he must, as any father would, to save his children from a terrible, nameless fate.

He made his way back to the camp-fire where Juson was preparing a supper of griddled bacon and doughbread. The three Abyss warriors were seated close by, speaking little, each presumably preoccupied with thoughts of what the next day would bring. After a few moments Rasgul and Harg came to join them.

As much to divert his mind as anything. Leth enquired of Rasgul, 'This morning at Ardbire Keep, what did you hope to achieve with your tales to Cerb of quests and adventures?'

'I hoped to keep my life, and yours too!' Rasgul half-smiled to himself, his pallid features eerily lit by the dancing orange flames of the campfire. 'Ah, Cerb Two-Heads! Always he bickers and carps! Never at peace with himself! In the past I have exploited this. I engage elements of his personality with my often fictional and greatly exaggerated exploits, to the extent that he has forgotten the prospect of eating me and has accompanied me as far as and even beyond the gate. But then his other self has risen to the fore, gained dominance and persuaded or browbeaten him back indoors. With a mixture of grumbles and apologies he has bidden me farewell and good speed, and tramped back to his fireside broodings, leaving me to continue on my way. Cerb was always a tricky fellow to deal with, pulled this way then the other by his conflicting urges. There have been occasions when I have felt my life was suspended by a mere thread, for he is generally hungry and loves nothing more a bellyful of fresh meat, be it human, Abyss warrior, lizard-guard or something other.'

'He eats his own guards?' asked Leth.

'If his larder is otherwise empty. They do not mind. They deem it an honour.' Rasgul chuckled harshly to himself. 'But never before, it goes without saying, has Cerb torn himself apart before my very eyes! Today has been an extraordinary day, one that will remain forever engraved upon my memory.'

The irony of these last words was not lost on Leth, knowing what he did of the Abyss warrior's background. But he was gradually coming to revise his opinion of Rasgul. Initially, at the Tower of

Glancing Memory, Leth had perceived him as a sombre, sullen fighter, a soldier, dull and obedient and little more. But in the last two days Rasgul's keen, if ruthless, intelligence and quietly commanding personality had begun to reveal itself. Given the doctoring that Urch-Malmain had performed upon the Abyss warrior, Leth wondered as to the nature of Rasgul's impressions of himself. He decided to probe Rasgul's memory gently, and Count Harg's also. 'You have passed through Ardbire Keep many times, then. For what purpose?'

Rasgul shrugged. 'I came with others from the Fortress of the Dark Flame. Initially it was to do Ascaria's bidding, for I was sworn to serve her.'

'But now you return determined to see her slain. How is that?'

Rasgul scarcely batted an eyelid. 'I was made to see that I had gone astray, that my previous allegiance had been grossly miscast. Now I know Ascaria for the evil force she is. My goal is to see her destroyed, and all those who willingly serve her.'

Leth took a breath. Rasgul was speaking with the conviction of a man who had experienced some form of epiphany. 'How were you made to see this?'

'Through the beneficences of my loving Master. He saw how I had erred, and made me see also.'

'It is Urch-Malmain whom you refer to?'

Rasgul gave a nod.

Leth sat back, and let his gaze flicker over the other three Abyss warriors. To have exchanged one form of evil for another, to be enslaved and incapable of knowing it. There was tragedy here, Leth saw, as well as something to be greatly feared. These warriors' lives were lived entirely according to the wishes of Urch-Malmain, who had instilled his own desires within their minds. They believed they possessed free will, yet their thoughts, desires, impulses were not their own. They could never truly know themselves or their potential. And their belief, almost certainly, was unassailable.

Leth was reminded of the factions of Enchantment's Edge, with whom he, as King, had so often come into conflict. Almost all of them taught unswerving, unquestioning obedience to so-called gods, the Higher Ones of Enchantment, of whom they truly knew nothing. His forebear, King Haruman, had vehemently opposed sectarian belief and the worship of deities whose existence and nature could not be proven. King Haruman had propounded an

Edict, banning such forms of worship. He had done so out of concern that it engendered ignorance and blind, dangerous fanaticism and hampered and even prohibited a genuine search for truth, knowledge and wisdom. Leth had fought, sometimes at great personal cost, to uphold Haruman's cause and keep the Edict in place.

And now he had actually encountered one of Enchantment's gods who, no doubt, in some form or other, had his followers in Enchantment's Edge. And he had discovered him to be, even in his weakened, dispossessed state, a creature of pure evil. A skilled and unprincipled manipulator of minds, a corruptor of souls, a creature at times quite cruelly capricious, who nevertheless entertained despicable goals which he intended to achieve by whatever means he deemed necessary.

Orbus, do you know that Urch-Malmain resides here within you? Do you know what he will do if I allow him to escape?

These thoughts passed through Leth's mind in a moment. He turned to Count Harg. 'And you, Harg. Do you also sing the praises of the loving and beneficent Master, Urch-Malmain?'

Harg smiled coldly and stabbed at a piece of meat with his knife. 'I owe allegiance to none but myself.'

'Still, you do Urch-Malmain's bidding.'

Was there just the tiniest flicker of doubt in those deep smalt eyes? Or did Harg honestly believe himself to be his own man?

Harg shook his head. 'Inasmuch as his wishes correspond with my own, but not more. Ascaria eats our world. You, Swordbearer, are here to prevent her. And I will aid you, not out of any kind of obedience to you, but in order that I may live on and pursue a life of brigandry, adventure and, eventually, ease.'

'And what were you before you took to this life? Tell me of your background. How do you recall your childhood?'

Harg's smooth brow furrowed momentarily. 'It has always been this way. I have never sought anything else.'

Leth turned his eyes to the flames. The company of these hollow creatures made him aware more than ever of the horrors Urch-Malmain could inflict if he returned to his own world.

'But what of you, Swordbearer?' Harg enquired archly. 'You are here from the Godworld, come to save us, are you not?'

'I will say only, as I have said before, that I am not what people here believe me to be,' replied Leth.

'But you *have* come to save us.'

Leth stayed silent.

'None but you can bear the Sword of the Orb,' Harg pressed. 'When I spoke with your companion, Lakewander, she affirmed that you had come after many years of petitions and summonings. You appeared suddenly, out of nowhere, so I understand.'

'I have said, I am not what people think. There is nothing I can add to that.'

Harg persisted. 'Tell us of the Godworld, Swordbearer. Is it so different to our own? Are all its peoples gods like yourself?'

'I do not know if the world I have come from is the world you would call Godworld,' Leth said after a pause. 'Certainly, its inhabitants are not gods.'

'But you, Swordbearer. What are you? You carry the Orbsword, yet are you mortal? Can you be slain?'

Leth met his blue gaze. 'You yourself have shown concern for my protection, at least until that time comes when our task is complete. Plainly, then, *you* consider me mortal. You have seen, and I have been made drastically aware, that I am susceptible to many of the perils that would afflict any normal inhabitant of this world. In the Meadows of Dreaming it was apparent that I was in as great a danger from the demons as any other of us. Certainly, I fear for my life when faced with dangers here just as I would in my own world. Hence, my assumption is that I am not invulnerable.'

'Ah, but to die here might be to rediscover existence in your own world.'

'I have considered that. I have considered, too, that perhaps I died in my own world and that this is my afterlife.'

'An intriguing notion!' Count Harg chuckled. 'And is there any among us who has not wondered about the nature of an afterlife, if such there is? Indeed, I have on various occasions helped some considerable number of persons to find an answer to that question!'

Juson sniggered at that. Harg grinned at Leth, his eyes glittering.

'I don't doubt that your victims have been many, Harg,' Leth said.

'And I imagine you would derive some satisfaction from personally launching me on my own voyage of discovery into the afterlife,' said Harg, halving an apple with his knife.

'I am not a murderer, Harg. Nor is it my place to visit summary justice upon any offender. If you are guilty of crimes – and I know that you are – I would by choice have you taken into custody and given a fair trial before your accusers. The evidence and facts as they are known would be presented. Should you be found guilty then I would have no hesitation in passing a sentence upon you that was considered by the law of the land to be commensurate to the magnitude of your crimes.'

'Law of the land?' Harg raised his eyebrows, coolly sardonic. 'We are in the Death Abyss. There is no law here, save for survival of the most able.'

'Even here the laws of common humanity must apply.'

Leth turned away. He had not intended to be drawn into confession, speculation or debate. But a question arose which he had not considered before. Could Harg genuinely be said to be guilty of – and therefore deserving of punishment for – those crimes he had committed solely as a result of the changes wrought upon his personality by Urch-Malmain? Harg had once been a different man, so Lakewander had avowed. Even a good man. Now he murdered and thieved as he willed, without conscience, presumably because it had amused Urch-Malmain to create such a monster and set him free. Was the process reversible? And whether or not it was, was Harg truly deserving of punishment?

Leth shook his head wearily. Imponderables beset him at every turn; he was in no mind to philosophize. He rose and stretched. 'I am tired. I think I will sleep now.'

'That is a pity, Swordbearer. I was just beginning to enjoy our little talk.'

'Another time, perhaps.'

'I will look forward to it.'

Leth moved away to spread his blanket upon the ground, then lay down. The clouded sky above him was starless, featureless, invisible, drawn into the enclosing night. He closed his eyes.

'Sleep soundly, Swordbearer,' he heard Harg say. 'Tomorrow we ride for the Fortress of the Dark Flame.'

III

The morning came far too soon. Leth woke, feeling that he had barely slept. Without enthusiasm he ate a breakfast of salted fish and bread and, with the others, harnessed his horse. Without further delay they set out upon the broad plain.

The day was chill and virtually still. Not a breath of breeze stirred the leaves upon the trees from beneath which they rode. The cold penetrated deeply into the flesh, seemed to seep through into the bones themselves so that the whole body felt numb and brittle and deprived of energy. The plain was bleak and featureless, a perfectly flat expanse of hard, even ground beneath a thin covering of sour pale dust. Far ahead an abnormal haze obscured the opposite wall of the Death Abyss, and within that haze, directly in front, was the dark bloody glow that signified the hidden presence of the Fortress of Ascaria, the Kancanitrix, the Dark Flame of Orbus's world.

Rasgul, riding alone at the head of the party, was hunched forward in the saddle. He peered constantly ahead, alert and intent, as though expecting something. The other three Abyss warriors, too, were more tense than they had been previously during their descent. They had spread out to either side of Leth, Harg and Juson, and their gaze was focused outwards, swinging across the plain to either side and to the distant haze ahead, searching.

To Leth it seemed that this was a dead place. The ground was unrelentingly even and hard beneath its layer of dust. No plants grew upon its surface; not even thistle, mat-grass or brown clover. There was no scrub to be seen, not a single stunted tree. There were no rocks, pebbles or clumps of earth, just the unrelieved brown-grey dust that rose in quick dry plumes around the horses' feet and settled quickly back to the lifeless earth again. Leth wondered to himself if it could be Ascaria's influence, her very proximity, that rendered the plain so barren and inhospitable to life. His mind flew back to the End of the World that Lakewander had revealed to him as they stood upon the wild Shore of Nothing. He flinched at the recollection. Even now, to merely think of the Nothing that he had been forced to confront, to try to embrace it within his mind, was to unleash an emptiness within himself that he shrank from reflexively. It was unembraceable; even in memory he needed to avoid it. And he wondered, surprisingly almost for the first time, what manner of creature Ascaria could be, who could wreak such utter devastation upon a world and its inhabitants.

Harg came up alongside him and broke the brooding train of his thoughts. 'Rasgul and I talked last night. Rasgul's intention is to lead the three of us – you, Juson and myself – into the Fortress of the Dark Flame as though we are his prisoners. He believes that will get us past the outer defences at least.'

Leth stiffened at this. 'We will be defenceless?'

'Not entirely. He and his men will take our main weapons, though anything that can be concealed about our persons, such as daggers, we will keep. The Orbsword will be strapped to Rasgul's mount.'

Leth shook his head. 'No!'

'It is merely to allay suspicion while we enter the Fortress, Swordbearer. The Orbsword will be free in its scabbard. No other can wield it, and you can summon it to you at will. And if we are threatened or discovered, that is exactly what you must do. That is the point at which we will begin fighting for our lives.'

Leth was still less than easy with the thought. 'Is Rasgul's defection not known?'

'He and the others have been absent for some weeks. He is confident that he can bluff his way in, at least in the initial stages. He is an officer of the Fortress garrison and is known by his men. Bringing captives from the High Lands will add to his credibility. Of course, we will be discovered soon enough. When we are closer he wants you to don your helm. You will draw the guards' attention and they will be less attentive to details than they otherwise might.'

'Are we to be bound?'

'Our hands will be tied loosely behind our backs, so that we can free ourselves quickly. At a cursory glance it will appear that we are bound fast. This is where your appearance and the impression it makes upon the guards will be most effective.'

'I do not like it.'

'It is the only way, Swordbearer. We are but seven; I think we are not likely to meet with success if we attempt to storm the Fortress. Or perhaps you think we should just ride up to the main gate and request entry of the guards for the purpose of a little sojourn?'

'I dislike the idea of riding helpless like a babe into my enemy's maw.'

'Trust me,' said Harg.

Leth looked aside at him and saw that he was grinning, his deep blue eyes alight with irony.

There came a shout from Rasgul up ahead, a guttural, wordless sound. He wheeled his horse around and galloped back to join them.

'There is the first,' he rasped, and pointed.

Leth peered in the direction he was pointing, directly ahead of them, but could see nothing but the haze and the strange red glow of the still hidden fortress. The glow was of notably greater height and breadth than it had been when they set out, but Leth did not think it was this that had excited the Abyss warrior.

'What is it? What do you see?'

'Wait!'

They carried on, following the same course. The other three Abyss warriors, Huuri, Dembarl and Fhurn, had drawn closer in following Rasgul's call, though their eyes still scanned the bare landscape ahead and to either side.

'There!' declared Rasgul, pointing again. 'Do you see now?'

Leth craned his neck, squinting as he peered hard into the watery distance. The ground was addled and indistinct where it merged into the haze, and at first, still, he could see nothing. And then – he blinked, his eyes watering with the strain of staring so hard – yes! He did not know what it was. A tiny blot. Something pale and still, standing out against the bleakness of the plain. Was it really still? It seemed to move against the haze, but that could have been a visual distortion. Was it large or small? From this distance it appeared tiny, but he could not judge the distance. He could not tell.

'What is it?' He was coming to realize that Rasgul's eyesight, and perhaps that of the other three as well, was keener than his.

'It is a child,' Rasgul said. 'The first one.'

Leth's heart kicked. He stared ahead again, but could make out nothing of the figure, or object, that he saw. But a sudden stricken, almost panicked feeling rushed through him. He made to dig his heels into his horse's flank and urge it forward into a gallop, but

Count Harg had anticipated him. Harg reached out and grasped Leth's rein close beside his horse's muzzle. The mount ramped, snorted, and turned in a half-circle.

'Wait, Swordbearer,' said Harg. 'This is not a time for impetuousness.'

Leth struggled against the tumult of feelings within him.

Galry! Jace!

The urge to draw forth the Orbsword and smite Harg's hand from his wrist was overpowering, but he fought, fought, drawing deep, long breaths to instil at least a semblance of calm. Reluctantly he could only admit that Harg was right. To rush forward now, no matter the reason, was potentially to place himself in danger. He knew nothing of what lurked within that haze. And the child standing so still up ahead, if child it was, could be anyone. Anyone's child.

Leth nodded, barely able to speak.

Harg eyed him a moment longer, then released his grip. They continued along their way, keeping the same pace, the eyes of all four Abyss warriors scanning the distance.

The haze seemed never closer. Leth was reminded of the vast, towering wall that curved around the perimeter of Orbus's blue domain. How he had walked for so long towards it, yet no matter how far he went the wall had seemed endlessly to retreat, never nearer, never further away.

Mercifully, after a while, he saw that it was not the same here. Infinitely slowly they were drawing closer to the distant figure. Leth could not take his eyes from it. Then he was aware that Fhurn reached out and touched Rasgul's arm and pointed, away off slightly to their left. Leth allowed his gaze to shift, following the direction of Fhurn's arm, and he saw another figure, similar in size and form to the the first. Harg was looking too. Then he turned to Leth, and there was no trace of irony or humour in his eyes. 'Prepare yourself, Swordbearer.'

Leth swallowed. A sensation of dread was slowly gathering, spreading right through him.

Galry! Jace!

The first figure was still not near enough to allow him to make out much detail. It was human, without question; he could see that much now. Standing against and partially swathed in the eerie backdrop of the misty blood-red glow, it wore a long smock-like garment, the colour of oatmeal. Its hair was fair, as far as Leth could make out –

like Galry's. It appeared to be unusually small and slight of stature, almost certainly a young child. And it was standing motionless upon the empty plain, gazing towards them, though whether it could actually see them or not Leth was unable to tell.

He could barely restrain himself, so powerful was his need to ride forward and identify the solitary figure. The Abyss warriors maintained their eager vigilance; Rasgul was half-standing in the saddle.

At last they drew close. The child – for child it was – was not quite motionless, Leth now saw. Though it stood more or less in one place, it was shuffling, just a step, forward then back, to one side then the other. It seemed not to be aware of the seven slowly advancing upon it. The child's face was slightly downturned, its arms wrapped about its upper body. The child was a boy, Leth now saw, aged about six or seven – Galry's age. He was dreadfully thin and pale. With ambivalent feelings shaking him to the core, Leth saw that it was not Galry.

Something was drastically wrong, that much was readily apparent. The boy's demeanour was lifeless and unnatural. He did not even glance up at the seven riders approaching. He displayed basic motor functions and virtually nothing else. As they came beside him Leth slipped from the saddle, his limbs stiff with cold, and went to kneel beside him. The boy's lips were in motion, but he made no sound. Nor did he seem aware of Leth's presence. His eyes stared dully at the floor. He continued his strange shuffling motion, a step back, one forward; another to the right, one to the left, without any pattern.

Leth knelt and put a hand on his shoulder. The boy ceased moving but failed to look up. His lips continued to move soundlessly.

'Son, what is your name?'

Leth's question elicited no response, not even a flicker in the glazed dull brown eyes. Gently Leth shook his shoulder. Still nothing.

'Boy, I am here to help you.'

'He is beyond help, Swordbearer,' came Count Harg's voice from behind.

Leth ignored him. He shook the shoulder again, gently slapped the boy's ashen cheek. It had no effect. Once more, harder. Then, so concerned was he to draw some kind of response, he took the child's thin arm and pinched the flesh between his finger and thumb. The pressure he applied was sufficient to have made any normal child cry out in protest, but this child was insensitive even to pain.

Leth stood again, letting go of the boy. The boy resumed his shuffling motion.

'They are less than shells, Swordbearer. Their dreams are gone; they have no imagination, no thoughts. Truly, they are no longer among the living.'

Leth stood still. His relief that this diminished creature was not Galry had been swiftly followed by a sense of guilt. For the boy was someone's: somewhere, someone must grieve for the loss of this child. Probably they did not know what had become of him. Which was worse, to not know or to be aware that this was what their son had become?

'There must be something we can do,' he said.

'There is nothing. I have seen them before.'

'You have been here before?'

Harg shook his head. 'By some miracle these children have from time to time found their way up from the Abyss. It is rare, but it has happened.'

'And what did you do with them?'

'Me? I did nothing, for I am untouched by such things. But I know that others tried, to no avail. They can be kept alive for a time, but that is all. Most remain here, though. Others . . . well, others are made into warriors. Children deprived of dreams.'

Leth fought back his anger. Rasgul spoke, showing no emotion at Harg's pointed insinuation. 'He is right, Swordbearer. You can do nothing.'

Leth remounted. He looked again at the tragic child, then his thoughts flew ahead. Where were Galry and Jace? In the Fortress that lay somewhere before him? Alive – that was, fully alive – or had they too been reduced to ambulant corpses or transformed into just as mindless child-warriors?

'Let us move on!' he ordered.

They had not gone more than a few yards before he realized the worst. The boy had not stood alone on the plain. Now Leth saw the others emerging out of the strange haze. There were scores of them; possibly even hundreds or more, for the haze, closer upon the riders now, revealed nothing beyond a distance of a hundred paces or so away.

The children's ages ranged from fifteen or so down to tiny

infants barely able to walk. They stood, sat, lay prone upon the cold dusty plain. Alone or in small knots and groups – it made little difference for they were unaware of one another's presence and no communication passed between them. Some of them walked in slow, foot-dragging circles, others meandered aimlessly. Some, like the first, shuffled from foot to foot but never left the spot where they stood.

And there were the dead. The plain was strewn with corpses, new and decaying, and small skeletons clad in tatters and rags.

And the silence . . .

It was in some ways almost the worst thing. So many children. Their noise, their boisterousness, the spontaneous youthful celebration of living that could rise so naturally over almost any hardship – all this was so terribly and completely absent.

Leth stared with leaden eyes at the faces of those they passed close to, dreading that at any moment he might recognize the sweet, ruined features of his own child.

'Have faith that yours are not among them, Swordbearer,' said Rasgul.

Leth was haggard. 'Faith?'

'You cannot stop and examine every one. They are lost. They are too many, and every second spent here diminishes the hopes of those still imprisoned within the Fortress. It is those whom you must consider now, the ones that Ascaria has not yet fed on.'

Deep within himself Leth acknowledged the truth of this. Jace's and Galry's one hope was that the Kancanitrix had not yet touched them and that he might still reach them before she did.

The air had taken on a faint reddish tinge now. Everything was toned by a dull bloodlight. The seven had entered the outermost fringe of the area touched by the red glow that Leth had first spied from the road to Ardbire Keep. They were far out upon the floor of the Death Abyss now. At almost any moment, Leth knew, he would be setting eyes for the first time upon the Fortress of the Dark Flame, and the monstrous creature that it housed would be separated from him by no more than the thickness of its protective walls.

IV

Rasgul, at the fore again, raised his hand abruptly. They were well into the red haze now. They halted. Leth brought his horse alongside the Abyss warrior. 'What is it?'

'I must take your weapons now.'

Leth could see only fifty yards or so in any direction. The haze was deeper, closer all around. It had become oppressive, a weird light that played upon Leth's nerves. Children wandered within it like ghouls, or stood stock still, darkly bloodlit shadows, some with lips moving soundlessly like the first, none acknowledging the seven riders in their midst in any way.

'I am not happy with this.'

Rasgul's features were set. 'We have come this far; this is the only way if we are not to turn back. Do you wish to turn back?'

'You know I cannot.'

'Very soon now we will encounter warriors from the Fortress. They must see that I am bringing back captives.'

Leth turned in the saddle and saw that Harg and Juson were giving up their swords. With a resigned sigh he unbuckled the scimitar that Harg had given him and handed it to Rasgul. Then he unbuckled the Orbsword. Dembarl dismounted and came to take it from him. He staggered under its sudden weight and looked up in some surprise at Leth, then bore it over to Rasgul's horse and held it while Rasgul strapped it behind his saddle.

'You see, the hilt is unharnessed,' said Rasgul to Leth. 'Summon it and it will fly to you.'

Harg and Juson were having their hands tied behind them. Rasgul approached Leth with a short length of cord. 'Don your helm, Swordbearer.'

Leth did so, then crossed his wrists behind his back. Rasgul bound his wrists and said, 'Check it. It is a slip knot, and not tight. You can pull free with the minimum of effort, as you must do if we are found out.'

Leth tested the binding and found that Rasgul was right. Rasgul readjusted the knot then climbed back upon his horse. Now they rode forward with Rasgul at the fore and Leth, Harg and Juson coming behind in single file. Dembarl and Huuri rode guard, one upon each flank, and Fhurn brought up the rear.

The flat plain dipped a little. Huge, strangely conformed boulders stood out here and there, emerging suddenly as if thrust up out of the ground. The dark red luminescence grew more intense. Leth watched the children still, peering into the faces of those he was close enough to make out. He calculated that he had already passed more than one hundred, plus countless dead. Of the living, not a single one showed a spark of inner life, either shambling slowly or standing silent and still, eyes cast sightlessly to the dust. He wondered how many more there could possibly be; how many Ascaria needed to fulfil her aims.

Rasgul uttered a sharp word of warning. A party of Abyss warriors was riding up the slope towards them. Leth slumped forward a little in the saddle to give the appearance of dejection.

The warriors, six in number, halted and their leader greeted Rasgul in harsh, guttural tones. They exchanged a few words; Rasgul jerked his thumb back, indicating the three 'captives'. All the warriors' eyes were on the three, though most pointedly on the knight in sapphire armour and helm. Leth heard brief, coarse laughter, then the Abyss warriors went on their way, filing slowly past him, their pale faces curious. Rasgul signalled forward and they continued on.

'It bodes well,' declared Rasgul a short distance on, when the Abyss warriors were well gone. 'They suspected nothing. Now, prepare yourselves. The greatest test is upon us.'

Though the glassy red light still persisted, the haze had lifted noticeably. Leth stared ahead to where the rough ground rose, some two hundred paces distant, to a long low ridge. Upon the ridge a dark, low form crouched: a huge castle of three levels, characterized by massive fortified walls and five wide, lowering rounded towers. The walls followed the contours of the ridge; the entire edifice was constructed of a dark, red-black stone, and it seemed to Leth that it was from the Fortress itself that the red luminescence radiated. Lights glimmered about its battlements. A long, exposed, elevated roadway led up to a colossal barbican. Leth felt his stomach tighten.

Rasgul looked back at him, his face sombre and haunted in the bloodlight. 'Are you ready, Swordbearer? Ascaria awaits you.'

FIFTEEN

I

Issul strained against her bonds. It was futile; she was securely bound and no amount of flexing, twisting and manipulating was going to permit her to break free.

More than an hour had passed since she had fallen into the hands of this band of – what were they? Disciplined cutthroats? Mercenary outlaws? She still did not know. They had not harmed her and she remained under the impression that they were unsure of what to do with her. From their failure to enquire as to her identity or her reasons for being here alone in the forest, however, she had come to believe that they had a reasonably sure idea of who she was.

She was intrigued by the disappearance of their commander, the man in the blue cloak. There had been something about him that she felt she knew, though she had not seen his face. Now she wondered, had his departure at the time of her capture been coincidence? That is, had he simply left at this time on pre-planned business, or had he deliberately absented himself for fear of being recognized by her? Her intuition inclined her towards the latter alternative.

Issul racked her mind, but she could not fit a face onto the body that she knew instinctively was not that of a total stranger.

She had been perfunctorily questioned three times. On each occasion it was the burly, black-bearded man whom she had seen earlier with the tracker who had interrogated her. His questions were gruff and to the point – he wanted to know the whereabouts of the chest she had carried. He showed interest in little else.

Each time she answered evasively, pretending ignorance. Though plainly frustrated by her attitude, Blackbeard had until now pressed no harder. His chilling parting comment had been, 'You *will* tell us. Be sure of that. We are patient just now, but we do not intend to wait forever. Think of what it will mean if you choose not to tell us.'

They knew about the chest, but not what it contained. They knew it to be significant, but not what its precise significance was. This much she was able to deduce – Blackbeard's interrogation skills were rudimentary, and he gave away more than he was aware of.

The last two times that he had come across to question her, Issul noticed something. Prior to his approaching her another member of the gang, whom she took to be on sentry duty, had arrived. They had conferred briefly, heads together with the other gang-members. Then Blackbeard had come over and put his questions to her. When he left her the men spoke again quickly, then the sentry made off once more into the trees.

Issul wondered, was the sentry conveying the content of her interrogation to another person? Did the mysterious blue-cloaked leader of this anomalous band wait somewhere close by, deliberately beyond her sight?

The afternoon wore on. Issul was left to ponder her predicament – deliberately, she supposed.

'Think of what it will mean if you choose not to tell us.'

Yes, those words had not been chosen lightly. They played upon her mind. She did not imagine they had originated from Blackbeard.

And it was not only the tortures and indignities that these men might inflict upon her that were implied here. Of equal if not greater importance were the consequences of her being led from this place without giving up the chest. The leader of this gang surmised the possibility, just as Issul herself knew, that if she was taken far from here she might never locate the chest again.

Issul weighed this over and over in her mind. She could not afford to leave without Orbus. Not under any circumstances.

But neither could she give him up to ruffians like these!

So what choice had she?

At the back of her thoughts hovered the unlikely prospect of some-how bringing these men around to the possibility of joining with her. It was a mad, absurd hope. She did not know who they were, or what precisely they wanted. Logically, they could not want to see the blue casket and Orbus destroyed, for his destruction, ultimately, was also theirs. They might not know this, of course. Unless . . .

Unless what? Might they be True Sept members? Unlikely. They did not speak or convey themselves in the manner of fanatics. Nor did she suspect them of working for the Krai. So ultimately – though she could not be totally certain – they should have nothing to gain by seeing the casket destroyed.

But so much mystery! Nothing could be relied upon!

Issul felt desperate and thwarted, but the knowledge that to lose Orbus was to lose everything kept bringing her back to clutch at the flimsiest of straws.

How might she win the confidence of men like these?

The answer was that she did not have to. She had to gain the confidence of their leader, who declined to show himself.

It had grown cold in the dwindling afternoon. The sun was low now, the forest shadows long and full. A few acutely slanting shafts of pale sunlight managed to stab through to the forest floor, but the uneasy dappled light they cast brought no warmth. The breeze, though light, still pierced the inactive flesh. Motionless for so long, Issul had begun to shiver and her fingers and toes grew raw and painful. She called out to the men, 'Is it your intention to have me freeze to death?'

As one they looked her way. They had lit no fire, presumably out of fear of drawing unwanted attention. From time to time they had been getting up, stamping their feet and performing exercises to stimulate their circulation. After a moment Blackbeard got up and came over to her. He drew a knife from his belt. 'I will free your ankles. You can stand and walk around a bit, warm yourself. No tricks, mind. We are watching you.'

He stooped and cut through the ligament binding her ankles. At that moment one of the other men called to him and made a signal with his hands. He seemed to be indicating the woods off to one side. Blackbeard straightened.

'Wait,' he told her gruffly, before she could stand. He walked back to the others. Issul gathered that he had acted without permission, and was being advised to seek his leader's approval before allowing her to walk. She flexed her ankles and toes but made no attempt to rise.

She cast her gaze around. Was it possible to make a break for it, even with her hands bound? The men were watching her keenly and she knew lookouts were close by. She dismissed the thought. And at that moment something extraordinary happened.

Without identifiable reason Issul was visited with the sudden conviction that her husband, King Leth, was close at hand. The thought was irrational, yet the impression was overwhelming, so much so that she could not prevent herself responding to it. She turned her head and peered hard into the shadows.

Leth?

Her heart pounded. She was so sure he was there.

Leth?

It was madness, yet . . . a glimmer of movement in the undergrowth a little way off.

Help me, Leth! Help me!

He was on horseback, beneath the trees. Without another thought for her guards Issul clambered to her feet and began to run towards him. 'Leth, help me! Quickly, free me! I am in trouble!'

The figure on the horse moved towards her. She saw, not Leth, but a warrior-knight in fabulous, gleaming, blue-tinged armour, an ornate horned and plumed helm upon his head. She stopped running, suddenly confused. There was something wrong. The horseman had also stopped. He was indefinite in form, a phantom. She did not know what to do.

There came the sound of pounding hooves. Out of nowhere a second horseman appeared, grim and pale-faced in black half-armour, bearing down upon her, a slender scimitar raised high. She turned away instinctively, but there was no time to get out of his path. She cried out.

She heard another cry: *'NNO-OOOOO!'*

Leth's voice – unmistakeable!

But now there was nothing.

Issul staggered back, stupefied. Both horsemen had disappeared. Or had they never been?

She turned. Blackbeard and the others were just behind her. They had obviously rushed to seize her. But they stood stock still now, their expressions mirroring her own.

'You saw it, didn't you?'

It was a relief. For she had wondered whether she alone had perceived the phantoms; whether she was mad.

Her captors eyed her warily. It struck her then: *They think I conjured this!*

She had been on the point of asking them what they had seen, to verify her own experience. Did they think it had meaning? Where had the phantoms sprung from? But now she kept silence, thinking that she might just turn their suspicion to her advantage.

Blackbeard came forward and grasped her arm. 'I told you, no tricks!'

His eyes flickered edgily past her, into the woods. His grip was tentative, almost gentle. She sensed that she was being treated with a new respect.

She allowed herself to be led back to the tree where she had been seated, too dazed to offer any resistance. One of the men spoke in a haunted voice, but she did not hear what he said. Blackbeard's grip became a touch firmer as his fears that she might yet strike him down with magic were dispelled. She sat down again.

What happened here? What just happened?

She thought of the Edge Riders, spoken of by Orbus: phantasmal creatures, awesomely powerful, which would come out of Enchantment, bringing with them a wake of chaos and destruction, paving the way for Enchantment to grow. Was that what she had just witnessed? The thought chilled her; *what will it mean if the first of the Edge Riders is free? Is there still time for us to act?*

Without consulting Orbus further she could be certain of nothing.

But why had she felt so certain of Leth's presence? Even now, despite everything, she felt him, as though he had somehow been close – and his anguished cry still echoed through her mind.

Her captors stood in a knot close by. They flashed her mistrustful glances and scanned the woods, apprehensive of another manifestation. Though they had obviously been shaken by what they had witnessed, their overall composure, individually and as a unit, impressed her. Typical bandits, even many soldiers, would have been panic-stricken at the sight of the phantom warriors. They would likely have fled. These men, though alarmed, had not for more than an instant been deflected from their purpose. Once again Issul found herself wondering who they were.

Issul let her head tip back against the tree-trunk and closed her eyes. She was sinking again into despondency, not knowing how she could escape this terrible situation and continue with her mission. She heard a heavy footfall in front of her and opened her eyes to see Blackbeard looming above her.

'Was that your doing?'

Issul hesitated. Should she continue with her bluff, let them believe she commanded elemental powers? Or was it better to admit the truth? Or could she work upon them with half-truth, a middle path by which she might yet lead them in the way she wanted? She elected for this latter. 'I am responsible inasmuch as such phenomena will recur again and again, becoming destructive and uncontrollable, if I am not permitted to continue on my way.'

Blackbeard digested this with a frown, clearly not sure what to make of her. She saw in his eyes an alert, if cold, intelligence. 'Do you threaten us?'

'I merely state how it is.'

'You mean it has to do with the chest, and what it contains?'

Again she balked, and realized that this was in fact not half-truth at all. It was indeed the way things were. She said, 'It has to do with many things. But I will tell you this: if I am prevented from continuing on my way, you will not survive. Nor will I. If you know anything of what you are about, you will be aware that there are immense and incalculable dangers here.'

She looked into his eyes and saw the lack of decision there.

'Do you know of Enchantment?' she asked.

'Enchantment?' A wariness. 'Of course.'

Issul nodded thoughtfully.

'Tell me more,' he said.

Issul shook her head. 'I want to speak to your leader.'

'I am leader here.'

'No, you are not. I speak of he who skulks yonder in the bushes, afraid to show his face.' She raised her voice and called, 'Come forth, mongrel! There are things we must discuss! Or are you too cowardly to face me?'

There was silence. Issul looked up angrily into Blackbeard's face. 'Well, understand this clearly: we are doomed. You are standing in the way of what must be done. There are factors involved which you cannot possibly comprehend, but you will bring down all the forces of Enchantment upon our heads if you do not help me. Now leave me. Begone!'

Blackbeard gave her a long appraising look, then withdrew, almost with reluctance. Issul sat alone and fumed. Perhaps it was impossible. Perhaps nothing she could say would sway these men. Why should they believe her, after all? They were treasure-seekers, nothing more. They had fought together as mercenaries in skirmishes here and there – hence their discipline and close co-ordination. They had seen that she carried a chest, and believed it held valuables that might make them rich. They had seen phantoms in the woods and suspected her of witchery. They were probably now debating the best way to kill her.

As she thought these glum thoughts there was a movement in the bushes off to one side. The blue-cloaked man stepped into the open before her. He was tall, broad of shoulder, deep-chested. Issul estimated him to be about thirty years of age. But she could not see his face, for he wore a mail coif which covered all but his eyes. Again she was struck by his familiarity, the way he moved and held himself.

He conferred briefly with Blackbeard, then strode over to her. He was swift and sure of himself. 'What is the nature of this quest that you are engaged upon?'

'Why do you hide yourself?'

'Please answer my question.'

'I think you have made a mistake. I think that whoever has employed you will not be pleased to learn what has happened here.'

'I wish to know what is in the chest that you were carrying, that you guarded so closely. And where is it now? And why do you speak of Enchantment?'

'I speak of Enchantment because it is the truth. And I will take you to the chest,' Issul said. She was thinking rapidly At all costs she had to get to Orbus. She had somehow to continue with him to the Farplace Opening. Somehow she had to get these men to accompany her, guard her, at least as far as the former Krai camp. It was absurd, but it was the only way. She had to make it utterly clear that if they obstructed her they would die.

'You will give it up?' queried the blue-cloaked man, clearly taken by surprise.

'No. And if you attempt to take it from me you will perish. Not by my hand, but as a natural consequence. Plainly you have followed me; I believe you know who I am. You know too that the chest is of incalculable value. Not monetary. It contains no treasure as such. But you will be aware from my actions back there—' she nodded in the direction from which she had ridden when she fled the grullag attack '—just how valuable I deem it to be. Thus I am willing to take you to it.'

She felt her nerve faltering. Did she dare confide in him? By what other means was she to get to Orbus?

The gang-leader nodded to himself and stepped back, straightening. 'Very well, take me. Is it far?'

She shook her head. He helped her to her feet. 'Let us go now.'

She led him and his men back the way she had come, through the deepening shadows of the forest. All the way her heart was in her mouth. If she was wrong . . .

They came to the grove and the thicket where she had hidden the chest. Issul pushed her way through the bushes.

'There,' she said, nodding. 'It is beneath that bush.'

At a nod from the leader one of the men dropped to the ground and probed beneath the bush. He withdrew, shaking his head. 'She leads us false.'

'No!' Issul felt her world dropping away. 'It is there! I hid it there!'

She fell to her knees. Her wrists were still bound behind her, so she could not feel beneath the bush. But she could see the worst. The man was right. The chest containing Orbus's blue casket had gone.

II

'Is this a joke?' the blue-cloaked commander demanded harshly.

'It is not! Look! There are my other things, just as I left them!' Her saddle and items of equipment remained undisturbed beneath the bushes. 'Somebody has been here and taken it!'

The gang-leader stood in a moment of indecision, but must have seen by her face that she was telling the truth. He snapped an order to his men to scour the nearby area. Issul was sick, her head spinning. She struggled desperately to bring order to her thoughts, at the same time unable to confront the full horror of what the theft of the casket meant. It was the loss of all hope; her children, Leth, Enchantment's Edge . . .

Who, or what, could have taken it?

'Are you all right?'

The words seemed to have no reference to her. Their sound enclosed her loudly, and the world had slewed, lurched. She felt her hands, disconnected, twitching and straining against some inexplicable restraint. A vast, rushing sensation, lifting her and turning her over, and a pounding, surging hiss. Everything blurred – the trees racing across the sky . . .

'Are you all right?'

She found she was staring at the sky through a black overhanging latticework of branches. She blinked, not clear about what had happened, a terrible hammering in her head. She realized she was slumped upon the earth, half on her back. One of her captors was kneeling at her side. The blue-cloaked commander towered over her.

'Are you all right?'

She nodded, and the movement of her head felt ridiculously exaggerated, as though she had no control over her movements. Abruptly she was both embarrassed and furious at herself, for she realized what had happened. She had fainted. *Fainted! In front of these men!* The shock of the loss of Orbus's world, combined with everything else she had suffered today and in recent days, had been more than she could consciously stand. Issul struggled to sit up, hampered by her still-bound wrists.

'Untie me!' she demanded.

The commander bent and helped her to her feet. 'With respect, I think that would be unwise.'

'Do you know what you do here? Do you understand what has happened? If that chest is not found, we are lost! All of us!'

And it hit her just then. Who was most likely to have followed her and seen her hide the chest, if not these men?

Moscul! Grey Venger! Orbus was in the hands of the Legendary Child.

Issul saw the blue casket shattered into a thousand fragments.

The loss of all hope.

The commander was watching her silently, his face hidden except for cool, expressionless hazel eyes. 'We will find it again.'

She made a scornful sound. 'Why did you follow me? Why do you seek the chest? Had I not stopped to investigate you, I would have been away from here, the chest safe with me.'

'What does the chest contain that is so important?'

'I have told you. It contains your future.'

'That is no kind of answer.'

'It is the only answer!'

'Then, if my men are unable to recover the chest?'

'Hah!' Issul's lips twisted in bitter contempt. 'Then nothing matters any more.'

She stood rigidly, unable to find proper vent for her feelings. The commander stood in meditative silence. His gaze was unfocused as he mused upon his own thoughts. But she sensed that he grew uncomfortable under her scrutiny.

Who are you?

He shifted his stance slightly, angling his body away from her, his eyes studying the forest. And in that movement she was transported . . . back to the garden of a little cottage, hardly more than a hovel, in the village of Lastmeadow. Only – what – no more than three weeks ago! A soldier by the fence, turning away as she appeared, unwilling to reveal his face.

Gordallith!

The name shot through her mind; she almost spat it out.

So this was Fectur's doing!

It hardly came as a surprise.

Her thoughts raced. What would be Gordallith's mission? To shadow her, learn where she was bound. Yes, and discover by what means she hoped and intended to bring salvation to Enchantment's Edge.

And then? Was Gordallith instructed to murder her? Likely so, if her survival was found to be inessential to the task of saving Enchantment's Edge.

So, indeed, she had embarrassed Gordallith by falling into his hands. And now he did not know what to do with her.

She pondered a brief moment. Should she let him know that she had found him out? He was the Spectre's man, and would not acknowledge her authority. Leth was gone; if Fectur could learn Issul's secret and prevent her return he would have the power he aspired to. No, Gordallith would kill her if he realized she knew him. He would not permit her to return and arraign him on a charge of high treason.

The casket was lost. Gordallith, ignorant of everything that was at stake here, would return now to Enchantment's Edge. He would not take the Queen with him.

It was the end.

But was she prepared to let herself die here, passively, in anonymity, on a traitor's blade? Was she not going to fight? Through her hopelessness her fury rose. If all was lost, her children, her husband, Orbus . . . if Enchantment's Edge must fall, then the Spectre would pay! As long as the blood ran in her veins she would not allow him to gloat for a single minute!

She thought quickly. Gordallith and one of his men guarded her here in the grove; the others searched for the chest. If she was to do anything, it had to be now. There would be no opportunity later. Her hands were bound, yet . . .

She had been taught by an expert.

Issul twisted a little, bringing both Gordallith and the guard into her view. She settled her weight, then suddenly lifted one foot and thrust out in a vicious snap-kick. The edge of her foot slammed with all the force she could muster into the guard's unprotected face. As he fell back, before Gordallith could react, she spun and kicked again. The bony top of her foot rammed hard into Gordallith's groin. He doubled over with a groan of pain. Issul bent low and ran.

She ducked beneath the bushes, shouldering through branches and brambles. Her foot snagged, she fell to her knees, but was up again instantly, forcing through. She broke free of the thicket and raced off between the trees. She estimated she would have several seconds before either man recovered enough to give chase. And she gambled – correctly – that they would not shout out to the others, for fear of bringing the wrong kind of company down upon them.

If she could just get herself beyond their sight . . .

With her hands bound she was severely hampered, yet she made good speed. Her one hope was to outpace them, get far enough away, find a place to hide, a sharp rock on which to saw through her bindings. It was a less than slender hope, but she burned with fury, with blind hatred for Fectur and all he represented, and this kept her running, thinking only of the moment, dodging, weaving beneath the trees with no notion of direction, thinking of getting back to Fectur.

There was crashing in the bushes somewhere behind. Issul did not risk looking back. She veered off to one side, half-tumbled down a wet, muddy bank, made off along a shallow gully. Quite suddenly she rounded the massive earthy rootstock of a fallen beech and found one of Gordallith's men before her. He was not looking her way, but he heard her and turned.

Without pausing Issul threw herself at him, head low. He was slightly downslope of her, which gave her extra momentum. Her head cannoned into his midriff. He went down, but she slipped and fell too. She rolled over and used her motion to come cleanly to her feet. The man was scrambling up, reaching for his sword. Issul arced her foot around hard into the side of his head, sending him sprawling again. She ran on, leaping, veering, twisting, the breath coming harsh and painful to her lungs. She could not tell whether anyone was behind her.

Her legs were beginning to fail her. She gasped for air, her lungs burned. She scrambled up a slope, crested it. A figure loomed. A hand flew out. Before she could respond a fist caught her hard on the side of the head and sent her reeling to the floor. Her world spun with pain. She struggled to her feet. Something swished through the air, snaked around her ankles, tightened, jerked. Her feet were pulled away from beneath her and she landed hard upon her back. Dazedly she was aware of the tracker with the green fillet around his head, whom she had first seen searching for her close to the grove. His hand was upon his whip-stock, and he grinned down at her. In his other hand he held a sword.

'I think that's far enough, little lady.' He sheathed the sword, took a dagger, bent and pressed the point to her neck, then with his other hand wound the coil of his whip more tightly around her ankles. Then he straightened. Issul lay trussed and helpless.

Tracker turned to seek out his companions. There was a sudden blur of movement, a thud, a groan. Tracker fell. A shadow fell across Issul. Hands were at her ankles, uncoiling the whip. 'Majesty, roll over. Let me cut free your hands.'

'Shenwolf!'

'Quickly!'

Too stunned to do anything but comply. Shenwolf cut swiftly through her bonds then helped her to her feet. 'Come on, this way!'

Tracker lay upon the ground, a bloody wound at the base of his skull. Issul bent and took his sword, then ran with Shenwolf.

'This way! There are horses!'

Where was he leading her? Was this another betrayal? She could not think, she could only run with him. A hundred paces through the trees, and at the foot of a grassy slope a pair of horses stood tethered. Issul leapt into the saddle of the first, Shenwolf the other.

'Follow me!'

Shenwolf bore off in an easterly direction. Issul glanced behind but could see no pursuers. After a distance of another hundred yards or so Shenwolf suddenly slowed. He raised a hand.

'Wait!'

He threw himself from the saddle, ran into the trees and fell to his knees at the base of a tumble of mossy limestone boulders. She saw him reach into a black gap. A moment later he stood and made his way back towards her.

'The chest!' Issul gaped in astonishment and sudden joy. In his hands Shenwolf carried the wooden chest that held Orbus's world.

He passed it up to her, and grinned. 'Aye, the chest!'

'But what—? How —?'

'Later. For now let's get as far from here as we can while there is still a degree of daylight!'

Back in the saddle he put his heels to his horse's flanks. Together they made off at fullest speed beneath the towering trees.

SIXTEEN

I

They rode hard, deep into the forest, for the better part of two hours. At length, with only the pallid silvery beams of a slender moon to light their way, they paused in their flight. They were at the foot of a high, wooded bluff. Their horses were weary, steam rising from their hides.

'I think we will be safe from pursuit, at least until the morning,' said Shenwolf. 'These mounts belonged to those brigands who had abducted you. In stealing them I set the remaining steeds running free. The brigands may recapture them in time, but it will not be soon enough to permit them to mount a pursuit tonight.'

Issul nodded, but said nothing. Despite her rescue, she was not entirely easy with Shenwolf's company. Much explanation was demanded, and for the nonce she found herself reticent and somewhat on edge.

Shenwolf pointed. 'I think I see a cave. Perhaps we can shelter there for the night.'

They rode forward, then dismounted and tethered the horses to a bush outside what did indeed turn out to be a narrow black cavern entrance. The two mounts were well-equipped for travel, with saddle-packs filled with food, leather water-sacks, blankets and sundry items, including bound-cloth and pitch-drenched torches by which they might see at night. To one of these Shenwolf struck a flint, and with weapons drawn the two entered the cave. They found it to be deep and untenanted by either man or beast. Moreover, natural flues in the rock ceiling permitted the escape of smoke. So they brought the horses within and gathered wood and tinder for a fire. As Shenwolf set the fire to blazing and prepared to toast rabbit meat with bread, then biscuits and preserved fruit from the saddle-packs, Issul retired to one side of the cave and summoned Orbus forth. To her immense relief he had suffered no harm.

'Are you aware of what has happened?'

'To some extent. Friend Shenwolf found the chest where you had hidden it. He called me forth, then set off to discover what had become of you.'

'Do not be too ready to term him "friend". Did he explain himself?'

'Not entirely. There was little time for chat. Issul, before you make any judgement, hear him out. He has risked much to save you.'

'I intend to. But, no matter his actions this evening, many questions still hang in the air and cause me distinct unease.'

'Quite so.'

'Will you remain here while we talk?'

'Certainly.'

The food was ready; the cave had filled with the mouthwatering aroma of roasting meat. Shenwolf handed Issul a trencher piled with meat sprinkled with fresh herbs, and bread, then seated himself cross-legged before the fire. Issul toyed abstractedly with her food and consumed little, whereas Shenwolf dug in enthusiastically.

'Shenwolf, I have not yet expressed my gratitude for your action this afternoon. Without your intervention I would be a prisoner still, and quite possibly dead. Also, were it not for you, Orbus would now be in the hands of dangerous and irresponsible men, and who knows what that would bring. So let me say to you, as I have said before, I thank you. At the same time a cloud hangs over us. There are questions that I am bound to ask you.'

Shenwolf chewed upon his food and swallowed. 'I understand. That is, I do not truly understand what it is that has caused you to doubt me, but I have seen that you do. That hurts me, and I wish to know why you should feel this way when all I have done has been, as I thought, out of loyalty to you and to King Leth. I will gladly answer your questions, as truthfully as I am able, in the hope that we may by such means dispel all doubts and suspicions. But I must ask you to understand that there are some things I am quite unable to explain. This, one way or another, you will have to accept, as I have had to.'

Issul frowned. She glanced at Orbus, who leaned in silence upon his staff, faceless in his mass of rags and indistinct in the deep gloom beyond the fireglow. 'What do you mean?'

'I mean . . .' Shenwolf scratched his head. In the ruddy glow of the flames he was haggard. His uniform was scuffed and soiled; dried blood had caked in his hair above one ear. Issul studied him hard. She could not decide what to make of him. So many questions burned in her mind, and behind them the nagging fear that he was not to be trusted, that he might yet be leading her into a trap. For more reasons than she could quantify she did not want this to be so. 'I am not sure what I mean, because I am not sure about many things. I think it will be simpler if I try to explain as I answer your questions.'

'Very well. Let's start with this afternoon. How did you come to find the chest and blue casket, and then rescue me? Why are you alone? It does not augur well for my company's defence against the grullags.'

Shenwolf looked grave. 'I am sorry, but the company was torn to shreds, Majesty.'

'There are survivors, surely?'

'As many as twenty were killed, from what I witnessed. Many others took wounds. Perhaps fifteen or so emerged unscathed. It was a very savage attack. Fortunately the grullags withdrew quickly.'

'With Grey Venger?'

Shenwolf nodded. 'That was my impression.'

She watched his face, looking for clues. 'And what then?'

'When the battle was done I had two concerns. Most urgently I feared for you. But also I was troubled by the knowledge that the two of us had come into conflict. And we had been seen by the men to have come into conflict, and I had been accused by you of some unexplained crime or misdemeanour. I was under suspicion, therefore, and would almost certainly be stripped of my weapons and placed under guard. So in the fog of the battle's wake I elected to come after you alone.

'You were easy to track,' he continued. 'You had ridden off alone, the ground was soft and damp, and your horse had developed a limp. Hence I had little difficulty in discovering the grove and thicket where you had hidden the chest. The fact that you were not present alarmed me, and I called Orbus forth and through him learned that you and he had been disturbed and that you had gone off to investigate. I then followed your trail again, saw other footprints and feared the worst. I took the decision to remove Orbus to another location, as his safety had to be paramount. Then I went back to find you.

'To be brief, I was able to observe your plight without being observed myself, though it was a close call. Your captors were highly organized and admirably skilled; they had sentries well-concealed. It was sheer luck that I spotted one before he spotted me.'

Issul nodded, remembering her own humiliating experience when Gordallith's lookouts caught her.

'When they marched off with you to recover the chest they left one man guarding the horses,' Shenwolf continued. 'I crept down and slew him, took these two horses and freed the others, stripping them of their saddles and equipment that they might run further and freer. Then I went back for you.'

'Had I not broken free, what would you have done?' Issul asked.

'I do not know. It would have depended upon their treatment of you, I think. I did not relish trying to tackle them alone.'

Issul absorbed this. So far it had the ring of plausibility. She knew Shenwolf to be bold and resourceful, and an expert tracker. And as before, at the Krai camp and afterwards, he had demonstrated extraordinary fidelity to her and the Crown. But there was enigma here. Something still nagged, and demanded explanation.

She pulled forth the leather pouch from her tunic and held out the little ivory talisman on the flat of her hand. 'All very well. Now explain this.'

Shenwolf glanced at the talisman, then lowered his eyes. 'I cannot.'

'Cannot?'

'Not entirely. Not satisfactorily.'

'I do not understand, Shenwolf.' Issul's voice took on a brittle tone. 'You have already admitted that it is yours, and we know that you gave it to the Child beside the pond. So why can you now not tell me what it is, and why you gave it?'

'Majesty, it is as I said moments ago. There are some things that I am unable to explain fully. I will gladly tell you all I can, but that, I fear, will not be enough. When I am done you will know little more than you know already.'

'Let me be the judge of that.'

Shenwolf bowed his head. 'My difficulty is that I know so little myself. You see, in all truth, I have almost no recollection of my past life.'

'That is indeed unfortunate!' declared Issul scathingly. 'Convenient also, were there something you wished to keep concealed!'

'If anything is concealed, it is concealed from myself also. That is the truth, Majesty. I swear it. I fully believe that no torture known to men could draw from me more about my true background than I am about to reveal to you.'

'Then what of the story you told me days ago at the inn of the Green Ram in Crosswood?'

'It hardly constituted a story, as I recall it,' Shenwolf replied. 'I said only that I came from beyond the forest.'

'And that you were taught martial skills by your father from birth.'

'That is still very little. I admit, I was evasive. The fact is, I did not want to embellish the truth but I was afraid that you would not believe me if I admitted it. What memories I possess are vague, fleeting impressions; hauntings, even.' He put down his trencher and rose, then took several paces across the cave floor, his head bowed and his hands to his temples. 'It is as though my past resides in a haze, impenetrable by me, which, when a stiff breeze blows, shifts fleetingly aside to show me a glimpse of an aspect of the enigma, but a glimpse only, then it is gone. Try as I might, I cannot recover it.'

Orbus spoke. 'Perhaps, then, you should begin by telling us what you do know of recent weeks: how you came to meet the Child beside the pond; why you came to Enchantment's Edge; how you came upon this talisman. Can you tell us where you set out from?'

Shenwolf gave a shake of his head. 'No. My first clear perception is of finding myself upon my hands and knees in the forest. A nondescript place; it cannot be more than a few leagues from here. My head was spinning; I was dazed, and for some moments dazzled as if by a bright light. It was, quite genuinely, as though I had arrived there without having been anywhere before, for I knew almost nothing. And I recall . . . it is so hard to explain . . . there was, for a few instants only, a sensation of being surrounding by a shimmering purplish lucency. It faded, and as it did so the forest came into substance around me.'

'Describe this phenomenon,' said Orbus.

Shenwolf swept his hand across his crown. 'There is nothing more I can say. It was the impression of light surrounding me. Perhaps not even light, but a bright, glaring colouration or disturbance of the air.

I was dizzy, I recall, and felt that I had been thrown down upon the ground, as if from quite a height. I can tell you nothing more.'

Issul glanced again at Orbus. He made no further comment, so she said, 'Very well. What then? You were alone in the forest. Did you know where you were? What did you do?'

'I had no notion of my whereabouts, nor how I came to be there, nor where I had come from.'

'But you knew *who* you were?'

'I knew my name, and little else. However, it is perhaps odd, but I was not at all distressed and only moderately disorientated by this. It did not seem unnatural. When my head had cleared sufficiently I began to walk, taking an upward trail to some high ground. I ascended as high as I could, then climbed a tall elm to scan my surroundings. I saw nothing but forest in all directions with, occupying the southern range of my vision, the bright blazing peaks which I subsequently learned to be the borders of Enchantment. Those mountains impressed me as daunting – lonely, eerie and inhospitable. So I descended and struck off generally northwards.'

'And you had not yet acquired the talisman?'

'Oh yes. I had it with me.'

'It belonged to you?'

'I do not know if it was mine, but I was wearing it around my neck. I remember becoming aware of it and taking it off to examine it.'

'So it was unfamiliar?'

'Everything was unfamiliar, and yet, as I say, that did not trouble me. The talisman may have been mine; I simply do not know. Majesty, what is this thing? Why do you place such weight upon it?'

'Just continue,' replied Issul curtly.

Shenwolf looked at her for a moment, then said, 'I walked for the better part of a day, and came eventually upon a tiny hamlet called Arklie Hollow. The folk there were wary and fearful, not keen for me to stay. Still, from them I gleaned the name of this land and its king. I learned too of the Krai menace and King Leth's call to arms. Thus informed I set off to become what I have since become, namely a soldier in the King's Army.'

'And along the way it so happened that you met with the Legendary Child and bestowed this talisman upon him!'

'The Legendary Child? What is this?'

Could he be bluffing? Issul studied him closely. He was a fine actor, if he was. Still, she was not ready to rule it out. 'You gave this "ornament" to a child beside a pond. You have already confessed as much.'

'Yes. Majesty, believe me, that is just how it happened!' Shenwolf's eyes and expression declared him wounded by her tone. 'For three days and nights I walked on, following a woodland path pointed out to me by the folk of Arklie Hollow. At a certain point I was forced to leave the path, for I came upon a family of grullags and felt it wise to give them the widest possible berth. As luck would have it they spied me almost at the same moment that I spotted them, and came in pursuit. I fled rather than face them, and ran for perhaps half a league deep into the forest before finally losing them. It was some hours afterwards that, plying my way in the direction in which I hoped Enchantment's Edge lay, I broke out beside the pond where the old woman, Arene, was with the child and its warden.'

'And that is it? A simple chance encounter?'

'Just that.'

Issul looked sceptically at Orbus, then thrust her hand at Shenwolf again. 'Then why did you give this to the Child?'

'I was charmed by him, pure and simple. He was fair, bright-eyed and bonny; I took an instant liking to him and was prompted on the spur of the moment to give him a gift of some kind. This was all I had. But it was a gift, from a stranger to a child, nothing more.'

Issul peered hard at him. Could this be so? Sheer coincidence and nothing more? It was extraordinary, most especially in the light of Pader Luminis's having identified the talisman as originating within Enchantment, and Orbus subsequently linking it to his ancient adversary, Urch-Malmain. If Shenwolf were making it up, then it was a most audacious tale, for on the surface it appeared designed to arouse her doubts. But if it were true . . . Issul was almost too thrown by it to gather her thoughts.

Shenwolf stood forlorn in the dancing fireglow. 'Majesty, I am unsure of what I am being accused.'

Orbus glided forward and spoke softly to Issul. 'I think we should discuss this.'

She nodded. To Shenwolf she said, 'Orbus and I must confer. Excuse us, please.'

'I will wait outside.'

'No!' It came out quickly, more staccato than she had intended, and there was no disguising her meaning. She softened her tone, but could do nothing to diminish the force of her message. 'Take yourself off that way, into the cave. Take a torch to light your way.'

Shenwolf self-consciously lit a brand in the flames of the fire and moved off into the depths of the cave. Issul watched as his silhouetted figure diminished. Lit by the flames of the torch, she saw him seat himself somewhat stiffly upon a low shelf of rock some distance away. She and Orbus then spoke closely, in undertones.

'What am I to make of this?' Issul sighed, almost bereft.

'It is an extraordinary tale,' Orbus agreed.

'Do you believe him?'

The bundled figure shifted. 'It is hard to know what to make of it.'

'Is it plausible, that his meeting with the Legendary Child came about by pure hazard? Can this—' she held up the little talisman '—really be without significance?'

'I would not go that far,' said Orbus. 'The talisman almost certainly originated from Urch-Malmain, after all, though it may have been many places since. Shenwolf's tale has a ring of convenience, and yet it is imbued with a naïveté that makes it almost persuasive, for who would think of making up a tale like this? In himself he is most convincing, also. You have never spoken to him of the Legendary Child, I take it?'

Issul gave a shake of the head.

'Well, let us consider the evidence. Shenwolf has rescued you from danger and possible death more than once in recent weeks. Myself also, now. He has placed himself at great risk in doing so. If he acts with ill-intent he has a strange way of showing it.'

'Even so . . . And if he truly knows nothing of his past, what might be hidden there? Is he Urch-Malmain's creature?'

'It may be so,' Orbus said. 'And if it is, then it is also possible that he genuinely knows nothing of it. Such manipulations are consistent with my recollection of Urch-Malmain's methods.'

'But his cheerful disposition, his decisiveness, his skills, his acts of heroism – these are not the actions and attributes of a muddled and dispirited amnesiac.'

'Were this a case of a man rendered memoryless by shock, a blow to the head or some form of disease, I would expect sluggishness, befuddlement, acute anxiety, yes. But if, as I suspect is the case, Urch-Malmain has refined his techniques of old, he will be more than capable of modifying memory, instincts, urges and even perception, without truly deranging the innate personality.'

Issul threw a troubled glance across to where Shenwolf sat. 'Then Shenwolf is not truly himself?'

'It is hard to say precisely *what* he is, as things currently stand. But let us not leap to conclusions. His story, combined with his being in possession of this talisman, leads me to infer a connection in some form with Urch-Malmain, but I can be no more precise than that. Strange, though. Very strange. More than ever I feel Urch-Malmain's presence; more than ever he works himself upon my mind.'

'What would be Urch-Malmain's likely goal?'

'He is, as you know, one of the Highest Ones of Enchantment. Hence his goal is ultimately that of the others: to maintain conflict so that Enchantment may sustain itself and grow; to overwhelm the formed world. The strategies by which he plans to achieve this remain unknown.' Orbus paused, then said ruminatively, 'In regard to Shenwolf, there is something else I have noticed.'

'What is that?'

'His dedication to you. The very way he looks at you. I don't count myself an expert in these matters, but I think the high regard in which he holds you may extend beyond a soldier's simple desire to serve his queen.'

Issul lowered her eyes. 'I have felt that, too. That is, I had until this morning. Now, though . . . ?'

'What of you, Issul? Until this morning you trusted him utterly. You confided in him; in a literal sense you had placed him in physical proximity to you, after a relatively short acquaintance. You had become very close to him, had you not?'

Issul stood quickly, her cheeks growing warm. 'You are impertinent, Orbus.'

'I apologize.'

'I— I did trust him, yes. He had proven himself over and over. I found his counsel useful and even sometimes wise. He was gallant and personable. He carries with him an air of mystery which is intriguing, I admit. He is also a superb weapons-master and a natural leader whom others follow willingly. But that has been the sum total of my regard for him.'

'I understand.'

After a brief silence, during which she avoided looking at either

Shenwolf or Orbus, Issul said in a vexed tone, 'But what now? He may yet be my enemy. How am I to proceed?'

'You carry on, as before. You must. Nothing has changed.'

'But Shenwolf . . . ?'

'If he is willing, he should accompany you still.'

'Orbus, I am not sure about this.'

'If he is your enemy, would you rather have him at your side or trailing you somewhere out of sight? Or do you intend to execute him here and now? I suspect he will raise objections to that.'

'But do we let him continue with us now to the Farplace Opening?'

'Can we afford not to? He has been there before, after all.'

Issul regarded the bundled god pensively. 'You believe in him, don't you, Orbus?'

'I think I do. But I think we should talk to him some more.'

II

Little more was said that evening. Orbus, needing no sleep, offered to keep watch through the night. Issul spread her blanket upon the ground to one side of the fire, Shenwolf to the other. In the darkness, as the fire dwindled to embers, Issul lay awake, thinking. Quickly, though, her tiredness overcame her, her thoughts drifted and slid, and before she knew it she was awoken by the sounds of movement inside the cave and birds singing outside.

Shenwolf had built the fire up and was preparing a breakfast of porridge and fruit. He flashed Issul a wide grin as she sat up blearily. 'Majesty! Good morning! I hope you slept well. There is a little stream fifty yards beyond the cave entrance, if you care to wash.'

Issul had slept solidly, despite her concerns, and felt the better for it. She rose now and, accepting Shenwolf's advice, went out to find the stream. The morning was cool but bright, the sky streaked with a few wisps of high white cloud. The sun had not yet risen fully above the trees, so the forest was held in a penumbral light. Issul walked a little distance into the trees and came upon the stream, which flowed without hurry and to a reasonable depth, and could not resist the temptation to bathe. She removed her clothes quickly and immersed herself in the cold water, washing the sweat and grime of travel from her limbs. It was too cold to stay for more than a few moments, and she soon made her way back to the cave. The food was ready. Orbus waited silently to one side as Issul and Shenwolf ate. Issul gathered her thoughts, but it was Shenwolf who spoke first.

'Majesty, I understand that you may have doubts about me. I can only assure you that I have told you the truth. But if you feel at this time that you would be more comfortable dismissing me, I will agree to leave now and trouble you no more.'

Issul shook her head. 'I prefer for you to accompany me, Shenwolf. I need your assistance still.'

'I am glad of that.' He brightened, then his gaze became thoughtful. 'May I ask something?'

'Do.'

'The Legendary Child – what is this?'

'It is yet another factor that menaces us. More I cannot say, for I know far too little.'

'Then, what was happening at the poolside when I arrived?'

'You do not know?'

He shook his head.

'Arene was about to kill him.'

'The Child?'

'The Child. She had been sent here to do just that. At that time none but she and a few of her people knew what he was.'

Shenwolf's face fell suddenly. 'And I prevented her.'

'That is how it appears.'

'What will this mean?'

'We cannot yet say. It is complex, and too much is unknown.' Her mind flashed back to the battle in the forest. 'Yesterday, when the grullags attacked, did you see the Child?'

Shenwolf shook his head.

'He was there. He came with the grullags to free Grey Venger, who is his disciple.'

'They must have followed me back when I reconnoitred Ghismile.'

'I thought so, but have since discounted it. They attacked on more than one front. There was no time for them to have organized themselves so well had they come in your wake, for it was literally

moments after your return that they struck. I think rather that Moscul
– the Legendary Child – had been following us, anticipating our
movements. Did you see what became of Arene?'

'She was on the ground. I could not tell whether she was alive or
dead. Phis also was wounded, but he lives to fight another day.'

'I have wondered about going back, trying to locate the survivors
of my company.'

Orbus interposed sharply: 'That is inadvisable.'

'I know. Gordallith is between us and them; perhaps the grullags
too. But I am concerned that when we reach the old Krai camp we
will find it bristling with Krai.'

'It is likely,' Orbus said. 'But we must face that when we come
to it. We cannot go back.'

'Gordallith?' queried Shenwolf. 'Is he the bandit-leader who
captured you?'

'Those men were no bandits. Gordallith is Lord Fectur's man.'

'Fectur?' Shenwolf was astonished. 'He had you abducted?'

'And no doubt worse, had you not altered their plans. Remember
I told you at Enchantment's Edge, he is an enemy perhaps more
vicious and determined than any I may face.'

They finished eating and Shenwolf rose. 'I will take the horses
to the stream to drink. Then, if you wish, we will move on.'

When he had exited the cave Orbus said, 'You seem surer of
yourself after a sound night's sleep. And am I wrong in thinking
that you feel a greater confidence in him?'

'I don't know. I want to. Yes, I think I am drawn to believe
him. It saddens and disturbs me, though, to think he may yet be
Urch-Malmain's servant and possibly not know it. I don't know
how to tackle that.'

'As I said, I think it is best to have him close so that we might
observe him and be alert should anything reveal itself.'

Issul hesitated. 'Orbus, something very strange happened yesterday.'

She told him quickly about the phantom horse-warriors, and her
feeling of Leth's proximity. 'Can these be the Edge Riders, Orbus?'

'I would wager not. I would not expect to see Edge Riders taking
human form, though it is possible that you might perceive them
as such.'

'Then what happened? And why did I feel so definitely that Leth
was present?'

'I cannot say. Perhaps he was that close, even if physically he remains trapped. Recall, not so long ago you had an equally powerful sensation of your children.'

'I even heard him!'

Orbus half-shrugged his ragged shoulders. 'I can offer no further explanation. Except that we are close upon the borders of Enchantment, which is perhaps explanation enough.'

'Have you had any other impressions, Orbus? Any further sense of his presence, or the children's?'

'I am not sure. I sense him, yes. It is strangely similar to the manner in which I sense Urch-Malmain. But I am torn two ways, and I do not know quite why. And I sense another presence within me, something monstrous, dark and powerful which I cannot explain. I am, I feel, at war with myself. Perhaps this is a symptom of being trapped outside my world. I do not know, but I think it is taking a toll.'

'In what way?' asked Issul anxiously.

Orbus paused a moment before replying, 'I am weaker than I was. I feel we should hurry now.'

III

They made the decision, after hasty consultation, to make for the Krai camp via Ghismile Tarn. Both Issul and Shenwolf were reasonably certain of the direction of the tarn in relation to their current location, and Shenwolf was confident that from the tarn he could find his way through the forest to the Krai camp. Before the sun was fully up they were on their way, Shenwolf riding slightly ahead, Issul behind with the wooden chest balanced in front of her on the saddle.

They followed no set path, but allowed their judgement to guide them towards the shore of Ghismile Tarn. By Issul's estimation they would break out somewhere along the tarn's southernmost shore, the side furthest from Ghismile village where Issul had slain the brutish Ombo and which was now occupied by grullags and, presumably, Moscul and Grey Venger.

With a melancholic feeling Issul wondered about the fate of the villagers she had left behind there. They had suffered for years under Ombo's inhuman rule. She had given them but a few days of freedom, if that, and now their village was occupied once more by an enemy as deficient in humanity and compassion as Ombo had been. One of her companions, Aurfusk, had been left behind to recover from wounds received at the hands of the Krai. Issul had promised to send soldiers to recover Aurfusk and help administer the village. It had been her intention to do that now, leaving a handful of men at Ghismile while she and the greater part of her company rode on for the Farplace Opening. Such plans were now dashed; she held out little hope that Aurfusk or many – if any – of the villagers had survived. If they had she was powerless at present to help them, and the knowledge of this weighed heavily upon her.

At midday she and Shenwolf stopped briefly to rest. They ate strips of dried meat, cheese, bread and fruit, and drank watered-wine, all drawn from the saddle-packs on Gordallith's horses.

'Tell me again about your memories of yourself,' Issul said.

Shenwolf's look grew distant. 'I have told you all I know. There is nothing more.'

'But you have glimpses in the mist. If you concentrate is it not possible to push the mist back a little further?'

'I have tried, without avail.'

'The little that you did tell me, about being taught martial and hunting skills by your father, about pursuing brigands and survival in the wild; are these things true?'

'They are true inasmuch as those distant impressions reside within me. But as I have said, if I attempt to pursue or scrutinize them more deeply, they withdraw.'

Issul considered for a moment, then said, 'Does the name Urch-Malmain hold any meaning for you?'

Shenwolf compressed his lips and slowly shook his head. For the first time she saw the pain in his young face. His guard was down, and he seemed bare before her. In a moment of pure impulse, Issul reached out and laid her hand on his.

'Shenwolf, I want you to know that I believe in you.'

He raised his eyes and smiled at her, almost shyly. 'That is good to hear. Yet I sense a "But" hovering on the tail of that sentiment.'

She sat back, removing her hand. 'I am going to be candid with you. Orbus and I believe your story. It is extraordinary that you should have come upon the Legendary Child in such a manner, and perhaps there are forces greater than we can comprehend at work here. But essentially what you have told us has the ring of truth.'

'And I must carry the guilt of knowing that my appearing at that time prevented the Child being slain. Were it not for me it would be dead now and unable to menace you and your kingdom.'

'That may be so. Then again, who knows what would have happened? That child is no ordinary child. Be quite sure of that. Had Arene laid hands on him, he might well have been capable of retaliation far more effective than anything possessed by a normal infant. Indeed, it is difficult to believe he could be as helpless as he appeared. Your intervention may actually have saved Arene's life, not Moscul's.'

'I would that it were so.'

'But I want to discuss further the matter of your background.'

'My lady Issul, I have told you all I can, and that is the truth.'

'That is not what I mean. The fact is that the circumstances of your arrival and memory loss, combined with other indications, give Orbus and I cause to think that an enemy of old has stirred. I cannot say definitely, but it is possible that this person has tampered with you, with your mind. We do not know exactly how or to what end.'

An expression of horror spread across Shenwolf's face. 'Do you mean —'

'Wait.' Issul lifted a hand. 'Nothing is certain, and your loyalty to me is not in question. Beyond that though, there are unknowns. Are you, unwittingly, Urch-Malmain's instrument? Has he despatched you here, at this particular time, for a specific purpose? Or is there no connection with Urch-Malmain at all? We do not know, but I wish you to be aware of the dilemma we face.'

'I must go!' exclaimed Shenwolf suddenly. 'I must take myself as far from you as I can, lest I be drawn to harm you.' He stood up abruptly. 'No! It will not be! I will kill myself before I will allow that to happen!'

'You will not go, nor will you kill yourself,' said Issul steadily. 'Sit down and hear my words. I need you beside me, and until a link is proven or disproven you stand accused of nothing. But equally, until I know the truth, I must take certain precautions. Thus, I may not confide in you so freely as I might otherwise have done. It is a sadness, for I have come to hold your opinion and advice in high regard. But I must now be more guarded. Will you obey my orders without question?'

'Of course! Utterly!'

'And if I seek your opinion, will you give it freely?'

'You know that I will.'

'And if it seems that I do not confide or share with you, will you understand and accept, without doubt, affront or recrimination?'

Shenwolf nodded, regret in his eyes. 'I will. Of course I will.'

'It may even be that as we delve deeper into this mystery we will uncover the secret of your memory. Perhaps it can be restored to you. I hope it will be so.'

They rode on, again relying largely on animal tracks to find their way through the densest forest. The day permitted a golden light to penetrate through the greens and yellows, russets and tans of the overhead canopy. The smells of herbs, moss and dank earth pervaded the air. Small creatures scurried in the undergrowth and birds flitted among the branches. For a short period Issul began to feel almost at peace.

Shenwolf now seemed more sure of the direction of Ghismile Tarn than Issul, and she allowed him to lead the way. For a time she watched him, wondering, hoping that somehow he might prove to be what she had previously believed him to be; then her mind was drawn back to the prospect of the Krai camp ahead, and the strange secret in the bunker beneath it.

As the day drew towards a close Shenwolf brought the horses to a halt.

'The tarn lies no more than two leagues distant, if I am not mistaken. We should rest here for the night so that we can approach in daylight, the better to avoid stumbling into grullags or anything else that might be on the prowl, and to get our bearings before we proceed.'

They made camp, eating a cold, simple meal. Issul brought Orbus forth to keep watch once again, then crawled beneath her blanket. She lay for a while on her back, watching the stars drift in their courses, wondering, as she had wondered so often before, about their nature and the secrets they might hold, but her eyelids grew heavy and soon she fell asleep.

IV

On this night, with the limitless forest dark and silent all around her, Issul's sleep was visited by a succession of disturbing dreams, which kept her fitful and tossing. She seemed to drift back and forth over the borders of unconsciousness and waking, then would plunge suddenly and involuntarily into terrifying, vision-filled depths. There her tormentors were arrayed before her, one after another.

Moscul sat beside her upon a wooden stile: a little fair-headed boy, her beloved nephew, smiling and innocent, his tiny warm hand in hers. It was a comforting image – that is, it should have been. Instead Issul was filled with a creeping dread, and could not understand why. Something was terribly wrong. Something awful impended. She felt it in her bones. What was it about this situation, this child, her sister's son, that made her feel this way?

'You must look after me, Aunt Issul.'

'Yes, I will do that, Moscul. You need not fear.'

'Will you be with me always?'

'Of course.'

'Then why did you send me away?'

He turned to stare up at her with bright violet reproachful eyes. Issul was overcome with confusion; her dread turning to sudden inexplicable terror. Had she sent him away? She could not recall. Why? What was wrong here?

'My mother is dead.'

Oh, the spirits, yes! *Ressa! Poor, poor Ressa!*

Issul was transported to her parents' summer villa, Saroon. She was in Ressa's bedroom, and before her her sister lay dead upon her bed. And as she watched Ressa moved, alive in death. Her body twitched, then heaved and bucked, her legs splayed wide. Yet her face showed no animation. Her head was thrown to one side upon the pillow. *Oh, what is happening?* Issul backed away. Ressa's body, still limp after three days, arched, thrashed and the blood spread darkly red through her gown. And a cry, a thin, tiny cry, and Ressa was still again, but something else made the smallest movement beneath her gown. She knew what it was. Issul knew what it was. She stood there rooted to the floor as Moscul came forth and stared up at her.

'My mother is dead, Aunt Issul.'

'Yes, I know, Moscul.'

His eyes disturbed her so, and she did not know why.

'I remember everything.'

'Everything?'

'I remember you!'

And he laughed. His laugh was terrible to hear; no three-year-old's laughter, but that of something not wholly human. Issul looked around her at the forest, fearful, still not able to explain what was happening, except that this was at least half a dream. Yes. That thought comforted her. This had not happened. She dreamed and it was not real. But something moved beneath the trees and a figure stepped forward. Grey Venger came at her in a single bound, a wild shriek, face horribly contorted, fingers angled into claws. And there were more figures mustered there in the forest fringe. Hirsute man-creatures, or were they the pale, wrinkle-faced Krai warriors? So many of them, together, coming from the dark.

'We are the dead.'

Their bodies, gem-eyes faded, mute upon a hut floor.

She could not understand them.

'Aunt Issul, you will take care of me, won't you?'

'Yes. Yes.'

'It is your duty, you know.'

Duty?

The child laughed again. Issul wanted to run.

'Iss! Help me! Help me, Iss!'

With sudden wrenching guilt Issul recalled Mawnie. Poor Mawnie, whom she had managed to look in on for only moments when she had returned to Enchantment's Edge.

'It was me he wanted, Iss! It was me!'

'No, Mawnie. You are ill. You must rest.'

'Hugo's dead!'

'I know. I know.'

'Help me, Iss. You are all I have.'

But Mawnie was retreating, fading away. Suddenly, from around a corner came Fectur. And Issul could not move. She was trussed tight upon the forest floor, helpless as a babe. Her terror pounded in her chest; she strained and stretched against her bindings.

'Fectur, do you know what you are doing?'

She looked up and saw Fectur with Grey Venger leering down at her. Fectur's eyes were cold slits. 'They are gone. You will see them no more.'

Sudden panic. Her children! 'Galry! Jace!'

'Your husband too.'

And Grey Venger crowed, 'The Righteous have ranged themselves against the Unbelievers and their foul King Who Is Without A Soul! You will all be swept from this world!'

He spat, his phlegm warm and wet upon her cheek, And she retched. She could not grasp it. 'Fectur? Are you one of them?'

She twisted her head, looking for a way free. 'I don't understand! Shenwolf! Shenwolf! Who are you?'

Had he lied to her? Was her trust misplaced? What was happening here?

Leth! Leth!

'You are my aunt, Issul. Aunt Issul.'

'Moscul, I want to talk to you!'

'Issul. Aunt Issul.'

The dark beating of heavy wings as she struggled against her bonds. A young prisoner's screams as the slooths descended. A mutilated head upon the ground. Miseon, poor Miseon.

'Shenwolf! Shenwolf!'

'I am here, Jace.'

Jace?

'Who are you?'

'I am Shenwolf.'

She awoke suddenly. The forest was dark, the trees lightly hissing as a breeze shivered their leaves, the stars clouding bright overhead. Shenwolf was bent over her, smiling.

'Shenwolf.'

'It's all right. You were dreaming.'

Her terror began slowly to dissolve. She felt glad of his presence. She looked around her. 'Where is Orbus?'

'Over there, beneath the trees. Jace, are you all right now?'

'Jace? I am Issul.'

'Yes, but I have said, in my heart you will always be Jace. Does that offend you?'

She shook her head.

'Jace . . . Issul . . .' he said softly.

'Did I cry out?' she asked.

'Yes. Was it terrible?'

She nodded.

'It is all right, it has gone now,' he said. His fingers brushed her cheek, stroked her hair. 'I am with you.'

He was calm, his voice reassuring. She needed that. His face was just above hers. 'Shenwolf,' she whispered.

'I am here.'

His voice was soft, close in her ear. Before she knew it his lips touched hers, then he kissed her cheek, the side of her nose, her eyelids, the corner of her mouth, softly, so softly. It was wrong, she knew it, but she wanted him, wanted his kisses. 'Shenwolf!' Her mouth sought hungrily for his. One hand went to the back of his head, pulling him to her, the other slid over his back. Their lips glued, Shenwolf pulled aside her blanket and slipped beneath it. His body was deeply stimulating against hers; she clung to him, their tongues meeting, exploring, playing. His hand slid inside her tunic and found her breast. She tore at his clothing, wanting him naked as his kisses smothered her neck, her shoulders, her breasts. They strained together, and she knew it was wrong, she knew it but could do nothing about it, did not want to stop it, not now, not now . . .

She cried out, and suddenly was awake, the forest all around her, hissing like an ocean lapping at the shore, and the stars cloudy bright above her head. She pushed herself up, her heart pounding. Had she called out? What had happened?

Shenwolf lay sleeping a few yards away. She could see nothing of Orbus. Issul sat up, struggling to make sense of everything, gradually remembering where she was and why, constructing the reality out of the multitude of images that had beset her. She was breathing heavily. She closed her eyes, calming herself, dispelling the phantoms, then put her chin upon her knees and hugged her shins. After a few moments she put her blanket aside and rose.

'Issul, child, are you all right?'

It was Orbus, coming from the deep dark beneath a tree. She nodded. 'I can't sleep.'

'Do your dreams trouble you?'

The question made her nervous. 'Did I call out?'

'No, but you have been restless all night.'

She nodded and let out a long sigh. 'How long have I been asleep?'

'About five hours. It is a while yet before dawn. You should try to sleep some more.'

'Yes, I will. I just want to stretch my limbs a little and clear my head.' She picked up the water-sack which lay beside her litter, and drank. Then she said, 'Orbus, I am concerned about Fectur.'

'He is a devil, that much is plain. Still, with what you already knew of him his latest instance of skulduggery can have come as no great surprise.'

'That's so. What worries me is the lengths he is prepared to go to now. He craves power, but it is not in his nature to take unnecessary risks. At least, not as I know it.'

'Was it such a risk? You say yourself that his men did not intend to kidnap you, at least not at this stage.'

'But at some point they would have been prepared to murder me. That says much.'

'Even so, had he had you murdered here in the forest, far from home, none would have been the wiser.'

'He knows I have gone to seek out a means to save Enchantment's Edge. Does he wish to prevent that? Why? With the Krai poised to strike Enchantment's Edge, and the unknown quantity of the Legendary Child also in opposition, his actions seem to border on the irrational.'

'You think him mad?' enquired Orbus.

'I am beginning to wonder whether he truly knows what he is doing. Alternatively, does he know something that we do not?'

'Such as?'

'I do not know. But his intelligence-gathering faculties are extraordinary. And who really knows where his true loyalties lie, other than to himself? Could he have discovered some link with the Legendary Child? Could he actually be working with the True Sept? Or with the Krai? He had uncovered a Sept channel leading to Prince Anzejarl, I know that. Can he have found some way of surviving the threat and establishing power for himself? Or is he out of control?'

'I fear you will find the answer to that only when you return.'

V

Late in the morning, as Shenwolf had predicted, they came in sight of Ghismile Tarn shimmering through the trees. They eased the horses forward slowly until they stood in the shade of the trees close beside the shore. The air was still, and warmer than in previous days. A few winged insects flitted between the forest's fringe and the water's edge. Upon the still water a pair of elegant black swans glided, a number of coots and other water-fowl evident some way off, close to the shore.

Shenwolf pointed. 'It is more or less as I thought. Over there is the village. And that way, see, is the height by which we approached when we came last time.'

'Very good,' said Issul, and swung her horse towards the higher ground in the distance. 'Let us waste no time.'

Two hours later they were upon the low promontory from which they had first gazed down just over a week earlier and gained their first sight of Ghismile Tarn. Issul felt her anxiety growing. Before the day was out they would be at the Krai camp again. What would they find?

Late in the afternoon Shenwolf signalled a halt. 'We should dismount now and approach on foot. Will you lead the horses while I check for traps?'

She nodded.

'It may be a laborious process. Stay a good twenty yards behind me,' Shenwolf added. He began making his way forward with slow, cautious footsteps, his eyes assiduously scanning the ground at his feet, the tree-trunks and bushes to either side, the boughs and branches above. From time to time he glanced back and gestured for Issul to move forward with the horses. After an hour of this the light began to fade. Shenwolf paused and said, 'I had hoped we might reach the camp before dark. It cannot be more than a few hundreds yards away. But now I think it will be safer to rest here overnight. The failing light only increases the risk of falling foul of a trap. It would be a cruel irony to have come so far only to find ourselves plunging into a stake-filled pit or swinging by our ankles in a noose, either of which we might easily have avoided in daylight.'

With reluctance Issul agreed. They led the horses a little way back to a hollow they had passed, which was well-sheltered by trees and a low cliff. A small pool fed by a bubbling spring lay at its base. They unsaddled the horses and tethered them beside the pool, where they might drink and crop the grass. Then they settled down to wait for the dawn.

VI

The ruined camp appeared deserted. When Issul had left it less than two weeks earlier it had been in flames. Now, most of its guard towers fallen, its huts and palisades reduced to ugly charred black vestiges, it was a blot within the great concealing forest, anonymous and silent, barely hinting at what it had once been.

As far as Issul could make out, the camp had not been visited since her departure by anything other than wild beasts and birds. She lay prone beside Shenwolf in the cover of the trees at the edge of the clearing in which the camp was situated, alert for any indication of life. The chest containing Orbus's world was at her elbow, bow and arrows slung across her back. Shenwolf had discovered no traps in the surrounding woods, which seemed a further indication that the Krai had not reoccupied the camp. But this was curious. Slooths had flown from the camp when their Krai masters were overcome; Issul had assumed they would return to Prince Anzejarl's army and he would dispatch reinforcements. The Farplace Opening – which as far as she could tell was the Krai's main purpose for constructing the camp – was surely far too precious to be abandoned? If Anzejarl knew, why were his troops not here? Or had the slooths not alerted him?

Or was it possible that the Farplace Opening was no longer in the underground bunker?

Or were there troops here still, hidden, waiting?

She had lain here for an hour now in the cool early-morning air, barely exchanging a word with Shenwolf. Nothing moved. Nothing made a sound, save the birds in the trees and the light breeze stirring the foliage. But still they waited, just in case.

For Issul, and she supposed to some extent for Shenwolf too, it was an eerie experience to look again upon this place where she had endured so much, and had fought for and won liberty at so high a cost. She could barely believe she had left here only days ago. Her imprisonment in the camp had become almost a distant memory. So much had happened in so short a time.

'I think we are clear,' murmured Shenwolf, breaking the flow of her thoughts. 'If you like I will go forward and check more thoroughly. If it is safe I will beckon you.'

Issul gave a nod.

Shenwolf rose to a semi-crouch. 'I will move around a little, come from the south-east perimeter of the clearing. That way, if Krai or anyone else are hidden here they won't be led directly to your position.'

He made off silently through the undergrowth. A minute passed and Issul saw him emerge from the forest fringe south-east of where she lay. Looking all ways, he crossed the stream that ran beside the clearing, where Issul had strained her back and rubbed her fingers raw and numb scrubbing Krai garments in the icy, fast-flowing water. Shenwolf moved swiftly to the secondary gate, which stood more or less intact at the edge of the main compound. He crouched there for some moments, scanning the compound, then was briefly lost to sight as he rose and entered. She saw him through a gap in the burnt palisade, heading for a ruined hut – her former dormitory – swivelling on his heels as he went, checking in all directions. He moved to the burned-out wall, quickly inspected the interior, then cut across to the remains of the former command hut. Reconnoitring the entire main compound in this manner, he eventually beckoned Issul to him.

'I truly think we are in luck,' he said when she had joined him, the chest beneath one arm. 'They have not re-occupied.'

'But why not?' she mused, then: 'To the bunker, then, quickly.'

They passed from the main compound through the picket gate into what had been the work area. Issul felt anger return as she recalled the ferocious battle that had taken place here; how the Krai guards, discovering themselves attacked, had turned their weapons upon the defenceless, shackled prisoners. And she steeled herself at the thought of what lay here, beneath the surface of the compound. They came to the head of the stone steps that led down into the underground bunker.

'Ah, I had forgotten,' observed Shenwolf, taking in the earth, boulders, grass and brushwood that covered the steps and entrance. 'This entrance we barred as securely as we could. It will be easier to enter at the rear, via the slooth pens. The entrance there is wider and better concealed by the surrounding terrain. We only covered it lightly.'

They left the work-compound, passed back through the main area, through another gate and into a passage between two walls of sharpened stakes. Issul shuddered. The last time she had passed this way it had been with two Krai guards gripping her arms, leading her – as they believed – to her death in the charnel back-clearing of the slooths' feeding area.

With Shenwolf watching her back she advanced around a right-angled corner. Ahead was another gate, this one wrenched off its hinges, and a smashed, fire-blackened wooden portcullis beneath a burned-out guard tower. Through this they passed along a twisting grassy causeway between the trees, and came at length into the open. At once the stench of putrefying flesh hit Issul's nostrils, and she gagged. Tatters of meat and bones were strewn across the clearing, and at its centre two stout wooden posts stood, silent and terrible.

Issul clenched her teeth tightly. Shenwolf took her arm.

The carcasses of several slooths occupied one side of the clearing, picked at by crows. Issul found herself rooted to the spot, unable to tear her eyes away, until Shenwolf spoke softly beside her. 'Come, this way.'

He led her away from the sight of the carcasses, her hand covering her mouth and nostrils, then veered back towards the west wall of the camp. The faintest dirt trail led between bushes, and down. Shenwolf pulled aside undergrowth to expose an opening. 'This takes us directly into the brooding-pens. Remember?'

Issul nodded. Exploring the bunker for the first time, they had entered from the work compound. In the grim chamber of the slooth nesting-stalls they had seen a way leading upwards towards light. Shenwolf had investigated and declared it to be a way out into the forest.'

Suddenly he froze. *'Hssh!'*

Issul heard it at the same time. The clink of metal; the unmistakeable sounds of things moving in the trees to the other side of the clearing. She threw herself down; Shenwolf likewise. Moments later a mounted column of Krai troops began to emerge from the trees across the clearing.

'By the spirits, Anzejarl *has* sent a force to investigate!' Issul breathed.

The leading Krai halted. Issul could not see how many made up the force, but it looked considerable. The leaders seemed to be taking stock of the sight of the ruined camp.

'Quickly!' whispered Shenwolf. 'They will search the camp. We have little time.'

Even as he spoke there came a barked command from the Krai officer in charge. Several Krai dismounted, drew their swords and began to run across the clearing, accompanied by an equal number of warriors on horseback. Others began to fan out silently, notching arrows to bows.

Issul and Shenwolf slid down into the darkness of the slooths' brooding pen. The air was thick, musty, imbued with the stale, pungent stench of slooths. They could see barely a thing, but though Issul carried a torch upon her back they could not light it for fear of the sound of striking flint carrying to the Krai outside.

'I think this may be one of the last places they search,' whispered Shenwolf. 'They may not even know of it. I just hope there are not stray slooths still lurking down here.'

His sword was drawn. Issul gripped the weapon she had taken from Gordallith's man. Slowly they began to grope their way forward along the aisle separating the two rows of stalls where the slooths had nested. They could not see a thing. From outside came curt, muffled calls of the Krai.

'Wait.' Issul knelt. She set down the wooden chest, raised its lid and took out the blue casket. 'Orbus, come forth.'

The god materialized, bathed in a faint, misty blue lucency. Before he could speak Issul hurriedly explained the situation. 'The chamber of the Farplace Opening is less than twenty paces from where we stand,' she said in conclusion.

'I know. I can feel it,' replied Orbus. He gazed towards the opening by which they had descended, revealed by a shaft of weak grey light. 'I can do nothing about the Krai, but perhaps I can help relieve this darkness.'

He passed his hand before him in a circle. His blue aura intensified slightly, sufficient to throw a pale radiance for some short distance around him. Immediately Shenwolf moved off between the wooden stalls, investigating each one, until he reached the door at the end. This was barricaded: Shenwolf himself had nailed it closed and heaped earth and stones against it when sealing the bunker. Now he prised at the planks, using his dagger to lever them free. Issul joined him. Within a couple of minutes they had the door open.

'It is through that door,' said Issul as they stepped into the ante-chamber outside the chamber of the Farplace Opening. Orbus stared contemplatively. As Issul moved to the door, which was also barred with planking, Shenwolf darted into the passage on the right which led to the main entrance and the former work-compound. He quickly returned. 'I can hear them outside. The entrance remains secure for now.'

He worked with Issul to unblock the door. When they had done they were both perspiring and breathing heavily. Issul turned to Orbus. 'What now?'

'We enter,' said Orbus. 'You take me through the Farplace Opening.'

'But we cannot all go through. Yet neither can Shenwolf remain. The Krai will kill him.'

'You have with you Urch-Malmain's talisman. Give that to Shenwolf. I think it will give him some protection on the other side.'

'But you cannot guarantee?'

'I can guarantee nothing at this stage. Shenwolf must make a choice: to step through with the talisman, in the hope that it will protect him, or to remain here.'

'What of the Queen?' Shenwolf said. 'She requires the talisman for her own protection.'

'As long as Queen Issul remains with me I can shield her to some degree from Enchantment's immediate effects,' Orbus replied slowly. 'Now, there is little time. Make your choice.'

'I will come through with you,' stated Shenwolf without hesitation.

'Then let us go.'

Issul's heart was in her mouth as she pushed upon the door. It swung back and she stepped in, and gasped. The fabulous light oval hovered as before in the centre of the chamber, unearthly and blindingly beautiful to behold. But it was much bigger than before. It rose almost to the ceiling and was nearly as broad as the chamber was wide. Its radiance was of a far greater magnitude than when she had first set eyes on it; both she and Shenwolf were forced to shield their eyes with their hands. Opalescent, multi-toned colours fluxed and whorled in its incandescent depths, and the oval pulsed, dilating and reducing rhythmically, as though alive. As her eyes adjusted Issul saw within it something that had not been present before: a maelstrom of thousands of tiny, dazzling fibrils and scintillae, surging and darting in clouds of restless, constantly changing colours. The sight was mesmerizing, breathtakingly beautiful, and terrifying. Clutching the blue casket to her, Issul was transfixed.

'This is grave,' declared Orbus in forbidding tones, snapping Issul out of her trance.

'What do you mean?'

'It was not this way when you saw it first.'

'No. Why? What is happening, Orbus? Why has it changed?'

'An Edge Rider is preparing to break through.'

Issul's gut twisted in fear. 'Now? What can we do? Can you prevent it?'

Orbus hesitated, his spine bowed as he leaned heavily upon his staff. 'You said Triune guarded the Opening on the other side, that she had taken it from the god who aids the Krai?'

'That is what Triune told me.'

Orbus stared at the great pulsing globe. 'Something has changed.'

'What does that mean?'

'It means that we do not know what we will discover on the other side.'

Issul glanced to Shenwolf, then back. 'Can we not pass through?'

'Oh, we must. And we must go immediately. But I am saying I no longer know what to expect.'

'And the Edge Rider?'

'May be on the other side.'

'What, then?'

Orbus did not reply. It was silent in this chamber of the Farplace Opening – unnervingly so. Issul could hear nothing from above ground, and the great orb pulsed and dazzled but, eerily, made no sound at all. Issul heard only her own breathing, her pounding heart, the blood surging within her veins, and Shenwolf's breath beside her.

'Orbus, what then?'

She stood on the lip of the future, clutching at the single, slender, ever more distant hope of salvation. And before her was only peril and uncertainty – the Unknown.

Are we to die here now?

'Orbus!'

The ragged god turned his head slowly to her. 'We can only go on.'

Issul looked back at Shenwolf, and swallowed. 'Are you with us?'

He was pale and gaunt, his features taut. He nodded once. 'Aye.'

'Then we go.' She clasped the casket tightly in both hands, and stepped forward into the chamber and into the blinding flux of the Farplace Opening and whatever lay beyond.

SEVENTEEN

I

The great walls of the Fortress of the Dark Flame towered high over Leth's head. Far higher than he had thought when he had first viewed them from across the plain, though he had perceived them as formidable even then. Leth, his wrists still loosely bound behind him, was riding slowly with his villainous company up the exposed causeway to the Fortress's main outer gate. The air was addled and warm now, uncomfortably close, stifling inside his helm. Through the eye-slits in the lowered visor Leth, looking up, saw gigantic interlocking blocks of black-to-blood-red stone rising sheer to more than one hundred feet. Where the walls wound along the edge of the ridge Abyss warriors could be seen upon the battlements, where flaming cressets blazed strangely in the weird light.

Overhead the dense mantle of cloud burned murky bronze-red. The bloodlight stained the dead and empty landscape all around, somehow cast by the Fortress itself, though whether out of the rock that formed it or from something else within Leth could not tell. Below, across the plain, parties of Abyss warriors rode out upon unknown business. Leth and his companions had encountered three patrols as they approached the Fortress. None had submitted them to anything but the most cursory questioning. They accepted Rasgul's explanation, apparently finding nothing irregular about his extended absence. All of them subjected Leth to intense scrutiny as they rode on by. He did not know what Rasgul was saying about him but plainly he was deemed a significant prize. Given his circumstances and lack of confidence in his companions, this did nothing to set his mind at ease.

Leth wondered where the Abyss warriors were bound. They had

the appearance of raiding or foraging parties. Were there settlements
or communities of some kind here at the lowest level of the Death
Abyss? What kind of persons or creatures could survive here?

Elsewhere upon the plain, as far as the eye could see, were the
lost, pathetic figures of Ascaria's children, empty victims, deprived
of dreams, creatures without inner life. They wandered silently and
aimlessly and were absorbed by the surrounding red mists.

Some become warriors. Leth looked at the Abyss warriors who
rode at his side, and wondered.

The Orbsword was strapped upon Rasgul's horse, behind the
saddle. Leth carefully tested the cord binding his wrists, reassuring
himself that he could easily slip free when the need arose. He looked
up again, trying to see the airy heights above the Fortress itself. As
they had ridden across the final stretch of the dead plain Rasgul had
pointed to an area directly over the Fortress, and said something
which sent a quiver of fear down Leth's spine: 'She is almost ready
to eat again.'

Leth had seen, in the air above the Fortress, something darkly
shimmering, an amorphous thing, a nameless, hanging emanation
that seemed both present and not present.

'What is it?' he had asked. 'What do you mean?'

'The emergence. You see it? It is a sign that Ascaria is strong
once more; she has engorged and vitiated sufficient dream-energies,
transformed them into her own vile force. This she will now release,
and it will devour.'

'How long before she releases it?'

'That is hard to say. From its appearance now, I would say at
any time.'

'Will my slaying her prevent it?'

'If you destroy her before she lets go, I think so.'

Leth had kept his eyes upon the strange formless form as they
rode towards it, but it tricked and worried his vision, allowed him no
focus and he found his eyes shifting involuntarily away. Eventually
it was obscured by the looming mass of the Fortress itself.

Now they were approaching the great outer barbican. The causeway veered at a sharp angle to approach a drawbridge spanning a
deep ditch in which a still, thick greenish fluid rested, its scummy
surface occasionally disturbed as if by something of bulk stirring
beneath. Abyss warriors stood guard beside a long, massive arch
surmounted by three stone bartizans. Others peered down from

the walls and squat barbican towers, their pallid faces lit pinkly in the bloodlight. The portcullis was up, as was a second in the shadow of the other end of the arch. Rasgul led his band across the drawbridge and beneath the arch. An Abyss warrior strode forward, his hand raised for the party to halt. He spoke briefly with Rasgul, appraised the others of the group, most particularly Leth, then waved them on.

They entered a wide, walled way which led straight for some one hundred yards, following the course of the outer wall – a killing field, where any invading force might be trapped and picked off at leisure by Abyss archers fifty feet above. At the far end of the killing field was a second, inner barbican. Here the portcullis was down and the party was obliged to stop again and be passed before it was cranked high and they were allowed to proceed.

They were in a long outer ward, circumscribed by high walls and fortified towers. Inner walls extended to the company's left side. A short distance along was another fortified gate, through which they passed under watchful eyes but without obligation to pause.

The tension was near-unbearable. Leth, striving to maintain an attitude of dejection, found his back aching with the effort of slouching in the saddle, and a hot, prickling sweat poured down his face and neck and soaked his clothing beneath the sapphire armour. He expected at any moment that his deception would be discovered and a rain of arrows would fall upon the party. The sapphire armour might protect him, but the others would surely die and he could not hope to fight on alone and survive against so many.

Inside the close-fitting helm he could barely breathe. The deep, veiling red lucency was more intense here, as they rode into a wide inner court, and the air had grown even warmer. He sensed the tension in the others, saw by the stiffness of their postures that they were no more at ease than he.

As they made their way slowly on across the court to a large entranceway set in the wall of a massive keep on the other side, Rasgul fell back beside Leth and said, aside, 'So far all is good, but I cannot expect to get much further without arousing interest. Be prepared.'

'Where are you taking us?' asked Leth.

'Supposedly to the dungeons. I may be able to bluff my way deeper into the citadel. Stay alert and say nothing.'

They dismounted outside a door which let into one wing of the central complex of the fortress. Now they encountered a minor problem: the Sword of the Orb could barely be borne by anyone but Leth. After a moment's consideration Rasgul commanded them to wait, then disappeared inside. He emerged moments later, followed by a single Abyss guard. At his bidding the newcomer and Fhurn hefted the sword between them, and with Rasgul leading the party passed within.

A small ante-chamber gave onto a short flight of stone steps leading to a guard-chamber manned by four warriors. Unchallenged, Rasgul opened a door on the far side of the chamber and they passed through into a long passageway of smooth stone walls. Their footsteps reverberated as they walked on. The temperature had risen further now they were indoors; the air was utterly still and cloying, tainted with an acrid, unidentifiable smell. The passage turned sharply to the right and they entered a larger room, set with a pair of workbenches, numerous shelves, and various instruments and diverse bottles and containers. Leth took it for a laboratory or workroom of some description. Beyond this was another downward stairway. They descended, followed another short passage, passed through a second guardroom and came to a four-way intersection. Rasgul led them left. Now they ascended a long ramp to a tall double door, faced in silver figured with intricate designs and glyphs. This Rasgul pushed open, and strode through into a spacious chamber where a tawny-robed figure knelt before a low dais or altar surmounted by an ornate golden chalice in which a blue flame burned. The figure rose and turned, plainly startled by the sudden entrance.

'What is this? What do you want?'

'Prisoners,' replied Rasgul, without breaking his stride. 'They are to be delivered without delay to the person of the Kancanitrix.'

'This is irregular.' The robed figure was near-human, but had a smooth, bald, beaked birdlike head and small, round, black near-featureless eyes that were sunk deep into bony sockets. He cast a lofty gaze over the three prisoners, lingering on Leth. 'I have received no instructions to this effect. You will wait here while I check.'

'No, don't do that,' said Rasgul. He was drawing free his scimitar as he walked forward, and now hacked the man-bird thing to the ground with a single swift blow. Leth heard a scuffling sound and a sudden low groan behind him. He turned and saw Dembarl, his scimitar drawn and wet with blood, standing over the twitching corpse of the Abyss warrior who had helped carry the Orbsword.

'Free your hands and take your weapon, Swordbearer,' declared Rasgul. 'From this point on we must fight. But do not draw the Orbsword until you must. Once it is free of its scabbard Ascaria will be aware of you.'

Leth slipped his hands from the cord that bound them, relieved that his fears of betrayal had been unfounded. He quickly buckled the Orbsword about his waist and took up the scimitar of the slain Abyss guard. Beside him Count Harg and Juson were similarly equipping themselves with their own weapons which Huuri, the last of Rasgul's three warriors, had toted.

Harg glanced Leth's way with a smirking grin, and winked. 'Well, Lord Swordbearer, here we are, eh? What grand adventures we are having! What fabulous larks!'

His lips drew back slightly. In the pervasive red air, to Leth's eyes, he looked insane.

Rasgul had crossed the chamber to a recess in the far wall. He pressed upon a panel on the wall and a door slid open at the back of the recess. He looked within quickly, then turned back. 'Somewhere beyond this point the Kancanitrix waits. Where, I do not know, for this is the furthest I have ever been.'

'Then you should not have killed this creature,' replied Leth, nodding towards the corpse of the beaked man. 'He could have been useful.'

Rasgul shook his head. 'He was an Acolyte. They exist only to serve Ascaria. They are incapable of betraying her.'

As were you until Urch-Malmain found you, thought Leth, but said nothing.

'Come, drag the bodies in here. We should waste no time,' Rasgul said.

At that moment an arras on one wall quivered and was drawn back. Another of the tawny-robed Acolytes was revealed, stepping through an opening. He was younger than the first and was carrying an icon or instrument of some kind in his two hands. Seeing the intruders he gave a sharp gasp and froze. His red eyes took in the two corpses and with a shriek he turned and fled.

Rasgul, Dembarl and Harg bounded across to the passage into which he had vanished. Harg knelt and took aim with his repeating crossbow, then swore. The fleeing Acolyte had rounded a corner and disappeared from sight before he had been able to loose a bolt. The Acolyte's frantic yells resounded through neighbouring corridors.

'Quick!' ordered Rasgul, cursing as he raced back across the chamber to the second passage behind the recess-door. 'They will be swarming in here in moments.'

Disregarding the bodies now, the seven ran for the passage. Fhurn entered last and closed the door behind them.

'Which way?' queried Leth. They were in a low corridor, long and broad, which led off in three directions. The red glow illuminated it sufficiently to make out its details, or lack of them, but Leth saw nothing to indicate a preference over one way or the other.

'I know not,' Rasgul replied, scowling. 'Still, we must choose one . . .'

He struck out in the direction that led off slightly to the left. A smooth stone floor descended gradually to a wider area. Two Acolytes appeared suddenly around a corner ahead. Each carried a pair of javelins which blazed with some kind of magical flame. Rasgul cried out something. The two Acolytes knelt and hurled their javelins. Rasgul threw himself to the side, flat against the wall. The javelins, amethyst-flamed, shot past him. Leth also dodged. The javelins flew by him with an angry swarming sound. He felt a searing heat, heard a thud and an agonized shriek from behind him.

The Acolytes both reached for their second missile. Rasgul hurled himself forward with a great roar, scimitar high. Leth, just behind, followed suit. Something sighed past his ear. One of the Acolytes cried out, throwing wide his arms, and fell back writhing. Rasgul was upon the other, striking him down with his blade. Leth raced forward and finished off the fallen Acolyte, who was clutching at the stub of one of Count Harg's bolts that protruded from his chest.

'I'll have that back if you don't mind,' called Harg, rising from kneeling and approaching, crossbow in hand. Terrible shrieks still resounded from behind him. Leth saw one of the Abyss warriors – was it Dembarl? – squirming upon his back. The strangely blazing javelin rose erect from his belly, quivering. Steam rose in dense, sizzling bursts from the point of entry into his flesh. Juson stood close by, looking on helplessly.

'Don't touch the weapon!' warned Fhurn. 'You can do nothing.'

It seemed to Leth that the javelin's shaft was growing shorter. With horror he saw that it was actually burrowing into Dembarl's writhing body as though imbued with a life and will of its own. The Abyss warrior convulsed and kicked, dreadful sounds escaping his lips. Abruptly a great gout of steam burst through the flesh of his face, and he jerked and lay still.

'Swordbearer!'

Leth turned to see Rasgul at the corner of the wall. He had taken the two unused javelins from the Acolyte corpses and now signalled for Leth to move to the opposite corner. Leth did so and peered around. There was no one to be seen either way. A wide, low-ceilinged chamber opened before them, supported by two rows of thick, unadorned rectangular columns. Numerous openings of curious shape could be seen leading off to either side.

'You are in charge now, Swordbearer,' whispered Rasgul, his burned-amber eyes flickering mistrustfully across the chamber. 'The passages may lead anywhere or nowhere.'

Leth glanced behind, then spoke to Fhurn and Huuri, both of whom had shortbows slung across their backs. 'You two wait. Bring up the rear, and be alert for attack from behind. The rest, fan out but stay close together and move with me across the chamber.'

The party began to move slowly through the chamber, slipping from column to column, pausing to look around, peering into the openings as they passed them. They reached the further end of the chamber without incident, and faced a blank stone wall formed of massive ashlar blocks. Leth heard a faint hiss behind him. He wheeled about. A compartment had opened in the facing wall of one of the columns. Within it a bulbous, bloated thing hovered, resembling a massive, deformed red-purple ball, all loose, hideous fleshy growths, waving tentacles and a wide, bubbling froggy maw.

'Cacodaem!' shouted Rasgul as the thing floated forward from its compartment. At the same time three more of the terrible creatures emerged from similar compartments in neighbouring columns.

The maw of the first cacodaem, cavernous enough to almost engulf a man in one go, opened. Leth saw something begin to form inside it. A brown liquid globule flew out at him. He managed to throw himself to the side, out of its path, and heard it splash wetly against the wall behind him. As the cacodaem opened its maw to spit again Leth darted out of its way around the nearest column. There were yells and screams coming from off to one side. Peering around the column Leth saw one of his companions – he could not tell who – smothered in the brown eructation of another of the cacodaems. The stuff had formed an elastic mass around its victim, and seemed to be thickening by the moment. The man – whoever he was – struggled desperately to free himself, his movements painfully slow and laboured as he strove against the stretchy, hardening stuff. As he did so the cacodaem glided forward, froggy maw wide, and plucked him from the ground.

Leth was not close enough to intervene. He saw Count Harg throw himself at the monster, sword flashing, then Leth grew aware of the first cacodaem sliding slowly around the column, seeking him out. Before it could turn he rushed it, slashing hard with his scimitar. The blade bit deep. The cacodaem convulsed in the air, emitting a terrible roar, and wheeled on Leth as he struck again. He dived low, avoiding its plunging maw. His blows, while aggravating the cacodaem, seemed to be having no mortal effect. He glimpsed Rasgul rush out, brandishing one of the blazing javelins he had taken from the two dead Acolytes. He thrust it deep into the cacodaem's bloated corpus. The cacodaem bellowed and shot upwards, smashing into the ceiling, spinning. Its form began to distort and diminish, gobbets of steaming flesh flying in all directions as the javelin burrowed deep.

As the dying creature fell to the ground Leth rushed to aid Harg. The cacodaem he was attacking was roaring and twisting, trying to defend itself against Harg whilst attempting to swallow its victim fully, whose legs protruded from its maw. Leth hacked hard at its flesh. It turned and drew back. Again the swordblows seemed to do little more than enrage it. But with the warrior in its jaws it was unable to spit at its two assailants. It pulled away, but two others were coming forward. A mass of brown spittle flew at Juson, missing him by inches. The remaining Abyss warrior – Leth thought it was Huuri – attacked the cacodaem from behind. Leth was aware of Rasgul between the columns, hurling his last remaining javelin, which plunged into the side of one of the cacodaems, sending it shrieking and shivering to the floor.

But now Leth was aware of other enemies coming from the passages to either side of the large chamber. Vaguely human, featureless things, powerfully muscled, with pewter-grey scaly skin, brandishing radiant, beaked axes and combat pincers. They came forward stealthily, weaving between the two remaining cacodaems.

Rasgul cried out a warning. 'Goles! Move back!'

One of the goles rushed at Leth, thrusting at his head with the bill-head of its axe with one hand, the other, with the spiked pincers, snapping at his groin. Leth dodged both blows, swung with his scimitar and struck the gole in the shoulder. The blade went deep, but the gole showed no reaction, and as Leth pulled back he saw to his shock that he had left no wound.

'Draw the Orbsword, Swordbearer!' called Rasgul, who was retreating and fending off the blows of another gole. 'It is your only hope!'

Without hesitation, leaping back to avoid the gole's attack, Leth dropped his scimitar and drew free the Orbsword. It glowed bright, though much of its radiance was lost in the blood-toned air. But there came a gasp from the goles, and even the cacodaems seemed hesitant for a moment.

Leth seized the opportunity and lunged at the nearest gole. The Orbsword passed effortlessly through its chest. The gole's mouth sagged open, it issued a long sigh, and fell.

But there were as many as ten goles advancing upon them now, maybe more, as well as the two cacodaems. Recovering from the shock of the sight of the Orbsword they pressed forward again relentlessly. Beyond them Leth glimpsed several Acolytes running forward from the tunnel along which he had come, grasping pairs of deadly blazing javelins. With the others of his party he drew back, but the situation was hopeless. There was nowhere to retreat to. His was the only effective weapon, but even with the Orbsword he could not hope to fight off so many assailants.

A cacodaem gaped and ejaculated its wet brown mass. Leth glimpsed Harg hurl himself to one side, narrowly avoiding the sticky mass, which glued itself to the edge of the closest column. Rasgul was being hard-pressed by two goles. Leth slid across, lowering his body, and swung the Orbsword into the nearest gole's flank. The creature spun with sudden shock, then fell silently. At that moment Leth saw, beyond the gole, something glittering within one of the column compartments from which the cacodaems had emerged. Ducking another mass of flying spittle, Leth lunged for the compartment. On its side wall was a small silver knob. Without time for thought Leth reached in and grasped it, pressed, pulled, twisted . . . Something gave. He heard a low grinding sound behind him. Harg called out.

Leth turned. In the rear wall of the chamber a door had opened.

Beyond it nothing could be seen bar a flickering redness, predominantly darker than that which filled the chamber he now occupied. There was no time for consideration. Harg and the remaining Abyss warrior were already fighting their way back towards the new opening.

'Through there!' Leth yelled. Now the others of his party saw the opening. Desperately hacking, they fought their way back. One by one they slipped through. Leth came last, the enemy creatures crowding him, yet holding back slightly, wary now of the glowing sword he wielded. From behind them he saw an Acolyte draw back an arm and hurl a javelin. The thing wuzzed angrily past his ear into the opening behind him. Leth prayed it had struck none of his companions. A gole came at him suddenly, axe swinging, pincers snapping. Leth avoided the blows. Something grasped him from behind and dragged him back. Rasgul stood inside the opening, gripping a metal bar set into the wall. As Leth came inside the Abyss warrior pushed hard upon the bar and the door slid shut upon the chamber, leaving the cacodaems, goles and Acolytes on the other side.

II

They were in a spacious area bounded by walls both of hewn stone and natural deep red rock. Numerous tunnel entrances were revealed in the rock faces, leading off in various directions. The acrid smell that Leth had detected earlier was more forceful here. It burned the back of his nose and was mingled with a faintly sulphurous stench and a moist, sour-sweet odour of decay.

From somewhere unseen, away to their left, issued a terrible sound: a dreadful, dirgeful bellowing. It came semi-rhythmically, finding its way through the tunnels, an inhuman sound that ranged across the scale from a profoundly menacing, enraged basso rumble to a ruthless, tormented lowing which mounted remorselessly, reaching a blood-chilling alto shriek before breaking off, pausing, then resuming again. Leth felt his teeth on edge, his gut knotting, the muscles of his spine involuntarily clenching.

Rasgul bent to pick up the fallen Acolyte javelin, then straightened, glancing grim-visaged towards the direction of the maddening sound.

'She knows,' he said chillingly to Leth. 'The Great Sow has sensed the Orbsword. She knows you are here.'

Count Harg, re-loading his repeating crossbow, wryly observed, 'Ah well, she tells us in which direction she lies, at least. We should not run down too many wrong tunnels.'

'And we should waste no time,' said Rasgul. 'She will be more anxious now than ever to release her obnoxious force upon the world.'

They struck out into one of the nearer tunnels, whose black maw promised to take them at least some distance towards the source of the dreadful stridency. They were five in number now: Leth, Rasgul, Harg, Juson and Huuri. A small, tight but motley band made up of murdering thugs and merciless warriors, none of whom knew their own hearts or minds, and led by a desperate and brave young king who had been summoned as a god to rid a world of a nebulous evil of which he knew nothing.

With Leth and Rasgul leading they crept forward into the obscuring shadows. The area they were leaving seemed deserted, but each of them knew that anything might lurk there, within the tunnels or anywhere close by, and Huuri took it upon himself to bring up the rear, alert at all times for sudden attack from that direction.

The tunnel, though it twisted like a worm, proved to be no longer than fifty paces, and they emerged from it into a colossal subterranean cavern of cathedral proportions. The floor was predominantly level and paved with huge slabs of red-black cut stone, but the cavern itself was a natural formation. From its furthest side, beyond fields of stalagmites, tall twisting igneous pinnacles and wildly formed ledges and outthrusts of rock, the chthonic light burned more intensely than ever before. A raging cascade tumbled down the far wall, its sound muted by the din of the monster somewhere even further below. Spuming jets of spray glinted pinkly, splaying out, foaming and falling, and great clouds of rubescent vapour rose, draping much of the cavern in a fine patina formed of millions of tiny glimmering beads of moisture. Weird capering shadows were thrown across the lofty ceiling, the towering walls and floor. And within those shadows, within that obscuring light, Leth thought he saw movement, as if the rock walls and the cavern floor itself had come alive.

He blinked, peered hard, and realized he had been partly mistaken. The cavern had not come alive, but it was a host, a domain of some kind of life. Creatures were advancing, crawling and slithering down the wet rock walls, coming towards him and his companions, coming in their scores, perhaps their hundreds across the steaming cavern floor. Their approach seemed calculated and deliberate, as if they had no need for haste. And from beyond them, in a yawning gulf unseeable at the back of the cavern, out of which the weird light emanated, Ascaria's dreadful lowing, bellowing, wailing issued without surcease, causing the clamouring air to tremble.

'Prepare yourself, Swordbearer,' cautioned Rasgul, and his voice carried such a strange emotion that Leth turned to look at him.

'What are they?'

'It is not what they are that you must concern yourself with. It is what they are not.'

He knelt, unslinging his bow. The others had done the same, levelling bolts and arrows at the oncoming horde.

'We cannot kill them all!' declared Leth.

Rasgul glanced aside at him. 'No, we cannot.'

Leth craned his neck, straining to make out more clearly the obscure host that moved toward him. The nearest were perhaps forty paces away. And with a horror greater than anything he had experienced so far, Leth gasped, seeing suddenly what it was that he faced.

'No!'

'They are not what you think, Swordbearer.'

'I cannot!'

'They are transformed. They are lost. They are Ascaria's newest defenders. And they are coming to kill us.'

Leth gaped, twisting his head from side to side, something inside him crying out in mute outrage. For he was looking at children. Some were in rags, some in half-armour. All carried hand-weapons of some form or other. They came on at a chill, remorseless pace.

'Do not be deceived. They are children no more, Swordbearer,' said Count Harg, his earlier humour no longer evident.

'I cannot kill them!'

Rasgul yelled at him. 'She lies beyond! She awaits you! We must fight through. It is the only way.'

'No! There must be another way!'

'There is not!'

Leth turned furiously upon Rasgul. 'How? How can I?'

'They are not children, Swordbearer! Whatever they once were, they are monsters now!'

Leth looked out again at the oncoming horde. The child-warriors were close enough now for him to make out the glitter of their eyes in the bloodlight. Their ages ranged from perhaps six years up to youths of fourteen or fifteen. Their faces were uniformly ashen, set, cold, expressionless. He looked beyond them in anguish, as if some impossible solace might lie there. But there was nothing, only his own knowledge that whatever they were now, whatever they had become, whatever threat they undoubtedly were to him, he could not bring himself to wade among them, mowing down their small bodies with his lethal blade. He could not. They had been children once. *His own children might be among them!*

He let out an anguished sob. *There has to be another way!*

There came the thrumming snap of bowstrings from beside him. Four of the child-warriors fell. Others crowded forward, paying no heed to the fallen bodies. Another flight of arrows and bolts . . . another four dropped. But there were far too many of them ever to be halted by so few bowmen. They were less than twenty paces away now, a swarming determined mass. Leth desperately scanned the walls of the cavern, seeking a way around the encroaching children, another way in.

With horror he realized that Rasgul and the others were laying aside their bows and drawing their blades, preparing to wade into the horde.

'Swordbearer!'

Was it was conceivable that they might fight their way through? Conceivably so, if only just, Leth saw. Despite their numbers the child-warriors were lightly armoured, if at all; they came forward with an almost mindless intent, and he doubted that they would be expert fighters. Yet to win through would entail such blood-shed, such terrible carnage. He could not countenance it. And in their overwhelming mass the children had the overall advantage, most especially if they could surround the five and strike at their unguarded backs.

He scanned the faces of the foremost, his dread ever-growing that in their ranks his gaze might fall upon Galry and Jace.

'Swordbearer!' Rasgul glared back angrily over his shoulder at Leth.

Leth stood unable to move, the Orbsword gripped impotently in his hand. *I will not be their murderer! There has to be another way!*

He turned and raced back into the tunnel from which they had just emerged, oblivious to Rasgul's furious hailing. Just yards along he knew that he had saved his men's lives. Three goles were creeping up the tunnel. Within moments they would have launched themselves upon Leth and his companions from behind.

Without slowing, using his speed and momentum, Leth ran at the surprised goles. He lofted the Orbsword and struck as he passed the first gole, taking its head cleanly from its shoulders. His motion took him cannoning into the second of the creatures. It was sent flying back, hammering against the the tunnel wall. Dazed and winded, it tottered and sank to one knee. Leth stepped in and thrust his blade through its chest.

But the third gole was upon him. A heavy axe-blow smashed down hard behind Leth's right shoulder, felling him. As he slammed breathless into the ground his one thought was to keep moving. He rolled instinctively, and heard and half-glimpsed the billed axehead strike again, biting into the rock where his head had been, sending sparks and rock chips flying. With all his strength he swung upwards and heard the gole complain as the Orbsword carved deep into its unnatural flesh.

His head still rang from the gole's first strike. He pushed himself away, came bent-legged to his feet, blinking and shaking his head to clear his vision. The wounded gole was coming at him. Leth parried the first blow, thrust forward. And again! The gole drew back, widened its stance, swung, missed. Leth detected an opening, waited. The gole jabbed with the bill-head. Leth pulled away, then drove in suddenly, neatly flicking aside the arm bearing the combat pincers, and lunged. His blade pierced the gole's throat. The gole opened its mouth as if to speak, and staggered back. Leth struck again, ending its life.

He paused to take stock, breathing hard. The combat had brought him to the mouth of the tunnel. He peered out, scanning the wider area from which the other tunnel entrances ran off. There were no other assailants visible. He gazed down for a second at the last of the fallen goles. Its first blow, which had caught him from behind, had been powerful enough to maim, possibly even kill him. Certainly it should have signalled the beginning of the end of the combat, yet the sapphire armour had deflected or absorbed much of its energy. Leth found himself marvelling. The armour had not split; from what he could see it had barely even buckled.

He came from the tunnel mouth and ran to the nearest of the other entrances. It appeared to lead towards the same destination as the tunnel he had just left, yet there had been no other entrance in the cavern close to where he and the others had stood. A dead end, or did it lead elsewhere?

He ran on. In the depths of the next tunnel he spied stone stairs curving upwards. He raced in, desperately hoping. He took the stairs in long bounds. They twined sinuously through the raw, warm mottled red rock, and then suddenly burst out onto a slender ledge.

Leth found himself at the edge, staring down into the great cavern where, some fifty feet below and perhaps fifty paces distant, Rasgul and the other three battled against the milling child-warriors. They had held close to the cavern wall, preventing the child-warriors from getting at their backs. A swelling sea of children crowded them. The ground nearby was littered with young corpses, as many as a score. Leth could see that the men were beginning to tire.

He looked about him, quickly assessing his own situation. The ledge upon which he stood, barely inches in width, threaded its way along the bellying, glistening, red-lit cavern wall towards the far gulf from within which hidden Ascaria unceasingly bellowed. Leth could not make out its full extent, and as it wound into various clefts and folds, he could not see whether its width would support him along its entire length. But he knew he could only take it or go back. He would be exposed and vulnerable, forced to inch along the ledge with his back against the rock face, and he could not be certain that it would take him to Ascaria.

He glanced down into the cavern again. So far his presence was undetected. It was go now or not at all.

He sheathed the Orbsword, needing both hands free, and slipped out sidewise onto the ledge. Beneath him the carnage continued, and from time to time, when the Kancanitrix fell momentarily silent to draw breath, the noise of battle reached him: clashing weapons, Rasgul's enraged battle-roars, the yells and grunts of Harg and the others. The children fought with relentless, undying silence, like spectres or dead creatures.

And there was another sound between the Kancanitrix's breaths, a strange, wet, rapid slurping, sucking noise that made Leth's stomach turn.

The rock at Leth's back offered few handholds. Its knobs and edges were worn smooth, as if by eons of water passing over its surface. But the rock was relatively dry on this side of the cavern; the cataract and its clouds and jets of spray being on the other side. A few yards along the ledge the rock began to lean outwards at approximately shoulder height, forcing Leth to incline himself forward from the waist. He hung precariously over the battle below, with only empty space between him and the rock floor.

A glance ahead showed him that the ledge fell away a little distance on. He was forced to turn, with great difficulty, so that his head and chest were pressed to the rock, his legs uncomfortably bent as he groped for hand and footholds.

He inched his way painfully along, never knowing whether his next step would take him as far as it was possible to go along the cavern wall. Suddenly something smacked off the rock close to his head with a loud report, then clattered to the ground far below. Another object followed, then another. He had been seen! The child-warriors were hurling weapons: hand-axes, knives, rocks . . . Miraculously they appeared to have no proper missile weapons, and their aim was none too certain. Nevertheless the missiles they did possess were a dangerous distraction, and if one struck one of his exposed hands, or his helm or a groping foot, it could spell the end for him.

More and more of the weapons flew at him, beating an irregular tattoo off the wall, and he could do nothing but keep on, hoping, desperately hoping, that he would not find himself stranded.

Something struck him heavily on the thigh. He froze, fearful for a moment that he might be hurt. But his armour had protected him once again. The sweat streamed down his back; his fingers ached from gripping the harsh rock. A little way ahead he saw that the ledge reappeared. It wound its way a few yards further and disappeared into a large black fissure. Large enough for a man to slip within and shelter, if he could just get there – but did it lead anywhere?

A small carbuncle of rock at eye level offered a fingerhold. He leaned and stretched out. His fingers grasped the rock but slipped off and he saved himself from toppling only by pressing himself even harder against the face, adhering, he did not know how, for the vital heartbeats it took him to regain his balance and find a grip. More weapons hammered off the wall all around him. Several struck him, though none powerfully enough to do him serious harm. From behind and below he heard a sudden yell:

'Swordbearer! We see you! We are with you! Swordbearer, hang on! Hang on!'

With difficulty Leth inched his head around. Below him he saw Rasgul running, leaping from rock to rock, striking down children with his scimitar. Blood poured from wounds on his thigh and cheek, but he scrambled to a platform closer to Leth's position, and from there was able to draw the attention of the children who pounded Leth. Many now abandoned their attempts to dislodge Leth and turned to deal with Rasgul.

Count Harg, also blooded, now broke free from the main battle and followed Rasgul's example. He clambered to another vantage and similarly drew the child-warriors to him. Huuri and Juson fought on at the tunnel entrance.

Leth forced his way onward. The ledge was almost within reach now. He could not tell exactly what was supporting his weight, but knew that a single tiny miscalculation would bring him plunging down. The floor immediately below was a mass of boulders and stalagmites; if he fell he would almost certainly break limbs if not actually kill himself. He cursed the helm and sapphire armour. Though they protected him from the missiles that still struck him, no matter the armour's suppleness it made traversing this face immensely difficult.

At last his fingers gripped a narrow crevice above the ledge. He brought his rear leg up, skidding and fumbling until it found a toe-hold. Now he could bring his other leg up and rest the foot upon the ledge itself. He pushed with his other hand, managed somehow to get his weight onto the forward leg, hauled himself across and was at last balanced precariously on the ledge.

He risked a look down. Rasgul was whirling his scimitar, striking down the children who clambered towards him. Bloody bodies and limbs were piling up on the cavern floor, and between Ascaria's bellows the cavern was filled with the cries of the dying. The sight was too horrible to bear, and Leth forced down his fear, not daring to let rise into consciousness the knowledge that it could be his children who were being slain down there.

He turned back, made himself concentrate upon his task. The

fissure gaped just ahead of him, the ledge widening a little as it entered the dark. He hauled himself forward and at last collapsed exhausted upon his knees in the blackness between the folds of protecting rock.

He could afford no time to rest. Hardly regaining his breath he scrambled up and began to feel his way gingerly forward. At first he was in total darkness. He gripped the rock on each side of him, tested each step with one foot upon the uneven ground. A little way ahead of him a bleak jag of rosy light glimmered, showing a ragged outline of rock. He pushed on towards it.

The crevice narrowed. Leth was forced to his knees, squeezing between what had become hardly more than a crack in the warm rock wall. He removed the sapphire helm to ease his passage, and became more aware than ever of the heat of the air against his face. It seemed that the helm even offered some protection against that. Once through the crack he replaced the helm, feeling vulnerable without it.

He eased forward into the weak glow of light, and found himself at the lip of a chasm. He was at the far end of the great cavern, and beneath him was the gulf out of which the flickering dark bloodlight issued, more intense now than ever. Far off to the other side the great red cataract tumbled, its spumes and vapours rising high. He could no longer see the child-warriors, nor any of his companions: the main body of the cavern was obscured by a dark shoulder of rock humping out near to where he stood. Ascaria's baleful roars split his ears, louder, much closer. They seemed to fragment the very air about him.

At first Leth thought he was at a cul-de-sac, for the cavern face dropped away beneath him and there seemed no way forward. But then he noticed, beneath him, small steps roughly hewn into the rock, leading down into a dark vertical cleft that seemed to descend as far as the chasm floor. It was a dizzying descent, but the only one available.

He began to work his way down. The steps, though relatively evenly spaced, were barely wider than his two feet placed side by side, and his right hip and shoulder clipped the rock as he went, almost pushing him off. Fortunately, a short way down the smooth face inclined slightly inwards and he was able to lean into it, clinging with the flats of his hands and tips of his fingers.

He reached the bottom at last, drenched in sweat. The sulphurous fumes were stronger here, as was the stench of decay, making the air difficult to breathe. He stood within the cleft and could see nothing bar the shivering bloodlight above. Cacophony rattled off the rock to either side of his head, painful in his ears. Were Ascaria's bellows more intense, or was it merely that he was ever closer?

Leth crept forward, coming cautiously from the shadows of the cleft and peering all around. Then he stood stock still. The bloodlight shimmered, drenching him, drenching the walls all around, dazzling so that he could barely see. But what he could see held him rooted to the spot, powerless to react. He was on a flat, wide area where strange fires danced and threw weird shadows in the eerie, intense light. And facing him across the floor of the cavern was the Kancanitrix.

III

Nothing in his life had prepared him for this. Not in his wildest imaginings, his most delirious nightmares, had he envisaged anything like it. The sight left him agape, filled him with awe, cold, paralyzing horror and a deep, overwhelming revulsion.

Ascaria towered some seventy feet into the sweating, trembling red air. She was almost as wide as she was tall, and seemed formed of some utterly strange, fluid-like, fleshy stuff. She was a grotesque, obese mound, a vast mass of rolling, undulating, bloated flesh, mottled red through murrey to deep blood, veined pink with patches of filth-brown merging into grey and mordant black. It could be said that her shape was vaguely that of a gigantic female, squatting in a lake of glutinous liquidy stuff that seemed to be of the same substance that formed her. Four huge mammaries spilled from her chest and flabbed out limp and swollen across great rolling swathes of loose fat that formed the outer layer of her naked belly. The nipples were near-black, each distended and larger than a man's clenched fist. The face was a hideous mockery, half-woman, half-pig: a broad, blunt snout, eyes that were almost buried beneath waves of blubber, and a horribly wide, toothless mouth rimmed by loose, soft, drooling purple lips. She lacked a neck, the head being a relatively small blunt conical form rising out of shoulders like hills. From her skull, long twisting hanks of matted hair hung lankly, lifeless crimson weed reaching as far as her bloated abdomen. She squatted in the pink-red lake, and Leth saw that it bubbled, slowly, and churned and gathered about her great pendulous thighs and ankles, and drew at least some of its substance from a small river flowing from the base of the great cataract at Ascaria's back.

As he gaped Leth had the impression that she was not wholly formed. Her gross towering body had a fluid, unfinished quality, as though it might shudder and remould itself at will. Surrounding Ascaria and the lake in which she rested and out of which it seemed she truly was *formed*, was another utterly alien phenomenon. A barrier of swiftly leaping, licking, darting tongues, reaching perhaps to the height of a man's head. They were deep unreflective olive black in colour, and now that he saw them Leth stared at them, mesmerized, his mind swimming, for intuitively he understood that he was looking at fire. Black fire.

The Dark Flame.

The heat was formidable, the air choking and noxious. Leth's hand rested on the hilt of the Orbsword, but he could not draw it, for he could not find the will to move.

Ascaria, it seemed, had not seen him. She sat oblivious, bellowing and baying, her throat and lips quivering, slow waves of fatty motion coursing over her massive chest and bulbous abdomen, making the fluid stuff in which she sat shiver as if in protest. And now Leth discovered the meaning of the second sound he had heard, the loathsome slurping, sucking noise that was audible in those brief moments when Ascaria paused. For he watched, horrified, as she reached down with a massive, ballooning red hand and plucked forth something that was at first obscured by the dancing black flames and clouds of dense pink and red vapour that rose all around her. She brought it high. It squirmed in her grasp. She lifted it to her gaping mouth, placed its upper parts briefly between her obscenely soft lips. Her little piggy eyes closed in a moment of apparent ecstasy, and the vile slurping sound violated Leth's ears. Then she tipped back her great head and lowed. At the same time she released the thing she held, which tumbled, limply rolling over the bags of loose flesh that formed her, coming to rest in the viscous pink sludge beneath her. There it came dazedly to its hands and knees and began to crawl away towards a gap in the black flames to one side of the Kancanitrix.

A child, Leth saw, and felt his gorge rise. A child no more. Pathetic now, crawling imbecilic from Ascaria's abominable bulk, hardly even knowing that it lived.

The fury and horror rose, boiling Leth's blood. But so intent was he on the ghastly spectacle he was witnessing that he wholly failed to notice the Acolyte who crept up on his left flank, amethyst-flaming javelin poised.

Too late! Leth glimpsed the movement from the corner of his eye. He twisted towards it even as the Acolyte let the javelin fly. The flaring weapon hummed through the air, straight and true to its target. Leth made to propel himself to the side, but was unevenly balanced and had no time. The javelin buried itself into the ribbed plackart of his breastplate, which protected his lower ribcage. The force of the blow almost lifted Leth off his feet. It threw him back, crashing onto his buttocks on the ground.

He stared in horror. The sapphire armour had failed to block the missile. The shaft of the javelin protruded three feet from his ribcage, burning white and purple, vibrating in a blur of motion. A great moan escaped Leth's lips.

Is this it? Have I come so far only to die here at her feet?

He grasped the shaft and tried to wrench it free, but it was buried deep and would not shift. More, it was forcing itself deeper and he could not stop it. Why did he feel no pain? He braced himself, for it would surely come. The javelin's vibrations coursed right through him, through his armour, through his hands and arms, through his flesh, his very bones. It was alive and intent, burrowing obediently into him.

Oh Galry, Oh Jace, I am so sorry. Oh Issul, I have failed us all.

His head sagged forward. He felt suddenly weak and utterly exhausted, overcome with the terrible futility of it all. He dragged his eyeballs up to peer through the visor slits at his murderer. The Acolyte stood some score or so paces away, its head-cocked, regarding him with a quizzical expression upon its bland avian-human face. Its broad beak moved; Leth had the impression it was speaking, gloating perhaps, but its words were drowned by the dreadful noise of the Kancanitrix.

And still he felt no pain.

And something inexplicable was happening. The javelin was growing shorter, boring into him, but he seemed untouched. No pain, no spurts of boiling steam as it vaporized his innards. Its flame-radiance was crawling rapidly across the surface of his breastplate, and further, over the entire suit of the sapphire armour. Leth stared in astonishment. A light, purple-blue aura radiated from him. He felt it tingling upon his skin. The last stub of the javelin-shaft melded into the armour, and he still felt no pain. He was alive. *Alive!* The sapphire armour seemed to have taken the javelin's energy and somehow transformed and redistributed it across its own surface. And now it glowed, radiant with whatever magical force the javelin had stored within it.

The Acolyte was jabbering something, though its words were still inaudible. Its round black eyes were wide and alight with disbelief as it watched the enemy in the glowing armour climb to his feet. And Leth advanced, renewed now, with single-minded intent. He drew the radiant blade from its scabbard. In a dozen swift paces he was upon the Acolyte, who had begun first to back away in confusion, then turn and try to flee. It was not quick enough. With a single blow Leth struck it dead, then turned to confront Ascaria again.

She seemed oblivious to his presence. She had gathered up another child and placed its head between the sinuous red mass of her lips in the obscene dream-stealing kiss. And the opaque black flames licked high in front of Leth. They gave off no heat; their composition was a mystery. But between them there were occasional breaks letting onto narrow paths of the oozing liquid slurry out of which Ascaria rose.

Leth raced forward, passed through one of the breaks. The red-black ooze lapped about his ankles, slow and slightly viscous. But it grew no deeper as he advanced. The noxious stench was overpowering here, making him gag, the fumes scouring his throat and lungs. Leth rushed on, the Orbsword held high. Ascaria rose mighty and mindless above him, swathed in clouds of her own dreadful vapour. How could he hope to slay her? He stood at the point where the mass of her colossal sweating body merged with the liquid stuff. With all his might he swung with the Orbsword, striking cleanly and deeply into the 'flesh' of her knee. The Orbsword passed through, and out with almost no resistance. It was as though he had run it through a mound of aspic. It left no wound. Ascaria was unharmed. She seemed still to be completely unaware of him.

Could she feel? Could she even see?

What *was* she?

He struck again, summoning every iota of strength in his body, stabbing deep into her dreadful matter. The Orbsword penetrated to its hilt and beyond, so that Leth's hand sank into her as far as his wrist. The liquid meat gathered around him, jellified, quivering and searingly hot, but still Ascaria lowed and bellowed and showed no reaction to his assault or consciousness of his immediate presence. He withdrew his hand and the sword and stepped back in frustration.

How was he to kill her if she could not be killed?

Out of the corner of his eye he glimpsed something large and round floating towards him across the surface of the lake in which he stood. A cacodaem opening its maw to eject its wet brown mass. Three others came over the wall of dark flame some way behind. And there were running figures between the flames, goles and Acolytes, skirting the encircling flame, racing around to cut him off.

One eye on the cacodaem, he began to retreat towards the edge of the lake, to get himself onto the other side of the dark flames. But he could see the Acolytes and goles were coming in large numbers, from all sides. There were child-warriors among them. And there was nowhere he could run.

The cacodaem ejaculated its ball of sticky sputum. Leth darted back and it shot past him and splashed into the lake just beyond him. He ran, leaping through the gap in the flames and back onto the solid flat rock. Just before him the cliff face rose. Two goles were coming at him from his left. A terrible roar rose from deep within him, and he ran to meet them, struck once, twice, thrice, and they fell gasping before they had even struck a blow.

But others menaced him from forty paces away: goles, Acolytes, child-warriors and a pair of cacodaems. They had slowed, approaching him warily, fanning out across the flat rock causeway. Behind him a similar number came from the other direction. They were too many. There was nowhere he could go. He searched around him desperately, but there was no way out and he sensed that he was lost.

There was a brief moment of near-silence as Ascaria paused to gather breath. In the hiatus, a new sound, a shout from somewhere above. 'Swordbearer!'

Leth wheeled to look up. High above him the Abyss warrior,

Rasgul, stood wide-stanced upon a ledge of rock. His hands were cupped about his mouth. Leth saw his chest heave as he yelled out. Leth strained his ears. 'The Flame! You must —'

His words were drowned as Ascaria resumed her terrible cacophony. Leth spun to face the wall of black flames. As he did so a cacodaem rose over it and came towards him, its maw beginning to open. Leth ran at it, took it by surprise, and thrust the Orbsword deep into its bulk before it could eject its gross matter. The monster spun away, spluttering, vomiting its own flesh. Diminishing in form, it rose in a spiralling ascent above the pool, then dropped into the liquid behind the flames.

Leth wheeled around. On each side the goles, Acolytes and warrior-children had advanced ten paces or so. He sensed they were wary of him, yet confident that they could overpower him by sheer weight of numbers. The Acolytes no longer carried flaming javelins, fearful of using them after witnessing their effect on Leth's armour. Instead they held bright curved falchions or hand-axes and combat-pincers similar to the goles.

Leth swivelled from one group to the other, the Orbsword before him. How many could he hope to kill? Six, seven, before they overpowered him? Less if the cacodaems succeeded in trapping him in their spittle. They were all edging forward, fanning around him.

Again Ascaria's ear-splitting lowing ceased for a moment.

'Swordbearer! The Flame! It is the Flame you must destroy!'

Leth glanced up, confused. Rasgul was frantically pointing.

'The Flame! The Dark Flame!'

Leth stared at the wall of flame. Ascaria began another earth-shaking roar. Two volleys of dark brown spittle shot towards him.

The Flame? The Dark Flame?

He leapt to the side and rolled. The spittle squelched onto the ground behind him. He came to his feet, incredulous, not daring to hope. It seemed mad, yet it was all now that he could do.

He sped forward and plunged the Orbsword into the wall of Dark Flame . . .

IV

There was a moment of utter stillness.

Nothing moved, nothing breathed, nothing made a sound. It was as though all of Orbus's world itself had caught its breath.

And then life returned with shocking vigour.

From far above Leth's head came a roar like nothing he had heard before. The Kancanitrix threw back her great mottled red head, the flab of her mouth falling open, and she issued a sound like chthonic thunder. Her massive arms had risen high as if to clutch and claw the cavern roof, huge rolls of loose flesh rippling and swinging under gravity's drag. The entire congealed mound of her body arched and shuddered, its mass oscillating with a liquid, heavy sound.

Simultaneously the ring of black fire flared, just momentarily, and issued a noise like a far-off angry wind. Time stood still. The black flames trembled, became jagged and brittle in appearance. They began to entwine themselves around the glowing rose blade within them. The entire mass of encircling black flames gathered and began to pour, howling and whistling, into the sword. The sword jerked violently. Leth was thrown off his feet, losing his grip on the hilt. He landed on his back and could only stare, his mouth agape inside the helm.

Ascaria was writhing and thrashing. She was losing her form. Waves of fleshy substance flowed towards the ground and melted into the ichorous pool at her feet. She was half her former size now, and diminishing, bellowing incoherent ear-shattering protests as she went. The Orbsword jerked and twitched within the black flames, held up by its own force. And the flames were no longer flames. They had become a mass forming into a ring of sooty shapeless cloud, which sighed and wailed as it was sucked into the blade of the Sword of the Orb. Within moments nothing was left of the great wall of vibrant black fire that had surrounded the Kancanitrix. The last wisps and tails of black were drawn to the glowing blade, their sound fading as they vanished into it like smoke drawn into a vacuum.

And beyond where the flames had been, in the centre of the red lake, Ascaria's bulk subsided. It was no longer a recognizable form. Her mouth remained, a dark pit in the amorphous sweating bulb that had been her head, the lips forming sounds which emerged as a slurping, rumbling lament, then a feeble, plaintive wet moan, then nothing. She diminished, merging into the dirty red liquid pool of her substance, which rippled and lapped and then was still. All that could be heard now was the background drone of the tumbling cataract across the cavern.

Dazed, Leth climbed slowly to his feet. He was weaponless, but the goles and Acolytes no longer menaced him, nor the child-warriors. The cacodaems had vanished or been destroyed with the vanquishing of the Dark Flame. The goles had dropped their weapons and stood in disconsolate postures, silent and lifeless. The Acolytes and children, likewise, appeared to have lost all life and motivation. They shuffled silently to and fro, but made no move towards Leth.

Leth looked at the Orbsword.

'Don't touch it, Swordbearer!'

It was Rasgul who spoke. He was descending the bluff behind Leth, via a steep twisting walkway. He limped, his body gashed and bloodied. He came forward across the flat paved floor and laid his hand on Leth's shoulder. 'You did it!'

'*We* did it,' Leth corrected him.

Another voice hailed Leth from above and behind: 'Ha! A splendid show, Swordbearer! Absolutely marvellous! Your mother would be proud of you!'

Count Harg was coming down the same pathway, some distance behind Rasgul. As he approached Leth saw that he was hobbling too, and his face was streaked with blood, grime and sweat. Leth looked past him. At the lip of the bluff some of the warrior-children were visible. No longer showing signs of hostility, some stood, some sat or squatted passively, as if lost. Leth wondered how many had died.

As Harg drew close Leth said, 'Where are the others? Juson and Huuri?'

'They did not get this far,' Harg replied, and halted, grimacing, his body slightly twisted, evidently in some pain. Then he gave a thin smile. 'She is gone.'

Leth nodded to himself, still hardly believing. He looked across at the pool of pink slew, and realized that it was slowly draining or evaporating away. The Orbsword rested before him, hovering vertically in the air as if by some force of its own. The radiant blade pulsed, and within its surface Leth saw that its colour was now marred with mingling, fluxing tones of red and black.

'Why should I not touch it?'

'It may be that the force of what it has absorbed will be too great,' Rasgul replied. 'We should wait a while and see.'

Leth looked at the great cavern around him, and suddenly snapped into a re-awareness of why he had come.

The children!

He spun and began to make his way with long swift strides around the circumference of the lake, where the wall of black fire had raged. He shouldered through the uncomplaining Acolytes and goles, Count Harg hobbling behind him. Leth grabbed a discarded falchion as he went, not yet ready to believe that all was safe. He made for the far side of the circle, to the area from which he had seen Ascaria take her victims.

He arrived to find himself standing on a slightly raised area, looking down into an enclosure, ringed by high stone walls. At the back was a rough shelter of sorts. Gazing up from him out of the enclosure were children, fifty or more. Their eyes were wide, their expressions expectant, stunned, frightened. But their eyes shone, and some of them were crying. They could feel, they could think and imagine. Soon they would be able to dream again.

A short flight of steps hewn into the stone led down to a gate letting into the enclosure. Leth thrust the falchion into his belt and slowly descended, anxiously, fearfully scanning the mass of pale faces peering up at him, scarcely able to breathe. His heart pounded painfully against his ribcage; his legs threatened to buckle beneath him.

'It's all right. It's all right,' he reassured the frightened children softly as he descended. He opened the gate. The children shrank back. More began to shiver and sob. 'It's all right now. You are safe. No one will harm you.'

He moved among them, examining every cowed face, trying to reasure them as he went. His anxiety mounted, almost choking him. He worked his way through, then back, silently pleading, but in the end he reached the rear of the enclosure and Galry and Jace were not present.

He peered beneath the low wooden roof of the shelter. In the dense shadows in one corner there was a huddle of bodies. Leth bent under the roof and moved towards them. The children tried to scramble away. He reassured them with quiet murmurs, his hands held open, and moved close. They were five in number, a couple of them almost too weak to move. The shadows were deep and Leth could not make out their faces. He brought them one by one towards the light, holding their hands, but in the end his own were not there.

With a great, heavy sigh Leth sagged to the ground, his back against the wall, vaguely aware of many young eyes upon him.

Numb, empty. Where might they be? Up above? Slain? Out on the plain beyond the Fortress, dead shells, starvelings, corpses? His eyes closed as he tried to blot out the images and the heaviness that bore him down.

'Swordbearer?'

Rasgul had entered the enclosure. He stood in the light, bent, his hand upon the shelter-roof, peering in.

Slowly Leth began to rise.

'They are not here?'

Leth shook his head.

'I am sorry.'

Leth looked into that savage, pale face, and for a moment saw emotion there, a genuine sadness. But his heart was too full to speak. He cast his eyes once more around the shelter, then found the strength to say, 'We must do something for those who have survived.'

Rasgul nodded and moved away. Still bent beneath the low roof, Leth moved to follow him. His eyes were better adjusted to the gloom now. As he passed back into the enclosure something caught his eye. He ducked back, peering hard into the shadows. A small pile of sacking or something occupied one dark rear corner of the shelter. Leth crept towards it. Close examination revealed it to be discarded clothing and filthy rags. He pulled it aside, only to discover nothing but scuttling insects beneath.

He sighed, fighting back the tears and the will-sapping anguish that felt like it could rip him apart. He wished that it would; he was drained of all desire to carry on.

There was a small movement in the dark, near to the level of his bowed head. Leth tensed, staring hard into the blackness. Slowly he made out a narrow recess between wall and roof that the darkness had concealed. He pushed his face closer, heard another tiny shift of something.

Leth moved closer, cautiously, grasping the hilt of his falchion. Now he saw something within, pale and shapeless. A movement! Then a voice: 'Stay back!'

It was a child's voice. In the deep, dusty gloom Leth spied a small, round, pale and filthy face, the glint of wide, fierce, frightened eyes. A little white fist clutched a short stick, which the child thrust at Leth.

'Stay back! If you touch her I will kill you!'

Now, behind the first face, Leth saw a second, another child, cowering on its belly deep in the recess. The first child, also prone in the narrow space, had his arm thrown protectively in front of the second.

A vast wave of emotion flooded up from somewhere deep within Leth's core, and burst from him in a great, uncontrolled sob.

'Keep away!'

'Galry! Jace!' Leth could barely frame the words, so intense was his relief and the sudden surge of love and such pride at the brave little boy who in his darkest, most terrified moments, thought first of protecting his infant sister's life.

'Galry! Jace!' He wept. The tears flooded from his eyes and coursed down his cheeks. And then he remembered that he still wore the helm; the children could not see his face.

Leth tore the sapphire helm from his head and fell to his knees, sobbing out loud. He threw wide his arms. 'My babies! It is me! Your father! I have found you! Oh, praise all the spirits, I have found you!'

EIGHTEEN

I

For long minutes they clung to each other, all three sobbing with
the joy and relief of their longed-for reunion. They were afraid to
let go, fearful that the moment might not be true, nothing more
than a dream, and that to let go would mean to be cast back into the
horrors that had preceded it, separated once more. Leth's emotion
poured out of him unchecked as he revelled in the sensation of his
children's vital warm little bodies in his arms again. When at last
he rose and carried them both out of the shelter he found Rasgul
at the head of the steps outside the enclosure, looking down and
smiling, his own orange-brown eyes glistening with tears.

There were no words to be said. Leth ascended the steps; Rasgul
reached out and squeezed his shoulder. Leth stood and gazed around
the vast cavern, realizing for the first time that the bloodlight
was fading.

'What now?' he said at length. 'Are we safe here?'

'No one will attack us now that she is no more,' Rasgul said.

'What of the cloud that she was about to send forth?'

'It died with her.'

'Can you be so sure?'

'Even if she had released it before she passed, it requires her
living force to guide it,' Rasgul said. 'Whatever happened, it will
have broken and dispersed now.'

Leth nodded. He looked down at the forlorn faces of the children
in the enclosure, and at the others, the unfortunate ones about the
cavern. 'We must do something for them.'

'We will do what we can.'

Galry's body had grown slack and heavy. Leth smiled and kissed his head. He had fallen asleep. Jace too was nodding against Leth's chest. Their nightmare was past; safe in their father's arms they could allow exhaustion to finally overcome them. But for Leth the realization was returning that the nightmare was far from over.

They were in an alien world. They did not know how to get back home. And there remained Urch-Malmain.

Had he gone now that Ascaria was destroyed? Had he stepped through his portal in the basement of the Tower of Glancing Memory, to wreak havoc and mischief upon the world of Enchantment's Edge?

And what of the portal that, by Lakewander's and Master Protector's account, Ascaria had guarded somewhere here in the Fortress of the Dark Flame – the portal that would return Leth to his own domain?

Leth looked around him. 'Where is Harg?'

Leth nodded towards the great cataract. 'He went over there.'

Still carrying the children Leth began to walk towards the tumbling wall of water. Its noise resounded now, filling the cavern. Beside the river that it formed was a rocky pathway leading to an entrance in the rock. This Leth followed and found himself peering into a curving passage towards a dim green luminescence obscured by the angle of the rock. A short way down Leth found a small round chamber, and there he came upon Count Harg kneeling before a glowing circular device on the floor, engraved with complex symbols. The air above the device shimmered with a rippling blue-green intensity.

In Harg's hand was the small palm-held silver instrument which Leth had glimpsed when they rode out from the Tower of Glancing Memory. With it he was adjusting and realigning a series of small knobs and fluted dish-like depressions set around the rim of the circular device, at the same time consulting a chart laid before him on the ground. He glanced up as Leth entered. 'Just a moment, Swordbearer.'

'What are you doing?'

'I am—Just one more. Yes, that does it, I think!' He eyed the chart once more. 'Indeed, perfect.'

He touched one of the circular depressions, then gathered up the chart and stood stiffly, sighing with the pain of his injuries. The blue-green haze above the device began to flicker; a quiet, distant hissing, buzzing noise was audible. The hazy luminescence became smoky, then slowly changed to become dominantly magenta in hue. The sound died away as the purple-pink smoke stabilized.

Count Harg nodded to himself in satisfaction. 'Yes, that's done the trick.'

'What is this? What have you done?' demanded Leth.

'What have I done? I have established our way back.' Harg's smalt gaze fell upon the two sleeping children cradled in Leth's arms. He smiled emotionlessly. 'You have found your little ones. Marvellous. That brings me great joy.'

'Way back? To where?'

'Why, to the Tower of Glancing Memory, of course.'

'This is the portal, isn't it?' said Leth, heatedly. 'This is the way that Ascaria guarded.'

'That is so.'

'And what have you done? You have tampered with it.'

'Tampered? No. I have acted in accordance with Master Urch-Malmain's instructions. He is anxious for us to return. He wishes to speak with you again.'

'Where did it lead prior to your modifications?'

Count Harg gave him a mocking look and drew in air through his teeth. 'Who really can say?'

'I was told it was the way back to my own land.'

'And you would have stepped in, would you? Blindly? Trustingly? With your darling children? I think not, Swordbearer. It could have taken you anywhere, anywhere at all. Or nowhere.'

'And I am to believe you that your adjustments have now rendered it safe and reliable?'

'Oh, I think you will. After all, I am going to use it myself. Good Master Urch is very keen to see you again. He awaits you now. Farewell, then. I will see you on the other side.'

So saying Harg turned and stepped onto the device. The magenta haze shimmered and flared. Harg's image remained within it for a moment, then flashed briefly and was gone.

Leth stared as the haze regathered itself. He heard a breath close behind him, and turned. Rasgul stood there.

'Do you go, Swordbearer?'

'I do not know.'

Long moments passed. Something sputtered in the haze. A square of paper appeared out of nothing and fluttered to the floor before